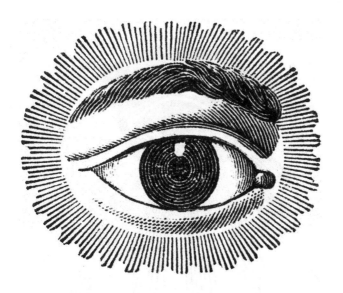

Hypnotism in Victorian and Edwardian Era Fiction
Volume 1.

Death by Suggestion

An Anthology of
19th and Early 20th-Century Tales of Hypnotically Induced Murder, Suicide, and Accidental Death

Edited by

Donald K. Hartman

THEMES & SETTINGS IN FICTION PRESS

Buffalo, New York

THEMES & SETTINGS IN FICTION PRESS

Buffalo, New York

First Edition, 2018

Layout and cover design
by David J. Bertuca

Publisher's Cataloging-in-Publication Data

Names: Hartman, Donald K., editor.
Title: Death by suggestion : an anthology of 19th and
  early 20th-century tales of hypnotically induced murder,
  suicide, and accidental death / edited by Donald K. Hartman.
Other titles: Hypnotism in Victorian and Edwardian Era
fiction ; vol 1.
Description: First Edition. | Buffalo, N.Y. : Themes & Settings
  in Fiction Press, 2018. | Includes bibliographical references.
Identifiers: ISBN 9781984128430 (softcover)
Subjects: LCSH: Hypnotism and crime—Fiction. |
  Hypnotism in literature. | Mesmerism in literature. |
  Animal magnetism—Fiction. | Murder—Fiction.
Classification: LCC PN6071.H9 D43 2018 | DDC 813.08
  D43--dc23

Contents

Introduction

The Victorian and Edwardian craze for hypnotism and mesmerism produced an enormous number of novels and short stories between the years 1850 and 1910. Much of this fiction was concerned with the anxieties people had with the relationship between hypnotist and subject and issues of mental power and control. A subset of this fiction dealt with hypnotism and crime, and a smaller subset with the notion of hypnotism causing death—either deliberate or unintentional.

This anthology contains stories of hypnotically induced murder, suicide, and accidental death. Most of the stories were written by minor and fairly obscure authors, but it also contains tales by a few prominent ones as well: Ambrose Bierce, Arthur Conan Doyle, and Julian Hawthorne (son of Nathaniel Hawthorne). You will find here stories that are preposterous; some that are slightly plausible; a few of them may make you shiver; and a couple may even make you laugh; but hopefully, you will find them all entertaining.

For those readers who need a brief overview on the history of hypnosis or are wondering if anyone has ever died or been killed through hypnotism (or allegedly died or been killed)—read on. For those who just want to get right into the stories themselves then, jump ahead to the first tale of hypnotic death: "The Tragedy of the Wedding."

Editor's note: The texts of the stories here are transcribed exactly as they originally appeared (you will notice many 19th-century spellings, especially words that were hyphenated then but not now, e.g. "to-day"); the only exception is the removal of footnotes from the story "The Crime of the Rue Auber." The notes added little to the story and only interfered with readability.

Hypnotism

Hypnotism has fascinated mankind even before a name was put to it, and yogis in India were placing themselves into states of hypnotic ecstasy before the time of Christ. The modern history of hypnosis begins with Franz Anton Mesmer. Mesmer, like many before him, tried to apply the principles of magnetism to mental and physical health. Mesmer claimed that with the use of magnetic wands, "magnetic fluid" could be directed at will, and the sick and infirm could be made healthy. Experiments conducted in 1784 by a royal commission headed by Benjamin Franklin led to the rejection of Mesmer's animal magnetism theory. Reports submitted by the commission stressed that magnetic fluid did not exist. The alleged therapeutic cures were dismissed as being due to "mere imagination." In spite of the commission's findings, mesmerism continued to flourish in Europe and America.

James Braid, a surgeon and a pioneer investigator of hypnosis, first introduced the term "hypnotism" from the Greek (*to sleep*) in 1842. Braid did much to dispel the superstitious aura surrounding the phenomenon of hypnosis. He disavowed Mesmer's magnetic fluid theory; rather, he advocated a physiological view that hypnosis is a kind of sleep. He thought the trance state differed from natural sleep and suggested the possible existence of a double consciousness in individuals. Braid was mainly interested in the curative possibilities of hypnosis and reported successful treatment of diseases such as rheumatism. Braid's views were taken up by the noted French neurologist Jean Martin Charcot. Charcot considered hypnosis a manifestation of hysteria, and he thought hypnotic trance and hysterical attack to be fundamentally equivalent phenomena. Sigmund Freud, who was influenced by Charcot, made use of hypnosis early in his career but later discarded hypnosis for other psychoanalytical techniques. [1]

Today, hypnosis is the subject of serious research. Hypnosis is accepted and used by many professionals in the areas of psychology, medicine, and dentistry. People in the 21st century remain as entranced and mystified by it as were their ancestors, and hypnosis is still popularized by many stage performers and charlatans. There are hundreds of self-help books that attest to the fact that we moderns have not lost our fascination for the "black art" of hypnotism. These books claim hypnosis can enhance one's sexual prowess; help break unwanted habits such as smoking or overeating; build poise; and improve one's ability and performance in just about every area of life. Currently the terms hypnotism and mesmerism are used synonymously, but mesmerism accurately defined is built around the theory of mesmeric "fluid," which was transferred from the operator to the subject, while hypnotism is based upon suggestion. Hypnotism deals with a state of passivity on the part of the subject; mesmerism deals with an actual force. The word "hypnosis" was not in common usage until the late 1880s—prior to that the terms use most often to describe the phenomenon were: animal magnetism, mesmerism, and hypnotism.

Hypnotism and Death

Hypnotism may seem benign to the denizens of the 21st century, but it provoked a fair amount of fear and anxiety for many folks living in the Victorian and Edwardian eras. Just the process of being hypnotized was thought by some to be physically and mentally harmful. The control of a subject's will by that of the hypnotist's led many to believe that hypnotism opened avenues for charlatans and criminals to exploit. The danger of being induced to commit a crime while under hypnotic influence aroused a particular dread for many people, and the thought that someone could use hypnotism to kill was especially abhorrent. [2]

Can hypnotism kill you?
Three real-life cases from the Victorian and Edwardian Eras

On a September day in 1894, at a castle located near Nyireghyhaza, Hungary, a dinner party was given by the castle's proprietor, Todor Salamon. After dinner, a hypnotist named Franz Neukomm was called upon to give a hypnotic séance and he selected as his clairvoyant medium Ella Salamon, the daughter of the party's host. During the séance, Neukomm placed Ella into a hypnotic trance and suggested to her that she was suffering from consumption; he had no sooner given this suggestion when Ella made a piercing shriek and fell heavily to the ground. One of the guests was a doctor who rushed to the young girl's assistance, but all his efforts to resuscitate her failed and she died on the spot. There was no doubt that Ella was dead, but had she died by hypnosis? [3-5]

The tale of Ella's death quickly spread throughout Hungary, and when foreign news wires picked up the story, her hypnotically induced death made international news. Sensationalized newspaper stories about the incident stirred public concerns about the use of hypnotism and only intensified the professional and social anxieties surrounding its use. Many people placed the blame of Ella's death on Neukomm, but when his case went to trial, Neukomm was cleared of the charge of gross negligence—the reason given for the verdict: death can occur suddenly at any time, to a hypnotized or non-hypnotized person.

Another death attributed to hypnotism occurred in 1897 to a 17-year-old boy named Spurgeon Young. Young, a resident of Jamestown, New York, died under circumstances that indicated his death was caused by experiments carried out by amateur hypnotists. The coroner involved in the case sent out inquiries to several prominent hypnotists asking them if they thought it possible Young's death could be the result of the strain he experienced during his hypnotic performances. A jury reviewed the answers provided by the leading hypnotists, and after making their own deliberations, they rendered a verdict that Spurgeon Young came to his death from diabetes and nervous exhaustion caused by the hypnotic practices used by the amateur hypnotists; their verdict also recommended that the New York State legislature pass a law prohibiting the practice of hypnotism. [6, 7]

On November 8, 1909, Robert Simpson was hypnotized by "Professor" Arthur Everton at a theater in Somerville, New Jersey. Simpson was a regular member of Arthur Everton's hypnotic stage performances, but at this particular performance, Simpson never awoke from the trance Everton had placed him in, even after physicians in the audience tried to revive him from his cataleptic state. Everton was arrested for manslaughter, but a Somerville grand jury eventually ruled that Everton wouldn't be prosecuted for causing Simpson's death. [8, 9]

Can a hypnotic subject be made an innocent and unconscious agent of murder? – Four real-life cases from the late 19th century

All of these cases of "hypnotic murder" received extensive newspaper coverage, most of it sensationalized, but the role hypnotism played in the courtroom was minimal, as compared to the role it played in hyped-up headlines and embellished and fabricated stories written by journalists. [10]

Eyraud-Bompard-Gouffé Case

Interest in hypnotism came to the fore with the trial of Gabrielle Bompard. In 1889, Bompard, in desperate need of money, conspired with her lover, Michel Eyraud, to kill Toussaint-Augustin Gouffé, a wealthy Parisian sheriff's bailiff. With the pretext of a sexual encounter, Bompard enticed Gouffé to her apartment and there she assisted Eyraud in strangling him to death. After the murder she and Eyraud escaped to America, but she later returned to Paris and confessed to her part in the crime. At her trial it was contended that she was under the hypnotic control of Eyraud when the crime was committed. Several experts in hypnotism were brought into the courtroom, and it was affirmed that no murder in real life could be attributed to hypnotic suggestion. Eyraud was sentenced to execution by guillotine, and Bompard was sentenced to 20 years of hard labor, but was released from prison in 1903. [11]

McDonald-Gray-Patton Case

On May 5, 1894, Thomas McDonald shot and killed Thomas Patton in Winfield, Kansas. McDonald was a farmhand and tenant of Anderson

Gray, a wealthy farmer and also a neighbor of Patton, the murdered man. Patton had been a witness against Gray in a legal case that involved considerable property. When McDonald's case went to trial, he freely admitted to killing Patton but claimed his employer Gray had exerted a strong hypnotic influence over him, and it was Gray's influence that led him to commit the crime. The jury in the case acquitted McDonald, and Anderson Gray was afterwards arrested, tried, and found guilty of planning the murder, and sentenced to death; Gray made an appeal to the Supreme Court of Kansas, the court however affirmed the verdict. Gray was not without influence, and with the assistance of family and friends, he finally received a pardon from Governor Edmund Morrill in 1897. [12]

Hayward-Blixt-Ging Case

Catherine Ging, a Minneapolis dressmaker, was shot to death on the night of December 3, 1894, by Claus Blixt. Blixt confessed that Harry Hayward, a socialite and professional gambler, had hired him to kill Miss Ging; Hayward had laid the plot to kill Ging in order to procure a life insurance policy he had on her that was payable to him. A unique feature of the case was that Blixt claimed that Hayward controlled both himself and Ging by hypnotism, that Hayward had compelled him to commit other crimes in the same manner, and that he couldn't resist Hayward's will, after Hayward would make a few hypnotic gestures at him. During the trial it was shown that Hayward was indeed the instigator of the murder, and even though Blixt had done the killing, Hayward was sentenced to death by hanging, and Blixt was given a sentence of life in prison. [13, 14]

Jones-Patrick-Rice Case

William Marshall Rice, merchant, financier, and founder of Rice University, was killed by poison on September 23, 1900. Albert T. Patrick, an attorney, and Rice's valet Charles F. Jones, were co-conspirators in a plot to steal Rice's fortune through forged documents and a bogus will. Jones initially asserted that Patrick had murdered Rice, but Jones then made a subsequent confession in which he said Patrick had hypnotized him (Jones) into giving Rice the poison; it was upon Jones's initial confession that Patrick was indicted for Rice's murder, convicted and sentenced to death by electrocution. Patrick appealed his conviction and was pardoned by New York State Governor John Alden Dix in 1912. [15-19]

Two modern cases of death via hypnosis

In September 1993 Sharron Tabarn, a 24-year-old mother of two, was found dead a few hours after being hypnotized at a stage show in Leyland, England. She was ordered to kiss a stranger in the audience and asked to perform a number of other harmless acts. She was brought out of the trance after it was suggested she was receiving a 10,000 volt shock. Ms. Tabarn died five hours later, after complaining of dizziness. Although her inquest found that it was an accidental death, the United Kingdom Home Office pathologist said it was hard not to believe there was a link between her death and being hypnotized. [20-22]

In 2011 three Florida teens died after being hypnotized by their high school principal, George Kenney. While he was principal at North Port High School, Kenney had hypnotized several students to help them achieve better test scores and prime athletic performance. Kenney admitted to hypnotizing Wesley McKinley the day before he committed suicide, and Marcus Freeman died in a car crash after a session of self-hypnosis, a technique Kenney had taught him. Another student, Brittany Palumbo, hanged herself a short time after being hypnotized by Kenney. In 2012, Kenney resigned from North Port High School and pleaded guilty to practicing hypnotherapy without a license; he also served one year probation. In 2015 the families of the dead teenagers received $600,000 ($200,000 per family) in a lawsuit settlement. Even though there had been no scientific evidence that hypnosis had directly caused the teens' deaths, the families hired an attorney to sue the school district because under Florida law, they could not sue Kenney directly because school employees are considered representatives of the school board. [23, 24]

Killing by Willing?

A listing of deaths attributed to hypnotic influence would not be complete without a mention of Anna Bonus Kingsford (1846-1888). Kingsford was a physician, spiritualist and anti-vivisection activist, and she claimed to have the ability to wish or will a person to death. One of Anna's first victims was Claude Bernard. Bernard, a French physiologist, was a great proponent of vivisection (he even vivisected his own pet dog); Kingsford was so outraged by Bernard's practices that she summoned a "spiritual thunderbolt" to strike him dead, and shortly after willing this to occur, Bernard did die. According to Edward Maitland, a fellow anti-vivisectionist and an author of a biography on Kingsford, Anna cast another death wish on physiologist Paul Bert who also succumbed to Kingsford's deadly will. Anna's next selected victim was Louis Pasteur. Pasteur, known today for his discoveries and breakthroughs on the causes and prevention of diseases, was heavily involved in vivisection, and his success with finding solutions for anthrax and rabies helped convince much of the scientific community and the public at large that vivisection was a useful tool in the fight against disease. Pasteur's extensive use of vivisection so inflamed Kingsford's wrath that she began a willful thought murder campaign against him, but she died of consumption before she could see her lethal vision come to fruition; Pasteur nearly died of a sudden illness during the time of Anna's baleful wishes toward him, but he did recover and went on to live for another eight years. Kingsford never claimed to be a hypnotist and was not known to have practiced hypnosis directly, but the ability to kill someone via willful thought alone, certainly would have been considered a species of hypnotism during Victorian times. [25-28]

NOTES

1. For general overviews on the history of hypnosis, see Alan Gauld's *A History of Hypnotism* (Cambridge University Press, 1992); Adam Crabtree's *From Mesmer to Freud: Magnetic Sleep and the Roots of Hypnotism* (Yale University Press, 1993); and Christopher Green's *Overpowered!: The Science and Showbiz of Hypnosis* (The British Library, 2015).

2. Palmer, John-Ivan. *The Origins of Mesmeric Death* (2009) [Available from: https://web.archive.org/web/20170713161714/http://www.whistling-shade.com/0901/mesmerism.html]

3. Lafferton, Emese. "Death by Hypnosis: An 1894 Hungarian Case and Its European Reverberations." *Endeavour*, Vol. 30, no. 2 (June, 2006): 65-70.

4. Ewin, Dabney M. "Death and Hypnosis: Two Remarkable Cases." *American Journal of Clinical Hypnosis*, Vol. 51, no. 1 (July 2008): 69-75. The 1894 Hungarian case being one, the other case took place in 1993 when a 24-year-old woman was found dead a few hours after volunteering as a subject at a stage hypnosis show; a hypnotic suggestion given at the show was believed by many to be a contributing factor to her death.

5. Hammerschlag, Heinz E. "A Case of Death under Hypnosis." In: *Hypnotism and Crime*. London: Rider and Company (1956): 49-55.

6. Bell, Clark. "The Case of Spurgeon Young." *Medico-Legal Studies*, Vol. 5. New York: Medico-Legal Journal (1898): 102-118. [Available from: https://babel.hathitrust.org/cgi/pt?id=uiug.30112023309492;view=1up;seq=132].

7. "J.W.S. Young's Death: Hypnotism Was a Contributing Cause According to the Jury." *Evening Journal* (Jamestown, NY) (Feb. 3, 1897): 5 [Available from: FultonHistory.com].

8. Gillette, Greg. *Hypnotized to Death* [Available from: https://web.archive.org/web/20150928074243/http://blogs.mycentraljersey.com/hillsborough/2011/02/23/hypnotized-to-death/].

9. "Begs a Dead Man to Come to Life: One Hypnotist Fails to Revive Victim of Another's Influence." *Spanish Folk Press* (Spanish Folk, Utah) (Dec. 9, 1909): 3. [Available from: http://chroniclingamerica.loc.gov/lccn/sn85058245/1909-12-09/ed-1/seq-3/].

10. Sherman, Roger. "Attitude of Courts Toward Hypnotism." *Suggestion* Vol. 8, no. 1 (Jan. 1, 1902): 1-8. [Available from: https://babel.hathitrust.org/cgi/pt?id=hvd.hc4hsp;view=1up;seq=7]

11. Levingston, Steven. *Little Demon in the City of Light: A True Story of Murder and Mesmerism in Belle Époque Paris.* New York: Doubleday (2014); also see Ruth Harris's "Murder Under Hypnosis." *Psychological Medicine* Vol. 14, no.3 (Aug. 1985): 477-505.

12. "On Hypnotic Murder." *Topeka State Journal* (April 10, 1895): 8 [Available from: http://chroniclingamerica.loc.gov/lccn/sn82016014/1895-04-10/ed-1/seq-8]; also: "Fake Stories in Kansas History." *The Inter Ocean* (Chicago), (July 7, 1912): 26. [Available from: https://www.newspapers.com/newspage/34585606/]

13. Wilhelm, Robert. *Murder by Gaslight: The Minneapolis Svengali.* (2010). [Available from: https://web.archive.org/web/20150905100102/http://www.murderbygaslight.com/2010/05/minneapolis-svengali.html]

14. Peters, Shawn Francis. *The Infamous Harry Hayward: A True Account of Murder and Mesmerism in Gilded Age Minneapolis.* Minneapolis: University of Minnesota Press, (2018).

15. *Murder Trial, 1900-1902: William Marsh Rice and the Founding of Rice Institute* [Available from: https://web.archive.org/web/20160506012716/http://exhibits.library.rice.edu/exhibits/show/founding/trial]

16. *Murder by Hypnotism: A Startling New Theory. Does It Explain the Rice Mystery?* [Available from: https://exhibits.library.rice.edu/files/original/d831dfd47fbbe-5a44f016cdcc8335e2a.pdf]

17. "Patrick's Four Years Fight for Life." *Washington Times* (June 18, 1905): 9. [Available from: http://chroniclingamerica.loc.gov/lccn/sn84026749/1905-06-18/ed-1/seq-21/]

18. *These Fingers All Point to Jones.* [Available from: https://web.archive.org/web/20170930035342/https://ricehistorycorner.com/2011/10/19/these-fingers-all-point-to-jones/]

19. Friedland, Martin L. *The Death of Old Man Rice: A True Story of Criminal Justice in America.* New York: New York University Press, (1994).

20. MacDonlad, Marianne. "Ministers to Review Hypnotic Stage Acts." *Independent* (Dec. 14, 1994). [Available from: https://web.archive.org/web/20150509191449/http://www.independent.co.uk/news/uk/ministers-to-review-hypnotic-stage-acts-1387404.html]

21. "In the Courts: Hypnotism Link to Daughter's Death." *Independent* (Jan. 20, 1998). [Available from: http://www.independent.co.uk/news/in-the-courts-hypnotism-link-to-daughters-death-1139727.html]

22. O'Keefe, Tracie. *The Case of a Woman Who Died After Being a Volunteer in a Stage Hypnosis Show* (Apr. 16, 2012). [Available from: https://web.archive.org/web/20180126180829/https:/tracieokeefe.com/the-case-of-a-woman-who-died-after-being-a-volunteer-in-a-stage-hypnosis-show/]

23. *Report Details How One Principal Hypnotized Students For Years*. (June 30, 2011). [Available from: https://web.archive.org/web/20170729190757/https:/www.npr.org/sections/thetwo-way/2011/06/30/137535891/report-details-how-one-principal-hypnotized-students-for-years]

24. Brown, Emma. "Three Teens Died after Being Hypnotized by Their Principal. Now Their Families are Getting $200,000 Each." *Washington Post* (Oct. 7, 2015). [Available from: https://web.archive.org/web/20180129205046/https://www.washingtonpost.com/news/education/wp/2015/10/07/three-teens-died-after-being-hypnotized-by-their-principal-now-their-families-are-getting-200000-each/?utm_term=.06986b64f71e]

25. "Killing by Her Willing: The Newest Kind of Murder a Cultured Science." *Los Angeles Herald* (May 24, 1896): 20. [Available from: http://chroniclingamerica.loc.gov/lccn/sn85042461/1896-05-24/ed-1/seq-20/]

26. Phelps, Norm. "Requiem for a Little Brown Dog" In: *The Longest Struggle: Animal Advocacy from Pythagoras to PETA*. New York: Lantern Books (2007): 129-147.

27. *Anna Kingsford, Psychic Assassin?* (April 22, 2013) [Available from: https://web.archive.org/web/20180207032655/http://strangeco.blogspot.com/2013/04/anna-kingsford-psychic-assassin.html].

28. Maitland, Edward. *Anna Kingsford, Her Life, Letters, Diary and Work*. London: John M. Watkin (1913). [Available from: https://catalog.hathitrust.org/Record/100884248]

The Tragedy of the Wedding

By Stanley Percival

AUTHOR'S NOTE.—The main incidents narrated in this story are based on scientific investigations, and apparent improbabilities do but portend what might be accomplished by an intellectual and unscrupulous man, who sought to commit crimes with the aid of hypnotism.

I.

"NAY, Sahib, thy medicine availeth naught; my time is at hand. Even now can I hear the voices calling to me. Ever hast thou been to me as a father and mother. Thou hast shown naught but kindness to me, thy unworthy servant. Sahib! I am not poor as thou thinkest. Nay, smile not! Ere I go, I would leave in thy hands the key of the hidden treasure of the Temple of Surya."

The bony, withered hand of the old Indian woman, wandered over her loose garment and nervously clutched a small piece of parchment, concealed within its folds.

"I have neither kith nor kin, and the secret would have died with me, but now will I show my gratitude for thy great goodness. Quick, Sahib, quick! open it, that I may read. This treasure is for you alone, Sahib Makyne. Trust not thy friend, the Sahib Belmont, for he has the eye of evil. And if thou dost trust him, surely then will harm befall thee."

Her eyes wandered over the yellow document which Makyne had unfolded, and she translated in a low, broken voice:—

"'In the Temple of Surya, in the plain of Seebpore, when the Queen of Night trailed her sable robes across the face of Varuna, the treasure of the Sonars was offered. Within the sweep of the arm is it hidden, guarded by the Sign of the Star.'

"Sahib — I am going — trust him not. I have spoken true talk—it is dark."

The eyelids closed, and her breath came in quick, short gasps, and, ere the next few minutes had passed, the old native woman, Nana, had crossed the "threshold of the world."

"Sorry she's gone," murmured Makyne; "I knew she couldn't last very long, when I saw her. Rather curious, this yarn of hers." And he looked at the parchment with its faded characters. "I can't read it. I'll show it to Belmont, he's rather keen on this sort of thing. Wonder if there's anything in it."

"This *is* curious," said Belmont, a couple of hours later, as he sat examining the document. "It's very old, in fact, I can hardly make it out. Now let's see," and he commenced reading word by word, translating into English as he proceeded.

"'In the Temple of Surya'—that's the Hindu Sun God, one of the Navagrahah, their planet gods—'in the plain of Seebpore'—that's probably outside the town of Seebpore, which lies about fifteen miles N.N.W. from here.

"The next phrase is evidently their way of meaning the moon, and 'the sable robes across Varuna's face'might be the shadows passing over an idol."

"Who the deuce was Varuna?" interrupted Makyne.

"That's the God of the Ocean, and probably there's an idol of the old chap in this temple."

"You seem to know all about it. But go on."

"Well, what I make out of the rest of it, is, that some treasure was hidden by the Sonars—they were goldsmiths, you know—but what the 'sweep of the arm'or the 'Sign of the Star'may be, we can't possibly guess until we see the place; but I should think it indicates the actual spot where the treasure was hidden. Anyhow we'll follow it up. I shouldn't be at all surprised if it's genuine. These old Hindus believed in offerings to their gods, and this one may have taken the form of jewels and gold, or something of that sort. I certainly propose that we go in search. What do you say?"

"Oh," laughed Makyne, "I'm game for a few days in the country, but as for making any wonderful discovery, I don't place much reliance on *that.*"

"Right. Then we'll go. By the bye, its yours of course, I've nothing to do with it; but I'm a bit hard up, as you know, and if you *do* strike it rich, you might lend me a bit to go on with."

"If we do find anything, we'll go halves, of course,"said Makyne promptly.

"Halves!" repeated Belmont, "that's awfully good of you, old man, but we'll find it first, and—and—then we can settle the division."

A hard look passed over his face, as a sudden thought came to his mind, and he strolled on to the verandah, and, settling himself in a lounge chair, lit his pipe.

"No, it's not enough," he said to himself, "not enough. I must have money, aye, and plenty of it, too. It there's anything in this old hag's tale, it'll take more than a simple fool like Makyne to keep me from getting it. Since the wife died, I've been going the pace pretty smart, and it'll be eternal smash if I don't ease up a bit. But there, she's dead now, and I've only my boy Arthur to think about, and by God, for his sake, I'd go to any ends—yes, any ends. How I hate that Makyne, he's always lucky. If I get hold of this money—and if it's there, I'm going to have it—I shall go over to the old country, and look after the youngster. I must get it, even if' but the remainder of the sentence was left unfinished. He sat motionless. His hands were tightly clenched and the hard lines on his face assumed an expression of fierce determination.

On the morning of the expedition, Belmont was moody and preoccupied, replying only in monosyllables to Makyne's remarks.

Towards evening they arrived at the ruined temple, and, too tired to commence exploring at once, threw themselves on the grass, and enjoyed a quite pipe.

They smoked for some time in silence. Miles away from the haunts of man, with the stillness of an Indian night coming on, the weird fantasies which wove themselves around the old ruin, seemed to Makyne to ring out, as a ghostly warning, Nana's last words, "Trust him not! Trust him not!" The words rang through his mind again and again, with such persistent reiteration, that at length it appeared to him as if Nana's spirit were hovering overhead in the rapidly approaching darkness. He tried to put the fancy away, but still it clung to him. At last he roused himself with an effort, and walked to the entrance of the temple. As he did so, the first faint streaks of the moon's pale light became visible, and Belmont exclaimed,

"At last she's come! We shall have enough light to work by directly."

The two men entered the temple, and Belmont, with his intimate knowledge of idols, soon discovered the one he sought.

"Here we are, here's Varuna, this with an arm raised, and by all that's holy we've struck it! I tell you, we've struck it! Here—look here," and he dragged his companion to the front of the idol. "Here's the shadow of the arm, and as the moon climbs higher and westward, it will move across the floor. 'The sweep of the arm,'see? It ought to fall in this direction, look out for anything like a star, within ten feet or so. Somewhere about here."

He was excited and flung himself on his hands and knees, minutely examining the rough floor, partly overgrown with grass and weeds, Makyne assisting, but still not thinking much of their prospect of securing anything of any value. After a long search they discovered a small slab in the shape of a star, let into the pavement.

"Got it!" shouted Belmont.

"Perhaps," returned Makyne; "wait until we see what's underneath, before we shout."

They removed the stone, and found a ring of iron, let into another and larger slab. They set to work with a will, Makyne's interest now thoroughly aroused, and after digging away the earth and stones, they managed to lift it away. Underneath was a rude cell, containing a curiously carved box or casket, with hinges and lock of pure gold.

"Well, I'm damned!" said Makyne.

"So am I," returned Belmont laconically.

They forced open the lid, and there, carefully wrapped in pieces of the finest silk, were jewels and precious stones of priceless value.

"Good luck!" said Makyne; "half of that little lot for each of us will make us rich men." He turned to place the casket on a marble ledge at his side, preparatory to replacing the slab.

With a savage cry, Belmont sprang at his companion, and gripped him by the throat.

"You'll give me half, will you?" he hissed. "But I'll have the lot."

Makyne struggled to free himself, but the grasp on his throat tightened, his eyes started from his head, his face became livid, until at last, with a frantic effort, he wrenched himself free.

He was too exhausted to offer further resistance, and Belmont, with an oath, drew a knife, and plunged it in Makyne's breast, who fell forward, gasping, "Nana was right, she warned me—Ah-h!" And he too, "crossed the threshold."

II.

Dr. Camro Makyne sat in his study at his house in Harley Street. In front of him was spread a collection of old newspaper cuttings, memoranda, and letters.

He turned them over, reading a line here and there, and, pausing over a slip from an Indian paper dated June 17th, 1864, he re-read the faded type:

"The body of Mr. John Makyne was found yesterday by some natives, lying in the ruined temple of Surya, on the plain of Seebpore. The unfortunate man had a severe knife wound in the left breast. No motive can be assigned for the crime, Mr. Makyne's personal property appearing to have been untouched. A small carved box was found close to the body, but whether it belonged to the victim, or was left by his murderer, it is not possible to determine. It has been suggested that Mr. Makyne had been decoyed by some means to the place by a native who stabbed him for the sake of what money and jewellery the deceased was carrying at the time, but who, alarmed immediately after striking the fatal blow, fled without securing his booty."

"Possibly," murmured the Doctor, "but they don't mention the fact that his friend, Belmont, went with him to the temple, and what they went there for. The poor old dad entered that in his diary the night before they started, and lucky it was he did so, and that his papers were sent home undisturbed, otherwise I might never have had a clue to work upon.

"I've been upon Belmont's track ever since I unearthed that entry. Strange that it escaped the notice of the authorities at the time. But now I think I've brought affairs to a climax. For the sake of clearness let me tabulate the data I have secured up to the present."

He jotted down a brief *resume* of the various papers that lay before him.

"'June 16th, 1864. J.M. murdered by party unknown, in Temple of Surya at Seebpore. Personal property untouched.'

"'Entry in J.M.'s diary, June 14th, to the effect that he and friend, Fred. Belmont, had become possessed of secret information regarding jewels hidden in a temple, and that they proposed to take a week's leave, with the intention of searching, and, if found, sharing treasure equally.'

"Then comes a gap of nearly four years, till I finished with the hospital work, and had time to look round me. Then we go on:—

"'Traced out movements of F. B. at time of murder. Found through agents that he had left district some time during the autumn of '64. Nothing known of his movements.'

"Let's see, next comes this cutting from a local paper in the North of England, Aug. 3rd, '84:—

"'It is with great regret'. . . H'm, we'll skip all the conventional editorial lies . . . 'death of Mr. Frederic R. Belmont, late of India, who passed away after a lingering illness . . . His son, Mr. Arthur Belmont, inherits the whole of his father's fortune.'

"'A.B. leaves England shortly after father's death, for tour through the U.S.'

"And I should have had him at New York, if my agents hadn't made fools of themselves, and let him slip through their fingers.

"That brings me up to the present moment," and he took up and glanced over a note he had that morning received from one of his confidential agents:—

"Mr. Arthur Belmont, living at 'The Chase,'Kneston, near Leicester. Father been in India, been dead some years. Son has good position in county. Has money. Am returning by first train tomorrow, and will give further details."

"Good man, Collins," said the Doctor. "He has the makings of an excellent detective in him. He ought to be here by now if he came by that train. I'll give him half-an-hour longer."

He lit a cigar, and sat musing over the papers, until the page announced that Mr. Collins wished to see him.

"Show him in. Well, Collins," the Doctor went on, as a neat, dapper little man entered the room. "I have your letter; what else have you to report, and how did you gather your information?"

"Went down as a stable-help, out of a job, Sir, and hung about the stables of 'The Chase,'doing odd jobs, and chatting to the men. Groom told me as how his master was coming up to town at the end of the month, but he didn't know where he was going to stay. So I loafed about for a few days, and came across Mr. Belmont's personal servant doing the grand one night, at a free and easy in the village pub. He wasn't above being treated by me though, but he was very close about his master's affairs at first, until I got him on a bit, and then he told me all I wanted to know.

"He said Mr. Belmont was coming up to town to be married to the Hon. Miss Shafton. Was going to stay at the Seeton Hotel until the wedding. Found out the names of several people Mr. Belmont knows in London— one of them's Major Dennis in Jermyn Street, where I've often been to take messages for you, Sir."

"Ah, yes, I remember," replied the Doctor. "Go on."

"I saw Mr. Belmont himself once, Sir," continued Collins. "He came into the stables one day when I was helping. He's a thin, fair-haired man of about forty, I should say. Light moustache, and looks delicate. That's all I could find out, Sir. I stayed there a week, and got back to town this morning."

"All right, Collins, you seem to have got all the particulars you could, but it's a matter of no consequence. I don't think it's the man I want, after all. That's all just now; I'll let you know when I want you again."

"Now," he said to himself, after the man had quitted the room. "It's just possible that this Arthur Belmont is the son of the man who murdered my father. It's probable he doesn't know anything of it himself, or how his father became suddenly rich. He must have been a child of barely ten, at the time Belmont, senior, came home directly after securing the jewels, thinking that the only two people in the world who knew of their existence were dead. Any tale he chose to concoct of having made a fortune would naturally be believed. Probably he gave liberally to the local charities, and was a 'pillar' of the particular church or chapel which he favoured with his patronage. That generally whitewashes a man, and makes people believe in him, whatever his past may have been.

"That's all perfectly clear, so far. I'd better see Major Dennis. He's a gossipy sort of fool, and I ought to get any further information I may want out of him, together with an introduction to this Arthur Belmont, and we'll see him, and make sure of the facts. And if he *is* the man who has had the use of the money which ought to have come to me, and the son of my father's murderer —well—God help him, that's all."

The man who was so interested in Arthur Belmont's history was a dark, keen looking man of about forty-four. More than twenty years before he had been left an orphan, with barely sufficient means to complete his education and to enable him to take his doctor's degree. As a youth he had been looked upon by his fellow-students as "Deuced clever, but infernally hard up, don't 'cher know!" And when, shortly after passing his final, he announced his intention of setting up as a fashionable doctor in the West End, their astonishment as to how he had procured the necessary capital was naturally great.

He explained that he had unexpectedly come into some money, but would give no further particulars.

A man of intense brain-power, he had, in his student days been attracted to the study of hypnotism. The fascination of the science had so grown upon him that he had devoted some years to its special study, and had become intensely skilled in its practice. He had an intimate knowledge of all the various schools of hypnotism that were in vogue on the Continent, his own system being that of suggestion, as taught in the School of Nancy.

His iron will, his strong self-control, the strength with which he had fought the battle of life against the heavy odds of poverty, all tended to make him coldblooded and heartless. Friends he had none; acquaintances by the score. And though he despised the men who courted his society, and the women who flattered him, he invariably met them with the polish of a man of the world, bland, suave and genial.

In spite of adverse public opinion he practiced hypnotism in his profession, using it with great success in various cases of functional neurosis.

In most instances, however, he merely adopted it with a view to an ulterior end, which end he carefully cloaked under an assumed sympathetic interest in the subject.

But deep in his keen, calculating brain was a tiny flaw—a flaw that had descended to him by the relentless law of heredity. His great-grandfather on the maternal side had been afflicted in early life with a slight trace of insanity, and the disease, latent during two generations, had reappeared in the third, in a curious and abnormal manner.

The inherited instability of his higher nerve-regions caused the stress of his earlier years of student's toil and professional worry to act with an effect that, had he been in easier circumstances, would, perhaps, never have been produced.

It found its expression in a bent of instinctive criminality, slight at first, but intensified by his extraordinary mental activity, and by the knowledge of his power over others. To him every kind of subtle, intellectual, scientific crime came as second nature. And with the skill to plan and execute came the skill to evade the consequences of his actions. Criminality was to him a hobby, a relaxation from severe scientific research. He brought his power-ful brain and brilliant inventive faculties to the subject, and it was to him as ordinary amusements are to other men. His utter lack of moral sensibility enabled him to commit crimes at which many hardened criminals would have recoiled, and caused him to manifest cynical and contemplative delight in inflicting suffering for the mere gratification of experiencing the emotion of power while so doing.

While he was yet a young man, he had come across the entry in his father's diary. He had been convinced then that Belmont was the murderer, and had vowed to some day hunt him down, and, if the treasure actually existed, to secure the share that should have descended to him, and become the avenger of his father at the same time.

Even now, when his professional success was assured, and he was fairly well off, his lust for revenge, and the chance of acquiring a possible fortune, were still ever in his thoughts.

III.

The next afternoon the Doctor strolled round to the club, where he knew Major Dennis was in the habit of indulging in billiards. He found him idly knocking the balls about.

"Hullo!" said Dennis, as the Doctor entered, "it isn't often you are out of your den this time of day."

"I came specially to see you, Major; just had the offer of a hack at a remarkably low figure, and I wanted to ask your advice on the matter, as I know you're a good judge of horseflesh."

"Delighted, my dear boy! I'll have a look at it whenever you like. Will you give me a hundred up? I'm just waiting for a game."

"With pleasure," replied the Doctor, choosing a cue.

"I say, Doctor, if you really want a first-class horse, there's a friend of mine in Leicestershire, who is getting rid of part of his stud, as he is going to be married shortly, and I've no doubt you would be able to pick one up cheap from him. He's coming up to town in a week or two, and is sure to look me up. I'll let you know when he's coming, and you can come round to my diggings one night, and see him about it."

"You don't mean Lascelles, of Leicester, do you? He has a good name up there for horses."

"No, it's Arthur Belmont. He lives at Kneston, just outside the town, and a fine place he keeps up, too. I never heard where he got his money from, but he's got enough of it—lucky devil! Besides his bank balances and investments, he has a second fortune in jewels. Makes a hobby of them, I believe. I've never seen such a collection of stones. But, there, I'll arrange for you to meet him."

"Thanks, Major," replied the Doctor, with a bland smile, "I shall be most happy to make his acquaintance. My shot? How's the score?"

"75 to 33; I lead. Any odds you like on me for this game, Doctor."

"Yes, I must pull up, or you'll run out." And he played a careful and finished break of 42, that showed his complete mastery over the balls when he chose to exert himself. He finished with a safety miss, and chuckled.

"There, Major, how are the odds now, eh? That makes it a better game —75 to your 76. I don't grudge you the odd one. Never bet unless you're certain. That's an excellent old rule in life as well as in billiards."

"Well, I'm damned; you're a perfect juggler with the balls. Just as I thought I had the game in my own hands, too!" And the Major screwed his eyeglass viciously into his eye, as he made his next shot. His attempt to score, however, was fruitless, and the Doctor, picking up his cue, ran out an easy winner.

"Thanks for the game, Major. I must be off; professional engagements won't wait for billiards, y'know. Give you your revenge another day."

"I'm really not surprised that Arthur Belmont is fond of jewels," he mused, as he walked homeward. "From what the Major says, I should think he's a bit of a collector and connoisseur. All the better; he'll be easier to draw. I really think my time is coming at last. What care I whether it be this man or his father who wronged me? The father's dead, and I'll take my revenge on the son. After all, he's merely a unit, an organism, and if I can make any use of him, I'll do it. I must get possession of my part of the property first, and then I'll consider whether it will be advisable to bring to an abrupt conclusion his adaptation to environment. That sounds better than saying, 'I'll kill him,' or rather, that I will be the means of his death. But let me forget all about the matter until I hear from Dennis. By Jove, what an exquisite bit of sky!" he added, glancing upward.

A week later Dr. Makyne received a note from Major Dennis, asking him to come round the same night to meet Arthur Belmont. Before leaving his house, he took from a jewel-case an antique Egyptian signet ring, with a curiously carved stone, which, set in a hoop of gold, revolved on its own axis. On one side was engraved the typical face of an Egyptian beauty, and on the reverse was the semblance of a death's head, in which the sockets of the eyes were set with emeralds, giving a ghastly and uncanny appearance to the wearer's hand.

"That's a ring that ought to excite his interest, if he's anything of the lover of jewels that Dennis says he is," he muttered, slipping it on his finger, with the death's head turned outward.

"Come in, Doctor, called out the Major, as the servant opened the door. "Let me introduce you to my friend, Belmont. I was just telling him that you wanted to buy a horse." And the three men fell to discussing horseflesh and stable lore.

"Well," said Belmont, finally, "if you will give me the pleasure of putting you and your wife up for a few days at my place at Kneston, after I return from my honeymoon, I shall be delighted, and then you can have your pick of the gees before they go up for auction."

"For my own part, I most readily accept; but as for my wife," the Doctor added, laughing, "you know, a bachelor isn't supposed to have one."

"Why, I certainly took you for a married man, Doctor. I thought most medical men were so, if only out of deference to Mrs. Grundy."

"My dear fellow, I ignore Mrs. Grundy entirely, and I have always looked upon my life, with its scientific interests and pursuits, as an exact mathematical problem, expressed in terms of precision and clearness, the corresponding sequences of which will be both logical and complete. Surely you would not have me introduce into this equation that unknown quantity—woman?"

"Bravo, Doctor!" chimed in the Major. "I don't know what you mean, but it's just what I think about it. I don't worry much about the logical sequences and mathematical problems, or whatever you call 'em, of my life— dodging bullets and looking after troop horses has been more in my line—but I think that woman's a damned nuisance, and I suppose that's just about what you mean, eh?"

"It's all very well for you two hardened bachelors to talk of woman in this way," said Belmont. "I think she's the choicest flower of earth. You know, 'God made man a little lower than the angels, and woman a little above 'em.'"

"Good idea," growled the Major, "only you've got it the wrong way round; but engaged men are permitted to rave, y'know. Where the deuce did you get that ring from, Makyne? It's been worrying me for the last ten minutes," he added, with his usual bluntness. "Let's have a look at it."

"There's a history connected with it, I dare say," replied the Doctor, as he handed it to the Major. "I picked it up at a sale a year or two ago. It has some amount of value, I believe."

"I should think it had," exclaimed Belmont, "It looks like an Egyptian; antique, too, I should say. Those revolving signets are very distinctive."

"I see you are something of a connoisseur," said the doctor, "I'm rather interested in jewels myself, I have a small collection, principally antique."

"Yes," returned Belmont, "I am rather keen on the subject. I have a very fair collection of old Indian specimens; they were brought home by my father a few years after the mutiny. How he got them, I never knew. One doesn't enquire too closely into the financial operations of those times. There were originally more, I believe, but he disposed of some, shortly after leaving India."

"Then you will be able to criticise mine. You must come round one day, I shall value your opinion."

"I will, with pleasure, I'm always glad to meet with a fellow-lover of old stones."

ɛɔɔʁ

"Good morning, Doctor," said Belmont's jovial voice, as he was ushered into Dr. Makyne's study, a couple of days later. "You see, I've kept my promise. I'm as bad as a society girl, when jewels are the attraction."

"Come in, my dear fellow, and make yourself at home," said the Doctor, shaking hands heartily. "You're just in time to join me in a cigar before lunch. I can offer you something choice in the way of Havannas; I flatter myself I'm a good judge in that line." And he pulled forward an easy chair, and made his visitor comfortable.

"I'm afraid my collection is not a very grand one, but I have one or two rather choice specimens," he went on, unlocking a cabinet and drawing out a box of Oriental workmanship, curiously carved, and apparently of great age.

"You've an uncommonly quaint box to keep 'em in, anyway," said Belmont, examining it with interest.

"Yes, it belonged to my father, and was sent home with his effects after he died in India. There is a strange story connected with it, that I will perhaps tell you some day." And the speaker chuckled to himself, as he thought how little his listener guessed that the story was of vital importance to him.

He took from the box a few rare specimens of rings, and chains, and Belmont criticised and approved with that zest of which only an enthusiast is capable.

"This is a fine piece of work," he exclaimed at length, holding up a delicate anklet, carved and pierced in a thousand fantastic shapes. "I have one almost identical, but mine is even finer in workmanship."

"Nonsense," said the Doctor; "why, I regard that as exceedingly fine, perhaps the finest specimen of that particular style extant. Modern gold-smiths seem to have lost the art of such delicate piercing, and most of the so-called genuine native work is manufactured to order in the Indian province of Birmingham."

"I'd like to bet you, Doctor, that mine's finer."

"I should be robbing you, my dear fellow. There isn't a finer in the world. But just for the sake of a friendly bet, I will wager you a box of cigars on it, and you can bring your collection round here one day, and we can compare."

"Right, I will. I have the jewels in town with me. They are keeping them in the safe at my hotel, until we get settled. I brought them up to let Miss Shafton make her choice from them for a wedding gift. I mean to surprise her," he added with a smile, "she doesn't even know I have them with me."

"That's a bet then, and as you're bound to lose, have another cigar now." And the Doctor smiled as he passed the box.

"No, no more, Doctor. They're excellent, but ever since I was thrown in the hunting field, a couple of seasons ago, I have been subject to attacks of giddiness, and smoking much before meals seems to bring them on. That one cigar, even, has made my head feel a bit dizzy."

"That's bad. What do you do for it? A little patching up would soon put you all right."

"Well, I thought I'd ask your advice on the matter;" and Belmont gave an account of his symptoms. "I heard from Major Dennis that you practise hypnotism for nervous complaints, and perhaps you can cure me by that. Everything I've tried seems no use."

"Certainly. Nothing easier. It is just in such cases as this that the value of suggestion becomes immense."

"I don't know much about mesmerism, or hypnotism, or whatever you call it, Doctor, but I've seen professionals do some queer things at the music halls."

"Three-fourths pure trickery. Very widely different from hypnotic suggestion as taught by the modern scientific schools. Put shortly, hypnotism is nothing more than a particular mental state in which susceptibility to suggestion is heightened. The use of hypnotism to medical men is founded on the premiss that many nervous diseases can be cured, or relieved, merely by making the patient believe that he will soon be better.

"Let me put you to sleep, and suggest that your giddiness will pass away, and you will be all right in five minutes.

"Now try to sleep, think of nothing but that you are to go to sleep. Lie back in that chair, you will be more rested and feel easier; you look tired already, your eyelids are beginning to close. You are feeling more and more fatigued all over—your head is so heavy that it is falling forward—your eyes are quite closed now, your thinking powers are getting dull and confused, you are nearly asleep, now you are quite off. Fast asleep!"

The Doctor kept his eyes fixed intently on his subject.

"You are still asleep?" he asked after a few moments.

"Yes," answered Belmont drowsily.

"Fast asleep?"

"Yes."

"But you can hear the ticking of this watch," and he held a sheet of paper to Belmont's ear.

"Yes, perfectly."

"Excellent," said the Doctor to himself. "An organisation most susceptible to hypnotic suggestion. Perfect hypnosis induced at first attempt. This ought to lead to some interesting experiments. But he will need some two or three weeks' training. He told me the wedding would not be for a month yet, that ought to give me ample time for— for any experiments I may deem advisable in the interests of science, or—of myself."

He stood motionless, gazing intently at Belmont. For years had he endeavoured to trace out the murderer of his father, and now at last, he had every reason to believe that the murderer's son was in his power; but of this he still required absolute proof.

"Arthur Belmont," he said, addressing the hypnotic, "were you with your father when he died?"

"Yes," Belmont answered in a quiet, steady voice, only a shade different from his normal tones.

"He died in '84, did he not?"

"Yes."

"He came from India, and had in his possession a valuable collection of jewels, I think?"

"Yes."

"Now—you are to tell me everything he said just before he died, everything that you heard.

"There's just a chance that old Belmont let drop some word about his secret," the Doctor went on to himself, "one word is all I want to make sure.

"Tell me," he repeated aloud.

Belmont started without any hesitation, and speaking freely and easily as though he were repeating some well-learned lesson.

"It was only for Arthur's sake I did it. The old woman was right—Curse you, I will have them all—How his eyes stared and his face turned livid—My knife!—Ha! Varuna has another offering—Poor old Jack, and no one knew. The papers said it was a native—"

"Stop," said the Doctor.

And Belmont ceased talking.

A smile of grim satisfaction played about the Doctor's hard lips. His search of years was ended, and before him, peacefully wrapped in hypnotic sleep, was the son of the man who had murdered and robbed his father.

"Your giddiness is passing off now," he said. "How do you feel? Better?"

"Yes, I think it is," Belmont answered; "I feel much better."

"It will be better still in a moment, and when you wake up, it will be quite gone, and you will forget everything you've said, and simply think you've had a little nap. Wake up now, and try another cigar."

Belmont opened his eyes, and stretched himself.

"I really beg your pardon, Doctor, I do believe I dropped off to sleep; I was extra late last night, and—"

The Doctor laughed.

"Don't apologise, my dear fellow, at all. How's your giddiness? Any better?"

"It's gone. Suddenly this time. These attacks generally last an hour or so."

"Well, next time you feel one of them coming on, give me a look up, and I'll cure you permanently in a week or two. I thought I could manage to take it away this time."

"Why—you don't mean to say you hypnotised me, surely?"

"No," smiled the doctor, "I merely suggested to you, while you were asleep, that you felt better, and you fell in with my suggestion. I told you hypnotism was nothing more than suggestion, you know."

"Well, it's served my turn this time. I'll certainly come and see you when next I feel at all queer, and I shall be glad if you will look upon me as a case for your skill."

"Thanks, I will. Now, have another cigar. It won't hurt you this time."

"Thank you, I don't think it will, though I haven't been able to smoke two cigars running since I had that smash. You've worked wonders, doctor."

"Science does sometimes," replied the doctor, with a slight smile.

Arthur Belmont felt instinctively attracted to Dr. Makyne. He had fallen under the spell of the geniality of manner, the intimate knowledge the doctor had of men and things, and the pleasant, easy familiarity with which he was welcomed to the house in Harley Street. He had had recurrences of the giddiness of which he had complained, and had, time after time, availed himself of Dr. Makyne's hypnotic power to relieve it.

But unconsciously he had by slow but certain degrees fallen under the domination of the superior will, for in each succeeding hypnosis the doctor had increased his power over his subject, and had brought him to such a state of hypnotic training, that Belmont's will and mind were entirely under the doctor's control, without the subject being aware of the fact in his waking moments.

It was some weeks after their first introduction, and but a few days to the wedding, that the doctor had asked Belmont to bring the jewels from his hotel for examination and comparison.

Belmont had readily consented, and the next evening the two men were sitting in the doctor's study deeply engaged in discussing the merits of the various specimens.

Dr. Makyne looked worried and anxious, so much so, that Belmont noticed it.

"Why, doctor, you're looking quite knocked up; I thought a brain like yours could stand any amount of hard work. You've been overdoing it."

The doctor laughed. "Yes," he replied, "I do feel a bit worried, I suppose. The fact is, I have an important experiment to undertake tonight, and if I fail, it might possibly affect my reputation."

"No fear of your failing, I should say. You high priests of science seem to have the power of invoking success in whatever you attempt."

"Thanks. I accept your compliment as an augury of my good fortune and success."

He half rose from his chair as he spoke. He was sitting opposite Belmont, the table, spread with the glittering and precious collection, between them.

"Arthur Belmont," he said, in a low penetrating voice, fixing his companion with his piercing, cold eyes, "these jewels, which you have brought to my house to-night, are not your own. They were stolen by your father from mine, and they are now coming back to their rightful owner, myself.

"Sit still! Your will is under my control, and you cannot move or prevent my actions. Your—will— is— under— my — control," he repeated slowly, settling himself back in his chair, but still keeping his eyes on his victim, fascinating him by their intense power.

Belmont sat huddled together, unable to move, save to follow the doctor's movements with his eyes. His face had grown pallid and lined with fear, and his eyes had that dumb look of agony at an approaching fate that the doctor had seen so often in those of a dog when he was slowly torturing it to death, "in the interests of scientific investigation."

"Listen;" he went on. "Years ago, in India, your father murdered mine for the sake of these very jewels. You gave me the final proof of that fact when you repeated the words that he uttered on his deathbed when I first hypnotised you. What did you think of those words at the time? Answer me."

"We thought he was raving; he had a touch of fever for some days before his death. I never thought, I never knew—oh, my God!"—the voice broke off in a wail of agony—"you—you are torturing me. I swear I never thought the words were true, or that it was of his own acts he was speaking."

"That may be so; it matters little now. What does matter is that I had to suffer for the lack of the money you were enjoying. Now it is my chance of adjusting the balance, and I mean to do so. I intend to regain my father's share of the treasure and to avenge his death at the same time. You will leave these jewels here, and when you go from this house, you will entirely forget that such jewels ever existed, except that, should the hotel people inquire after them, you will say that you have left them for better security at your London banker's. No other people here know you have them in town. You told me, I think, that you informed no one, as you wished to surprise your bride by letting her make a selection for her wedding gift.

"Afterwards, if your friends should ask—but that, I think, will be immaterial, when the next few days have passed—" and the doctor laughed a vicious little laugh which came to his lips but not his eyes, as if some hidden thought had suddenly appealed to him and amused him—

"Your memory of these jewels will be an absolute blank, and you will even forget that you ever were interested in such things," he repeated, to the crouching, shrinking figure in the chair before him.

"So much for the jewels. Now listen to me further, Arthur Belmont. I am a scientist, and the pursuit of scientific investigations is my very life. There is one experiment I have long wanted to undertake, but a suitable human organisation had not been found till I met you.

"I have studied your mental characteristics with the greatest care and completeness, since my good friend, Major Dennis, introduced you to me. I owe him a deeper debt of gratitude than I think he can ever be aware of, by the way. I have made full notes on the hypnoses that you have been in, and of your symptoms, and have come to the conclusion that you are an admirable subject for my purpose. You quite follow me so far?"

"I—quite—follow—you." The words were jerked out from the parched and whitened lips, as if some involuntary power, apart from the action of the throat, impelled their utterance.

"Very well. Next Thursday you will be standing before the altar with your bride. You doubtless know the form of the Marriage Service. I must admit that personally I am better acquainted with scientific rather than with religious formulae."

He took a Prayer-book from the bookcase and turned to the Form of Solemnization of Matrimony, and went on—

"You will come to the part where you plight your troth and will be required to say after the priest:—'I, Arthur Belmont, take thee ... in sickness and in health, to love and to cherish. . . .'"

The doctor stopped. Belmont still sat motionless in a condition of deep hypnosis, his widely staring eyes following the doctor with a look of intense horror and despair, which played over his face like a wave, distorting it in a ghastly and inhuman manner.

Dr. Makyne keenly observed the effect his words produced, and laid down the Prayer-book in order to note them in his case-book before going on speaking.

"'Mental emotion under suggestion produces similar results as physical.'I remember a woman we experimented on in the Bicetre at Paris years ago, to whom I suggested that her flesh was being torn off with red-hot pincers. Her expressions and reflexes were very similar to the present ones. This is worth noting."

He went on speaking to Belmont, leaning towards him and dropping his voice, that any chance servant passing the door might not hear.

"When you reach the next sentence at the word 'part,' you will" and he leaned still closer and whispered in Belmont's ear words that caused the whole expression of the hypnotic to assume a still more intense horror, and his face to twist and writhe, till it seemed to shrivel up, as if the blast of a furnace had passed over it.

Dr. Makyne drew back and watched the effect of his suggestion—at first with an unmoved face and then with a slight pleased smile, as of an artist who contemplates a neatly touched-in sketch.

"I think my experiment is in a fair way to succeed, and that it will clear up a point in hypnotism about which, I must confess, I have been somewhat sceptical. We shall know the result by Thursday, at any rate. At present we can do no more, except to replace these jewels in their old resting-place, from which they have been absent so long.

"I must awaken him gently and by degrees this time," he went on, as he thrust the box into the cabinet and locked it. "I have rarely seen such a deep hypnosis."

He paused a moment, and then spoke in a softer voice:

"You are looking better now, Belmont. You had a nasty touch of neuralgia, but it's wearing off. You will be quite free from pain in a minute. Here is a volume of Longfellow, my favourite poet," and he laid an open book on the table. "Presently, when you wake up, you will think you've been absorbed in reading, and be asking for a cigar, forgetting everything you have dreamed, until that moment I mentioned to you next Thursday. *Then* you will remember. Now," he added, glancing at the clock on the mantelpiece, which pointed to a few minutes to nine, "when the clock strikes nine, wake up."

He strolled to the other end of the room, and stood admiring the soft beauty of a water-colour, when the clock commenced chiming, and almost simultaneously came Belmont's usual clear, pleasant voice—

"Doctor, I think I'll try another of your cigars. I was so interested in the immortal Miles Standish that I've let this go out, and it spoils a good cigar to re-light it."

"Certainly," replied the Doctor, turning round; "help yourself. It's awfully good of you to come and help an old bachelor get through them. Oh, by the way, I want you to look at this old Indian bangle I bought at a sale. It's very ancient, and rather valuable, I believe. Are you a judge of such things?"

"Not I, Doctor. I can tell you the points of a good foxhound, or talk to you about the latest pattern on a gun, but I never took any interest in jewellery. Just wear a ring or two myself, but that's all."

"Ah! It's a very interesting subject, though," replied the Doctor, drily.

"Yes, "he added to himself, "I really think my experiment will succeed."

IV.

Dr. Makyne sat in his study, filling in some details to the notes he had made on the case of Belmont. He laid down his pen, and leaned back in the softly-padded chair, glancing at his watch, which he placed on the table in front of him.

"Ten minutes to twelve. I won't add the final note until I am certain, and that won't be for an hour or more yet. Let's see — wedding timed for twelve. The critical point will be reached by about twelve-fifteen. That's as near as we can estimate. Then they will wire to Fleet Street. Nearest telegraph office to St. George's Church is in Grosvenor Street, a short three-minutes' walk—say two, for an enterprising reporter in a hurry. That will catch the one o'clock edition nicely, and the boys will have the papers up here inside another ten minutes, now that they all ride machines. That's about an hour and a-quarter. Time for a cigar and a liqueur before lunch."

He rose, and going to a cigar cabinet on the sideboard, chose, with care, a choice cigar, lit it, and poured out a glass of Chartreuse.

Passing the bookcase, as he sauntered back to his seat, he paused a moment to select a volume from its well-stocked shelves, and then settled himself luxuriously in his easy chair.

"I believe in a perfectly equable enjoyment of life, as far as is possible in man," he would have said. "When I was poor and in hardship, I was happy, and now that I am rich and in comfort, I am exactly the same. It is only the environments that have altered."

He opened the book, and turned to the lines—

"I stood upon the hills, when Heaven's high arch
Was glorious with the sun's returning march,
And woods were brightened, and soft gales
Went forth to kiss the sun-clad vales. . . .
If thou art worn and hard beset
With sorrows that thou wouldst forget,
If thou wouldst read a lesson, that will keep
Thy heart from fainting and thy soul from sleep,
Go to the woods and hills! No tears
Dim the sweet look that Nature wears."

He re-read the words slowly, and laid the book down.

"Ah," he said to himself, "how exquisitely Longfellow has written of Nature's beauties! How his poetry appeals to one's sense of peace and harmony!"

⚬

"Happy the bride that the sun shines upon." And if the same remark applies to a bridegroom, Belmont should indeed have been happy, for the morning of the 16th June, in London, was as if it had been brought from the Sunny South.

The church was filled with that throng of fashionable people to whom a Society wedding is as attractive as a remnant sale to the ordinary British matron. The sunlight streamed in through the stained glass windows, adding a further charm to the many and delicate shades of the silks and satins with which the average Society woman seeks to rival "Solomon in all his glory."

Belmont was laughing and chatting in the vestry with his best man, waiting the moment when he should join his bride at the altar.

"Never felt better in my life," he said, in reply to a query.

"That's all right, then. And so you ought, marrying a girl like that, you lucky devil. Now I'm responsible for you for the next few minutes, until you *are* married, so just do as I tell you. Don't drop the ring when I pass it to you, so that I have to go on my knees and grovel for it; and if you want to sneeze at all, just arrange that it shan't happen when the Parson Johnny asks you if you'll have her; and, above all, when he tells you to take her hand, don't ask, 'What's trumps?' Sounds bad, y'know."

"All right," said Belmont, laughing; "I'll remember. Look out! here they come!" And they left the vestry to meet the bride and her father.

The service started. The first responses had been made, and the bridegroom commenced repeating after the officiating clergyman—

"I, Arthur Belmont, take thee, Violet Neville Shafton, to be my wedded wife—"

With some surprise the best man noticed a slight hesitation in Belmont's speech, and a sudden pallor that overspread his face. The hesitation and pallor, however, both appeared to be but momentary, and he continued in a firm, clear voice:—"to have and to hold, from this time forward, for better, for worse, for richer, for poorer, in sickness, in health, to love and to cherish, till— death—do—us—part"

The soft stillness of the church was suddenly broken by a piercing shriek from the bride; for the words "till death do us part" had been uttered by the bridegroom in a voice growing gradually slower and slower, until the last word came with a horrible gasp, an expression of intense mental agony passing over his face, as he fell, with a low moan, across the altar steps, his head striking the sharp edge, and staining their fair whiteness with a dull stream of crimson.

෯෬

In his study the Doctor sat wrapped in thought, pondering over his Longfellow, as he had so often done before, when he was aroused from his reverie by the clock chiming a quarter past one. He put the book down, and paced the room, straining his ears to every sound in the streets.

Suddenly he stopped, and flung up the window and listened intently, as he heard the newsboys shrilling the words of their contents bills:

"Speshul 'dishun! 'Orrible tragedy at fashionable wedding! Bridegroom drops dead at the altar!"

He bought a paper as the lad passed the window, and turning to the stop-press telegram, read with a satisfied smile: "At the wedding of Mr. Arthur Belmont and the Hon. Violet Shafton, at St. George's Church, this morning, the bride-groom dropped dead, from heart disease, at the altar steps."

He walked to the table, and completed his memoranda on the case, with the sentence—

"On the 16th of June, Arthur Belmont died from cardiac failure."

He blotted the words, and locked the papers away in his safe.

"My theory is proved, then. Death can be caused by post-hypnotic suggestion."

He rang the bell, and the page appeared.

"Is luncheon served yet?" he asked.

"Yes, sir, it's just going in."

And Dr. Makyne strolled in to lunch with a calm and contented manner—and a most excellent appetite.

The Irishman's Story

By Julian Hawthorne

Few people are aware of the existence of a small hostelry near Slyne Head, on the west coast of Ireland. The coal-black rocks and precipitous promontories of that desolate region render the scenery imposing; and the storms, which are frequent, form a spectacle that is nothing less than magnificent. The whole force of the Atlantic breaks against those awful cliffs, and the half-wild inhabitants of the region will tell you that, in winter, the spray is sometimes dashed three hundred feet in the air. Fishing is almost the sole occupation of the natives. The nearest railway station is at Westport, thirty miles away, whence the explorer must travel either on foot or upon the dilapidated "jaunting-car" that serves as a stage, and is driven by Pat Maguire, who is also the proprietor of the inn. But explorers are as few as snowflakes in June; and for several years previous to the date of this story, Dr. Griffith Gramery had been the only visitor.

The doctor was not a comely man. He had a big, square head, covered with grizzled red hair, which stood upright; thick eyebrows hanging far down over a pair of small but extraordinarily piercing eyes; a large nose and mouth, and a broad, short chin. His head was set low down upon broad shoulders; his arms were long, but his body rather small and short. The peasants held him in superstitious awe and respect, believing him to be in league with Satan, probably because he had once or twice exercised upon them a remarkable magnetizing power that he possessed. But as all his dealings with them had been beneficent, they mingled their awe with affection. A man may be hand-in-glove with the Evil One, and yet a very good fellow at bottom.

This season, Dr. Gramery arrived, as usual, about the first of October; but he explained to Pat Maguire that a young lady and gentleman, friends of his, would come on the seventh of the month, and would expect Pat to be at Westport railway station to drive them over. The doctor, it seems, had met Mr. and Mrs. Roger Mowbray in London during the previous season, and had sung the praises of Slyne Head so eloquently that the young couple—they were in their honeymoon—had promised to come over and spend a week there. They proved as good as their word, and on the evening of the appointed day they drove upon the jaunting-car, and were cordially welcomed at the inn door by the doctor.

The moon was close to the fall, and the air soft and mild. After supper the three friends strolled out on the cliffs; and Roger Mowbray and his wife both confessed that they had never seen so grand a sight. The rocks are full of caves, some midway in the face of inaccessible precipices, some so low down as to be covered at high-water. The coast is everywhere jagged and irregular. Slyne Head itself is a beetling pinnacle of rock, overhanging its base, which is four hundred feet below its summit. The party made their way thither and sat down to contemplate the prospect. The ocean, rising in its vast sweep to the horizon, was luminous beneath the moon; and where the surf broke on the ragged teeth of the rocks far below it looked like great drifts of snow against the blackness.

"How glorious and terrible it is!" exclaimed Mrs. Mowbray. "After this, I can understand and almost believe in all the legends of ghosts and hobgoblins that Ireland is famous for!"

"None but spirits of light and loveliness should become visible to you, fair lady," said the doctor, who had a courtly, chivalrous way with women, which, partly on account of the odd contrast with his ugliness and eccentricity, made him a favorite with the sex. "But the people hereabouts are certainly very superstitious; and, to confess the truth, I have occasionally amused myself by playing off a few juggleries upon them. They take me for a magician; and it keeps them from bothering me when I want to be undisturbed. I have only to make a few cabalistic passes, and they run as if the devil were after them."

"I recollect your alluding, in London, to your powers in that direction," observed Roger. "You promised to give us an illustration some time. What more fitting time could there be than this?"

"Oh, I wish you would, Dr. Gramery!" exclaimed Mrs. Mowbray. "I never saw anything of that sort."

"And I fancy your husband doubts whether anybody ever saw anything of the sort," returned the doctor, laughing, and fixing his brilliant eyes on the young man's face. "He is a skeptic."

"Say an agnostic," rejoined Roger, with a smile. "I will believe what I see."

"If that be your only stipulation, I could easily astonish you," the doctor answered. "The eyesight and all the senses are readily deceived. Moreover, unless I am much mistaken, yours is a temperament that lends itself to such impressions. I should expect to be more successful in deceiving you than your wife; though she looks half a spirit already, while you have the thews and sinews of an athlete."

"Well, all I can say is, I am prepared for the test," replied Roger, still smiling, though with somewhat of an effort. The doctor's eyes had a singular sparkle. It was difficult to look away from them.

For a full minute, the doctor remained silent and immovable, gazing in a preoccupied manner at Roger Mowbray, who gazed back at him. Mrs. Mowbray, meanwhile, had become interested in watching the flight of a great seabird, which, alter poising itself in the air on a level with their position, suddenly swooped downward, and alighted on a rock, surrounded by waves, near the foot of the cliff.

"Look at me!" abruptly cried the doctor, in a sharp, imperious tone, springing to his feet. "I am going to jump down the precipice, and stand beside that sea-fowl. Look! Roger Mowbray, I'm off."

Roger started up with a gasp of horror and amazement. "Good God! the man is killed!" he cried out in a wild tone. He stood gazing fearfully and breathlessly over the cliff, peering downward as if following the descent of a heavy body through the air. But after a moment he raised himself, trembling and aghast, the sweat standing on his forehead. "It's a miracle!" he said, huskily; "such a thing was never known! He fell four hundred feet, and now there he stands at the bottom, nodding and waving his hand! Merciful Heaven! what a thing to see!"

"Why, Roger!" exclaimed his wife, half laughing and half alarmed, "how absurdly you act! Any one would think you were crazy! What are you saying about the doctor being down the cliff, when he has not moved a foot away from you? Why, what's the matter with you?"

Her husband paid not the slightest attention to her. He continued to stare down at the rock on which the sea-bird was seated, emitting ever and anon inarticulate ejaculations.

"He does not hear you, Mrs. Mowbray," remarked the doctor, speaking aside to her. "He is in what may be termed an abnormally imaginative state, in which one mistakes fancies for facts. He really believes that I jumped off the cliff and alighted on that rock; and nothing that you could say to him would change his conviction. Curious, is it not?"

"But what is the cause of it? He was never like this before!" cried she, becoming more and more alarmed. "Can nothing be done? Roger!" She laid her hand on her husband's arm, but he moved away from her. "He doesn't know me!" she exclaimed in terror. "Oh, what shall I do?"

"My dear Mrs. Mowbray," interposed the doctor, smiling comfortably in the moonlight, "give yourself no uneasiness; it is the simplest thing in the world. Your husband is partially asleep, that is all. A certain portion of his brain—that which discriminates between truth and imagination—has temporarily ceased to operate; it has been inhibited, to use the scientific term ; or, if you want another phrase, your husband is in a hypnotic trance. Of course you have heard of hypnotism, and you are aware how commonly it is now practiced, and how amusing some of its manifestations are. It also has the advantage of being entirely harmless. The trance can be broken as easily as it can be induced."

"Oh, but I don't like Roger to be hypnotized!" she protested, still agitated. "I want him to know me and hear me! Please make him come back to me, Dr. Gramery."

"Your word is law, my dear lady," said the good doctor, with perfect amiability. He turned to the young man, and drawing him a little to one side appeared to whisper something in his ear. Then he clapped his hands sharply together, and called out, "Hello, Mowbray! Here we are!"

Mowbray glanced up, yawned, passed his hand over his forehead, and then, looking at the doctor with evident perplexity, said: "Aren't you wet? How did you get up here again?"

"You see," said the doctor, the next morning after they had talked and laughed a good deal over the event of the night before, "hypnotism is the real explanation of all the marvels of magic and enchantment that we read and hear about. The magician's first act is to hypnotize the spectator or spectators; that done, they will see—imagine they see—any miracle he may choose to suggest to them."

"Do you mean to say," demanded Roger, "that he can put more than one person at a time into the trance?"

"A hundred as easily as one; and perhaps a thousand more easily than a hundred. Why not? Consider the phenomena of panic—the unreasoning fear that seizes upon a multitude, though each separate man of the crowd, if alone, would have retained his presence of mind; or look at the wild enthusiasm or rage to which an eloquent orator can arouse a vast audience, though any one member of it would listen to him coldly. So I doubt not it would be easier to hypnotize a large assemblage than a single individual; and the Eastern jugglers seem to do it. You have heard of the famous Indian 'Basket Trick' as it is called? There an audience of any number of persons severally and collectively witness a transaction that their reason assures them is preposterously impossible, at the same time that their eyesight convinces them it takes place. What is the explanation? Simply, that they are all hypnotized before the trick is performed; and then, of course, the 'trick' is reduced to merely inducing them to believe that something is done which is really not done at all."

"After my experience of last night, I don't feel like disputing anything you say, doctor," observed Roger Mowbray. "But I should like to know how a man can hypnotize a crowd of people, and also how they can recover from the trance without recognizing that they have been in it."

"If the conditions be favorable, nothing is more easily performed than hypnotism," the doctor replied. "Simply to fix the attention for a few moments is often sufficient; and any juggler can do that. I hypnotized you last night only by inducing you to look intently at me for sixty seconds. Then as to your second point, the trance may be of various degrees, from light to profound. The light trance is sufficient for complete self-deception, and the transition from that to waking is so easy as not to be perceived."

"I certainly believed I saw you jump over the cliff," said Roger, "and after I came to, I still could hardly persuade myself that you had not done it. Rachel, here, says she spoke to me, but I didn't hear her. But is it not rather alarming that such a power as you possess should exist?"

"Indeed, if I didn't know the doctor was a good man, I shouldn't feel safe for a moment," Rachel said.

"Luckily, I am harmless," remarked he, with a peculiar smile. "But there's truth in your suggestion, Mr. Mowbray. Hypnotism might give terrible powers. If I had told you, last night, to jump over the cliff, you would have done it, or if, while you were still in the trance, I had commanded you to do, or to see, or not to see, a certain thing at a certain future time,—say, at five o'clock this afternoon,—you would have obeyed punctually at the appointed hour, without any further action on my part."

"Dear me!" said Rachel, with a nervous laugh, "I remember you whispered something to Roger last night, before you woke him up. What did you tell him to do?"

"You said a person could be ordered 'not to see' anything," broke in Roger. "Do you mean that a concrete object could be rendered actually invisible to one in the hypnotic trance?"

"Certainly!" replied the doctor. "Anything that is told to the patient, he is bound to believe. If I were to tell you that the big tree yonder had been dug up and carried away, it would immediately become invisible to you; and neither your sense of touch nor any other means could persuade you that there was anything there. But I see this conversation is distressing Mrs. Mowbray; let us change it. Do you know, Mr. Mowbray, that you bear a strong resemblance to your late father?"

"I have been sometimes told so. But I was not aware that you knew him."

"Yes, I knew him well, many years ago, when we were both about your age. Afterward, circumstances separated us. When I met you the other day in London the likeness startled me; it was as if a buried generation had come to life again. Your father's wife was a Miss Clayton, I think?"

"Yes, that was my mother's name."

"Ah! I was not thinking of her as your mother. I do not trace her features in you. However, that is neither here nor there. Thinking over those old days has recalled another person to my mind—one John Felbrigge. I fancy you have never heard of him."

"I think I remember the name," said Roger, "but I never saw him. Unless I'm mistaken, my father and he were not good friends."

"They were friends until, for some reason, they had a bitter quarrel, and parted. It was the general opinion that Felbrigge was in fault. He was certainly a cross-grained fellow, whereas your father was always very suave and engaging. The quarrel occurred before your father's marriage, and the occasion of it, I think, was some affair of the heart. Naturally, Felbrigge would get worsted there!"

"What became of this Mr. Felbrigge?" inquired Rachel.

"He was a student, and after the quarrel he devoted himself to abstruse researches, and lived on the Continent, and afterward in India. He ought to have died long since, I suppose."

"The woman in the case was not my mother, was it?" asked Roger.

"She was not the lady your father married, I think," the doctor replied. "It was probably some earlier affair; he was a dangerous man," he added, laughing. "Now that I recollect, the other woman's name was Mercy— yes, Mercy Holland. You never knew of her?"

Mowbray shook his head.

"No, of course not!" said the doctor. "And what interest have these old stories for you young people? Come, I have something to propose! What do you say to our taking our luncheon with us, and spending the day down on the rocks? There are some curious caves I want you to see; and there is a romantic legend about one of them. Shall we go?"

The others willingly consented, and they made their preparations and set out. Instead of climbing to the top of Slyne Head, as on the previous evening, they descended to the shore, above which the stupendous crags hung as it about to topple over. In a crevice of the rocks, just above high water mark, the doctor picked up a fragment of chain with handcuff attached to it. It was but slightly rusted, and evidently could have been left there but a short time before. Mowbray and his wife were much interested in the discovery, and speculated as to how it could have got there.

"Is there a jail anywhere in this neighborhood?" Roger inquired.

"None nearer than Galway, that I know of," replied the doctor. "But I believe there have been some evictions going on in this neighborhood, and this handcuff may have been put on a prisoner who escaped. He must have had assistance in freeing himself from his fetters, however. This handcuff, as you see, shuts by a spring, and can be opened only by taking two hands to it. The person to whom it was attached could not unfasten it unaided. It is certainly odd that the fugitive should have shaped his course in this direction. In these thinly settled regions concealment is more difficult than in cities."

"What a strange feeling it must be to be fastened to a chain, and know that you can't get away," observed Rachel, examining the steel manacle with curiosity.

"People get used to even that," rejoined the doctor; "and after all, we are all fettered in some way, though the links may be invisible." He put the relic in his pocket, and they continued their journey along the beach. The way was rough and tortuous, the bowlders lying irregularly, and the pebbles of which the beach was composed offering a slippery and wearisome foothold. They were nearly an hour in going no more than a mile; but they were rewarded, at the end of their journey, by coming to a large cave, hollowed out in the seaward extremity of a promontory that formed one of the natural divisions of the beach. Its mouth was only about seven or eight feet in diameter; but inside it expanded into a chamber of fair size and height, draped with seaweed, and pervaded by the clean, salt smell of the sea. The day had been somewhat close and oppressive, and the coolness of the cave was grateful, after their arduous walk. The interior was lighted up by the rays of the declining sun, for it was already afternoon.

Using a large flat stone as a table, they unpacked their basket, and lunched at their leisure. The doctor was in capital spirits, and made himself, highly agreeable. He related many stories of his own past life and adventures; he had traveled in all parts of the world, and had lived several years in Northern India, where he had seen strange sights. Finally, the conversation got round to the spot where they then were, and the traditions connected with it.

"And, by the by, one of the best yarns is about this very cave," he remarked. "Many years ago a powerful noble lived near Slyne Head, and he married a young and beautiful woman. For a time, all appeared to go well; but finally the husband became suspicious of the attentions to his wife of a neighbor of his who was visiting him. He watched, and his suspicions were confirmed. He concealed his emotions, whatever they were and on some pretext invited his wife and the friend to this cave. He had had an iron ring fastened to the rock at the back part of the cave, with a chain attached to it. Pretending to be in sport, he induced them to let him fasten this chain around them, and then, telling them to be happy together to their hearts' content, and replying to their shrieks and entreaties only by peals of laughter, he bade them farewell and left them. The tide was rising, and a storm was coming on. A couple of hours later the cave was submerged, and the lovers were, of course, drowned. What do you think of that legend, Mrs. Mowbray? Would you like to know what the young people said to each other, when they were left alone, and the first wave threw its spray over them?"

"It is fearful to think of," said Rachel, with a shudder. "Was it really this very cave?"

"Undoubtedly; and if you want any further proof, the ring to which they were chained still hangs to the rock behind you. See—the sunlight has just reached it!"

Rachel turned with a start, and then all three approached the ring and examined it. It was hanging to a bolt driven into the face of the solid rock, at the furthest extremity of the cave. It was about seven inches in diameter, and appeared to be at least an inch in thickness, though it was so bearded with green seaweed and roughened with rust and limpets that an exact estimate was difficult. At all events, it looked strong enough to hold an ox, much more a pair of terrified lovers. Beneath the ring was a shallow ledge, forming a rude seat, and Rachel, who was fascinated by the picturesque horror of the thing, sat down upon it. The setting sun shone on her charming face, and gave it the semblance of a rosy blush. Her husband thought she had never looked more lovely.

The doctor took the handcuff from his pocket, and passed the chain through the ring, fastening it by springing one of the links over another. "That will enable us to realize the situation better," he remarked, turning to Roger with a smile, and putting the handcuff in his hand. "Imagine Mrs. Mowbray to be the lady in question, and you the wicked earl."

"Shall I manacle you, Rachel?" asked her husband, playfully.

She held out her wrist at once. "Do!" she said; "I am not afraid."

"Don't be too sure of your nerves," put in the doctor; "it might give you a turn."

"Oh, my husband will not desert me," she replied. "Put it on, Roger."

He slipped it on and fastened it. "There—now you are a prisoner," said he.

"And now all you have to do is to imagine that you are to stay there until this time to-morrow," the doctor added, "when some fisherman, perhaps, will discover your drowned and bruised body. You are looking for the last time on yonder setting sun. Do you hear the plunging of the surf? In another hour it will be at the mouth of the cave; an hour more and it will have filled it to the roof. You will be alone, and death will come slowly and frightfully. You will struggle and strain, and tug at your fetters; the steel will cut into your flesh, but you cannot break it. The cold water will creep slowly to your knees, your waist, your throat. You will scream—ah! what screams! but the rocks will echo them back, and they will die away upon the sea. You will think of the sweetness of life, of your warm and familiar home, of the love of your friends, and of your husband—and then the wave will lap over your face and gurgle into your mouth, and strangle your breath; you will be nothing but a lump of lifeless flesh, and this pleasant, luxurious world will know you no more!"

Doctor Gramery must have had a good deal of the actor's talent; he had begun his speech lightly enough, but as he went on his voice became hoarse and incisive; he made strange gestures, and there was something terrible and ominous in his aspect. Rachel sat gazing at him with parted lips and widening eyes. As he finished she rose to her feet, and stretching out her hand to her husband, faltered: "Let me go!"

By a sudden, forcible movement the doctor interposed himself between them.

"Five o'clock!" he exclaimed, in a stern, commanding tone.

Roger stood motionless for a few moments, while a dazed expression came over his face. The doctor now moved to one side; the husband and wife were within a couple of paces of each other, and his eyes rested upon her. But there was a queer, vague look in them, and presently he said, in a sluggish tone, "Where is Rachel?"

"Here I am—here!" she exclaimed. "Here in front of you! What ails you, Roger? Take off this manacle—it hurts me! Don't you hear me?"

"It is very odd," said Roger, turning to the doctor. "What has become of Rachel? She was here just now, and I didn't see her go out. How was it?"

"Mrs. Mowbray?" responded the doctor, coolly. "Why, my dear fellow, she just went out of the cave. Is it possible you didn't notice her? See!" he added, pointing outward, "there she stands on that rock at the entrance, beckoning to us! Come on, it's getting damp, and we shall be catching our death of cold. We have a long walk before us."

The two men moved together toward the mouth of the cave, Roger walking like a man in a dream. Suddenly a piercing shriek filled the cave. "Roger! my husband! my love! Hear me! Come to me!" Then came another shriek.

Mowbray and the doctor were now at the mouth of the cave, and the latter pointed along the beach to the right. "There she goes!" he said. "Let us hurry and catch up with her. She will stumble among these slippery stones and hurt herself."

"Oh, God!" said a husky voice, strained and unnatural. The chain rattled and strained; there was a groan. Mowbray had moved out of sight. The doctor turned and looked into the cave with a hideous expression; then he, too, vanished.

A storm had been gathering during the afternoon, and soon after five o'clock it burst over Slyne Head, with frequent crashes of thunder and zig-zags of lightning. The rain hissed down in torrents. Six o'clock had passed when Roger Mowbray, his clothes soaked through, and a scared, drawn look on his face, walked hastily into the inn, and called for Pat Maguire. After the summons had been repeated once or twice, with increasing emphasis,

Mrs. Maguire appeared from the kitchen, wiping her hands on her apron. "What would ye be pleased to want, sorr?" said she. "Sure, Misther Maguire stepped out an hour ago; he was after fearin' ye'd be caught in the rain, and 'twas warnin' ye to come home he'd be. Didn't ye meet him at all, at all?"

"No. Has Mrs. Mowbray—my wife—has she returned?"

"Yer wife, is it? Indade, then, she has not, sorr! Ye're the first in this night."

"Doctor Gramery—has not he got back? We parted on the beach—he took another path up the cliff. Have you seen nothing of either of them?"

"Not I, Misther Mowbray—hide nor hair av 'em. But there was a bit av a letter the doctor left this mornin', an' he was tellin' Misther Maguire to give it ye at six o'clock—not sooner. Maybe that'll explain things—more betoken 'tis six o'clock now, an' afther. Wait till I fetch it!"

She disappeared into the kitchen, and returned in a moment with a letter in her hands. Roger opened it, and this is what he read:

"Roger Mowbray:—When you read this I shall have accomplished the purpose for which I brought you down here, and for which I have waited many years. You know me as Griffith Gramery, but my true name is John Felbrigge. Thirty years ago your father took away the woman I loved, Mercy Holland, and ruined her. She bore him a child; by his cruelty and neglect she died in childbed. At that time he had already married; but his wife being an invalid, and incapable of raising up children for him, he caused you to be put forward as her son, thereby keeping the estates in the family. But you have no more right to your name than any other base-born waif of the gutter.

"I waited a long while for the proper time and means for retaliation; but when I heard that you were married, I saw my way. Last night I proved my power over you; to-day, in the cave, I shall put it into practice. At the moment you read this, your wife, chained to the rock by the manacle I have provided for the purpose, will be drawing her last breath in loneliness and agony—an agony as great, I trust, as that which your father caused Mercy Holland to endure. And you, realizing that you abandoned her there, misled by the be-wilderment I put upon your senses, will understand something of the despair I felt when I knew that the woman I would have made my wife had died in shame and misery. May you live to endure that despair as long as I have done! As for me, you will never see me again. I have my place of retreat provided where I shall spend many years in ease and comfort, happy in the assurance that all I desired has been brought to pass. Blessed be hypnotism!

"Yours to command,
"John Felbrigge."

Roger Mowbray slowly laid the letter down on the table, and looked up with a ghastly countenance. At that moment there was a hurried step on the threshold, a sound of voices, and the door was thrown open. In swept the storm, with wind and rain; a clap of thunder shook the house; and there stood Pat Maguire, red in the face and breathless, and leaning on his arm, weak and tottering, her clothing drenched and torn, her wet hair hanging about her shoulders, her wrist bruised and bloody—there was Rachel Mowbray, rescued at utmost need, with the sea leaping at her very throat, by the worthy Irishman whom chance had brought within hearing of her final outcry. There she was, no phantom of a bewildered brain, but true flesh and blood, alive and safe—and in her husband's arms!

Next morning, when the storm had cleared away, the dead body of Doctor Gramery, alias John Felbrigge, was found lying at the foot of Slyne Head, crushed and disfigured. How he came to his death, whether by accident or design, was never known. He may have lost his way and missed his footing in the storm; or the horror of the deed he had done may have proved too much even for his iron nerves, and he sought oblivion in suicide. He was buried where he fell, and the great cliff is his gravestone; but the peasants avoid the spot, and in the roaring of the waves they sometimes fancy that they catch the fearful outcry of a lost soul.

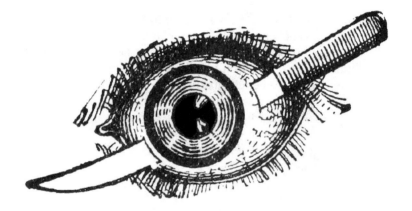

Suggested Suicide

by Erckmann-Chatrian

At that time—said Christian—I was as poor as a church mouse, and had taken refuge in the gable end of an old house on the Strasse Minnesinger at Nuremberg.

I dwelt in the angle of the slated roof, and could only stand upright in the middle of my room with its sloping walls. To reach my window I had to walk over my straw pallet, but this window had a magnificent unbroken view of city and country. I could see the cats gravely promenading in the gutters, the swans on the distant river bringing food to their devouring young, the pigeons with their tails spread like fans whirling to the depths of the street below, and when the Angelus bell called the world to prayer they would come and perch on my roof crooning their melancholy song. I could see the good burghers sitting before their doors, smoking their pipes, and the young girls in their short red petticoats with their pitchers on their arms, laughing and talking around the fountain. I would watch the windows of the city light up, one by one; then gradually all would fade away, the shadow queen, Night, would lay her mantle on the earth and sky, the bats come flitting from their hiding places, and I would go to sleep in sweet solitude.

The old second-hand dealer, Toubac, knew the way to my garret as well as I knew it myself. He was not afraid to climb my ladder, and every week his goat-like head, surmounted by a reddish wig, would peer through my trap-door, his fingers clinging to the edge of my loft, as he said, "Ach Himmel, Master Christian, have you anything new?"—to which I would reply, "Come in, come in; I am about finishing a little landscape for you. Then with a silent laugh his great lank body would lengthen, lengthen, until he touched the roof.

To do Toubac justice, he never chaffered with me. He bought all my sketches, one with another, at fifteen florins, and sold them for forty. Oh! he was an honest Jew.

This kind of life pleased me. I was happy and content, when one day the whole city of Nuremberg was startled by a strange, mysterious event. Not far from my dormer window, a little to the left, was the Inn of the Boeuf-Gras, an old inn very renowned throughout the country. There were always three or four wagons standing before the door, loaded with sacks and barrels. The country people on their way to market all stopped at the Boeuf-Gras for their tipple of beer.

The gable end of this inn was remarkable for its peculiar form. It was very narrow and pointed; the sides were cut in saw-teeth, and grotesque carving—intertwined serpents—ornamented the cornice and windows. But what was more remarkable, the house facing it had exactly the same carving, the same ornaments, even the same iron rod for the sign-board. You could almost imagine that these two old dwellings reflected each other, only behind the inn a great oak spread its shadowing leaves above the roof, while the roof of the other house was clearly outlined against the sky. Again, as the Boeuf-Gras was gay and animated, the other house was dark and silent. On one side, crowds of drinkers were incessantly coming and going, shouting, singing, and cracking their whips, on the other side, were silence and solitude. Only once or twice a day, the heavy door would open to let an old woman pass through, her back bent like a bow, her chin long and pointed, her robe clinging to her hips, and an enormous basket on her arm.

The physiognomy of this old woman struck me forcibly; her little green eyes, her thin sharp nose, her great flowered shawl, which seemed at least a hundred years old, the lace on her bonnet falling down to her eyebrows, all seemed so fantastic that she interested me in spite of myself. I wanted to know what this lonely old woman was doing in that great, deserted house. I imagined she lived a life of good works and pious meditations.

But one day I stopped in the street a moment to look at her; she suddenly turned and gave me a glance so horrible in expression, distorting her face with such hideous grimaces, that I fairly shuddered. Then walking off, shaking her trembling head, and drawing her great shawl about her, she disappeared behind the heavy door. "She is mad," I said, "a wicked old madwoman. I was stupid to interest myself about her. But truly, I should like to catch that expression. Toubac would willingly give me forty francs for it."

This jesting did not reassure me. The horrible glance of that old woman pursued me everywhere. When I climbed the perpendicular ladder to my garret, I imagined that she was crouching somewhere in the darkness, waiting to catch me by my coat tails and pull me backward.

I related these fancies to Toubac, who, far from laughing, gravely said, "Take care, Master Christian. Beware of this old woman. Her teeth are sharp, pointed, and of marvellous whiteness, which is not natural at her age. They say she has the evil eye, the children fly from her, and the people call her the Flittermouse, or bat."

I admired the perspicacity of the Jew, and his words gave me food for reflection. But after some weeks, having frequently met the Flittermouse without any evil consequences, my fears disappeared, and I thought no more about her.

Well, one evening when I was sleeping a heavy, dreamless sleep, I was awakened by a strange harmony, a sweet melodious vibration, like the breeze sighing among the leaves. I listened a long time, almost breathless, afraid to move for fear of losing this tremulous musical sound. Finally I turned toward my window, and saw two wings beating against the glass. At first I thought it was a bat caught in my room; then the moonbeams gleaming on the transparent filigree of the wings showed me a magnificent "butterfly of the night." Sometimes the vibrations were so rapid that I could scarcely distinguish them, then the rhythmic movement would cease and the creature would repose upon the glass like a delicate tracery of lace.

This aerial apparition in the silence of the night thrilled my heart with sweet emotions. It seemed to me some pitying angel, touched by my solitude, come to soothe my loneliness, and the thought softened me to tenderness and tears.

"Rest tranquil, sweet captive," I said, "I will not retain thee against thy will. Return to liberty and Heaven." I opened my little window. The night was calm, millions of stars sparkled in the sky. One instant I contemplated this sublime spectacle, the words of prayer naturally trembling on my lips, when, imagine my amazement and horror, on lowering my eyes, I saw a man hanged to the rod which supported the sign of the Boeuf-Gras, his straggling hair, stiff arms, and legs stretched to a point, casting a gigantic shadow on the street below.

The immobility of that figure in the cold moonlight was something frightful. I tried to cry out, my tongue seemed frozen in my mouth, my teeth clashed against each other. I do not know what mysterious power drew my eyes to the shadowy depths beyond, where I dimly saw the old woman crouching at her window contemplating the hanged man with diabolical satisfaction.

I was seized with terror. All my strength failed me, and I recoiled against the wall and fell on my bed unconscious. How long I remained in this death-like sleep I do not know. When I came to myself, it was broad day, and my hair was wet with the dews of the night. A confused noise came up from the street below. I looked out. The burgomaster and his secretary were standing before the door of the inn. People were coming and going; some would stop a moment to look, then continue on their way. The good women of the neighborhood, sweeping before their doors, gazed up and down the street, and talked among themselves. At last a litter, and upon that litter a body covered by a woollen cloth, came out of the inn, borne by two men. As they went down the street, the children ran behind them. Then the crowd dispersed, and all was quiet.

The window of the inn in front of me was still open. A bit of rope hung from the rod of the sign board. It was not a dream. I had seen the "butterfly of the night "—the hanged man—and the old woman crouching at her window.

Toubac made me a visit that day. As soon as his great nose was on a level with my floor, he cried out, "Master Christian, have you anything for me?"

Seated upon my only chair, my hands on my knees, my eyes fixed on vacancy, I paid no attention to him. Surprised at my silence, Toubac called still louder, "Master Christian!" Then striding across my loft, he slapped me on the shoulder: "Ach Himmel! What's the matter with you?"

"Ah! Is that you, Toubac?"

"Well, I should think so. Are you sick?"

"No, I am thinking."

"What in the devil are you thinking of?"

"Of the hanged man."

"Ah! ah!" cried the old second-hand dealer, "then you saw him. Poor boy, what a strange story; the third one in the same place!"

"How? The third?" I exclaimed.

"Yes. I should have told you, but it is time enough yet; there will be the fourth to follow his example."

As Toubac spoke, he seated himself on the edge of my chest, and lighting his pipe sent trailings of blue smoke along the bare walls.

"Mein Gott!" he continued; "I am not a coward, but before I would pass a night in that room, I would go and hang myself elsewhere. Just think of it, Master Christian; nine or ten months ago, a good man from Terbingen, fat and jolly, a dealer in furs, stopped at the Boeuf-Gras, demanding supper and lodging. He ate well, drank well; they put him to sleep in that chamber, the green chamber, as they call it. Next morning he was found hanged to the rod of the sign board. Well, if he were the only one, there would be little more to tell. The coroner was summoned, and they buried him in the strangers' grave at the end of the garden.

"But about six weeks afterward, a brave soldier from Neustadt came along. He had his definite discharge in his pocket, and was so happy at the thought of seeing his native village again. All the evening as he emptied his beer glass he talked of nothing but his home, and the dear little cousin waiting to marry him. At last they put this brave man to bed, and that same night, as the watchman passed along the Minnesinger, he perceived something on the rod of the sign board. He raised his lantern, and there hung this brave soldier, his definite discharge in his pocket, his hands pressed close to his thighs as if he were on parade.

"' Bless my soul,' said the burgomaster. 'This is extraordinary. What can it mean?'

"They examined the chamber, replastered the walls, and sent a mortuary report to Neustadt of 'sudden death.' All Nuremburg was indignant against the innkeeper. Some wanted to force him to take down his iron rod, saying it inspired people with dangerous ideas. But old Nikel Schmidt would not hear of it.

"'That rod,' said he,' was put up there by my grandfather. It has carried the sign of the Boeuf-Gras for more than a hundred years. It has done no harm to any one, not even to the hay wagons that pass under it. All those who don't want to look at it can turn their heads.'

"Well, the excitement passed away, and for many months there was nothing new. Unhappily a student from Heidelberg, on his way from the University, stopped at the Boeuf-Gras day before yesterday. He was the son of a pastor. Now do you suppose the son of a pastor would think of hanging himself on the rod of a sign board, just because a great Meinherr and a brave soldier had hanged themselves there? You must acknowledge. Master Christian, it is not reasonable. Ah, well—"

"Stop! stop!" I cried. "There is some frightful mystery under all this. It is not the rod, it is not the chamber."

"What! do you suspect the innkeeper, one of the most honest men in the world, belonging to one of the oldest families of Nuremberg?"

"No. God preserve me from unjust suspicions, but there are depths of darkness we cannot fathom."

"You are right," said Toubac, astonished at my excitement. "Let us talk of something better, Master Christian,—of our landscape."

This brought me back to reality, the affair was soon arranged, and Toubac descended the ladder very well satisfied, charging me to think no more of the student of Heidelberg. I would most willingly have followed his counsel, but when the devil mixes himself up in our affairs, it is not easy to be rid of him.

II.

Alone in the solitude of my room, this strange story returned to my mind with frightful pertinacity.

"The old woman," I said, "is the cause of all this. She alone has conceived and consummated these crimes. But by what means? Has she resorted to artifice, or the assistance of supernatural powers?"

I walked up and down my narrow loft, a voice within me crying out: "It was not in vain that Heaven permitted you to see the Flittermouse contemplating the agony of her victim. It was not in vain that the soul of the poor young man came to you in the form of a butterfly of the night. No, it was not in vain. Heaven has imposed a terrible task upon you, Christian, and if you do not accomplish it, take care! You will fall into the toils of the old woman yourself. Perhaps at this moment she is weaving her net in the shadowy darkness."

For many days these frightful thoughts pursued me without ceasing. I could not sleep. It was impossible to work; the brush fell from my hand, and—horrible to say—I frequently found myself viewing the iron rod with complacency.

At last I could stand it no longer. One evening I leaped down my ladder, four steps at a time, ran out into the street, and crouched behind the door of Flittermouse to surprise her fatal secret.

From this time, there was not a day that I was not in the streets, watching the old woman, never letting her out of my sight; but she was so crafty, and had such subtle instincts, that, without turning her head, she knew when I was following her and caught me at all my schemes. Nevertheless she pretended not to see me, would go and return from the market like any good woman, only now and then she would hasten her steps, and mutter confused words to herself.

At the end of a month, I saw that it was impossible to attain my end by this means, and the conviction filled me with inexpressible sadness.

"What must I do? The old woman divines my projects; she is always on guard; everything fails me; the old vixen already believes that I am at the end of my rope. What must I do?"

As I asked myself this question, a bright thought came into my head. My attic overlooked the dwelling of the Flittermouse, but there was no window on that side of my room. I lightly raised one of the slates of my roof, and could scarcely contain my joy; the whole interior of the old building was open to my view. "At last I have you," I cried; "you cannot escape me now. From here I can see all your movements, the habits of the fox in his den. You will not suspect this invisible eye, this eye that will surprise your crime at the moment of consummation. Oh, justice marches slowly, but surely."

Nothing could be more sinister than the interior of this old building. A dark court, paved with greenish mouldy slabs; in one corner a pool of sickening, stagnant water; a rickety stairway leading to a gallery with a wooden railing; on this railing old clothes, rags, and the empty case of a worn mattress. On the first floor to the left was a stone sink, indicating the kitchen; on the right, were high windows looking upon the street, with some pots of withered flowers on the sills. Everything was gloomy, dilapidated, and mouldering. The sun never penetrated the depths of this court, never brightened the old cracked walls, the worm-eaten gallery, or dust-tarnished windows. It was truly an asylum for bats. Flittermouse must have been well pleased.

I had scarcely finished these observations when the old woman entered. She had returned from the market. I heard the heavy door grind on its hinges, then Flittermouse appeared with her basket. She seemed fatigued, and out of breath; and she held to the banisters as she climbed the stairs.

It was suffocatingly hot, and one of those days when the insects come out of their hiding-places and fill the air with their rasping sounds. The old woman softly crossed the gallery like a ferret. Spying a struggling fly, she caught and delicately presented it to a bloated spider squatting in a corner of the gallery, then passed into the kitchen, returned in a few minutes, shook out the old clothes on the railing, made a few strokes with her broom on the steps, then suddenly raised her head, her green eyes searchingly scanning my roof.

By what strange intuition did she suspect something? I could not tell, but I softly lowered the slate, and gave up the position of spy for that day.

For six weeks I could discover nothing singular in the Flittermouse; sometimes she would peel her potatoes, sometimes spread her linen on the railing, sometimes spin a little; but she never sang, as is the custom of good old women, whose quavering voices blend so well with the buzzing of the wheel.

Silence reigned around her; not a sparrow came to light on her window sill; the pigeons in flying over her court seemed to spread their wings with greater velocity. Everything shunned her. Only the spider seemed pleased in her society.

You cannot conceive of my patience in these long hours of watching; nothing escaped me; at the least noise I would raise my slate, stimulated by curiosity and indefinable fear.

In the mean time Toubac complained:

"Master Christian, how in the devil do you pass your time? In other days you gave me something every week. Now it is scarcely one a month. Ah, these painters! It is a true saying, 'Idle as a painter.' As soon as they get a few kreutzers in their pocket, they go to sleep."

I began to lose courage myself. In spite of all my spying and watching, I could discover nothing extraordinary. I said, "The old woman can't be so very dangerous after all. Perhaps I am wrong to suspect her." I found myself making many excuses for her, when one evening with my eye to my hole I abandoned all these benevolent reflections.

The scene suddenly changed. Flittermouse passed across the gallery like a flash. She was no longer the same. Her back was straight, her head erect, her jaws were firmly set, she walked with a quick step, her gray hair floating behind her. "Oh, ho," I said, "something has happened."

That night, when the noise of the city had died away, when silence and mystery had settled on the old dwelling, I threw myself on my pallet and suddenly saw that the window in front of me was lighted; a traveller occupied the green chamber, the chamber of the hanged. Then all my fears returned; the agitation of Flittermouse was explained; she scented a victim.

I slept no more that night; the rustling of a straw, the nibbling of a mouse under the floor, made me shiver. I got up, perched myself at my window, and listened. The light in front of me was finally extinguished, but a moment before, whether it were reality or illusion, I thought I saw the old vixen also waiting and listening. I watched through the long hours until the gray dawn lay on city and distant hill. Then, worn out with fatigue and excitement, I slept, but my sleep was short; by eight o'clock I was at my post of observation.

It appeared that the night of Flittermouse had not been more peaceful than mine. When she opened the door on the gallery, a livid pallor covered her face and meagre neck; she had on only her chemise and a woolen petticoat, and her gray hair was tumbling on her shoulders. She looked over to my side with a dreamy air, but saw nothing; she was thinking of other things. Suddenly she descended, leaving her old shoes at the top of the stairs, no doubt to assure herself that the lower door was securely fastened; she quickly ascended the stairs, leaping three or four steps at a time—it was frightful. She darted into a neighboring room, I heard something like the opening of a great chest, then Flittermouse appeared on the gallery dragging a manikin behind her—and the manikin was dressed like the student of Heidelberg.

The old woman with surprising dexterity suspended this frightful object to a beam overhead, then she descended to contemplate her work from the court. A peal of abrupt laughter escaped her lips. She ascended and descended again and again like a maniac, every time uttering new cries and fresh bursts of laughter.

A noise was heard in the street; the old woman bounded forward, unhooked the manikin, carried it away, returned, and, leaning on the banister, her neck stretched, her eyes gleaming, she listened intently. The noise passed by, the muscles of her face relaxed, she drew a sigh of relief. It was only a passing carriage. Evidently the old vixen was frightened. Then she re-entered the chamber, and I heard the lid of the chest closed.

This strange scene amazed me. What did the manikin mean? I became more watchful than ever.

Soon after this Flittermouse went out with her basket. I watched her to the turn of the street. She had retaken her air of trembling old age, walked with tottering steps, turning from time to time to see if any one noticed her.

She remained out five long hours, while I restlessly tramped up and down my loft. To me the time was insupportable; the sun beating down on my roof seemed to scorch my brain.

I saw the good man who occupied the fatal chamber sitting at his window, calmly smoking his pipe. He was a good-natured looking peasant from Nassau, with a three-cornered hat and a scarlet waistcoat, and evidently had no thought of harm. I wanted to cry out, "Take care, my good man; beware of the old woman."

But he would not have understood me.

In about two hours Flittermouse returned. I heard the closing of the great heavy door. Then she appeared in the court, seated herself on the lower step of the stairs, and placed her enormous basket before her. At first she drew out some packages of herbs and vegetables, then a scarlet waistcoat, a folded three-cornered hat, plush breeches, a pair of long woollen stockings—the exact costume of the peasant from Nassau.

I had a revelation, flames actually passed before my eyes. I recalled those precipices which draw you with irresistible power, wells you feel forced to throw yourself into, depths of darkness you dare not gaze upon for fear of being drawn into their rayless gloom. I remembered the contagion of suicide and murder, the fantastic allurement of example, which makes you yawn when others yawn, suffer when you see others suffer, and take your life because you see another take his life. My hair stood on end with horror.

How the Flittermouse, this low, degraded creature, had been able to divine this profound law of nature, I could not conceive. How she had found means to make it subservient to her sanguinary instincts, I could not understand. Without reflecting any further upon this strange mystery, I determined to turn this fatal law against herself, to draw the old vixen into her own trap; so many innocent victims were crying for vengeance.

I immediately started to carry out my plans, ran to all the old clothes dealers of Nuremberg, and late that evening arrived at the Boeuf Gras with a great bundle under my arm.

Nickel Schmidt knew me well. I had painted the portrait of his wife.

"Ah, Master Christian; what happy circumstance has procured me the pleasure of seeing you?"

"Well, to tell the truth, Master Schmidt, I have a desire to pass a night in that chamber." As we were standing at the door of the inn, I pointed above to the green room. The good man gave me a suspicious glance.

"Do not be afraid," I said, "I have no thought of hanging myself."

"Ah, that is well. It would be a great pity to lose a painter of your talents. When do you want the room, Master Christian?"

"To-night."

"It is impossible; it is occupied."

"The gentleman can have it immediately," said a voice behind us; "I don't want it any longer."

We turned around much surprised. It was the peasant from Nassau, his great three-cornered hat on the back of his head, his bundle on the end of his stick. He had heard the story of the three suicides, and was fairly trembling with rage.

"Rooms like yours'" he stammered, "ought to—ought to—it's murder—assassination—you deserve to be sent to the galleys."

"Come, come; be quiet," said the innkeeper. "It has not prevented you from sleeping well."

"No, thank God! I said my prayers last night; if it had not been for that, where would I be? Where would I be?" and he went off holding up his hands to heaven.

"Ah, well," said Master Schmidt, very much astonished, "the chamber is vacant, but you are not going to play me a bad trick, I hope."

"It would be worse for me than for you, my dear sir."

I handed my package to the servant and took my place among the drinkers. I had not felt so calm and happy for a long time. After so much anxiety, I seemed to be nearing the end, the clouds were breaking, some invisible power seemed upholding me.

I lighted my pipe, emptied my glass of beer, and leaning my elbow on the table listened to a band playing in the Strasse. Lost in a kind of dreamy wakefulness, I would every now and then note the hour, and ask myself if the weary past was not a dream. But when the watchman warned us that it was time to leave the hall, other and more serious thoughts filled my mind, as I followed the little maid who preceded me with a lighted candle.

III.

We ascended to the third story. Placing the light in my hand, she pointed to a door, saying "There it is," and hastily descended the stairs.

Opening the door, I found the green room like all other rooms of an inn, the ceiling very low, the bed very high. I explored it at a glance, and glided to the window. Nothing was yet to be seen at the house of Flittermouse, only in a long obscure chamber a dim light was burning.

"That is well," said I, closing the curtains. "I have sufficient time."

I opened my package, took out a woman's bonnet with deep hanging lace, and put it on, and placing myself before the glass I began with a sharp-pointed brush to trace my face with wrinkles. This took me nearly an hour, and when I put on the robe and great flowered shawl, I was actually afraid of myself. There was Flittermouse looking at me from the depths of the glass.

Just then the watchman cried, "Eleven o'clock!" I quickly took out the manikin I had brought, dressed it in the costume of the old woman, and placed it near the window.

After all I had seen of the old vixen's craftiness, her infernal cunning, and artful deviltry, nothing would have surprised me. I parted the curtains and waited in some trepidation.

The dim light I had noticed in that long, dismal chamber cast its yellowish rays on the manikin of the Nassau peasant. It was cowering at the foot of the bed, the head hanging upon the breast, the three-cornered hat drawn over the face, the arms dragging as if plunged in the depths of despair.

The light was managed with such diabolical skill that only part of the figure appeared, but the red waistcoat with its great buttons was plainly visible. This motionless, pathetic figure in the silence of night struck the imagination with wonderful power. Even I, although forewarned, felt cold shivers down my back. How then would it be with a poor countryman, unexpectedly confronted with this dismal spectre? He would become so terrified that he would lose all self-control, and the spirit of imitation would do the rest.

I could see Flittermouse crouching in the shadowy darkness, but was careful not to let her see me. Softly opening the curtains, I raised the manikin and made it appear as if it were advancing toward her. Then suddenly, seizing a light, I threw the window wide open and stood in full view of the old vixen, *the living image of herself.*

In her amazement she dropped the manikin of the peasant and looked at me in stupefied terror. A horrible pantomime commenced. She extended her finger—I extended mine; her lips trembled—I made mine tremble; she leaned forward—I did the same. I cannot describe this frightful scene. It was like the madness of delirium and insanity. It was a struggle between two wills, two minds, two souls, which should conquer the other, and in that struggle I had the advantage, for the poor victims in shapes of horror aided me.

After imitating the movements of Flittermouse for a few moments, I drew a rope from under my petticoat, and fastened it to the rod of the sign board.

The old woman watched me with gaping mouth as I passed the rope around my neck, her wild-beast eyes gleaming, her features convulsed.

"No, no," she cried in a stifled voice.

I continued with the coolness of an executioner.

Then she was seized with a fit of rage; clinching the window-sill with her hands, she howled:

"Old fool—old fool."

I did not give her time to finish; suddenly extinguishing my light, I bent down like one about to take a sudden leap, and seizing the manikin I had already prepared, I dashed it into space.

A terrible cry from across the street, then all was silent.

I listened a long time, great drops of sweat beading my brow; then I heard far, far away in the distance the voice of the watchman crying: "Past twelve o'clock!"

"Now justice is done," I murmured; "the three victims are avenged. God pardon me!"

Just a moment after the cry of the watchman I had seen the old woman leap from her window, a rope around her neck, and hang suspended from the iron rod, her body writhing in the contortions of death. And the calm, silent moon, looking over the high, pointed roof, cast her cold, pale rays on the distorted face and long, floating hair.

Just as I saw the poor young man, I now saw the Flittermouse.

Next day all Nuremberg knew the bat had hanged herself. It was the last event of that kind on the Strasse Minnesinger.

John Barrington Cowles

By Arthur Conan Doyle

It might seem rash of me to say that I ascribe the death of my poor friend, John Barrington Cowles, to any preternatural agency. I am aware that in the present state of public feeling a chain of evidence would require to be strong indeed before the possibility of such a conclusion could be admitted.

I shall therefore merely state the circumstances which led up to this sad event as concisely and as plainly as I can, and leave every reader to draw his own deductions. Perhaps there may be some one who can throw light upon what is dark to me.

I first met Barrington Cowles when I went up to Edinburgh University to take out medical classes there. My landlady in Northumberland Street had a large house, and, being a widow without children, she gained a livelihood by providing accommodation for several students.

Barrington Cowles happened to have taken a bedroom upon the same floor as mine, and when we came to know each other better we shared a small sitting-room, in which we took our meals. In this manner we originated a friendship which was unmarred by the slightest disagreement up to the day of his death.

Cowles' father was the colonel of a Sikh regiment and had remained in India for many years. He allowed his son a handsome income, but seldom gave any other sign of parental affection—writing irregularly and briefly.

My friend, who had himself been born in India, and whose whole disposition was an ardent tropical one, was much hurt by this neglect. His mother was dead, and he had no other relation in the world to supply the blank.

Thus he came in time to concentrate all his affection upon me, and to confide in me in a manner which is rare among men. Even when a stronger and deeper passion came upon him, it never infringed upon the old tenderness between us.

Cowles was a tall, slim young fellow, with an olive, Velasquez-like face, and dark, tender eyes. I have seldom seen a man who was more likely to excite a woman's interest, or to captivate her imagination. His expression was, as a rule, dreamy, and even languid; but if in conversation a subject arose which interested him he would be all animation in a moment. On such occasions his colour would heighten, his eyes gleam, and he could speak with an eloquence which would carry his audience with him.

In spite of these natural advantages he led a solitary life, avoiding female society, and reading with great diligence. He was one of the foremost men of his year, taking the senior medal for anatomy, and the Neil Arnott prize for physics.

How well I can recollect the first time we met her! Often and often I have recalled the circumstances, and tried to remember what the exact impression was which she produced on my mind at the time. After we came to know her my judgment was warped, so that I am curious to recollect what my unbiassed instincts were. It is hard, however, to eliminate the feelings which reason or prejudice afterwards raised in me.

It was at the opening of the Royal Scottish Academy in the spring of 1879. My poor friend was passionately attached to art in every form, and a pleasing chord in music or a delicate effect upon canvas would give exquisite pleasure to his highly-strung nature. We had gone together to see the pictures, and were standing in the grand central salon, when I noticed an extremely beautiful woman standing at the other side of the room. In my whole life I have never seen such a classically perfect countenance. It was the real Greek type—the forehead broad, very low, and as white as marble, with a cloudlet of delicate locks wreathing round it, the nose straight and clean cut, the lips inclined to thinness, the chin and lower jaw beautifully rounded off, and yet sufficiently developed to promise unusual strength of character.

But those eyes—those wonderful eyes! If I could but give some faint idea of their varying moods, their steely hardness, their feminine softness, their power of command, their penetrating intensity suddenly melting away into an expression of womanly weakness—but I am speaking now of future impressions!

There was a tall, yellow-haired young man with this lady, whom I at once recognised as a law student with whom I had a slight acquaintance.

Archibald Reeves—for that was his name—was a dashing, handsome young fellow, and had at one time been a ringleader in every university escapade; but of late I had seen little of him, and the report was that he was engaged to be married. His companion was, then, I presumed, his *fiancée*. I seated myself upon the velvet settee in the centre of the room, and furtively watched the couple from behind my catalogue.

The more I looked at her the more her beauty grew upon me. She was somewhat short in stature, it is true; but her figure was perfection, and she bore herself in such a fashion that it was only by actual comparison that one would have known her to be under the medium height.

As I kept my eyes upon them, Reeves was called away for some reason, and the young lady was left alone. Turning her back to the pictures, she passed the time until the return of her escort in taking a deliberate survey of the company, without paying the least heed to the fact that a dozen pair of eyes, attracted by her elegance and beauty, were bent curiously upon her. With one of her hands holding the red silk cord which railed off the pictures, she stood languidly moving her eyes from face to face with as little self-consciousness as if she were looking at the canvas creatures behind her. Suddenly, as I watched her, I saw her gaze become fixed, and, as it were, intense. I followed the direction of her looks, wondering what could have attracted her so strongly.

John Barrington Cowles was standing before a picture—one, I think, by Noel Paton—I know that the subject was a noble and ethereal one. His profile was turned towards us, and never have I seen him to such advantage. I have said that he was a strikingly handsome man, but at that moment he looked absolutely magnificent. It was evident that he had momentarily forgotten his surroundings, and that his whole soul was in sympathy with the picture before him. His eyes sparkled, and a dusky pink shone through his clear olive cheeks. She continued to watch him fixedly, with a look of interest upon her face, until he came out of his reverie with a start, and turned abruptly round, so that his gaze met hers. She glanced away at once, but his eyes remained fixed upon her for some moments. The picture was forgotten already, and his soul had come down to earth once more.

We caught sight of her once or twice before we left, and each time I noticed my friend look after her. He made no remark, however, until we got out into the open air, and were walking arm-in-arm along Princes Street.

"Did you notice that beautiful woman, in the dark dress, with the white fur?" he asked.

"Yes, I saw her," I answered.

"Do you know her?" he asked eagerly. "Have you any idea who she is?"

"I don't know her personally," I replied. "But I have no doubt I could find out all about her, for I believe she is engaged to young Archie Reeves, and he and I have a lot of mutual friends."

"Engaged!" ejaculated Cowles.

"Why, my dear boy," I said, laughing, "you don't mean to say you are so susceptible that the fact that a girl to whom you never spoke in your life is engaged is enough to upset you?"

"Well, not exactly to upset me," he answered, forcing a laugh. "But I don't mind telling you, Armitage, that I never was so taken by any one in my life. It wasn't the mere beauty of the face—though that was perfect enough—but it was the character and the intellect upon it. I hope, if she is engaged, that it is to some man who will be worthy of her."

"Why," I remarked, "you speak quite feelingly. It is a clear case of love at first sight, Jack. However, to put your perturbed spirit at rest, I'll make a point of finding out all about her whenever I meet any fellow who is likely to know."

Barrington Cowles thanked me, and the conversation drifted off into other channels. For several days neither of us made any allusion to the subject, though my companion was perhaps a little more dreamy and distraught than usual. The incident had almost vanished from my remembrance, when one day young Brodie, who is a second cousin of mine, came up to me on the university steps with the face of a bearer of tidings.

"I say," he began, "you know Reeves, don't you?"

"Yes. What of him?"

"His engagement is off."

"Off!" I cried. "Why, I only learned the other day that it was on."

"Oh, yes—it's all off. His brother told me so. Deucedly mean of Reeves, you know, if he has backed out of it, for she was an uncommonly nice girl."

"I've seen her," I said; "but I don't know her name."

"She is a Miss Northcott, and lives with an old aunt of hers in Abercrombie Place. Nobody knows anything about her people, or where she comes from. Anyhow, she is about the most unlucky girl in the world, poor soul!"

"Why unlucky?"

"Well, you know, this was her second engagement," said young Brodie, who had a marvellous knack of knowing everything about everybody. "She was engaged to Prescott—William Prescott, who died. That was a very sad affair. The wedding day was fixed, and the whole thing looked as straight as a die when the smash came."

"What smash?" I asked, with some dim recollection of the circumstances.

"Why, Prescott's death. He came to Abercrombie Place one night, and stayed very late. No one knows exactly when he left, but about one in the morning a fellow who knew him met him walking rapidly in the direction of the Queen's Park. He bade him good night, but Prescott hurried on without heeding him, and that was the last time he was ever seen alive. Three days afterwards his body was found floating in St. Margaret's Loch, under St. Anthony's Chapel. No one could ever understand it, but of course the verdict brought it in as temporary insanity."

"It was very strange," I remarked.

"Yes, and deucedly rough on the poor girl," said Brodie. "Now that this other blow has come it will quite crush her. So gentle and ladylike she is too!"

"You know her personally, then!" I asked.

"Oh, yes, I know her. I have met her several times. I could easily manage that you should be introduced to her."

"Well," I answered, "it's not so much for my own sake as for a friend of mine. However, I don't suppose she will go out much for some little time after this. When she does I will take advantage of your offer."

We shook hands on this, and I thought no more of the matter for some time.

The next incident which I have to relate as bearing at all upon the question of Miss Northcott is an unpleasant one. Yet I must detail it as accurately as possible, since it may throw some light upon the sequel. One cold night, several months after the conversation with my second cousin which I have quoted above, I was walking down one of the lowest streets in the city on my way back from a case which I had been attending. It was very late, and I was picking my way among the dirty loungers who were clustering round the doors of a great gin-palace, when a man staggered out from among them, and held out his hand to me with a drunken leer. The gaslight fell full upon his face, and, to my intense astonishment, I recognised in the degraded creature before me my former acquaintance, young Archibald Reeves, who had once been famous as one of the most dressy and particular men in the whole college. I was so utterly surprised that for a moment I almost doubted the evidence of my own senses; but there was no mistaking those features, which, though bloated with drink, still retained something of their former comeliness. I was determined to rescue him, for one night at least, from the company into which he had fallen.

"Holloa, Reeves!" I said. "Come along with me. I'm going in your direction."

He muttered some incoherent apology for his condition, and took my arm. As I supported him towards his lodgings I could see that he was not only suffering from the effects of a recent debauch, but that a long course of intemperance had affected his nerves and his brain. His hand when I touched it was dry and feverish, and he started from every shadow which fell upon the pavement. He rambled in his speech, too, in a manner which suggested the delirium of disease rather than the talk of a drunkard.

When I got him to his lodgings I partially undressed him and laid him upon his bed. His pulse at this time was very high, and he was evidently extremely feverish. He seemed to have sunk into a doze; and I was about to steal out of the room to warn his landlady of his condition, when he started up and caught me by the sleeve of my coat.

"Don't go!" he cried. "I feel better when you are here. I am safe from her then."

"From her!" I said. "From whom?"

"Her! her!" he answered peevishly. "Ah! you don't know her. She is the devil! Beautiful—beautiful; but the devil!"

"You are feverish and excited," I said. "Try and get a little sleep. You will wake better."

"Sleep!" he groaned. "How am I to sleep when I see her sitting down yonder at the foot of the bed with her great eyes watching and watching hour after hour? I tell you it saps all the strength and manhood out of me. That's what makes me drink. God help me—I'm half drunk now!"

"You are very ill," I said, putting some vinegar to his temples; "and you are delirious. You don't know what you say."

"Yes, I do," he interrupted sharply, looking up at me. "I know very well what I say. I brought it upon myself. It is my own choice. But I couldn't— no, by heaven, I couldn't—accept the alternative. I couldn't keep my faith to her. It was more than man could do."

I sat by the side of the bed, holding one of his burning hands in mine, and wondering over his strange words. He lay still for some time, and then, raising his eyes to me, said in a most plaintive voice—

"Why did she not give me warning sooner? Why did she wait until I had learned to love her so?"

He repeated this question several times, rolling his feverish head from side to side, and then he dropped into a troubled sleep. I crept out of the room, and, having seen that he would be properly cared for, left the house.

His words, however, rang in my ears for days afterwards, and assumed a deeper significance when taken with what was to come.

My friend, Barrington Cowles, had been away for his summer holidays, and I had heard nothing of him for several months. When the winter session came on, however, I received a telegram from him, asking me to secure the old rooms in Northumberland Street for him, and telling me the train by which he would arrive. I went down to meet him, and was delighted to find him looking wonderfully hearty and well.

"By the way," he said suddenly, that night, as we sat in our chairs by the fire, talking over the events of the holidays, "you have never congratulated me yet!"

"On what, my boy?" I asked.

"What! Do you mean to say you have not heard of my engagement?"

"Engagement! No!" I answered. "However, I am delighted to hear it, and congratulate you with all my heart."

"I wonder it didn't come to your ears," he said. "It was the queerest thing. You remember that girl whom we both admired so much at the Academy?"

"What!" I cried, with a vague feeling of apprehension at my heart. "You don't mean to say that you are engaged to her?"

"I thought you would be surprised," he answered. "When I was staying with an old aunt of mine in Peterhead, in Aberdeenshire, the Northcotts happened to come there on a visit, and as we had mutual friends we soon met. I found out that it was a false alarm about her being engaged, and then—well, you know what it is when you are thrown into the society of such a girl in a place like Peterhead. Not, mind you," he added, "that I consider I did a foolish or hasty thing. I have never regretted it for a moment. The more I know Kate the more I admire her and love her. However, you must be introduced to her, and then you will form your own opinion."

I expressed my pleasure at the prospect, and endeavoured to speak as lightly as I could to Cowles upon the subject, but I felt depressed and anxious at heart. The words of Reeves and the unhappy fate of young Prescott recurred to my recollection, and though I could assign no tangible reason for it, a vague, dim fear and distrust of the woman took possession of me. It may be that this was foolish prejudice and superstition upon my part, and that I involuntarily contorted her future doings and sayings to fit into some half-formed wild theory of my own. This has been suggested to me by others as an explanation of my narrative. They are welcome to their opinion if they can reconcile it with the facts which I have to tell.

I went round with my friend a few days afterwards to call upon Miss North-cott. I remember that, as we went down Abercrombie Place, our attention was attracted by the shrill yelping of a dog—which noise proved eventually to come from the house to which we were bound. We were shown upstairs, where I was introduced to old Mrs. Merton, Miss Northcott's aunt, and to the young lady herself. She looked as beautiful as ever, and I could not wonder at my friend's infatuation. Her face was a little more flushed than usual, and she held in her hand a heavy dog-whip, with which she had been chastising a small Scotch terrier, whose cries we had heard in the street. The poor brute was cringing up against the wall, whining piteously, and evidently completely cowed.

"So Kate," said my friend, after we had taken our seats, "you have been falling out with Carlo again."

Only a very little quarrel this time," she said, smiling charmingly. "He is a dear, good old fellow, but he needs correction now and then." Then, turning to me, "We all do that, Mr. Armitage, don't we? What a capital thing if, instead of receiving a collective punishment at the end of our lives, we were to have one at once, as the dogs do, when we did anything wicked. It would make us more careful, wouldn't it?"

I acknowledged that it would.

"Supposing that every time a man misbehaved himself a gigantic hand were to seize him, and he were lashed with a whip until he fainted"—she clenched her white fingers as she spoke, and cut out viciously with the dog-whip—"it would do more to keep him good than any number of high-minded theories of morality."

"Why, Kate," said my friend, "you are quite savage today."

"No, Jack," she laughed. "I'm only propounding a theory for Mr. Armitage's consideration."

The two began to chat together about some Aberdeenshire reminiscence, and I had time to observe Mrs. Merton, who had remained silent during our short conversation. She was a very strange-looking old lady. What attracted attention most in her appearance was the utter want of colour which she exhibited. Her hair was snow-white, and her face extremely pale. Her lips were bloodless, and even her eyes were of such a light tinge of blue that they hardly relieved the general pallor. Her dress was a grey silk, which harmonised with her general appearance. She had a peculiar expression of countenance, which I was unable at the moment to refer to its proper cause.

She was working at some old-fashioned piece of ornamental needlework, and as she moved her arms her dress gave forth a dry, melancholy rustling, like the sound of leaves in the autumn. There was something mournful and depressing in the sight of her. I moved my chair a little nearer, and asked her how she liked Edinburgh, and whether she had been there long.

When I spoke to her she started and looked up at me with a scared look on her face. Then I saw in a moment what the expression was which I had observed there. It was one of fear—intense and overpowering fear. It was so marked that I could have staked my life on the woman before me having at some period of her life been subjected to some terrible experience or dreadful misfortune.

"Oh, yes, I like it," she said, in a soft, timid voice; "and we have been here long—that is, not very long. We move about a great deal." She spoke with hesitation, as if afraid of committing herself.

"You are a native of Scotland, I presume?" I said.

"No—that is, not entirely. We are not natives of any place. We are cosmopolitan, you know." She glanced round in the direction of Miss Northcott as she spoke, but the two were still chatting together near the window. Then she suddenly bent forward to me, with a look of intense earnestness upon her face, and said—

"Don't talk to me any more, please. She does not like it, and I shall suffer for it afterwards. Please, don't do it."

I was about to ask her the reason for this strange request, but when she saw I was going to address her, she rose and walked slowly out of the room. As she did so I perceived that the lovers had ceased to talk and that Miss Northcott was looking at me with her keen, grey eyes.

"You must excuse my aunt, Mr. Armitage," she said; "she is odd, and easily fatigued. Come over and look at my album."

We spent some time examining the portraits. Miss Northcott's father and mother were apparently ordinary mortals enough, and I could not detect in either of them any traces of the character which showed itself in their daughter's face. There was one old daguerreotype, however, which arrested my attention. It represented a man of about the age of forty, and strikingly handsome. He was clean shaven, and extraordinary power was expressed upon his prominent lower jaw and firm, straight mouth. His eyes were some-what deeply set in his head, however, and there was a snake-like flattening at the upper part of his forehead, which detracted from his appearance. I almost involuntarily, when I saw the head, pointed to it, and exclaimed—

"There is your prototype in your family, Miss Northcott."

"Do you think so?" she said. "I am afraid you are paying me a very bad compliment. Uncle Anthony was always considered the black sheep of the family."

"Indeed," I answered; "my remark was an unfortunate one, then."

"Oh, don't mind that," she said; "I always thought myself that he was worth all of them put together. He was an officer in the Forty-first Regiment, and he was killed in action during the Persian War—so he died nobly, at any rate."

"That's the sort of death I should like to die," said Cowles, his dark eyes flashing, as they would when he was excited; "I often wish I had taken to my father's profession instead of this vile pill-compounding drudgery."

"Come, Jack, you are not going to die any sort of death yet," she said, tenderly taking his hand in hers.

I could not understand the woman. There was such an extraordinary mixture of masculine decision and womanly tenderness about her, with the consciousness of something all her own in the background, that she fairly puzzled me. I hardly knew, therefore, how to answer Cowles when, as we walked down the street together, he asked the comprehensive question—

"Well, what do you think of her?"

"I think she is wonderfully beautiful," I answered guardedly.

"That, of course," he replied irritably. "You knew that before you came!"

"I think she is very clever too," I remarked.

Barrington Cowles walked on for some time, and then he suddenly turned on me with the strange question—

"Do you think she is cruel? Do you think she is the sort of girl who would take a pleasure in inflicting pain?"

"Well, really," I answered, "I have hardly had time to form an opinion."

We then walked on for some time in silence.

"She is an old fool," at length muttered Cowles. "She is mad."

"Who is?" I asked.

"Why, that old woman—that aunt of Kate's—Mrs. Merton, or whatever her name is."

Then I knew that my poor colourless friend had been speaking to Cowles, but he never said anything more as to the nature of her communication.

My companion went to bed early that night, and I sat up a long time by the fire, thinking over all that I had seen and heard. I felt that there was some mystery about the girl—some dark fatality so strange as to defy conjecture. I thought of Prescott's interview with her before their marriage, and the fatal termination of it. I coupled it with poor drunken Reeves' plaintive cry, "Why did she not tell me sooner?" and with the other words he had spoken. Then my mind ran over Mrs. Merton's warning to me, Cowles' reference to her, and even the episode of the whip and the cringing dog.

The whole effect of my recollections was unpleasant to a degree, and yet there was no tangible charge which I could bring against the woman. It would be worse than useless to attempt to warn my friend until I had definitely made up my mind what I was to warn him against. He would treat any charge against her with scorn. What could I do? How could I get at some tangible conclusion as to her character and antecedents? No one in Edinburgh knew them except as recent acquaintances. She was an orphan, and as far as I knew she had never disclosed where her former home had been. Suddenly an idea struck me. Among my father's friends there was a Colonel Joyce, who had served a long time in India upon the staff, and who would be likely to know most of the officers who had been out there since the Mutiny. I sat down at once, and, having trimmed the lamp, proceeded to write a letter to the Colonel. I told him that I was very curious to gain some particulars about a certain Captain Northcott, who had served in the Forty-first Foot, and who had fallen in the Persian War. I described the man as well as I could from my recollection of the daguerreotype, and then, having directed the letter, posted it that very night, after which, feeling that I had done all that could be done, I retired to bed, with a mind too anxious to allow me to sleep.

Part II.

I got an answer from Leicester, where the Colonel resided, within two days. I have it before me as I write, and copy it verbatim.

"DEAR BOB," it said, "I remember the man well. I was with him at Calcutta, and afterwards at Hyderabad. He was a curious, solitary sort of mortal; but a gallant soldier enough, for he distinguished himself at Sobraon, and was wounded, if I remember right. He was not popular in his corps— they said he was a pitiless, cold-blooded fellow, with no geniality in him. There was a rumour, too, that he was a devil-worshipper, or something of that sort, and also that he had the evil eye, which, of course, was all nonsense. He had some strange theories, I remember, about the power of the human will and the effects of mind upon matter.

"How are you getting on with your medical studies? Never forget, my boy, that your father's son has every claim upon me, and that if I can serve you in any way I am always at your command.—Ever affectionately yours,

EDWARD JOYCE.

"P.S.—By the way, Northcott did not fall in action. He was killed after peace was declared in a crazy attempt to get some of the eternal fire from the sun-worshippers' temple. There was considerable mystery about his death."

I read this epistle over several times—at first with a feeling of satisfaction, and then with one of disappointment. I had come on some curious information, and yet hardly what I wanted. He was an eccentric man, a devil-worshipper, and rumoured to have the power of the evil eye. I could believe the young lady's eyes, when endowed with that cold, grey shimmer which I had noticed in them once or twice, to be capable of any evil which human eye ever wrought; but still the superstition was an effete one. Was there not more meaning in that sentence which followed—"He had theories of the power of the human will and of the effect of mind upon matter"? I remember having once read a quaint treatise, which I had imagined to be mere charlatanism at the time, of the power of certain human minds, and of effects produced by them at a distance. Was Miss Northcott endowed with some exceptional power of the sort? The idea grew upon me, and very shortly I had evidence which convinced me of the truth of the supposition.

It happened that at the very time when my mind was dwelling upon this subject, I saw a notice in the paper that our town was to be visited by Dr. Messinger, the well-known medium and mesmerist. Messinger was a man whose performance, such as it was, had been again and again pronounced to be genuine by competent judges. He was far above trickery, and had the reputation of being the soundest living authority upon the strange pseudo-sciences of animal magnetism and electro-biology. Determined, therefore, to see what the human will could do, even against all the disadvantages of glaring footlights and a public platform, I took a ticket for the first night of the performance, and went with several student friends.

We had secured one of the side boxes, and did not arrive until after the performance had begun. I had hardly taken my seat before I recognised Barrington Cowles, with his *fiancée* and old Mrs. Merton, sitting in the third or fourth row of the stalls. They caught sight of me at almost the same moment, and we bowed to each other. The first portion of the lecture was somewhat commonplace, the lecturer giving tricks of pure legerdemain, with one or two manifestations of mesmerism, performed upon a subject whom he had brought with him. He gave us an exhibition of clairvoyance too, throwing his subject into a trance, and then demanding particulars as to the movements of absent friends, and the whereabouts of hidden objects all of which appeared to be answered satisfactorily. I had seen all this before, however. What I wanted to see now was the effect of the lecturer's will when exerted upon some independent member of the audience.

He came round to that as the concluding exhibition in his performance. "I have shown you," he said, "that a mesmerised subject is entirely dominated by the will of the mesmeriser. He loses all power of volition, and his very thoughts are such as are suggested to him by the master-mind. The same end may be attained without any preliminary process. A strong will can, simply by virtue of its strength, take possession of a weaker one, even at a distance, and can regulate the impulses and the actions of the owner of it. If there was one man in the world who had a very much more highly-developed will than any of the rest of the human family, there is no reason why he should not be able to rule over them all, and to reduce his fellow-creatures to the condition of automatons. Happily there is such a dead level of mental power, or rather of mental weakness, among us that such a catastrophe is not likely to occur; but still within our small compass there are variations which produce surprising effects. I shall now single out one of the audience, and endeavour 'by the mere power of will' to compel him to come upon the platform, and do and say what I wish. Let me assure you that there is no collusion, and that the subject whom I may select is at perfect liberty to resent to the uttermost any impulse which I may communicate to him."

With these words the lecturer came to the front of the platform, and glanced over the first few rows of the stalls. No doubt Cowles' dark skin and bright eyes marked him out as a man of a highly nervous temperament, for the mesmerist picked him out in a moment, and fixed his eyes upon him. I saw my friend give a start of surprise, and then settle down in his chair, as if to express his determination not to yield to the influence of the operator. Messinger was not a man whose head denoted any great brain-power, but his gaze was singularly intense and penetrating. Under the influence of it Cowles made one or two spasmodic motions of his hands, as if to grasp the sides of his seat, and then half rose, but only to sink down again, though with an evident effort. I was watching the scene with intense interest, when I happened to catch a glimpse of Miss Northcott's face. She was sitting with her eyes fixed intently upon the mesmerist, and with such an expression of concentrated power upon her features as I have never seen on any other human countenance. Her jaw was firmly set, her lips compressed, and her face as hard as if it were a beautiful sculpture cut out of the whitest marble. Her eyebrows were drawn down, however, and from beneath them her grey eyes seemed to sparkle and gleam with a cold light.

I looked at Cowles again, expecting every moment to see him rise and obey the mesmerist's wishes, when there came from the platform a short, gasping cry as of a man utterly worn out and prostrated by a prolonged struggle. Messinger was leaning against the table, his hand to his forehead, and the perspiration pouring down his face. "I won't go on," he cried, addressing the audience. "There is a stronger will than mine acting against me. You must excuse me for to-night." The man was evidently ill, and utterly unable to proceed, so the curtain was lowered, and the audience dispersed, with many comments upon the lecturer's sudden indisposition.

I waited outside the hall until my friend and the ladies came out. Cowles was laughing over his recent experience.

"He didn't succeed with me, Bob," he cried triumphantly, as he shook my hand. "I think he caught a Tartar that time."

"Yes," said Miss Northcott, "I think that Jack ought to be very proud of his strength of mind; don't you! Mr. Armitage?"

"It took me all my time, though," my friend said seriously. "You can't conceive what a strange feeling I had once or twice. All the strength seemed to have gone out of me—especially just before he collapsed himself."

I walked round with Cowles in order to see the ladies home. He walked in front with Mrs. Merton, and I found myself behind with the young lady. For a minute or so I walked beside her without making any remark, and then I suddenly blurted out, in a manner which must have seemed somewhat brusque to her—

"You did that, Miss Northcott."

"Did what?" she asked sharply.

"Why, mesmerised the mesmeriser—I suppose that is the best way of describing the transaction."

"What a strange idea!" she said, laughing. "You give me credit for a strong will then?"

"Yes," I said. "For a dangerously strong one."

"Why dangerous?" she asked, in a tone of surprise.

"I think," I answered, "that any will which can exercise such power is dangerous—for there is always a chance of its being turned to bad uses."

"You would make me out a very dreadful individual, Mr. Armitage," she said; and then looking up suddenly in my face—"You have never liked me. You are suspicious of me and distrust me, though I have never given you cause."

The accusation was so sudden and so true that I was unable to find any reply to it. She paused for a moment, and then said in a voice which was hard and cold—

"Don't let your prejudice lead you to interfere with me, however, or say anything to your friend, Mr. Cowles, which might lead to a difference between us. You would find that to be very bad policy."

There was something in the way she spoke which gave an indescribable air of a threat to these few words.

"I have no power," I said, "to interfere with your plans for the future. I cannot help, however, from what I have seen and heard, having fears for my friend."

"Fears!" she repeated scornfully. "Pray what have you seen and heard. Something from Mr. Reeves, perhaps—I believe he is another of your friends?"

"He never mentioned your name to me," I answered, truthfully enough. "You will be sorry to hear that he is dying." As I said it we passed by a lighted window, and I glanced down to see what effect my words had upon her. She was laughing—there was no doubt of it; she was laughing quietly to herself. I could see merriment in every feature of her face. I feared and mistrusted the woman from that moment more than ever.

We said little more that night. When we parted she gave me a quick, warning glance, as if to remind me of what she had said about the danger of interference. Her cautions would have made little difference to me could I have seen my way to benefiting Barrington Cowles by anything which I might say. But what could I say? I might say that her former suitors had been unfortunate. I might say that I believed her to be a cruel-hearted woman. I might say that I considered her to possess wonderful, and almost preternatural powers. What impression would any of these accusations make upon an ardent lover—a man with my friend's enthusiastic temperament? I felt that it would be useless to advance them, so I was silent.

And now I come to the beginning of the end. Hitherto much has been surmise and inference and hearsay. It is my painful task to relate now, as dispassionately and as accurately as I can, what actually occurred under my own notice, and to reduce to writing the events which preceded the death of my friend.

Towards the end of the winter Cowles remarked to me that he intended to marry Miss Northcott as soon as possible—probably some time in the spring. He was, as I have already remarked, fairly well off, and the young lady had some money of her own, so that there was no pecuniary reason for a long engagement. "We are going to take a little house out at Corstorphine," he said, "and we hope to see your face at our table, Bob, as often as you can possibly come." I thanked him, and tried to shake off my apprehensions, and persuade myself that all would yet be well.

It was about three weeks before the time fixed for the marriage, that Cowles remarked to me one evening that he feared he would be late that night. "I have had a note from Kate," he said, "asking me to call about eleven o'clock to-night, which seems rather a late hour, but perhaps she wants to talk over something quietly after old Mrs. Merton retires."

It was not until after my friend's departure that I suddenly recollected the mysterious interview which I had been told of as preceding the suicide of young Prescott. Then I thought of the ravings of poor Reeves, rendered more tragic by the fact that I had heard that very day of his death. What was the meaning of it all? Had this woman some baleful secret to disclose which must be known before her marriage? Was it some reason which forbade her to marry? Or was it some reason which forbade others to marry her? I felt so uneasy that I would have followed Cowles, even at the risk of offending him, and endeavoured to dissuade him from keeping his appointment, but a glance at the clock showed me that I was too late.

I was determined to wait up for his return, so I piled some coals upon the fire and took down a novel from the shelf. My thoughts proved more interesting than the book, however, and I threw it on one side. An indefinable feeling of anxiety and depression weighed upon me. Twelve o'clock came, and then half-past, without any sign of my friend. It was nearly one when I heard a step in the street outside, and then a knocking at the door. I was surprised, as I knew that my friend always carried a key—however, I hurried down and undid the latch. As the door flew open I knew in a moment that my worst apprehensions had been fulfilled. Barrington Cowles was leaning against the railings outside with his face sunk upon his breast, and his whole attitude expressive of the most intense despondency. As he passed in he gave a stagger, and would have fallen had I not thrown my left arm around him. Supporting him with this, and holding the lamp in my other hand, I led him slowly upstairs into our sitting-room. He sank down upon the sofa without a word. Now that I could get a good view of him, I was horrified to see the change which had come over him. His face was deadly pale, and his very lips were bloodless. His cheeks and forehead were clammy, his eyes glazed, and his whole expression altered. He looked like a man who had gone through some terrible ordeal, and was thoroughly unnerved.

"My dear fellow, what is the matter?" I asked, breaking the silence. "Nothing amiss, I trust? Are you unwell?"

"Brandy!" he gasped. "Give me some brandy!"

I took out the decanter, and was about to help him, when he snatched it from me with a trembling hand, and poured out nearly half a tumbler of the spirit. He was usually a most abstemious man, but he took this off at a gulp without adding any water to it. It seemed to do him good, for the colour began to come back to his face, and he leaned upon his elbow.

"My engagement is off, Bob," he said, trying to speak calmly, but with a tremor in his voice which he could not conceal. "It is all over."

"Cheer up!" I answered, trying to encourage him. "Don't get down on your luck. How was it? What was it all about?"

"About?" he groaned, covering his face with his hands. "If I did tell you, Bob, you would not believe it. It is too dreadful—too horrible—unutterably awful and incredible! O Kate, Kate!" and he rocked himself to and fro in his grief; "I pictured you an angel and I find you a——"

"A what?" I asked, for he had paused.

He looked at me with a vacant stare, and then suddenly burst out, waving his arms: "A fiend!" he cried. "A ghoul from the pit! A vampire soul behind a lovely face! Now, God forgive me!" he went on in a lower tone, turning his face to the wall; "I have said more than I should. I have loved her too much to speak of her as she is. I love her too much now."

He lay still for some time, and I had hoped that the brandy had had the effect of sending him to sleep, when he suddenly turned his face towards me.

"Did you ever read of wehr-wolves?" he asked.

I answered that I had.

"There is a story," he said thoughtfully, "in one of Marryat's books, about a beautiful woman who took the form of a wolf at night and devoured her own children. I wonder what put that idea into Marryat's head?"

He pondered for some minutes, and then he cried out for some more brandy. There was a small bottle of laudanum upon the table, and I managed, by insisting upon helping him myself, to mix about half a drachm with the spirits. He drank it off, and sank his head once more upon the pillow. "Anything better than that," he groaned. "Death is better than that. Crime and cruelty; cruelty and crime. Anything is better than that," and so on, with the monotonous refrain, until at last the words became indistinct, his eyelids closed over his weary eyes, and he sank into a profound slumber. I carried him into his bedroom without arousing him; and making a couch for myself out of the chairs, I remained by his side all night.

In the morning Barrington Cowles was in a high fever. For weeks he lingered between life and death. The highest medical skill of Edinburgh was called in, and his vigorous constitution slowly got the better of his disease. I nursed him during this anxious time; but through all his wild delirium and ravings he never let a word escape him which explained the mystery connected with Miss Northcott. Sometimes he spoke of her in the tenderest words and most loving voice. At others he screamed out that she was a fiend, and stretched out his arms, as if to keep her off. Several times he cried that he would not sell his soul for a beautiful face, and then he would moan in a most piteous voice, "But I love her—I love her for all that; I shall never cease to love her."

When he came to himself he was an altered man. His severe illness had emaciated him greatly, but his dark eyes had lost none of their brightness. They shone out with startling brilliancy from under his dark, overhanging brows. His manner was eccentric and variable—sometimes irritable, sometimes recklessly mirthful, but never natural. He would glance about him in a strange, suspicious manner, like one who feared something, and yet hardly knew what it was he dreaded. He never mentioned Miss Northcott's name—never until that fatal evening of which I have now to speak.

In an endeavour to break the current of his thoughts by frequent change of scene, I travelled with him through the highlands of Scotland, and afterwards down the east coast. In one of these peregrinations of ours we visited the Isle of May, an island near the mouth of the Firth of Forth, which, except in the tourist season, is singularly barren and desolate. Beyond the keeper of the lighthouse there are only one or two families of poor fisher-folk, who sustain a precarious existence by their nets, and by the capture of cormorants and solan geese. This grim spot seemed to have such a fascination for Cowles that we engaged a room in one of the fishermen's huts, with the intention of passing a week or two there. I found it very dull, but the loneliness appeared to be a relief to my friend's mind. He lost the look of apprehension which had become habitual to him, and became something like his old self. He would wander round the island all day, looking down from the summit of the great cliffs which gird it round, and watching the long green waves as they came booming in and burst in a shower of spray over the rocks beneath.

One night—I think it was our third or fourth on the island—Barrington Cowles and I went outside the cottage before retiring to rest, to enjoy a little fresh air, for our room was small, and the rough lamp caused an unpleasant odour. How well I remember every little circumstance in connection with that night! It promised to be tempestuous, for the clouds were piling up in the north-west, and the dark wrack was drifting across the face of the moon, throwing alternate belts of light and shade upon the rugged surface of the island and the restless sea beyond.

We were standing talking close by the door of the cottage, and I was thinking to myself that my friend was more cheerful than he had been since his illness, when he gave a sudden, sharp cry, and looking round at him I saw, by the light of the moon, an expression of unutterable horror come over his features. His eyes became fixed and staring, as if riveted upon some approaching object, and he extended his long thin forefinger, which quivered as he pointed.

"Look there!" he cried. "It is she! It is she! You see her there coming down the side of the brae." He gripped me convulsively by the wrist as he spoke. "There she is, coming towards us!"

"Who?" I cried, straining my eyes into the darkness.

"She—Kate—Kate Northcott!" he screamed. "She has come for me. Hold me fast, old friend. Don't let me go!"

"Hold up, old man," I said, clapping him on the shoulder. "Pull yourself together; you are dreaming; there is nothing to fear."

"She is gone!" he cried, with a gasp of relief. "No, by heaven! there she is again, and nearer—coming nearer. She told me she would come for me, and she keeps her word."

"Come into the house," I said. His hand, as I grasped it, was as cold as ice.

"Ah, I knew it!" he shouted. "There she is, waving her arms. She is beckoning to me. It is the signal. I must go. I am coming, Kate; I am coming!"

I threw my arms around him, but he burst from me with superhuman strength, and dashed into the darkness of the night. I followed him, calling to him to stop, but he ran the more swiftly. When the moon shone out between the clouds I could catch a glimpse of his dark figure, running rapidly in a straight line, as if to reach some definite goal. It may have been imagination, but it seemed to me that in the flickering light I could distinguish a vague something in front of him— a shimmering form which eluded his grasp and led him onwards. I saw his outlines stand out hard against the sky behind him as he surmounted the brow of a little hill, then he disappeared, and that was the last ever seen by mortal eye of Barrington Cowles.

The fishermen and I walked round the island all that night with lanterns, and examined every nook and corner without seeing a trace of my poor lost friend. The direction in which he had been running terminated in a rugged line of jagged cliffs overhanging the sea. At one place here the edge was somewhat crumbled, and there appeared marks upon the turf which might have been left by human feet. We lay upon our faces at this spot, and peered with our lanterns over the edge, looking down on the boiling surge two hundred feet below. As we lay there, suddenly, above the beating of the waves and the howling of the wind, there rose a strange wild screech from the abyss below. The fishermen—a naturally superstitious race—averred that it was the sound of a woman's laughter, and I could hardly persuade them to continue the search. For my own part I think it may have been the cry of some sea-fowl startled from its nest by the flash of the lantern. However that may be, I never wish to hear such a sound again.

And now I have come to the end of the painful duty which I have undertaken. I have told as plainly and as accurately as I could the story of the death of John Barrington Cowles, and the train of events which preceded it. I am aware that to others the sad episode seemed commonplace enough. Here is the prosaic account which appeared in the Scotsman a couple of days afterwards:—

"*Sad Occurrence on the Isle of May.*—The Isle of May has been the scene of a sad disaster. Mr. John Barrington Cowles, a gentleman well known in University circles as a most distinguished student, and the present holder of the Neil Arnott prize for physics, has been recruiting his health in this quiet retreat. The night before last he suddenly left his friend, Mr. Robert Armitage, and he has not since been heard of. It is almost certain that he has met his death by falling over the cliffs which surround the island. Mr. Cowles' health has been failing for some time, partly from over study and partly from worry connected with family affairs. By his death the University loses one of her most promising alumni."

I have nothing more to add to my statement. I have unburdened my mind of all that I know. I can well conceive that many, after weighing all that I have said, will see no ground for an accusation against Miss Northcott. They will say that, because a man of a naturally excitable disposition says and does wild things, and even eventually commits self-murder after a sudden and heavy disappointment, there is no reason why vague charges should be advanced against a young lady. To this, I answer that they are welcome to their opinion. For my own part, I ascribe the death of William Prescott, of Archibald Reeves, and of John Barrington Cowles to this woman with as much confidence as if I had seen her drive a dagger into their hearts.

You ask me, no doubt, what my own theory is which will explain all these strange facts. I have none, or, at best, a dim and vague one. That Miss Northcott possessed extraordinary powers over the minds, and through the minds over the bodies, of others, I am convinced, as well as that her instincts were to use this power for base and cruel purposes. That some even more fiendish and terrible phase of character lay behind this—some horrible trait which it was necessary for her to reveal before marriage—is to be inferred from the experience of her three lovers, while the dreadful nature of the mystery thus revealed can only be surmised from the fact that the very mention of it drove from her those who had loved her so passionately. Their subsequent fate was, in my opinion, the result of her vindictive remembrance of their desertion of her, and that they were forewarned of it at the time was shown by the words of both Reeves and Cowles. Above this, I can say nothing. I lay the facts soberly before the public as they came under my notice. I have never seen Miss Northcott since, nor do I wish to do so. If by the words I have written I can save any one human being from the snare of those bright eyes and that beautiful face, then I can lay down my pen with the assurance that my poor friend has not died altogether in vain.

CRIME SUGGESTED BY HYPNOTISM.

Hypnotism With a Vengeance

By Ichor

Chapter I.

Considerable obscurity still involves some of the phenomena attending the practice of hypnotism, but that the business may be fraught with quite unexpected dangers is clearly proved by the following narrative.

The barque Calypso, Captain Davis, was on her way from England to Cape Town, where she had to deliver a portion of her cargo. From thence she would proceed to Western Australia to discharge the remainder, and to land some seventy or eighty steerage passengers. She was a comfortable, well-found ship, with a good seaman for her commander; but he was of a gloomy, morose disposition, and a most rigid disciplinarian, officers and crew alike standing in great awe of him. At the same time he was perfectly just, never finding fault without reason, and his harsh nature was largely attributable to a sad occurrence which had embittered his life. He had seen his only son dragged down by a shark while bathing, and from that hour he declared war against the rapacious monsters, never missing an opportunity of destroying one, and even sometimes delaying his vessel a little in order to effect his purpose. As soon, however, as the brute was fairly hooked and noosed his interest in it ceased, and he did not even look at it being hauled on board and despatched, but retired to his cabin, or to the extremity of the ship, where he sat down to brood over his sorrow, after adding another figure to his record of sharks destroyed.

Owing to emigrants being taken upon this voyage the Calypso required a doctor, and the owners fulfilled the law by engaging at a very moderate cost the services of one who desired a holiday, and to make a sea trip. Dr. O'Leary, as he was called on board—though he did not possess the letters M.D.—was not in large practice, and he could easily arrange for a *locum tenentem*; but he had a decided hobby, and this was—mesmerism.

O'Leary quickly realised the fact that the captain would stand no nonsense, and he feared that he would not be able to indulge his hobby. Neither with the emigrants, who were berthed forward, nor with the crew did he dare to play any pranks; but there was one person upon whom he cast longing eyes, as he seemed from his physique to be a likely subject, and that was Binks, the cabin boy. Unfortunately, however, he was the one person for whom the captain called more frequently than for any one else in the ship, so that O'Leary could never have been sure of him for five minute together.

Although Binks was rated as cabin boy, he was quite 17 years of age, or more, but he looked much younger, owing to his short stature and slight frame. He was a gentle, harmless lad, almost verging on weakness of intellect, though he could not positively be set down as defective in that respect, and the captain had taken him out of charitable consideration for his widowed mother. He neither bullied the youth himself nor did he allow anyone else to do so.

Captain Davis had an old custom of taking a long sleep in the afternoon, when his ship had reached warm latitudes, and was in the trade winds, so that his attention might be relaxed. This lasted exactly an hour and a quarter, if nothing occurred to disturb it, and the captain had acquired such a habit of awaking to the minute that his reappearance could be counted upon as if it had been timed by a clock. O'Leary, hearing that this was a regular institution, determined to take advantage of it.

The Calypso had no saloon passengers, though she could accommodate half a dozen or so, and while the captain took his siesta the vicinity of the cabin was generally undisturbed. O'Leary easily persuaded Binks to be his subject, and he was able to obtain a clear hour each afternoon, using an empty state-room, where there was a good sofa, though the bunks had been dismantled.

The weather on the whole had been propitious, but when the Calypso was about four days' sail from Cape Town there were indications of a change, not so pronounced, however, as to prevent the captain and others not in the watch on deck who cared to follow suit from taking their repose. O'Leary was engaged as usual, and he had reached a highly interesting point, with Binks in a satisfactory state of trance. He had never yet been able to make the latter speak while in that state, but to-day he thought, from certain signs, that he would succeed in so doing.

Early in the day a sail had been made out to the eastward, and before Captain Davis retired this was seen to be a brig, bound south. She was closing with the Calypso, either with the object of speaking, or possibly, because she did not intend to call at Cape Town.

When Captain Davis had been asleep for half an hour the brig signalled, and she was ascertained to be the Hope, from Cardiff for Cape Town. Her captain's leg had been accidentally broken on the previous day, and she asked whether the Calypso had a doctor on board who could come to set the limb.

Just as the request had been interpreted, O'Leary, who had heard some unusual sounds, slipped out of the cabin in order to ascertain whether he would have to awaken Binks and beat a retreat. The chief officer, whose name was Ray, told him what was going on, and said that he was about to call the captain.

This startled O'Leary, who saw that he must get rid of Binks before the captain was approached. He therefore said that he would call the latter, as he was going back to the cabin.

But alas for O'Leary! As he was on his way, not to the captain's room, but to the other end of the cabin in order first to dispatch Binks, the former opened his door, and asked what was the matter. His practised senses, even in sleep, had told him that something unusual was happening.

Then O'Leary had to stop and tell what had occurred. The captain, still yawning, sat down to listen, and then told him to bear a hand, and get ready quickly to board the brig. O'Leary had to hurry off to obtain what he wanted from the dispensary, with no excuse for going to the room where Binks lay, but he still hoped to have an opportunity of awakening him. When he returned, however, although the captain had gone on deck, he had sent the steward to the cabin to expedite the doctor's movements, so that Binks had to be left to take his chance.

A boat had already been hoisted out, and soon O'Leary was on his way to the brig, both vessels being hove to. Captain Davis called to him to be as quick as he could, the weather having a threatening appearance.

Long before the operation was completed a heavy squall came on, and though there was a slight lull afterwards it was but momentary, the wind beginning to blow strongly. The sea rose quickly, rendering it impossible for the boat, which was the smallest belonging to the Calypso, to return until the weather moderated.

The gale was sharp while it lasted, but it blew itself out in twelve hours. During the night both crews had their hands full, and when daylight came the vessels were not in sight of each other. It was annoying to Captain Davis to lose his boat's crew and doctor, but he recovered them at Cape Town, where the Hope arrived a day later than he did.

Of course Binks had been wanted, but he was called for in vain. The steward suggested that he had perhaps accidentally broken something, and was hiding, in order to be out of the way when it should be discovered. He was expected to turn up by the next morning at latest, and in the meantime the captain, though annoyed, was too busy to give much thought to the matter.

The steward, like a sensible man, turned in to sleep pretty much as usual, his duty not requiring him to wait upon gales; but he dreamed that Binks came to his coach, and by the dim light in the companion way he saw that he was dead. The figure, after looking at him mournfully for a few moments, disappeared in the darkness of the cabin. When the steward arose next morning he saw that Binks had returned, and was lying in his berth, this being simply a corner of the sofa in the saloon. He went to him and shook him roughly, but the lad did not rise, and then the appalled steward saw that he was stiff and cold. His face was that of a corpse, but the teeth were tightly clenched, and the eyes, which were slightly open, seemed fixed and lustreless.

The captain, who had been on deck all night, was then lying down, but the steward made his report to Mr. Ray, who came to look at Binks and pronounced him to be dead. The supposed dream must have been a reality, Binks in his trance having an intense desire to return to his own sleeping place, which enabled him to perform the act of somnambulism. He stopped for a moment by the sofa where the steward lay, and after reaching his own place he relapsed into deeper trance than before. The steward, being almost asleep, believed that this was a dream, and told it as such.

Ray was unwilling to disturb the captain, but the latter was not long in appearing, and he also when he saw Binks said that he was dead. It was a mysterious affair, but one thing was certain, that the body must be buried. Poor Binks in his living death was sewn up in canvas, with his clothes on and a lump of coal at his feet, and launched over board.

The steward was cautioned to say nothing about his dream to the sailors, but he had already told it with embellishments, and the cabin thenceforth had a ghost. O'Leary was fearfully shocked at the tragical end of his experiments, but he took care to keep his secret, and in his own mind he could account for the steward's dream.

Chapter II.

On reaching Western Australia Captain Davis found a return freight ready, with prompt despatch, so that the Calypso went home by the way she had come. No one regretted this but O'Leary, who wished to see the Pacific; but of course he was not consulted, and indeed, the emigrants having left, he was no longer required. The ship, however, had engaged to bring him home, so Captain Davis advertised for saloon passengers, with the inducement of a surgeon being carried, and obtained four, all of the male sex. They were pleasant, genial fellows, but although O'Leary became pretty intimate with them he never once touched upon his favourite topic, having had enough of mesmerism to last him for a long time. The steward, however, confided the ghost story to them, though he asked them not to speak of it to the captain or officers.

The Calypso did not touch at the Cape a second time, and a week or so after passing it she was near the spot where she had fallen in with the Hope on the outward voyage. Light baffling winds prevailed, and the vessel made little progress, but there seemed to be a prospect of some excitement, as a huge shark had been seen. For some reason, however, it was shy and would not approach very near to the ship, though it hung about her neighbourhood, having now been visible for three days. Only one had been seen at a time, and the men were sure that it was always the same shark following the ship for some mysterious reason, as it had behaved throughout in a uniform manner, rushing towards the vessel until it was within a few fathoms, and then sheering off to remain out of sight for perhaps an hour or two.

Of course the fishing tackle had been brought out, and Captain Davis was particularly anxious to destroy this shark, as its movements exasperated him. It was all to no purpose, however, the creature declining to be tempted.

On the third day there was a dead calm, the sails flapping idly to the lazy roll of the vessel. While waiting for breakfast two of the passengers were lying on a rug under the awning spread over the quarter-deck, and one was relating to the other a strange experience of the previous night.

He had slept badly owing to the heat, and at one time, when lying awake, he had heard the sound of loud whispering in the saloon, which induced him to rise and look out of his cabin, thinking that some of his fellow passengers were up, being, like himself, unable to sleep. He saw nothing, though he still heard the whispering, apparently coming at one time from his right side and at another from his left; now seemingly close to him, and again far away. Much mystified, and feeling rather creepy as he remembered the "ghost story," he returned to his bunk, fancying, moreover, that he had made out the words continually repeated—*"For heaven's sake, release me, and let me die."*

The captain appearing at that moment, the story was repeated to him, and met with loud ridicule. "Why, man," he said, "one hears all sorts of sounds in calms like this. Your whispering was the gentle rubbing of the ropes, and your fancy made out the words. There are no ghosts in this ship."

It was odd that the captain should have been so positive, since the steward had brought him a precisely similar tale that morning, and he had told him roughly not to be a fool, nor to spread any such nonsense in the ship. But he was puzzled when he heard that the words had sounded the same to two independent hearers, and he felt vaguely uncomfortable about the matter.

The doctor was not very well that morning, and turned up just in time for breakfast, looking worried and out of sorts. The whispering ghost was discussed at table, and laughed at by all except the passenger who had heard it. O'Leary scoffed with the rest, and thought it unnecessary to mention that he, also, had not only heard the sound, but had *recognised the voice.*

The shark came nearer to the ship on this morning than it had previously done, moving slowly past, almost alongside. It was a huge brute, nearly 20ft. long, with greedy eyes, but still it did not take the bait readily; passing to and fro, and listlessly regarding it, as if beneath its notice. At last it turned on its side, and the morsel vanished in the great chasm of a mouth.

Never was there such a cur of a shark. He showed scarcely any fight, and seemed to have had very little vitality to begin with; as he was lying on deck disabled, with his tail severed, in far less than the usual time for such a monster. His appearance was strange, as he was greatly emaciated, but in the region of the stomach his body was much swollen, and one old sailor remarked to another of the hands, "It's my belief, Bill, that that 'ere beggar's swallowed a barrel, and has starved because he had no room to stow any grub."

Then the stomach itself was carefully opened, and out rolled a large lump of coal, but the bulk of the cargo was to come. "I'm blessed if there ain't a plaster himage inside," said the boatswain as he tugged out something which looked very like it. It was, in fact, a human figure, quite nude, and seemingly made of chalk, until the touch revealed its softness. No human artist, however, could have produced so realistic a statue, perfect even to the eyelids and the long hair.

Every one pressed forward to see this strange sight. If it had not absorbed all attention O'Leary's appearance could not have failed to attract notice as, withdrawn from the circle, he leaned sick and faint against the bulwarks. At the first glance he had recognised the body of Binks, and the consequent revulsion was too much for him.

Chapter III.

The captain was not present at this stage of the proceedings, having withdrawn as soon as the shark was fairly secured, but the steward was among those who stood by. "By Jingo!" he said after attentively looking at the blanched features, "I believe it is poor Binks. Yes, I'm sure it is, for there is the mole on his cheek." At this the sailors all recoiled, falling back a step or two, and murmurings about a Jonah, and an unlucky voyage, began to rise. There was a pause, broken by the mate saying, "He had better go back into the sea."

"Yes, heave the—thing overboard," more than one of the men replied; and, though there was general disinclination to touch the body, two of them at last stepped forward to carry out the suggestion, when O'Leary interposed.

He had had time to recover his equanimity, and he had determined to do his duty, although he fully expected that exposure and disgrace would be the result to himself. He now said, "No, the matter must be looked into since it is out of reason for a body to remain unchanged for so many months. Carry it to my cabin."

At this the mate fired up. "Are you boss here, or am I?" he said. Then, turning to the men, he continued, "Do as I tell you."

O'Leary stepped between. "I don't pretend to be boss over you or anyone else, but that body must *not* go overboard. I appeal to the captain."

No one, not even Ray, desired the presence of the captain, who was sitting aft in a brown study, and the former sulkily replied, "If he wants the stinking thing in his cabin let him have it. He may eat it, if he likes, for me."

O'Leary persuaded two of the hands to wash the body and convey it to his room, where he locked himself in. The body had been coated with a cheese-like deposit, and the skin was bleached as white as paper, which had given it the appearance of wet chalk. After the lapse of a quarter of an hour O'Leary called to the steward for some brandy, and he then shut the door again.

There was a yell of horror, and a quick stampede of one or two men who were about, when, some time afterwards, O'Leary issued from the passage leading to the cabins, holding Binks by the hand. The latter wore a blanket cloakwise, and walked extremely well for a corpse, or even for a ghost, but his physical powers were almost unimpaired by his trance, with the single exception that he was quite blind. His lips had recovered their natural tint, and there was a slight colour in his cheeks, but otherwise the chalky whiteness remained, and altogether he was a ghastly object.

O'Leary took Binks up on the quarter-deck to the captain, who had been apprised of the finding of the body, but who nevertheless stared in open-mouthed astonishment, not unmixed with dread, when it walked up to him. He began to pour a volley of questions into the doctor, who, however, interrupted him by saying that he would take Binks back to the cabin before discussing him.

This done, O'Leary, who had already ascertained that Binks had scarcely any recollection of having been mesmerised, and none whatever of subsequent events, gave his explanation to the captain. The lad had fallen into a cataleptic state closely resembling death, although he was still living. When he was thrown into the sea the shark swallowed him before he sunk far, and, being so large a brute, he did so at a gulp without injuring the body. Binks, in his trance, required neither food nor air, and the shark soon found that he had a tenant who was more than a match for him. The canvas covering and all clothing had been quickly digested, but the now naked body defied the action of the gastric juice, inasmuch as it was living flesh, as did also the lump of coal. These two bulky articles would have killed the shark in time by starvation, as he could not take sufficient food.

The blindness, O'Leary thought, would be but temporary. It probably arose through the skin of the eyeballs being clouded, and when this regained its normal condition the sight would be restored.

Binks believed that he was still on the outward voyage, and he continued to think so until the ship was near England, and his sight was returning. To avoid too great a shock he was cautiously told that he had had a severe illness, with a long period of unconsciousness. Some of the men were cruel enough to tell him of his having been swallowed by the shark, but he took this for an attempt to hoax him. O'Leary did not try to mesmerise him again, having no desire to awaken awkward recollections; and Binks's complexion for a long time after his arrival was, to say the least of it, remarkable.

A Scientific Revenge

By Marie Madison

"Do you remember the murder of the banker Halliday, about seven years ago? It has always remained shrouded in mystery. The best detectives were detailed on the case. Every clue, however slight, was investigated to the fullest extent; but nothing came of them. The police were compelled to confess themselves baffled. To this day they are as much in the dark regarding it as ever. It is not a mystery to me, however, but I can't go with my story to the authorities. They would laugh at me and ask for proof, which is beyond my reach."

I must confess that I was playing the part of an eavesdropper, and that these words were not spoken for my benefit. If this reaches the eye of the gentleman who uttered them, I am sure he will be as much surprised as I was on hearing the story which followed this introduction.

I was seated at a table in the cafe of the Manhattan Club, sipping a delicious claret punch, when the above startling words reached my ear. I turned and looked at the speaker and his companions. The latter awoke no interest within me—they were ordinary men about town—but the one who had spoken at once brought to life every inquisitive instinct of my nature. He was a man long past his prime, yet younger in mind and heart, by far, than the two blase, worn out individuals who sat with him. He looked like one who had stored up his vitality, who had not wasted one hour of his time, either in useless thought or more useless dissipation, and, as I studied his striking face more closely, through the clouds of smoke from my cigar, I felt a double interest in his words and prepared myself the more successfully to play the eavesdropper by changing the position of my chair, and while apparently absorbed in the enjoyment of my claret punch, drank in every word of the following story:

"There has been a great deal said of late in the New York papers about hypnotism, but I doubt if many people who read of the various tests have much faith in them. To show you what a dangerous weapon may be made of hypnotism, I'll relate to you an incident which came under my own observation, and which is closely connected with the Halliday mystery. Indeed, I may say I played a part in the drama, the leading character of which was a woman.

"Halliday had an only child, a daughter, just budding into womanhood at the time of his death. Being an intimate friend of the family, I often called at his home, when I had ample opportunity to study the girl. I first met her after her return from abroad, where she had been attending school. She was not particularly beautiful, but there was a subtle charm about her that rivalled beauty and in spite of myself I would find my glance wandering toward her whenever she was present. There was a peculiar look in her soft grey eyes that puzzled me, and I became fascinated with something in her manner that I could not analyse. She was a slight, delicate girl, yet every move, turn, and glance suggested power, but I was confident that it was a power of which even she herself was not cognizant. Owing to my studies of the occult forces and hypnotism I was as great a curiosity to the girl as she was to me, for whenever I looked toward her I invariably found her glance bent upon me in a searching, inquiring way. Whenever we were alone she fell to questioning me about some scientific problem that would not have interested many men. Halliday was a man of wonderful mental vigor, and I was not surprised to find the girl uncommonly bright, though her choice of subjects for study and conversation astonished me. You would have said that there was something uncanny about her.

"Do you remember anything about the murder? Halliday was found seated at his desk, his head lying on his outstretched arms, shot through the head with his own revolver. It was after hours, but he often remained alone in the bank when he went over the books, keeping everything securely locked meanwhile. He was a most pains-taking worker, superintending most of the business of the bank himself. He went over the books periodically to see that there were no deficiencies; investigated doubtful securities—indeed, it was to his indefatigable industry that the firm owed its reputation and stood solid during the panic, eight years ago, when so many banks went under. He was quiet and cautious, and never made any display of his habits. Judging from the appearance of the bank, no one would have dreamed that Halliday was sitting in his office, pouring over accounts, and keeping track of his millions—except the murderer.

"Truly whoever committed that crime was familiar with the habits of the banker. Robbery seemed to be the motive, for a large amount of money was stolen from the dead man's pockets, though the vaults and safes were untouched. It is believed that the robber was frightened away by the watchman, for Halliday had not been dead more than five minutes when he was found lying across his desk, his head resting upon an open journal and ledger, which were saturated with the life blood that poured from a bullet hole in his temple.

"The crime created the greatest sensation of the year. The murdered man had been popular, both in business and society, and had always been charitable and just. So far as was known he had not an enemy on earth. Though large rewards were offered for a clue to the murderer, the case became one of the great mysteries of New York, and finally people ceased to speak of it. I doubt if one person out of a hundred will even remember it.

"As soon as possible after the death of her husband Mrs. Halliday and her daughter Helen sailed for Europe. They were about three years absent, and when they again returned to America I received an invitation to attend a reception to be given in honor of Helen, who on that occasion was to make her formal debut into society.

"When I entered the drawing-room, and again stood before my interesting young friend, I was both surprised and delighted. She had developed into a tall, stately woman. There was something in her attitude, her stride, her whole appearance, that suggested the tragedy queen, and I knew that the 'old power' which I had discovered in the girl had developed in the woman, till I felt almost sure that she must be aware of its existence.

"She was above the usual height of woman, and her figure had filled out in what artists term 'curves of grace.' A calico gown would have hung in regal folds from those shoulders, and it needed little imagination to change the fan she bore into a sceptre, so royally did she wield it. During the course of the evening I offered her my arm, and requested the pleasure of a few moments' social chat—as in the old days. I suggested that we seek the wide veranda, which had been so profusely decorated with palms and flowers as to present the appearance of some tropical garden.

"'You know I don't dance,' I said, 'but if you will honor and old cavalier with a few moments' conversation, he will try to dream that he is young again.'

"She declared herself glad of an opportunity to rest awhile, and, as she said, 'to renew some of the old subjects which were so fascinating to me when I was too young to enjoy them to the full.'

"I led the way to the coolest spot, and for a few moments we sat speechless under the palms, looking out on the scene before us, where the garden surrounding the house had been decorated with Japanese and Chinese lanterns that swayed in the soft breeze, flickering and sputtering, and threatening to become extinguished at every stronger gust of wind.

"I broke the silence, saying—

"I hear you have become a famous horsewoman since you went abroad.'

"Yes?' There was a peculiar smile on her lips as she said this word, in a half assertive half questioning tone. 'I love horses, and they—well, if they don't love me they obey me.'

"Obey!' She had struck the keynote of her power.

"I believe it,' I said. 'Few living creatures could look into your eyes and not obey you.'

"'What do you mean?' There was something almost of suspense in the way she spoke those words, and I could not but feel surprised.

"'I mean that you have great power, though you may not know it. You have heard of Mesmer—?'

"'Have I heard of Mesmer? Then I have hypnotic power, you mean?'

"To a wonderful degree, and I thank heaven, for that reason, that you are a good woman.'

"'But I have never hypnotised anyone.'

"That is because your power is undeveloped. You do not know how to control it yourself. If you wish to become my pupil I will teach you how to use it, and you may be able to do a great deal of good.'

"No, no.' I saw her recoil at the thought. 'I should be afraid. I am not always good. If anyone wrongs me I want to be revenged. I don't think it would be safe!' These last words were spoken in a light tone, and ended with a laugh, but I felt there was more in them than appeared from her manner at that moment.

"'But,' she added, more seriously, 'there is one gift which I possess that I have cultivated. I say nothing to my friends about it, for they, will laugh at me. But you will not professor; you understand me. I found out by accident that I was capable of reading what was in another's mind. At first I was surprised to find, during conversation with someone, that I occasionally was about to speak the very words they uttered, or would speak them in unison. This happened so often that I began to question myself the meaning of it, and to experiment, until at last I seemed to be able to read the thoughts of those about me; but I have left every one in the dark as to how I have learned much that I know, from the dread of being laughed at.'

"'You must be a martyr and endure the ridicule of the ignorant for the sake of science,' I said. 'However, if you will agree to a plan I have in mind, I will arrange a way in which you can give a test of your powers without running the risk of being laughed at.'

"'You mean that you will apparently be the controlling spirit, and thus cloak my art, or whatever you would call it, under your own science. You would feign to hypnotise me, and thus allow me to read the mind of a subject without arousing suspicion toward myself.'

"I looked up in astonishment. She had read my thought as plainly as if it were written in legible characters.

"'You are right. That is my plan, and you have either a very keen insight into the methods of a man or you are a marvel in the science of mind reading.'

"We agreed upon a plan, and returned to the drawing-room. In a short time a little group that had formed about the attractive debutante was plunged into an animated discussion of the occult forces, and especially hypnotism. I had adroitly led them into that channel, and finally volunteered to give an exhibition of the power of mind over matter. Soon the large room was filled with expectant guests, all ready for an impromptu entertainment. I gave several amusing tests then, turning to my young friend Helen, said:

"'I will now give you a slight idea of the use of hypnotism in the science of mind reading. Miss Helen, will you assist me?'

"Without hesitation the young girl came forward and seated herself before me. I made several passes before her face, then looked steadily into her eyes, as though placing her under a spell. Strong as my power is I found it drifting away from me as I gazed into those deep grey orbs. I whispered to Helen to obey me implicitly and to pretend to be under my influence. Then, turning to our audience, I looked about for a suitable subject. Seated near in a languid attitude, with a sceptical smile on his face, was Bruce Halliday, a second cousin of Helen's whose good looks and quiet ways had made him a universal favorite with the gentler sex, and I heard that night, through the gossip of the quests, that he was desperately in love with his fair cousin.

"I had never liked Bruce Halliday. His lazy, indolent air exasperated me. Whenever I saw him I felt I would like to shake some life into him. His manner at that supreme moment was almost maddening to a sensitive person. He seemed so sure of himself—so doubtful of others. Nothing was sacred to him, science nor religion, and as I saw the supercilious smiles which curved his lip I hated him intensely.

"'I will teach you a lesson, my friend,' I said mentally, then aloud:

"'Mr. Halliday, I believe you are sufficient of a sceptic to make an excellent subject for I the young, lady. Will you come forward?"

"He arose and advanced toward me with a manner that said as plainly as words:

"'Watch me show this old fraud up.'

"In spite of herself, Helen smiled faintly when Bruce came toward her, and I placed her hand upon his wrist. I smiled also; it suggested a betrothal, and I believe many of the guests thought the same thing, for there was a suppressed titter among them.

"To all but myself Helen was in a hypnotic sleep, and I watched her eagerly, waiting to hear what she would say to verify my belief in her.

"A moment passed. I saw a look of annoyance come over Bruce's face, followed by one of dismay, and he endeavored to draw his hand away from the detaining grasp of his cousin. I looked quickly at Helen.

"'What do you read in this man's mind?' I asked, but instead of speaking the girl gave a quick, sharp gasp, and, opening her eyes, looked up into the startled face of young Halliday with such an expression of horror and doubt that it seemed to justify my hatred for the man, then, throwing his hand from her, she sprang to her feet and dashed away out of the room.

"It is needless to say that her action created a sensation, till some bright wit suggested that this was part of the performance, and that I was very clever to find such a way out of a failure. It had all been fixed up beforehand.

"I did not mind having the laugh on me. I was too anxious about Helen to pay any attention to the remarks of the jokers. I suggested to Mrs. Halliday that she had best follow her daughter, and learn if any harm had come to her. She did as I bade, and in a few moments a servant announced that Miss Helen would have to be excused from again returning to the drawing-room that evening, as she was very ill.

"That broke up the festivities for the night. I afterwards learned from Mrs. Halliday that on going upstairs she had found Helen lying in a dead faint across the threshold of her boudoir.

"About a week after the reception I was seated in my study when the bell rang, and a moment later Helen entered the room. She had recovered from her indisposition, but still looked somewhat pale.

"I motioned her to a chair, but stood before her, with my elbow on the mantel, and studied her face.

"'You gave us quite a scare the other night,' said I.

"'Foolish of me, wasn't it?' she answered.

"'No, it is easily explained, I assure you. It often happens that mind readers fall into a state of catelepsy while under intense strain.'

"'And you think that is all that ailed me?'

"'Undoubtedly. You must not overdo yourself. Your subject was too strong, but that was my fault. If I had allowed you to choose someone for yourself you probably would not have made that mistake.'

"For, after several hours' puzzling thought over the strange turn affairs had taken on the night of her debut, I had arrived at this decision.

"'I am glad you think that is all that ailed me,' said Helen, seeming relieved. 'And now, I am going to accept your proposition. I want to become your pupil. Teach me to be a hypnotist.'

"But you told me you did not wish to develop your power; you were afraid of yourself.'

"'I have changed my mind. I have come to the conclusion that if I have power enough to control the will of others, I ought surely to be able to control my own when it leads me in the wrong direction.'

"'True, and will you?'

"'Of course. When will we begin?'

"'To-morrow?'

"'Yes.'

"'That will suit me.'

"'Thanks. I will be here at eleven."

"True to her word, and punctual to the moment, Helen rang my bell.

"I took great pleasure in teaching her the methods of the different masters with whom I was familiar. I had not made a mistake in her. She had the strongest will I had ever found in a woman, and I thanked heaven, as I saw it develop under my instruction, that she was a pure, noble-minded girl.

"In three months she was my master, but before that three months were over she became engaged to her cousin Bruce. I was pained when I heard of the betrothal, for I thought her worthy of a far better man, but she declared that she loved him, and against the wishes of all—even of her mother—she had promised to become his wife. The wedding was to take place eight months from the time she had given him her word. It was to be on the anniversary of her debut into society. I was glad, at any rate, that there was to be no hurried marriage, and secretly hoped that something would occur to prevent it before the time had elapsed.

"About five months after the betrothal I passed the evening at Mrs. Halliday's. It was a rainy night. I always chose bad weather in which to make my calls on the Hallidays, in hopes of finding them alone. On this evening only Bruce and a friend of Helen's were present. I had not seen young Halliday since his betrothal, and was surprised to find him quite changed. A spirit of unrest seemed to have taken possession of him. His eyes were dark and sunken, his cheeks pale and so drawn that the cheek bones showed with ghastly prominence. He had lost that supercilious air that so exasperated me, and seemed to be suffering. Much as I disliked him, I could not but feel sorry for him.

"Helen seemed, to partake, of the indisposition of her lover, for her face had grown thinner, and a weary look about the mouth told of sleepless nights. To me she gave the idea of one supported only by her will. During the evening Mrs. Halliday spoke of the changed appearance of her son-in-law to be. She told me she believed the marriage would never take place, for Bruce seemed to be in decline. He had become a victim of melancholia, and she would not be surprised if it developed into insanity. I felt that I had read the young man's character aright, and said to myself that this change was the result of dissipation, and I feared that Helen, with her ability to read the mind, was aware of the truth.

"A month later Bruce Halliday was dead—a suicide.

"The papers were full of the case. They spoke of the young man's family, his betrothal to the heiress, his good looks, his decline, and finally of the mad act which ended his life, making much of the fact that he was found in the same attitude as Helen's father—his arms extended over his desk and his life blood staining the pages of a book upon which his head was resting—that book the Bible, which lay open at the Ten Commandments, while the index finger of his left hand pointed to the sentenced: 'Thou shalt not kill.'

"Little was seen of Helen after that. I called to express my regrets, but she was not at home. Later I heard that she was going to Europe again, and went, to bid her good-bye. She had grown much paler and thinner since I had last seen her, and I felt that grief for her betrothed, though not made manifest, was wearing her life away.

"After a short call I bade the mother and daughter good-bye and left, wondering if I should ever see my interesting pupil again.

"I sat musing on the strange fate that had robbed this young girl of the man she loved, in the very dawning of their life, when I was surprised to suddenly find her standing before me.

"Her face was even paler than usual, and her eyes moved restlessly to and fro as she stood waiting for me to speak.

"'Miss Halliday,' I exclaimed, as soon as I recovered sufficiently from my surprise to find my voice. 'What is it? You look ill. Has anything happened?'

"I seized her arm, and placed her gently in the chair from which I had arisen. She did not reply for a moment, but, fixing her dark eyes upon mine, looked at me in a strange, reproachful manner. Suddenly she startled me by saying—

"Never teach a woman the power of hypnotism again. You place a dangerous weapon in the hands of the most irresponsible possessors in the world—not unscrupulous, but impulsive. None should know it save those who value earth's possessions lightly—who harbor no revenge. You are not to blame that I became your pupil, for I promised you sacredly that I would do no harm, but listen till I tell you what I have done.'

"You remember the night I made my debut? You also remember our experience in mind reading? I rushed out of the drawing-room and fell in a faint on the threshold of my own room. You said it was the strain. No, it was not. It was what I read in Bruce Halliday's mind. When I took his hand he was thinking of his love for me, but, suddenly, the current of his thought changed, and I saw a picture in his mind that drove the blood out of my heart. I saw my father seated at his desk in the banking office, going over his books—they were, however, the books Bruce kept at the bank. I read down the page with him. I saw deficiencies that were there to cover systematic robberies committed by my cousin in my father's bank. I saw the guilt of the theft in Bruce's mind, and I saw him, look furtively back at my father, as he left with the other clerks, and Banker Halliday was alone. Then, I saw him return, unseen. I saw him as he demanded the books of my father; a stormy scene ensued; Bruce tried forcibly to gain possession of those tell-tale books; he was choking my father into insensibility, when father drew his revolver from the desk drawer and endeavored to turn it upon the wretched thief. Bruce wrested it from him and shot him through the head. My father fell back in his chair, dying, the red blood pouring from a wound in his temple. Bruce saw that he was dying, and he laid him across the desk as he was found shortly afterwards, arranging his head in such a position that the life blood would obliterate the evidence of guilt in the books which lay open on the desk. He dare not destroy them; that would place the suspicion of murder upon him; and to further prevent this, he robbed the pockets of the dying man as he breathed his last, and then made his escape. That is what I saw in Bruce Halliday's mind. That is why I promised to be his wife. That is why I wished to develop my hypnotic powers. I have had my revenge. I killed Bruce Halliday as he killed my father. You look at me as if you thought I was mad. Don't you understand me? I killed him by my will. From the moment I learned how to use my mesmeric power I began to torture him with the memory of his crime, of which hitherto he seemed to be utterly indifferent. I put the idea in his mind to take his own life. You see how I have succeeded. No one can convict me, yet I am a murderess—no, perhaps I am an executioner. You look horrified, my friend. Perhaps you think I may have made a mistake. Here, are proofs that I did not! Here is a confession Bruce Halliday left, in which he describes the cowardly murder of my father just as I saw it, so I know that I was right. And now good-bye, professor. I am going to France and shall probably never return to America.'

"'And what became of her?'

"She still lives in her adopted country. At last accounts she was studying for the medical profession, and wrote me that she believed that in that calling she would find opportunity to put her hypnotic power to use in doing good."

EXTRAORDINARY STORY OF HYPNOTISM AND ABDUCTION.
ROMANTIC ADVENTURE OF A YOUNG LADY.

How I Committed My Murder

By H. Thomlinson

Any break in the monotony of life in the little seaside village of Pygwyllion was rare, and when posters were put up stating that Professor Schlafmacher, of Berlin, the renowned hypnotist, would give a lecture in the schoolroom, and exemplify his powers on any who cared to go upon the stage, there was considerable excitement amongst all the population. All, that is to say, except Captain John Tompkins and myself, Robert Jones, both late of the merchant service. We had each, on our retirement, settled down in this remote little place, where I had purchased a small cottage, whilst Tompkins boarded in the schoolmaster's house. We had not previously known each other, but we naturally soon became acquainted, and our having been in the same profession, together with a community of taste in tobacco and other matters, had in the course of seven years ripened the acquaintance into a close friendship, and a day seldom passed in which we were not to be seen in one another's company. Tompkins and I had, of course, seen a good deal of the world in our way, and we rather prided ourselves on being hard headed, practical men of experience, who could see as far as most people and were not to be imposed on. Therefore, when the rest of the village was anxiously looking forward to the approaching lecture we remained calm and unmoved, took our pipes, grog, and walks as usual, and betrayed no excitement.

We talked about it to one another, though. "Ever seen any of this hypnotism, Bob?" asked Tompkins. I said I had once been to a performance where a man had pretended to mesmerize a woman, and made her tell how many shillings someone in the audience—a confederate, no doubt—had in his pocket, and so on. "All arranged before-hand, of course," I concluded.

"Nothing genuine, eh?"

"Well, not quite that, perhaps. He got two girls up on the stage and gave them some beans, which he said were chocolate creams, and just as they were going to eat them he told them they were black beetles, and, by Jove! You should have seen them drop those beans and jump on the chairs and shake themselves. I think that was genuine. They looked a mighty weak-minded lot."

"That sort of thing wouldn't do with you and me, would it, Bob?"

"Not much," said I. "I should like to come across the man who could hypnotize either of us, Jack!"

"It wouldn't be a bad joke to go and see the show, would it?" said he.

"All right," said I. "Let's go." And so, when the afternoon arrived, to the astonishment probably of many of the audience, Tompkins and myself put in an appearance.

Punctually to the moment the lecturer stepped on to the platform. He was a man of about forty-five, or perhaps fifty, and there was nothing remarkable about him except his eyes, which had a peculiar expression of depth which I cannot attempt to describe. I had never seen any eyes like them. He spoke in very good English with somewhat of a foreign accent, and his manner was perfectly quiet and free from affectation. In a few opening remarks he explained that he trusted we should not regard him as wishing to impose on us by any deception, but simply as the exponent of certain powers possessed, more or less, by all, but little known and less cultivated, which were capable of working the greatest benefits to the world when properly exercised. Any confederation was, as we could see for ourselves, impossible, since the whole audience were practically known to one another, and it was from them only that the subjects of his experiments would be taken. He begged us to judge what we might see with impartiality, and then to ask ourselves whether he was in any sense exaggerating the tremendous possibilities which might result from a more general and intelligent recognition of his science.

The lecturer then asked that some of the audience would come on to the stage. As there seemed to be some hesitation in complying with this, he said, "Perhaps there is some lady present who will play us a little tune upon the piano? Will anyone be so kind?"

Hereupon a little girl, the daughter of the schoolmaster, stepped forward, after some urging from her mother, and was helped on to the platform by the professor. He opened the piano and placed a seat for her. But here a hitch occurred. It appeared that the intending performer could not recollect her piece, and her music was at home.

"Ach! that is very awkward," said the professor. "But, tell me, is your music in a book?"

She said it was, in a book "about so big" (holding out her hands), and with a green cover.

There were some books on a shelf near the piano, and the professor, taking down one of about the size described, with a brown cover, on which was inscribed in large letters, "Copy Book," placed it before her, and, touching her head lightly with his hand, said, "Is this not the same book as yours? Yes? That is very fortunate. Will you please find the place, for you see I do not know which is your tune?" The little girl turned over six or seven pages rapidly, and then, keeping her eyes fixed on a statement, in large text hand, that "Honesty is the best policy," played her little tune through carefully and correctly. When she had finished the lecturer thanked her politely, and, taking her hand, led her to the steps.

"I think," he then said, "that the piano will perhaps be in the way of the performances presently. Will anyone be so good as to help me to move it back a little?"

Two hulking youths at once started forward; but, to our great astonishment, no sooner had they mounted the platform than one immediately thrust his hand into his waistcoat after the manner of a sling, whilst the other limped to the nearest chair and, sitting down, put one foot on his knee and nursed it most tenderly; the faces of both wearing an expression of intense pain.

"Dear me," said the professor, "this is very sad, and so very sudden! Please let me look at your foot." He went to the youth on the chair, and after looking at him a moment said, "My young friend, you are either very foolish or you play a little joke on me. You have not hurt this foot at all. It is the other one that pains you." Instantly the young man dropped the foot to the ground with a crash of his heavy boot, and seizing the other one placed it most gingerly over the other knee, whilst he groaned heavily.

"That is better," said the professor; "and now, my friend, let me see your wrist. Ach! yes! I must make you a proper sling for it." He turned away for an instant, and then, facing them again, said, pointing to a corner of the stage, "Will you please move the piano over there? I think that will be the best place." Both youths at once jumped up, and the instrument was placed in the desired position; after which they returned to their seats in the room, apparently wondering what on earth there could be to excite the roars of laughter in which the audience indulged.

I cannot give an account of all the experiments. Suffice it to say that people were made to shiver with cold, or wipe their foreheads from heat; that they shot imaginary bears with walking sticks, and ran from visionary mad dogs. Those sang, or at least tried to, who never sang before; and the sexton, a preternaturally solemn person, danced a hornpipe on the table. Tompkins and I regarded it all with openly superior smiles. The professor had got a wonderfully soft lot!

After about an hour the lecturer again addressed us. Though such exhibitions might seem, he said, to some of us to have something of the marvellous about them, there was, he assured us, nothing of the sort in reality. All the results which we had seen were caused merely by the imposition of his will for the time on the person operated on. The strength of the will-power, like the strength of the muscles, could be greatly developed by constant practice. At the same time, as a very strong man might at some period or other be confronted with one still stronger, so it might happen that the trained hypnotist might meet with a subject with will-power equal to or greater than his own, over whom he might fail to exercise any influence. Such an occurrence at a lecture like the present was, of course, inconvenient; but any genuine professor of hypnotism who, as it were, challenged a whole audience must be, of course, prepared to face the possibility. Admitting the power of the operator to be sufficient, he desired to call our attention to the fact that as it was possible, as we had seen, to induce sensations of pain, it was also possible in many cases to remove it by the same agency, often permanently. Such cures were, however, not suitable for public exhibition, and he was happy to think, judging from their appearance, that his present audience were not in need of such treatment. This was, however, a most important part of his science, and one which ought to receive far more attention than had been at present accorded to it. Time was drawing on, and he must shortly leave; but he had still some minutes to spare, and would be pleased to see a few more of the audience on the stage, if any were disposed to come.

"Bob," whispered Tompkins, "I'm going up."

"Right, old man," said I. "I'm with you."

The professor bowed politely as we appeared on the platform, but looked at us, I thought, doubtfully, as at possibly difficult subjects.

"Kindly be seated, gentlemen," he said.

We took chairs on either side of the stage, and facing one another. The professor kept us waiting whilst he was apparently looking for something in his pockets. He didn't seem to find it, and I got so tired of waiting to be operated on that I closed my eyes. I fancy that, strangely enough, I must have dozed off for a moment, for I woke up with a start just in time to see Tompkins open his eyes and stare at me. Just then the professor spoke.

"I am extremely sorry, gentlemen, but I find that I have mistaken the time. Allow me to ask your pardon, and to express my great regret for the trouble I have given you; I trust you will excuse me."

Of course, we returned to our seats, and the professor, after briefly thanking the audience for their attention, hurried out to his cab and drove off to the nearest station.

"Thought he wouldn't tackle us, Bob," said Tompkins, when we got outside. "Wouldn't have done to fail just at the end. All bunkum about the time, you know. Had a quarter of an hour more, easy." I agreed with him. Indeed it was such a palpable case of running away that I felt quite sorry for the professor.

If I live to be a hundred I shall never forget the awakening the following morning; the first drowsy feeling that something had gone wrong, the clearer impression that the something was very serious, and then the full recollection of the whole horror. Could it be but a dream? Alas! no. Too well did I recall the dreadful details. I sat up in bed, and the whole ghastly sequence of events repeated itself.

I had gone to bed, and to sleep, but had woke again. I had looked at my watch. It was just after eleven, I felt wide awake, and after tossing about restlessly a short time I determined, finding sleep impossible, to go out for a stroll. I dressed, and let myself quietly out, I walked on slowly, without thinking where I was going, till I found myself on the small wooden pier that runs out into the bay—a favourite resort of Tompkins and myself. What was my astonishment to see Tompkins standing there. He explained that he, like myself, could not sleep, and preferred strolling out to a wakeful night in bed. I was very glad to see him, and we walked up and down and smoked together. The night was fairly light, but somewhat cloudy. Our conversation turned presently on the lecture that afternoon.

"You did get just a little bit queer when you were on the stage, though, didn't you?" said Tompkins.

"What do you mean?" said I.

"Why, you shut your eyes," said he.

"I didn't," said I—but I knew this was not true.

"I saw you," said he.

"I saw you open yours," said I.

"You didn't," said he.

"I did," said I.

"That's a lie," said he. And then some devil got hold of me, and—we were walking by the edge of the pier and Tompkins was on the outside—I gave him a push, and over he went into two fathoms of water.

He couldn't swim, and I can't either, and he fell too far out for me to reach him, even had I tried. But I didn't. I must have been mad, I suppose. I just stood there and saw him go under once, twice, and the third time. The clock struck twelve as he sank finally. And then I had walked home and gone to bed.

This was the recollection the morning brought me—I had committed a foul and dastardly murder. I had slain one who was as a brother to me, and the brand of Cain was on me for ever.

How I got up and dressed I don't know. My brain was all in a whirl, the one clear idea being that I must try to conceal my crime. There were no witnesses. No one had seen me go out or come in, and if Tompkins's body were found there was no reason for supposing he had been thrown in by anybody at all. He might very easily have fallen in. No; I had only to keep cool and collected, and no suspicion could possibly attach to me. If anyone were suspected, it would certainly not be his best friend.

I nerved myself, therefore, to swallow some breakfast, after which I took my hat and coat and told my servant I was going over for the day to the neighbouring town, where I had a little business to attend to. I actually forced myself to turn back, as if by an afterthought, and say that if Captain Tompkins should call he was to be told that I might not be home till late, but would see him in the morning. Once clear of the village I walked as if my life depended on it. Where I went I hardly know. I believe I had some food somewhere, but it was mostly walk, walk all day. I knew I must return at night, and intuitively I made my way back in the evening.

And then, as I neared the village, came the awful feeling that I must go down to the pier and see if Tompkins's body were there. It was late for Pygwyllion—about ten—and there would be no one about. The more I resisted this gruesome impulse the stronger did it grow. The hideous attraction that the scene of his crime has for the murderer was upon me, and I was compelled to yield to it.

I went down to the pier, and stood there with my eyes wide open for any observer, and my ears alert for any sound. There was neither one nor the other. Except for the soft plash of the water all was silent as the grave. I hesitated for an instant, and then stole softly on to the pier. The structure, as explained, was of wood and built on piles, and near its outer end there were steps at either side leading down to a sort of lower platform, used for a landing from boats. It was my idea to go down to this platform, where I might see the body if, as was very possible, it had been washed in amongst the piles. I climbed carefully and quietly down the slippery steps—and there, standing against the railing and looking down into the water, was a dark form.

The figure turned its head at the sound of my footsteps. Its face was of a ghostly pallor, and its features were the features of Tompkins. The eyes appeared to me to gleam with concentrated hate as it gazed at me, and I felt each individual hair of my head assume an erect position as I stared in turn at the awful apparition.

"Why are you here?" whispered the spectre, in scarcely audible tones, which seemed to tremble with rage. "Why are you here?"

I hardly know how I forced myself to reply, but I managed to stammer out, "I c—c—came to look for you."

"To look for me!" echoed the apparition.

"Yes! I have always heard so. There is no peace for the murderer. None! Haunted! Always haunted! Haunted till he dies from the terror. Yes! day and night I shall see you. No darkness can shut from the eye of the murderer the presence, the constant presence, of his victim's spirit. Oh! the horror of it!"

I gave a dismal groan. It was awful.

"I'll go to the police," I began; but the spectre interrupted me.

"I shall do that," it said. "You forget that they wouldn't see you; no one sees you but me. You're dead, you know; since last night, when I threw you over the pier. I saw you go down three times; and I never even tried to save you, when perhaps I might have done so. But I'll give myself up in the morning. I'd rather be hanged than haunted. And when I am perhaps you'll be at rest."

The sudden relief I felt was almost too much for me. It was evident that it was not Tompkins's spirit, but Tompkins in the flesh that I had found, and I was therefore not a murderer in fact, although I certainly had been one in intention. On the other hand, it was clear that Tompkins, having in some way got out of the water (although I could have sworn I saw him drown), had lost his wits from the shock and become insane. This, however, was my salvation, for so long as he imagined himself to be the murderer and not the intended victim, as he really was, he certainly would not bring any charge against me. It was evidently my cue to avoid in any way disturbing this illusion, and, indeed, to foster it carefully. I should have, to explain to him that I was not dead, but had escaped in some extraordinary way. Thereupon Tompkins would fall on my neck and shed tears of joy, whilst I should magnanimously forgive him and he would remain indebted to me for life. It seemed perfectly simple, I began at once, in a solemn voice.

"Why did you throw me off the pier last night?"

"Torture me not," cried Tompkins, in a tone of agony. "I know you will haunt me till I'm hanged, but don't keep on like this. It's not regular. You oughtn't to speak. Dead people don't talk, you know."

"Answer me," I replied. "I command you."

"You know very well," said he. "We quarrelled about that show yesterday, and you told me I'd been to sleep on the stage, and I told you it was a lie; and then you said—but what is the use of going over it again? I threw you in, and you're dead."

"What would you give to know I was alive?" said I.

"Give? Why, anything. But you're as dead as Moses, you know. You can't swim—I mean you couldn't when you were alive."

"Tompkins," I said, "would you be surprised to hear that I'm not dead? That by I—er—that I learnt to swim—er—last week, and I—er—dived, just to frighten you—and climbed out when you went away?"

"Don't mock me," cried Tompkins, reproachfully. "I murdered you. You're dead; and I'm going to give myself up."

"I'm not dead," I said.

"You are," he persisted.

"Feel my hand," said I, and I made a step towards him.

He recoiled in horror. "Keep off!" he almost screamed. "I won't! I can't! You're only an appearance. You ought to vanish now and let me go home, and then come in the night again and stand over me. You shouldn't go on this way."

"Look here," I said, rather loudly, for I was getting irritated—a man who insists on calling himself a murderer when the body is alive and wanting to shake hands with him is an annoying person— "don't call me an appearance. I'm as solid as you are. What's this?" and I sprang on him suddenly and gave him a couple of smart blows on the chest.

Now this kind of thing is not usually soothing in effect, but the look of intense relief that came over Tompkins's face as he received the thumps I have never seen equalled. The deadly pallor fled; and, if he did not literally fall on my neck, he wrung my hands till they ached, and the moonlight showed something very like tears in his eyes.

Soon, however, his face fell. "Bob, old man," he said, sadly, "I *meant* to drown you. It's no credit to me that you're alive. I shall go and give myself up for attempted murder."

"Don't be an idiot," I returned. "You haven't any proof. You don't suppose I'm going to charge you, do you?"

"You must," he said.

"Must, be blowed," said I. "There is no harm done. That sort of thing is quite common—amongst friends. A little temper, that's all. Why, I might have done it to you, instead."

"Aren't you going to do anything, then?" he asked, doubtfully.

"Yes," I said, "I am. I'm going home to have a drink, and you're coming with me."

And so it happened that, ten minutes later, two retired merchant skippers, each of whom regarded himself as the would-be murderer of the other, might have been seen marching amicably up the little street of Pygwyllion, arm in arm, to the residence of one of them, on liquid refreshment bent.

On arriving at my cottage I called to my old servant, Mary, to bring whisky and glasses. Now, Mary had lived with us during my wife's lifetime, and remained with me ever since, and on the strength of long service claimed privileges, one of which was to find fault with me whenever she pleased—which, to tell the truth, was pretty frequently. She always insisted on remaining up till I was at home and, as she considered, safe for the night, and held ideas about late hours which she made no scruple of expressing. Possibly my tone of voice was lacking in that humility suitable to a return home somewhat later than usual, and exhibited inappropriate cheerfulness. When a man suddenly finds that he has not committed a murder of which he believed himself guilty, and that, moreover, he is not to be called to account even for the attempt, there is undoubtedly something inspiriting in the situation, and it is possible that my voice may have been unduly jubilant. At any rate, old Mary appeared to think so. She set the bottle and glasses on the table with as much banging as was consistent with their safety, and delivered herself of the following : —

"A nice hour for a respectable gentleman to come home, Captain Jones, certainly! And I suppose you'll be sitting up the best of the night now. You'd better make the most of the whisky; there's no more. And for goodness' sake don't forget to bolt the door after you've let Captain Tompkins out. Perhaps he'll sleep on the sofa, though. And when you do go to bed I hope you'll make less noise than you did last night, keeping me awake with your snoring and grunting and talking in your sleep till the clock struck twelve. And now I'll wish you good-night."

"Did you hear that, Bob?" said Tompkins, when she had gone. "Old lady had the nightmare badly. Why, at twelve o'clock last night you were just drow—I mean diving—down by the jetty."

"Never mind that, old man," said I. "It's all over. Take some grog."

Now, what glorious luck! I thought to myself. If my dear friend here should ever, which Heaven forbid, find out the rights of the matter, what a witness for an alibi! Unsolicited testimony to my being at home. And the old girl would swear to it with the best conscience.

"Bob, old chap, here's your health, and Heaven bless you for a kind-hearted fellow!"

Just then old Mary put her head in at the door and snapped out, as she threw a letter on the table, "This came for you this evening; I forgot it."

When the door was closed I took the letter up and examined it. It was addressed in a strange hand, and bore the postmark of a town some miles distant. On opening the envelope an inner cover appeared, on which was the following inscription: —

"To Captains Jones and Tompkins,

"Pygwyllion.

"The writer begs that the enclosed may be read by the above-named gentlemen in the presence of each other."

The letter itself I here give in full :—

"Gentlemen,—In adopting the profession of a hypnotist, I did so not so much as a means of making money as from a desire to benefit my fellow-creatures, and to bring about a more extended belief in the marvellous powers of an art in relation to which such general ignorance prevails. With this end in view it has been my custom often to visit small towns and villages where the very existence of the science was perhaps unknown. It has been my good fortune to open the eyes of many to the enormous benefits offered to the human race by the legitimate practice of my profession, and I am thankful to say that I have in many cases effected radical cures when the patient had been given up by the faculty. Towards honest, if sceptical, inquiry I have always been patient; but to the pig-headed, obstinate self-sufficiency of half-educated people—like yourselves, gentlemen—I have sometimes, as in your case, administered a sharp lesson. I will explain myself. When you came on the stage last night you did so in obedience to the exercise of my will, although you did not think so; and I may here inform you that you proved yourselves two of the easiest subjects to influence that I have met with. The smallest exertion only on my part was necessary. I must call to your recollection that you both felt a momentary sensation of sleepiness, after which I apologized for dismissing you. That instant, gentlemen, allowed me to impress on your minds (which in such matters are abnormally weak) the idea that each of you had murdered his friend by throwing him off the jetty. But this is not all. I willed that this impression should not come into force until you were asleep last night. Whether this has happened as I intended I leave it to yourselves to say. I fear you may, perhaps, have been inconvenienced, but I can assure you that after the receipt of this letter you need fear no further interference in your affairs from me.

"I will merely add that I should strongly advise you not again to oppose your puny and untrained wills to a power the extent of which your very narrow intellects are quite incapable of realizing. In the hands of an unscrupulous operator the results to you might be much more serious than those caused by   "Yours faithfully,

"Karl Schlafmacher,

"Professor of Hypnotism."

We looked at one another, but for some time nothing was said. When at length Tompkins broke the silence his remark seemed to be somewhat wanting in relevancy.

He said, "Bob, my boy, pass the grog."

An Adventure at Brownville*

By Ambrose Bierce

*(This story was written in collaboration with Miss Ina Lillian Peterson, to whom is rightly due the credit for whatever merit it may have).

I taught a little country school near Brownville, which, as every one knows who has had the good luck to live there, is the capital of a considerable expanse of the finest scenery in California. The town is somewhat frequented in summer by a class of persons whom it is the habit of the local journal to call "pleasure seekers," but who by a juster classification would be known as "the sick and those in adversity." Brownville itself might rightly enough be described, indeed, as a summer place of last resort. It is fairly well endowed with boarding-houses, at the least pernicious of which I performed twice a day (lunching at the schoolhouse) the humble rite of cementing the alliance between soul and body. From this "hostelry" (as the local journal preferred to call it when it did not call it a "caravanserai") to the schoolhouse the distance by the wagon road was about a mile and a half; but there was a trail, very little used, which led over an intervening range of low, heavily wooded hills, considerably shortening the distance. By this trail I was returning one evening later than usual. It was the last day of the term and I had been detained at the schoolhouse until almost dark, preparing an account of my stewardship for the trustees—two of whom, I proudly reflected, would be able to read it, and the third (an instance of the dominion of mind over matter) would be over-ruled in his customary antagonism to the schoolmaster of his own creation.

I had gone not more than a quarter of the way when, finding an interest in the antics of a family of lizards which dwelt thereabout and seemed full of reptilian joy for their immunity from the ills incident to life at the Brownville House, I sat upon a fallen tree to observe them. As I leaned wearily against a branch of the gnarled old trunk the twilight deepened in the somber woods and the faint new moon began casting visible shadows and gilding the leaves of the trees with a tender but ghostly light.

I heard the sound of voices—a woman's, angry, impetuous, rising against deep masculine tones, rich and musical. I strained my eyes, peering through the dusky shadows of the wood, hoping to get a view of the intruders on my solitude, but could see no one. For some yards in each direction I had an uninterrupted view of the trail, and knowing of no other within a half mile thought the persons heard must be approaching from the wood at one side. There was no sound but that of the voices, which were now so distinct that

I could catch the words. That of the man gave me an impression of anger, abundantly confirmed by the matter spoken.

"I will have no threats; you are powerless, as you very well know. Let things remain as they are or, by God! you shall both suffer for it."

"What do you mean?"—this was the voice of the woman, a cultivated voice, the voice of a lady. "You would not—murder us."

There was no reply, at least none that was audible to me. During the silence I peered into the wood in hope to get a glimpse of the speakers, for I felt sure that this was an affair of gravity in which ordinary scruples ought not to count. It seemed to me that the woman was in peril; at any rate the man had not disavowed a willingness to murder. When a man is enacting the rôle of potential assassin he has not the right to choose his audience.

After some little time I saw them, indistinct in the moonlight among the trees. The man, tall and slender, seemed clothed in black; the woman wore, as nearly as I could make out, a gown of gray stuff. Evidently they were still unaware of my presence in the shadow, though for some reason when they renewed their conversation they spoke in lower tones and I could no longer understand. As I looked the woman seemed to sink to the ground and raise her hands in supplication, as is frequently done on the stage and never, so far as I knew, anywhere else, and I am now not altogether sure that it was done in this instance. The man fixed his eyes upon her; they seemed to glitter bleakly in the moonlight with an expression that made me apprehensive that he would turn them upon me. I do not know by what impulse I was moved, but I sprang to my feet out of the shadow. At that instant the figures vanished. I peered in vain through the spaces among the trees and clumps of undergrowth. The night wind rustled the leaves; the lizards had retired early, reptiles of exemplary habits. The little moon was already slipping behind a black hill in the west.

I went home, somewhat disturbed in mind, half doubting that I had heard or seen any living thing excepting the lizards. It all seemed a trifle odd and uncanny. It was as if among the several phenomena, objective and subjective, that made the sum total of the incident there had been an uncertain element which had diffused its dubious character over all—had leavened the whole mass with unreality. I did not like it.

At the breakfast table the next morning there was a new face; opposite me sat a young woman at whom I merely glanced as I took my seat. In speaking to the high and mighty female personage who condescended to seem to wait upon us, this girl soon invited my attention by the sound of her voice, which was like, yet not altogether like, the one still murmuring in my memory of the previous evening's adventure. A moment later another girl, a few years older, entered the room and sat at the left of the other, speaking to her a gentle "good morning." By *her* voice I was startled: it was without doubt the one of which the first girl's had reminded me. Here was the lady of the sylvan incident sitting bodily before me, "in her habit as she lived."

Evidently enough the two were sisters.

With a nebulous kind of apprehension that I might be recognized as the mute inglorious hero of an adventure which had in my consciousness and conscience something of the character of eavesdropping, I allowed myself only a hasty cup of the lukewarm coffee thoughtfully provided by the prescient waitress for the emergency, and left the table. As I passed out of the house into the grounds I heard a rich, strong male voice singing an aria from "Rigoletto." I am bound to say that it was exquisitely sung, too, but there was something in the performance that displeased me, I could say neither what nor why, and I walked rapidly away.

Returning later in the day I saw the elder of the two young women standing on the porch and near her a tall man in black clothing — the man whom I had expected to see. All day the desire to know something of these persons had been uppermost in my mind and I now resolved to learn what I could of them in any way that was neither dishonorable nor low.

The man was talking easily and affably to his companion, but at the sound of my footsteps on the gravel walk he ceased, and turning about looked me full in the face. He was apparently of middle age, dark and uncommonly handsome. His attire was faultless, his bearing easy and graceful, the look which he turned upon me open, free, and devoid of any suggestion of rudeness. Nevertheless it affected me with a distinct emotion which on subsequent analysis in memory appeared to be compounded of hatred and dread—I am unwilling to call it fear. A second later the man and woman had disappeared. They seemed to have a trick of disappearing. On entering the house, however, I saw them through the open doorway of the parlor as I passed; they had merely stepped through a window which opened down to the floor.

Cautiously "approached" on the subject of her new guests my landlady proved not ungracious. Restated with, I hope, some small reverence for English grammar the facts were these: the two girls were Pauline and Eva Maynard of San Francisco; the elder was Pauline. The man was Richard Benning, their guardian, who had been the most intimate friend of their father, now deceased. Mr. Benning had brought them to Brownville in the hope that the mountain climate might benefit Eva, who was thought to be in danger of consumption.

Upon these short and simple annals the landlady wrought an embroidery of eulogium which abundantly attested her faith in Mr. Benning's will and ability to pay for the best that her house afforded. That he had a good heart was evident to her from his devotion to his two beautiful wards and his really touching solicitude for their comfort. The evidence impressed me as insufficient and I silently found the Scotch verdict, "Not proven."

Certainly Mr. Benning was most attentive to his wards. In my strolls about the country I frequently encountered them—sometimes in company with other guests of the hotel—exploring the gulches, fishing, rifle shooting, and otherwise wiling away the monotony of country life; and although I watched them as closely as good manners would permit I saw nothing that would in any way explain the strange words that I had overheard in the wood. I had grown tolerably well acquainted with the young ladies and could exchange looks and even greetings with their guardian without actual repugnance.

A month went by and I had almost ceased to interest myself in their affairs when one night our entire little community was thrown into excitement by an event which vividly recalled my experience in the forest.

This was the death of the elder girl, Pauline.

The sisters had occupied the same bedroom on the third floor of the house. Waking in the gray of the morning Eva had found Pauline dead beside her. Later, when the poor girl was weeping beside the body amid a throng of sympathetic if not very considerate persons, Mr. Benning entered the room and appeared to be about to take her hand. She drew away from the side of the dead and moved slowly toward the door.

"It is you," she said—"you who have done this. You—you—you!"

"She is raving," he said in a low voice. He followed her, step by step, as she retreated, his eyes fixed upon hers with a steady gaze in which there was nothing of tenderness nor of compassion. She stopped; the hand that she had raised in accusation fell to her side, her dilated eyes contracted visibly, the lids slowly dropped over them, veiling their strange wild beauty, and she stood motionless and almost as white as the dead girl lying near. The man took her hand and put his arm gently about her shoulders, as if to support her. Suddenly she burst into a passion of tears and clung to him as a child to its mother. He smiled with a smile that affected me most disagreeably—perhaps any kind of smile would have done so—and led her silently out of the room.

There was an inquest—and the customary verdict: the deceased, it appeared, came to her death through "heart disease." It was before the invention of heart *failure*, though the heart of poor Pauline had indubitably failed. The body was embalmed and taken to San Francisco by some one summoned thence for the purpose, neither Eva nor Benning accompanying it. Some of the hotel gossips ventured to think that very strange, and a few hardy spirits went so far as to think it very strange indeed; but the good landlady generously threw herself into the breach, saying it was owing to the precarious nature of the girl's health. It is not of record that either of the two persons most affected and apparently least concerned made any explanation.

One evening about a week after the death I went out upon the veranda of the hotel to get a book that I had left there. Under some vines shutting out the moonlight from a part of the space I saw Richard Benning, for whose apparition I was prepared by having previously heard the low, sweet voice of Eva Maynard, whom also I now discerned, standing before him with one hand raised to his shoulder and her eyes, as nearly as I could judge, gazing upward into his. He held her disengaged hand and his head was bent with a singular dignity and grace. Their attitude was that of lovers, and as I stood in deep shadow to observe I felt even guiltier than on that memorable night in the wood. I was about to retire, when the girl spoke, and the contrast between her words and her attitude was so surprising that I remained, because I had merely forgotten to go away.

"You will take my life," she said, "as you did Pauline's. I know your intention as well as I know your power, and I ask nothing, only that you finish your work without needless delay and let me be at peace."

He made no reply—merely let go the hand that he was holding, removed the other from his shoulder, and turning away descended the steps leading to the garden and disappeared in the shrubbery. But a moment later I heard, seemingly from a great distance, his fine clear voice in a barbaric chant, which as I listened brought before some inner spiritual sense a consciousness of some far, strange land peopled with beings having forbidden powers. The song held me in a kind of spell, but when it had died away I recovered and instantly perceived what I thought an opportunity. I walked out of my shadow to where the girl stood. She turned and stared at me with something of the look, it seemed to me, of a hunted hare. Possibly my intrusion had frightened her.

"Miss Maynard," I said, "I beg you to tell me who that man is and the nature of his power over you. Perhaps this is rude in me, but it is not a matter for idle civilities. When a woman is in danger any man has a right to act."

She listened without visible emotion—almost I thought without interest, and when I had finished she closed her big blue eyes as if unspeakably weary.

"You can do nothing," she said.

I took hold of her arm, gently shaking her as one shakes a person falling into a dangerous sleep.

"You must rouse yourself," I said; "something must be done and you must give me leave to act. You have said that that man killed your sister, and I believe it—that he will kill you, and I believe that."

She merely raised her eyes to mine.

"Will you not tell me all?" I added.

"There is nothing to be done, I tell you—nothing. And if I could do anything I would not. It does not matter in the least. We shall be here only two days more; we go away then, oh, so far! If you have observed anything, I beg you to be silent."

"But this is madness, girl." I was trying by rough speech to break the deadly repose of her manner. "You have accused him of murder. Unless you explain these things to me I shall lay the matter before the authorities."

This roused her, but in a way that I did not like. She lifted her head proudly and said: "Do not meddle, sir, in what does not concern you. This is my affair, Mr. Moran, not yours."

"It concerns every person in the country—in the world," I answered, with equal coldness. "If you had no love for your sister I, at least, am concerned for you."

"Listen," she interrupted, leaning toward me. "I loved her, yes, God knows! But more than that—beyond all, beyond expression, I love *him*. You have overheard a secret, but you shall not make use of it to harm him. I shall deny all. Your word against mine—it will be that. Do you think your 'authorities' will believe you?"

She was now smiling like an angel and, God help me! I was heels over head in love with her! Did she, by some of the many methods of divination known to her sex, read my feelings? Her whole manner had altered.

"Come," she said, almost coaxingly, "promise that you will not be impolite again." She took my arm in the most friendly way. "Come, I will walk with you. He will not know—he will remain away all night."

Up and down the veranda we paced in the moonlight, she seemingly forgetting her recent bereavement, cooing and murmuring girl-wise of every kind of nothing in all Brownville; I silent, consciously awkward and with something of the feeling of being concerned in an intrigue. It was a revelation—this most charming and apparently blameless creature coolly and confessedly deceiving the man for whom a moment before she had acknowledged and shown the supreme love which finds even death an acceptable endearment.

"Truly," I thought in my inexperience, "here is something new under the moon."

And the moon must have smiled.

Before we parted I had exacted a promise that she would walk with me the next afternoon— before going away forever—to the Old Mill, one of Brownville's revered antiquities, erected in 1860.

"If he is not about," she added gravely, as I let go the hand she had given me at parting, and of which, may the good saints forgive me, I strove vainly to repossess myself when she had said it—so charming, as the wise Frenchman has pointed out, do we find woman's infidelity when we are its objects, not its victims. In apportioning his benefactions that night the Angel of Sleep overlooked me.

The Brownville House dined early, and after dinner the next day Miss Maynard, who had not been at table, came to me on the veranda, attired in the demurest of walking costumes, saying not a word. "He" was evidently "not about." We went slowly up the road that led to the Old Mill. She was apparently not strong and at times took my arm, relinquishing it and taking it again rather capriciously, I thought. Her mood, or rather her succession of moods, was as mutable as skylight in a rippling sea. She jested as if she had never heard of such a thing as death, and laughed on the lightest incitement, and directly afterward would sing a few bars of some grave melody with such tenderness of expression that I had to turn away my eyes lest she should see the evidence of her success in art, if art it was, not artlessness, as then I was compelled to think it. And she said the oddest things in the most unconventional way, skirting sometimes unfathomable abysms of thought, where I had hardly the courage to set foot. In short, she was fascinating in a thousand and fifty different ways, and at every step I executed a new and profounder emotional folly, a hardier spiritual indiscretion, incurring fresh liability to arrest by the constabulary of conscience for infractions of my own peace.

Arriving at the mill, she made no pretense of stopping, but turned into a trail leading through a field of stubble toward a creek. Crossing by a rustic bridge we continued on the trail, which now led uphill to one of the most picturesque spots in the country. The Eagle's Nest, it was called—the summit of a cliff that rose sheer into the air to a height of hundreds of feet above the forest at its base. From this elevated point we had a noble view of another valley and of the opposite hills flushed with the last rays of the setting sun.

As we watched the light escaping to higher and higher planes from the encroaching flood of shadow filling the valley we heard footsteps, and in another moment were joined by Richard Benning.

"I saw you from the road," he said carelessly; "so I came up."

Being a fool, I neglected to take him by the throat and pitch him into the treetops below, but muttered some polite lie instead. On the girl the effect of his coming was immediate and unmistakable. Her face was suffused with the glory of love's transfiguration: the red light of the sunset had not been more obvious in her eyes than was now the lovelight that replaced it.

"I am so glad you came!" she said, giving him both her hands; and, God help me! it was manifestly true.

Seating himself upon the ground he began a lively dissertation upon the wild flowers of the region, a number of which he had with him. In the middle of a facetious sentence he suddenly ceased speaking and fixed his eyes upon Eva, who leaned against the stump of a tree, absently plaiting grasses. She lifted her eyes in a startled way to his, as if she had *felt* his look. She then rose, cast away her grasses, and moved slowly away from him. He also rose, continuing to look at her. He had still in his hand the bunch of flowers. The girl turned, as if to speak, but said nothing. I recall clearly now something of which I was but half-conscious then — the dreadful contrast between the smile upon her lips and the terrified expression in her eyes as she met his steady and imperative gaze. I know nothing of how it happened, nor how it was that I did not sooner understand; I only know that with the smile of an angel upon her lips and that look of terror in her beautiful eyes Eva Maynard sprang from the cliff and shot crashing into the tops of the pines below!

How and how long afterward I reached the place I cannot say, but Richard Benning was already there, kneeling beside the dreadful thing that had been a woman.

"She is dead—quite dead," he said coldly. "I will go to town for assistance. Please do me the favor to remain."

He rose to his feet and moved away, but in a moment had stopped and turned about.

"You have doubtless observed, my friend," he said, "that this was entirely her own act. I did not rise in time to prevent it, and you, not knowing her mental condition—you could not, of course, have suspected."

His manner maddened me.

"You are as much her assassin," I said, "as if your damnable hands had cut her throat." He shrugged his shoulders without reply and, turning, walked away. A moment later I heard, through the deepening shadows of the wood into which he had disappeared, a rich, strong, baritone voice singing "*La donna e mobile*," from "Rigoletto."

Paul Vargas: A Mystery

By Hugh Conway

During the course of my professional career I have met with many strange things. The strangest, the most incomprehensible of all, I am about to narrate. Its effect upon me was such, that, without pausing for investigation or inquiry, I turned and fled from the town—even from the country in which I witnessed it. It was only when I was some thousands of miles away that I recovered from my terror sufficiently to think calmly over what had happened. Then I vowed a self-imposed vow that for many many years I would mention the matter to no one. My reasons for secrecy were these:—

In the first place I was, as I am now, a doctor. Now I am fairly well-to-do, and have little anxiety about the future. Then I was struggling hard to make a living. Such being the case, I argued that the telling of an incredible, monstrous tale—the truth of which, however, I should be bound to uphold in spite of everything and everybody—would do little towards enhancing my reputation for common sense, or improving my professional prospects.

In the second place I determined to wait, in the hope that, some time or another, matters might be explained to my satisfaction.

So it is that for twenty years I have kept my own counsel. My first reason for silence no longer exists; whilst, as to the second, I have now given up hoping for an elucidation. The one person who might make things clear I have never seen since.

Although nearly a third of a man's allotted years has passed, there need be no fear of my magnifying or mystifying anything. The circumstances are still fresh in my mind; moreover, in the fear that memory should play me false, I wrote down at the time, all that happened—wrote it with a minuteness and technical detail which would be out of place here.

My story concerns a man whom I saw but thrice in my lifetime; or, I should rather say, saw during three brief periods of my lifetime. We were medical students together. His name—I do not change it—was Paul Vargas.

He was a tall, dark-haired, pale-faced young man; strikingly handsome in his own peculiar style. His nose was aquiline and well-formed; the broad forehead betokened great intellectual power, and the mouth, chin, and strong square jaw all spoke of strength of will and resolution. But had all these features been irregular and unpleasing, the eyes alone would have redeemed the face from plainness. More luminous, eloquent, expressive eyes I have never seen. Their dark beauty was enhanced by a distension of the pupil, seldom met with when the sight is perfect as was Vargas's. They possessed in a remarkable degree the power of reflecting the owner's emotions. Bright as they always were, they sparkled with his mirth, they glittered with his scorn, and when he seemed trying to read the very soul of the man he looked at, their concentrated gaze was such as few could bear with perfect ease.

This is a description of Paul Vargas as I remember him when first we met. I may add that in age he was two years my senior; in intellect a hundred.

Of Vargas's family and antecedents his fellow-students knew nothing. That he was of foreign extraction was clearly shown by his name and general appearance. It was supposed that Jewish blood ran in his veins, but this was pure conjecture; for the young man was as reticent concerning his religious opinions as he was about everything else connected with his private history.

I cannot say he was my friend. Indeed, I believe he had no friends, and I think may add, no enemies. He was too polite and obliging to make foes; although there was usually a calm air of superiority about all he said and did, which at times rather nettled such an unlicked lot of cubs as most of us were in those days.

Yet, if we were not bosom friends, for some months I saw a great deal of Paul Vargas. He was an indefatigable student, and, as if the prescribed course of study was not enough for him, was engaged during his leisure hours on some original and delicate experiments, conducted simply for his own pleasure. Wanting some one to assist him he was good enough to choose me. Why, I never knew. I flattered myself it was because he thought me cleverer than my fellows; but it may have been that he thought me duller and less likely to anticipate or forestall his discoveries.

Under this arrangement I found myself two or three nights in every week at his rooms. From his lavish expenditure in furniture and scientific apparatus, it was clear that Vargas had means of his own. His surroundings were very different from those with which the ordinary medical student must be contented.

All our fraternity looked upon Paul Vargas as abnormally clever; and when the closer intercourse began between us, I found at first no reason to differ from the general opinion. He seemed to have all the works of medical and surgical authorities at his finger ends. He acquired fresh knowledge without effort. He was an accomplished linguist. Let the book or pamphlet be English, French, or German, he read it with equal ease, and, moreover, had the valuable knack of extracting the gist of the matter, whilst throwing aside any worthless lumber which surrounded it. From my average intellectual station I could but admire and envy his rapid and brilliant flights.

He made my visits to him pleasant ones. Our work over for the evening, it was his custom to keep me for an hour or two smoking and chatting; but our talk was not the confidences between two friends. Indeed, it was little more than scientific gossip, and the occasional airing of certain theories; for Vargas, if silent about himself and his private affairs, at least, expressed his opinions on the world in general openly and freely.

He had resolved to become a specialist. He poured out the vials of his scorn on the ordinary general practitioner—the marvellous being who, with equal confidence, is ready to grapple with fever, gout, consumption, blindness, deafness, broken bones, and all the other ills and accidents which afflict mankind.

"It is absurd!" he said. "As well expect the man who made the lenses for that microscope to make the brass work also—as well ask the author of this treatise to print and bind it! I tell you one organ, one bit of the microscosm called man, demands a life's study before the cleverest dare to say he understands it."

Certainly the organ selected by Vargas for his special study was the most complex and unsatisfactory of all—the brain. Any work, new or obsolete, which treated upon it—anything which seemed to demonstrate the connection between mind and body, he examined with intense eagerness. The writings and speculations of the veriest old charlatans were not beneath his notice. The series of experiments we were conducting were to the same end. I need not describe them, but something of their nature may be guessed at, when I say it was long before the time when certain persons endeavoured to persuade the world that scientists were fiends in human shape, who inflicted unheard of tortures on the lower orders of animals, solely to gratify a lust for cruelty.

We had been engaged on our researches for some weeks—Vargas's researches I should call them, as by this time my conjectures as to what he aimed at had come to an end. I grew tired of groping in the dark, and was making up my mind to tell him he must enlighten me or seek other assistance. Besides, I began to think that, after all, my first estimate of his ability was not quite correct.

He certainly talked at times in the strangest and most erratic way. Some of his speculations and theories were enough, if true, to upset all the recognised canons of science. So wild, indeed, that at times I wondered if, like many others, his genius was allied to madness.

At this time a wave of superstition crossed the country—one of those periodical waves, which, whether called mesmerism, clairvoyance, electro-biology, spiritualism, or thought-reading, rise, culminate, and fall in precisely the same manner.

Paul Vargas, although ridiculing the new craze, read everything that touched upon it, even down to the penny-a-liner's accounts of mysterious occurrences.

"The truth may be found anywhere," he said; "if there is a diamond in the ground the most ignorant boor may, unwittingly, dig it out."

One night I found him in a strange preoccupied mood. He did his work mechanically, and I could see that his thoughts kept straying away. We finished earlier than usual, and for a while he sat opposite to me in silence. Then he raised his eyes and asked me a question.

What that question was I have never been able to remember. I have racked my brain again and again, but have never recalled the purport of it. All I know is, it was, from a scientific point of view, so supremely ridiculous that I burst into a peal of laughter.

For a moment Paul Vargas's eyes positively flamed. Feeling that our relations were not friendly enough to excuse the indiscretion on my part, I hastened to apologise. He was himself again directly, and, with his calm superior smile on his lips, assured me I had done nothing which demanded an apology. He then changed the conversation, and during the remainder of my stay talked as rationally and instructively as the most methodical old lecturer in the schools.

He bade me good-night with his usual politeness, and sent me away glad that my ill-timed mirth had not offended him. Yet the next morning I received a note saying he had decided to discontinue that particular series of researches in which I had given him such invaluable assistance.

I was somewhat nettled at this summary dismissal. Vargas asked me to his rooms no more, and he was not the man to call upon uninvited. So, except in the schools and in the streets, I saw nothing more of him.

It was predicted by those who should know best that Paul Vargas would be the scholar of the year. I alone dared to doubt it. In spite of his great talents and capacity for work, I fancied there was that in his nature which would defeat these high hopes. There was something wrong—something eccentric about him. In plain English, I believed, if not mad now, Vargas would end his days in a madhouse.

However, he never went up for his last examination. He had a surprise in store for us. Just before the final trial in which he was to reap such laurels he vanished. He went without a word of warning—went bag and baggage. He left no debts behind him. He defrauded no one. He simply, without giving a reason for his departure, went away and left no trace behind him. Some time afterwards it was reported that he had come into a large fortune. This explanation of his conduct was a plausible one, and was generally accepted as correct.

After the nine days' wonder had died away I, like others, ceased to think about the missing man. The years went by, I passed my examination creditably, and was very proud and hopeful when duly authorised to place M.D. after my name.

I have narrated how I first met Paul Vargas. I had no expectation of again seeing him, nor any great wish to do so. But we met a second time. It was in this wise.

When I took my medical degree I was far from being the staid, sober man I now am. Having a little money of my own I resolved to see something of the world before I settled down. I was not rich enough to be quite idle, so I began by making one or two voyages as doctor to an emigrant ship. I soon grew tired of this occupation, and being in England, but not yet cured of roving, I cast about for something professional to take me abroad. I had not long to wait. Cholera was raging in the East. A fund had been raised to send out a few English doctors; I tendered my services which were accepted.

At Constantinople I was detained several days waiting instructions. One day, whilst idly strolling through the streets, I came face to face with Paul Vargas.

Although he wore the fez and was in appearance more Turkish than English, I knew him at once and accosted him by his name. Surprised as he looked at my salutation, he had evidently no wish to deny his identity. As soon as he recognised me he greeted me cordially, and having learnt what brought me to Constantinople, insisted that I should pay him a visit. I willingly consented to do so. I was most curious to ascertain why he had thrown up the profession so suddenly. The day being still young I started then and there with him for his home.

Naturally, almost my first question was why he left us so mysteriously.

"I had my reasons," he said.

"They must have been powerful ones."

He turned his dark eyes full upon me.

"They were," he said. "I grew sick of the life. After all, what did it mean? Work, work, work, only to find out how little one really knew or ever could know by study. Why, in one half-hour I learned more by pure chance than any one else has yet dreamed of."

I questioned him as to the meaning of his arrogant assertion, but he evaded me with all his old adroitness; then we reached his house, and I forgot all save admiration.

His house was just outside the city. House! it might be called a small palace. Here he lived in true Oriental luxury. Judging from the profusion which surrounded him, and from the lavish scale on which his establishment was conducted, I felt sure that the report of his having inherited a fortune was quite correct. All that money could buy, all that an intellectual Sybarite could desire, seemed to be his. Books, paintings, statuary, costly furniture, rich tapestries, the choicest dishes, and the rarest wines. Only a man in the enjoyment of a princely income could live in such style and splendour.

He led me from room to room, until he opened the door of one more beautifully garnished than any of the others. A girl was sitting at the window. As we entered she sprang forward with a cry of joy, and threw her arms round Vargas.

He returned her passionate embrace; kissed her, whispered some words of love in a strange, musical language, then gently disengaging himself, said—

"Myrrha, welcome an old friend of mine, an Englishman."

She turned towards me. Her beauty absolutely dazzled me. She was tall and majestic; coil upon coil of jet black hair crowned her well-poised queenly head. Her cheek had the clear brown tinge of the south. Her eyes were glorious. Never before had I seen such a splendid creature. The perfection of her form, the look of splendid health and glowing vitality would have been enough to make her an object of the greatest interest to any one of my own profession.

The bright colours of her rich dress well became her. Although in years she was but a girl, the gold and jewels which covered her hands, arms, and neck, seemed quite in keeping with her beauty. As I looked at her I felt that Paul Vargas's earthly paradise ought to be complete.

She came forward with unembarrassed grace, smiled a bright smile, and giving me her hand, bade me welcome in English, correct enough, although tempered by a slight foreign accent.

After a little while Vargas suggested that I should walk round the gardens with him. As we left the room, the look which passed between him and the girl was quite enough to show the complete love they bore one another.

"Your wife, I suppose?" I said, when we were alone. "She is very beautiful."

"My love, my life, my very soul!" he exclaimed passionately. "But not my wife in your sense of the word."

I said no more, feeling the subject was a delicate one to handle. Who Myrrha was, or why she should live, unmarried, with him was none of my business.

I had not been long in his society before I discovered that Paul Vargas was, in some ways, much changed—I may say improved. He seemed altogether a better sort of fellow than the man I had known of old. No less polite, but more natural. His invariably charming manners were enhanced by the addition of something like friendliness. In an hour's time I felt that I had made more progress with him than I had in the whole of our previous intercourse. I attributed this change to the power of love, for, wife or no wife, it was plain that the man loved his beautiful companion with all the force of his strong nature.

Yet it shocked me to discover that all the old ambition was dead. I mourned that such a highly-gifted man could at his age withdraw completely from the battlefield, and seem only to strive to make life as soft and sensuous as it might be possible for wealth to make it. I spoke once or twice to this effect, but the darkness of his brow and the shortness of his answers told me I trod on forbidden ground. For his own sake I hoped that the day would come when he would weary of his voluptuous existence and long for the bracing tonics of hard work and the struggle for success.

I was detained in Constantinople three days longer. Vargas pressed me to take up my abode with him. It was not worth while to do this, as at any moment I might be ordered away. But I spent several hours of each day with him. He was always glad to see me. Perhaps the sweetness of his seclusion was already beginning to pall upon him, and the occasional sight of a common-place work-a-day face was a welcome one.

The route came at last. I bade my friend good-bye, and sighed as I thought how grimly the scenes of death and misery to which I was about to pass would contrast with the Elysium I was quitting. Vargas accompanied me to the steamer by which the first part of the journey was to be made.

"Do you mean to live here all your life?" I asked.

"No, I shall grow weary of it—very soon, I expect."

"And then?"

"Then I shall sell everything and try another land."

"You must be rich to live as you do."

"I was rich. I had sixty thousand pounds—but in the last year or two I have spent two-thirds of my fortune."

"Two-thirds of your capital! What folly!"

He shrugged his shoulders, and smiled that old superior smile. Then a deep gloom settled on his handsome face.

"I have plenty left—plenty to last my time," he said.

"What nonsense you talk! What do you mean by your time?"

He leaned towards me, placed his hand on my arm, and looked at me with an expression in his eyes which thrilled me.

"I mean this," he said, slowly. "I could, if I chose, tell you the exact day—if not the exact hour at which I shall die. You see how I live, so can understand that if I have money to last my time, that time is short."

"My dear fellow!" I exclaimed, "have you any complaint—any secret malady!"

"None—I am hale and sound as you. Nevertheless I shall die as I have said."

His absolute conviction impressed me more than I cared to show. "A man must die of something specific," I said. "If you can predict your illness, can you not take steps to prolong your life?"

"Prolong my life!" he echoed as one in a dream. "Yes, I can prolong my life—but I will not."

I could only conclude that Paul Vargas meditated self-destruction.

"Why should you not care to live?" I urged.

"Care to live?" he cried bitterly. "Man, I revel in life! I have youth, strength, love—fame I could have if I wished for it. Yet it is because I may have fewer temptations to prolong my life that I am squandering my wealth—that I let ambition beckon in vain—that, when the moment draws near, I shall forsake the woman I love."

It was as I guessed years ago, Paul Vargas was mad!

He sank into moody silence, broken only when the moment of my departure came. Then he roused himself, shook hands with me and bade me good speed.

"We shall meet again some day," I said cheerfully.

His dark eyes gleamed with all the old scorn they were wont to express when any one, whose words were not worth listening to, opposed him in argument.

"We shall meet no more," he said, curtly and coldly, turning away and retracing his steps.

He was wrong. We met again!

I worked through the cholera; saw many awful sights; gained much experience and a certain amount of praise. On my way home I inquired for Vargas, and found he had disposed of his house and its entire contents, departing no one knew whither.

Two years went by; I was still unsettled; still holding roving commissions. I blush to say that I had been attacked by the gold fever, and in my haste to grow rich had lost, in mining, nearly all I possessed. I cured myself before the disease grew chronic, but ashamed to return all but penniless to England, I sojourned for a while in one of those mushroom towns of America—towns which spring up almost in a night, wherever there is a chance of making money.

I rather liked the life. It was rough but full of interest. The town held several thousand inhabitants, so there was plenty of work for me and another doctor. If our patients were in luck we were well paid for our services; if, as was usually the case, they were out of luck we received nothing and were not so foolish as to expect more. Still, taking one with another, I found the healing art paid me much better than mining. My studies of human nature were certainly extended at New Durham. I met with all sorts of characters, from the educated gentleman who had come out to win wealth by the sweat of his brow down to the lowest ruffian who lived by plundering his own kind, and my experiences were such that when I did return to England I was competent to write as an authority on the proper treatment of gunshot wounds.

One evening I met the other doctor. We were the best of friends. As our community was at present constituted there was no occasion for professional rivalry. Our hands were always full of work. Indeed, if we manoeuvred at all against each other, it was with the view of shunting off a troublesome patient.

"I wish you'd look in at Webber's when you pass," said Dr. Jones. "There's a patient of mine there. He's going to die, but for the life of me I can't tell what ails him."

I promised to call and give my opinion on the case.

Webber's was a mixture of drinking bar, gambling hell, and lodging-house. Its patrons were not of the most select class, and the scuffles and rows that went on there made the house a disgrace even to New Durham. By this time I was too well known to fear insult even in the lowest den of infamy, so I entered boldly and asked to be conducted to Dr. Jones's patient.

A blowsy, sodden-faced, vicious-looking woman led me up stairs and turned the handle of a door.

"He ought to be dead by now," she said. "If the doctor can't cure him, or he don't die in two days, out he bundles."

I walked into the room, taking no notice of the brutal threat. There, on a wretched apology for a bed—with a look of heartrending despair in his large dark eyes, lay Paul Vargas!

I thought I must be dreaming. The man I had seen little more than two years ago, lapped in absurd luxury—spending money like water to gratify every taste, every desire—now lying in this wretched den, and if Jones's view of the case was correct, dying like a dog! I shuddered with horror and hastened to his side.

He knew me. He was conscious. I could tell that much by the light which leapt into his eyes as I approached.

"Vargas, my poor fellow," I said, "what does this mean?"

As I spoke I remembered how he had predicted his own death. He must have remembered it too, for although he made no reply, and lay still as a log, there was a look in his eyes which might express the satisfaction felt by a successful prophet, when one who has laughed at his forecast is bound, at last, to realise its correctness.

I addressed him again and again. Not a word did he answer; so at last I was compelled to think that his power of speech was gone. Then I went to work to thoroughly inspect him and ascertain the nature of his complaint.

I sounded him, tested every organ, examined every limb; but like my colleague was utterly unable to find the cause of his illness. Of course I laboured under the great disadvantage of being unable to get a word of description of his pains from the patient himself. I satisfied myself that he had absolutely lost the power of moving his limbs. This utter helplessness made me fancy the spine might be broken, but it was not so. Paralysis suggested itself, but the obviously clear state of the mind as shown by those eloquent eyes was sufficient to send this idea to the background. At last I gave up, fairly baffled. I could give no name to his ailment—could fix no seat for it. His bodily weakness was great; but weakness must be caused by something. What was that something? So far as my knowledge went there was no specific disease; yet I was as certain as Dr. Jones that Paul Vargas, if not dying, was about to die.

And underneath us was the din of drunken men and unsexed women. Ribaldry and blasphemy, oaths and shrieks, laughter and shouts, rose and penetrated the frail planks which bounded the small, dirty room in which the sufferer lay. At all cost he must be moved to more comfortable quarters.

I went down stairs and questioned the Webbers as to how he came there. All they knew was that late one night the man entered the house and asked for a bed. He was accommodated with one, and for two days no one troubled about him. Then some one looked him up and found him in his present deplorable state. One of the inmates who had a grain of kindness left fetched Dr. Jones. That was all they knew of the affair.

I managed to secure the assistance of four strong and almost sober men. I paid what reckoning was due at Webber's, then set about removing the poor fellow. He was carried carefully down stairs, laid on an extemporised stretcher, and borne to my house, which, fortunately, was only a few hundred yards away. During the transit he was perfectly conscious, but he spoke no word, nor, by any act of his own, moved hand or foot. I saw him safely installed in my own bed, and having satisfied myself that no immediate evil was likely to result from the removal, went out to look for some one to nurse him.

I was obliged to seek extraneous aid as my household consisted of an old negro who came of a morning to cook my breakfast and tidy up the place. Except for this I was my own servant.

Decent women in a place like New Durham are few and far between, but at last I found one to whom I thought I might venture to entrust my patient, and who, for a handsome consideration, consented to act as sick-nurse. I took her back with me and instructed her to do what seemed to me best for the poor fellow. She was to give him, as often as he would take them, brandy and water and some nourishing spoon meat.

Vargas was now lying with his eyes shut. Except that he undoubtedly breathed he might be dead. I watched him for more than an hour, yet found his state a greater puzzle than ever. So utterly at sea I was that I dared not prescribe for him, fearing I might do more harm than good.

It was growing late. I had a long hard day before me on the morrow. I had to ride many miles, and doubted whether I could get back the same day. Yet, late as it was, I did not retire to rest before I had thoroughly ex-amined the clothes and other personal matters which I had brought from Webber's with the sick man. I hoped to come across the name of some friend to whom I could write and make his state known. Money or articles of value I had little expectation of finding—such things would soon disap-pear from the person of any one who lay dying at Webber's!

The only scrap of writing I met with was a letter in a woman's hand. It was short, and although every word showed passionate love, it ended in a manner which told me that a separation had taken place.

"You may leave me," it ran; "you may hide yourself in the farthest cor-ner of the world; yet when the moment you know of comes and you need me, I shall find you. Till then, farewell."

On the flyleaf was pencilled, in Vargas's peculiar handwriting, "If I can find the strength of will to leave her, my beloved, surely I can die in secret and in silence."

There was no envelope, no date; no address; no signature to the letter. All it showed me was that Paul Vargas still clung to his morbid proph-ecy—that he had made up his mind he was to die, and it may be had been driven into his present state by his strange monomania. The mystery was—why should he leave the woman he loved and come here to die alone and uncared for. It was, of course, just possible that in some way he had learnt that I was in New Durham, and when illness overtook him was making his way to me.

This could only be explained by the man himself, and he was without power of speech.

After giving the nurse strict instructions to call me if her charge's condition showed any change, I went to the bed I had rigged up in my sitting room, and in a minute was fast asleep. After I had slept for about three hours a knocking at my door aroused me. I opened it and found the nurse standing outside. Her bonnet and cloak were on, and by the light of the lamp she carried with a tremulous hand I saw that her face was ghastly pale, but nevertheless, wearing a defiant, injured look.

"What's the matter?" I asked.

"I'm going home," she said, sullenly.

"Going home! Nonsense! Go back to the sick room. Is the man worse?"

"I wouldn't go back for a hundred pounds—I'm going home."

Thinking some sudden whim had seized her I expostulated, commanded, and entreated. She was inflexible. Then I insisted upon knowing the meaning of such extraordinary conduct. For a while she refused to give me any explanation. At last, she said she had been frightened to death. It was the man's eyes, she added, with a shiver. He had opened them and stared at her. The moment I heard this I ran to his room, fearing the worst. I found nothing to excite alarm; Vargas was quiet, apparently sleeping. So I returned to the stupid woman, rated her soundly, and bade her go back and resume her duties.

Not she! Horses would not drag her into that room again—money would not bribe her to re-enter it. The man had looked at her with those fearful eyes of his until she felt that in another moment she must go mad or die. Why did she not move out of the range of his vision? She had done so; but it was all the same, she knew he was still looking at her—he was looking at her even now—she would never get away from that look until she was out of the house.

By this time the foolish creature was trembling like a leaf; and, moreover, had worked herself up to a pitch bordering on hysteria. Even if I could have convinced her of her folly, she would have been useless for nursing purposes, so I told her to get out of the house as soon as she liked; then, sulkily drawing on my clothes, went to spend the rest of the night by Vargas's bed.

His pulse still beat with feeble regularity. He seemed in want of nothing; so I placed a low chair near the bed and sat down. As I sat there my head was just on a level with his pillow. I watched the pale still face for some time, then I fell into a doze. I woke, looked once more at Vargas, then again closed my eyes, and this time really slept, feeling sure that the slightest movement of his head on the pillow would arouse me, I did not struggle against drowsiness.

Presently I began to dream—a dream so incoherent that I can give no clear description of it. Something or some one was trying to overpower me, whether mentally or physically I cannot say. I was resisting to the best of my ability, the final struggle for mastery was just imminent, when, of course, I awoke—awoke to find Paul Vargas's luminous eyes, with strangely dilated pupils, gazing fully into mine. The whole strength of his mind, his very soul, seemed to be thrown into that fixed gaze.

I seemed to shrivel up and grow small beneath it. Those dark, masterful eyes, held me spell-bound; fascinated me; deprived me of volition or power of motion; fettered me; forbade me even to blink an eyelid. With a strong steady stroke they pierced me through and through, and I felt they meant to subjugate my mind even as they had already subjugated my body, and as their gaze grew more and more intense, I knew that in another moment I must be their slave!

With this thought my own thoughts faded. For a while all seemed dim, misty, and inexplicable, but even through the mist I see those two points glowing with dark sustained fire. I can resist no longer, I am conquered, my will has quitted me and is another's!

Then thought came quickly enough. I am ill—dying in a strange place. There is one I love. She is miles and miles away; but not too far to reach me in time. A burning desire to write to her comes over me. I must and will write before it is too late! Yet I curse myself for the wish as in some dim way I know that some fearful thing must happen if she finds me alive.

Then all consciousness leaves me, except that I have the impression I am out of doors and can feel the night air on my brow. Suddenly I come to myself. I am standing, bareheaded, close to the post-office, with a kind of idea in my bewildered brain that I have just posted a letter. I feel battered and shaken, large beads of perspiration are on my forehead. In a dazed way I walk back to my house, the door of which I find left wide open—an act of trustfulness scarcely due to New Durham. I enter, throw myself into a chair, and shudder at what has taken place.

No—not at what has taken place, but at what might have taken place. For I know that Paul Vargas, although speechless and more helpless than an infant, has by the exercise of some strange weird mental power so influenced me that I have identified myself with him, and done as he would have done. His unspoken commands may have worked no evil, but I shudder as I feel sure that had he ordered me, whilst in that mesmeric state, to murder my best friend, I should have done so.

It was only when annoyance and anger succeeded fear, I found myself able to return to him. I felt much mortified that I, in the full vigour of manhood had been conquered and enslaved by the act of a stronger will than my own. I went back to the sick-room, and found Vargas lying with closed eyes. I laid my hand on his shoulder, bent down to his ear and said—

"When you recover I will have a full explanation of the jugglery you have practised upon me."

I resumed my seat, fearing his strange power no longer. Now that I knew he wielded it I was armed against it. I flattered myself that only by attacking me unawares could he influence me in so mysterious a manner. When next he opened his eyes I did not shun them. I might well have done so—their expression was one of anguish and horror—the expression one might imagine would lurk in the eyes of a conscience-stricken man to whom had just come the knowledge that he had committed some awful crime. Every now and then they turned to me in wild beseeching terror, but they bore no trace of that strange mesmeric power.

Paul Vargas, if he was to die, seemed doomed to die a lingering death. For some ten days longer he lay in that curious state—his symptoms, or rather absence of symptoms, driving Jones and myself to our wits' end. We tried all we could think of without beneficial results. Every day he grew a little weaker—every day his pulse was rather feebler, than on the preceding day. Such stimulant and nutriment as I could force down his throat seemed to do no good. Slowly—very slowly—his life was ebbing away, but so surely that I was fain to come to the sad conclusion that in spite of all our efforts he would slip through our fingers. By this time he had grown frightfully emaciated, and although I am convinced he suffered little or no bodily pain, the look of anguish in his staring dark eyes was positively painful to encounter.

I had obtained the services of another nurse, and was thankful to find that, to her, the dying man was not an object of dread; although, after my own experiences, I could not blame her predecessor.

Hour after hour, day after day, Paul Vargas lay, unable to move or speak; yet I felt sure in full possession of his mental faculties. Several times I noticed, when the door was opened, a look of dread come into his eyes. He breathed freer when he saw that the new-comer was the nurse or myself. This puzzled me, for if, as I suspected, he had willed that I should write a letter and send it to the proper place, his look should have been one of hope and expectancy, instead of its displaying unmistakable signs of fear.

Although Vargas often gave me the impression that he was trying to subject me again to that strange influence, it was only once more that he attained anything like success. One day, grown bold at finding I had as yet avoided a repetition of my thraldom, and, perhaps egged on by curiosity, I met his strange fixed gaze half-way and defied him to conquer me. In a moment or two I found I had miscalculated my powers, and—although I blush to say it—I felt that in another second I must yield to him, and as before, do all he wished. At that critical moment the nurse entered the room and spoke to me. Her voice and presence broke the spell. Thank God, it was so! Vargas was sending an impulse into my mind—urging me in some way which I knew would be irresistible—to perform, not some harmless task, but to go to my medicine chest and fetch a dose of laudanum heavy enough to send him to sleep forever. And I say, without hesitation, that had the woman not entered the room at that very moment, I should have been forced to do the man's bidding.

Yet I had no wish to cut his few last days short! If I had given him that poison it would have been suicide, not murder!

Although he had predicted his own death, why was Paul Vargas so anxious to die, that he had endeavoured to make me kill him? Unless their tortures are unbearable, few dying persons seek to precipitate matters; and this one, I am sure, suffered little or no pain. His death was lingering and tedious, but not painful.

After this fresh attempt to coerce me, I was almost afraid to leave him alone with the nurse. I even took the precaution of being present when Dr. Jones, out of professional curiosity, paid him an occasional visit.

The tension on my nerves grew unbearable. I prayed fervently for the man's recovery, or, if recovery was out of the question, for his death. At last the time came when the latter seemed to be drawing very very near— so near that Jones, whose interest in the case was unabated, said, as he left me in the evening—

"He will die to-night or before to-morrow is over. I believe he has only kept himself alive the last few days by sheer force of will and determination not to die."

I assented gloomily, wished my colleague good-night, and went to rest.

Next morning, just after breakfast, I heard a rap at my door. I opened it and found myself face to face with a woman. She was tall, and even the long black cloak she wore did not hide the grace and symmetry of her figure. A thick veil covered her face. Thinking she had come for advice I begged her to enter the house.

I led her to my sitting-room. She raised her veil and looked at me. I knew her in a moment. She was the lovely girl who had shared with Vargas that luxurious eastern paradise—the girl whom he called Myrrha.

She looked pale and weary, but still very beautiful. Her sombre attire could not diminish her charms. My one thought, as I gazed at her was, how any man, of his own free will, could tear himself from such a creature? Yet, for some unknown reason, Paul Vargas had done so.

It was clear that I was entirely forgotten. No start of recognition showed that my face was anything but that of a stranger. I did not wonder at this. I was much changed; bronzed and bearded; was, in fact, as rough looking a customer as many of my own patients.

For a moment she seemed unable to speak. Her eyes looked at mine as though they would anticipate what I had to tell her. Her lips trembled, but no words came from them.

At last she spoke. "There is a gentleman here—dying."

"Yes," I replied. "Mr. Vargas is here."

"Am I in time?—is he still alive?"

"He is very, very ill, but still alive."

A wretch reprieved on the scaffold could not have displayed more delight than did Myrrha when she heard my words. A look of indescribable joy flashed into her face. She clasped her hands in passionate thankfulness and tears of rapture filled her eyes. Poor girl, she had little enough to rejoice at! She was in time—in time for what? To see her lover die. That was all!

"Take me to him at once," she said, moving towards the door.

I suggested a little rest and refreshment first. She declined both, peremptorily.

"Not a moment must be wasted. I have travelled night and day since I received his letter. Quick, take me to him, or it may be too late!"

I asked her to follow me. She threw off her long cloak, and I saw that her dress beneath it was plain black. No ribbon, jewel, or ornament broke its sable lines. With a look of ineffable joy on her face she followed me to Vargas's room.

"Let me go first and prepare him," I said.

"No," she replied, sternly. "Let me pass."

She laid her hand on the door, opened it, and preceded me into the room.

Paul Vargas's eyes were turned—as, indeed, they had for the last few days been mostly turned—towards the door; yet the look which leapt into them was not one of joy and welcome. It was a look of woe—of supreme agony. A convulsive shudder ran across his face, and I expected his next breath would be the last.

Why should the advent of his beautiful visitor so affect him? Had he treated this woman so evilly, that he dreaded lest she came to his deathbed to heap reproaches on his head. Yet, he himself had summoned her—brought her from afar——by the letter which he had willed me to write.

Injured or not, Myrrha came to console, not reproach. My doubts on this point were at once set at rest. With a cry of passionate grief she threw herself on her knees beside the bed; clasped the poor wasted hand in hers, and covered it with tears and kisses. In a strange tongue—one unknown to me—she spoke words which I knew were words of fervent love. The musical voice, the thrilling accent, the gestures she used, were interpreters sufficient to make me understand that she was rejoicing that death had spared her lover long enough for her to see him once more.

A soft look, a look that echoed her own came over the sufferer's face—a look of infinite tenderness and deathless love. But it was transient. His eyes grew stern. I fancied they tried to drive her away; then, as she heeded not his commands, they besought and appealed to her. In vain—the strange girl laughed joyfully as a bride who welcomes her bridegroom. She kissed her lover again and again. Then, with a weary sigh, Paul Vargas closed his eyes—never, I thought, to reopen them. I went to his side.

He was not dead; but he bore infallible signs of approaching dissolution. Practically, it was of little moment whether he died now or in an hour's time. Nothing could save him. Still, the wish one always feels to prolong the faintest nicker of life prompted me to speak to Myrrha.

"The excitement will kill him," I whispered.

She sprang to her feet as if stung. She threw me a glance so full of horror that I started. Then, bending over Vargas, she satisfied herself that he still breathed.

"Go," she whispered, fiercely. "Leave me alone with my love. Take that woman with you."

I hesitated. I wanted to see the end. But I could not dispute the sacred claims of love and grief, or help sympathising with the girl in her desire to be alone with the dying man. My duties were ended. I had done all I could; but death in his present mysterious garb had conquered me. The man must die. How could he die better than in the arms of the woman he loved?

I motioned to the nurse to leave the room. I followed her through the door; then turned to take my last look at Paul Vargas.

He was lying apparently unconscious. Myrrha had thrown herself on the bed by his side. His poor pale face was drawn close to her full red lips. Her bosom beat against his. Her arms were wreathed around him, holding him to her. The contrast between life and death—between the rich, strong glowing life of the young girl, and that of the man now ebbed away to its last few sands, was startling. I closed the door reverently. My eyes filled with tears and I sighed for the sorrow which was about to fall on the devoted, passionate creature. How would she bear it! Then I went about my duties, knowing that when I returned home, I should have a patient the less.

I rode some miles into the country, to set a miner who had met with an accident which would most likely prove fatal. Just as I reached his cabin my horse fell suddenly lame. I led him the rest of the way and, having done all I could for the injured man, started to return home. There was nothing for it but to leave my horse to be fetched the next day, and walk back to New Durham.

I strode on as briskly as the nature of the track would allow. As I trudged along I thought of Myrrha and Paul Vargas, and wondered if by any chance I should find him alive on my return. I was so pre-occupied with these thoughts that, not until I was close to him, did I notice a man lying on the side of the track.

At first I thought it was one of the common sights of the neighbourhood; a man dead-drunk, but as I stood over him I found, for a wonder, it was not so. The man's back was towards me; his face was buried in the herbage; but I could hear him sobbing as if his heart was about to burst. As he lay there he threw his arms out with wild gestures of despair—he dug his fingers into the ground and tore at it as one racked by bearable torture. He was evidently a prey to some fearful bodily or mental distress. Whichever it might be, I could not pass without proffering my assistance.

His agitation was so great that he had no idea of my proximity. I spoke, but my words fell unheeded. Sob after sob burst forth from him.

I stooped and placed my hand on his arm. "My poor fellow," I said, "what is the matter?"

At my touch he sprang to his feet. God of Heaven! shall I ever forget that moment. Before me stood Paul Vargas, well and strong, as when we parted some years ago in Constantinople!

What saved me from fainting I cannot tell. The man stood there before me—the very man I had left an hour or two ago at his last gasp! He stood there and cast a shadow. He did not fade away or disappear as a vision or hallucination should do. There was life and strength in every limb. His face was pale but it was with the pallor of grief; for, even now the tears were running from his eyes, and he was wringing his hands in agony.

Speak! I could not have fashioned a word. My tongue clave to my palate. My lips were parched and dry. All I could do was to stare at him, with chattering teeth, bristling hair and ice-cold blood.

He came to my side. He grasped my arm. He was still flesh and blood. Even in that supreme moment his strong convulsive clutch told me that. He spoke. His voice was as the voice of a living man—yet as the voice of one from whom all joy of life has departed.

"Go home," he said. "Go home and learn how the strongest may tremble at death—at what a cost he will buy life—how the selfish desire to live can conquer love. You asked me once if I could not prolong life. You are answered. You brought her to me—you yielded then, but not the second time when I would have undone the deed. "Go home, before I kill you."

Something in his whole bearing struck me with deadly terror—a natural human terror. I turned and fled for my life, until my limbs refused to bear me farther. Then I sank on the ground and, I believe, lost consciousness.

When I recovered I made the best of my way home, telling myself as I walked along that overwork and want of sleep were acting on me. I had dreamed an absurd horrible dream. Nevertheless I trembled in every limb as I opened the door of the room in which I had left Paul Vargas, dying in the arms of the woman who loved him.

Death had been there during my absence. I knew the meaning of that long shapeless form stretched out on the bed, covered by the white sheet. Yet I trembled more and more. The words I had heard in my supposed dream came to me clear and distinct. It was some time before I could summon courage enough to move the covering from the dead face. I did so at last and I believe shrieked aloud.

Lying there in her black funereal dress, her fair hands crossed on her breast, her waxen face still bearing a smile, lay the girl whom I knew only by the name of Myrrha—dead!

The Harmony of Horror:
A Pianist's Most Terrible Experience

By Havelock Ettrick

"YOUR carriage awaits you, monsieur."

"Thanks. I shall not, however, require it. I am walking."

So saying, I wrapped my warm fur mantle closer about me, and stepped out into the brilliant night. The evening had been one of wild intoxicating success, and I thought that the walk across Paris would help to soothe my nerves, naturally too highly strung; and now, with the cries of an applauding multitude still ringing in my ears, strained to a tension that was unbearable, I must be alone.

The air was keen and frosty, the sky clear, the brilliant stars scintillated and sparkled like diamonds in the hair of some dusky beauty; the gleaming constellations appeared twice as radiant, surpassing in magnificence their usual appearance.

I heard the clock in the Tour de St. Jacques strike the quarter before three as I rapidly made my way along the deserted street. The elation of my spirits, the wild exultation of my heart, was but intensified by the loneliness; the clear frosty air was as champagne in its power to keep buoyant my throbbing brain. I was wildly, intensely happy, I trod on glorified air.

And yet, had I not cause for happiness?

The ceaseless toil for many years, the drudgery and hardships to which I had been no stranger, had brought at last their reward.

I was famous, and Paris, the world, lay at my feet!

The wheel of fortune had turned, and I, the poor obscure student of Dresden Conservatoire, the half-starved, always penniless aspirant for musical fame, was the darling of Paris! After having met with unqualified success both at Berlin and Budapest, I had taken Paris by storm, and the musicians, critics, and high-born dames, composers, all alike, of the gay city, hung over my chair drinking in with delight the liquid notes as they dropped from my long, supple fingers.

Occupied with these pleasing reflections, I turned into the Rue Royal, which was by this time utterly deserted, save for a few prowling cabs on the search for night fares. I passed, and left on the right, the great church of the

Madeleine, and struck into the labyrinth of quiet streets that lie between the Boulevard Haussmann and the main avenue of the Malesherbes.

Deep sunk in thought, I scarcely noticed that the footsteps of a man had been gaining rapidly upon me, and it was only upon hearing them almost at my side that I turned round to see who it was that shared my nocturnal peregrinations. As I did so, however, an arm was thrust into my own, and I saw my uninvited comrade, a pleasant voice at the same time exclaiming—

"Ah, Monsieur Raoul Kaiservitch, you walk quickly! I left the *Châtelet* but a few moments after yourself, and I have had the greatest difficulty to overtake you. I see," he continued, "that you do not recognise me. Well, more people know a celebrity than a celebrity knows. I was present to-night at the supper given in your honour, and am one of the many humble worshippers at the shrine of genius."

"You are very amiable," was my rejoinder. Glancing again at my companion, I saw that he wore a dark moustache and imperial, but otherwise his face was invisible, being enveloped in the heavy fur mantle that the chilliness of the night rendered welcome; a broad slouched hat shaded the upper portion of his face, and I could but dimly perceive the dark flashing eyes that occasionally met my own.

"You are bound for the Rue des Sept Chiens, is it not so?" he inquired.

"That is my destination; I trust I am not taking you out of your way," I replied.

"Far from it, our roads lie together: this little street that we are approaching is a short cut for both of us. I fancy that I know Paris better than you," my companion said, laughingly. "I was born and bred on the boulevards."

"True," was my rejoinder, "I have only been here for the best part of a month; but I begin to find my way about with ease, though I generally confine myself to the main streets; I have no bump of locality."

Thus chatting, we turned up the quiet side street mentioned by my companion.

What followed I am almost at a loss to describe; the incidents are fused into one hazy remembrance, and at this length of time are well-nigh lost to my recollection.

I can recall a scuffle of feet, a hurried whispering; then I was thrown violently to the ground, and a heavy wrap deadened my cries for help. I had no doubt but both my friend and myself had fallen into the hands of a band of robbers, and that such money as I possessed was the motive for the attack.

I was lifted from the ground, and placed on the seat of a carriage which would appear to have been in waiting. Helpless, and the victim of a plot evidently prearranged, I could do nothing but await developments. I was held in my seat by four powerful hands, the owners of which, apparently anticipating some resistance on my part, prevented the smallest movement. The drive was a silent one, and seemed to me of interminable length; the jolting and bumping over the rough cobbles told me that the main streets were being avoided, and that our course lay along the quieter and less frequented byways of Paris.

At length, with a sudden jolt and the throwing of the horse upon its haunches, the vehicle came to a standstill. Swiftly and in perfect silence I was lifted from my seat, and conveyed into a house, a heavy door closed behind me, and I knew that, whatever the reason of my abduction, I was completely in the power of my captors.

I felt myself hurried along a passage, and pushed into a room, the agreeable warmth of which at once struck me.

The heavy cloak that enveloped my head was removed, a glare of light struck my dazzled eyes; then, recovering myself, I looked around me.

When my eyes had become accustomed to the blaze of light with which the room was flooded, I saw that it was for some definite purpose that I had been brought thither; I was evidently expected.

A group of men, numbering perhaps some two dozen, sat in semicircular fashion round a full concert grand piano. I saw with surprise that upon the book-rest stood one of my own programmes. Was it, I asked myself, the custom in Paris for artists to be violently assaulted and dragged against their will to give compulsory performances in the small hours of the morning?

A second glance at the faces of the men, who sat in stolid silence around the piano, told me instinctively that it was for no ordinary musical performance that they waited.

The men were none of them of less than middle age, many of them wore grey beards and possessed but scanty locks. Upon the faces of all there was a strange look of determination, in some cases it amounted to fierceness; they were men, I felt sure, whom one might fear, but shrink from useless appeals to their sense of mercy; men who conveyed swiftly to my brain the impression that they carried their lives in their hands!

To what place had I been brought? As my eyes travelled round the silent group, they were arrested by the sight of one man; the fashion of the chair in which he sat, and the manner of his occupation of it, was such as I had never before seen.

The chair was placed at the back of the room some yards away from the piano with its surrounding audience, and was in the shade. The strong lamps, that cast such a glare down upon the fierce resolute faces that conveyed such a disagreeable impression to my mind, left the end of the room in comparative darkness, and I could but dimly see its outline. It seemed to be fashioned of some dully gleaming metal, and was raised upon two steps of what appeared to be glass. The man was bound hand and foot by leather straps, which rendered the smallest movement an impossibility; upon his head was placed a metal cap to which was attached a wire which ran up to the ceiling of the room. The man was pale and livid, giving no signs of life except from his black beady eyes, which followed my smallest movement with intense anxiety.

The audience had their backs turned to the mysterious chair and its occupant; only the player at the piano would face in their direction.

Who was the man thus bound?

What was the meaning of the silent audience, the piano, the entrapped musician?

As I stood irresolute, the figure of a man rose from a chair placed close beside the piano, and advanced with outstretched hand towards me. He struck me as being of about fifty years of age, and he wore a full black beard, and was dressed entirely in dark clothes.

"Welcome, Monsieur Kaiservitch! You will excuse the somewhat peremptory manner in which you have been brought into our midst."

"Is it the custom in Paris to waylay musicians, monsieur? I judge from the open piano that my professional services are expected. I cannot deny that I would choose any time rather than the present for giving them."

"Unfortunately, Monsieur Kaiservitch, we have no option but to require your artistic services at the present time. It is for this reason that you were followed from the *Châtelet* Theatre and brought hither. I speak in the name of my comrades when I assure you that if you will do as we counsel you, no harm of any description will come to you, and that you will be safely at your residence within the space of one hour from now."

"I thank you," was my reply, "for the assurance. May I ask what is required of me?"

"Simply to play on the piano that you see before you—and which, let me add, you will find no mean instrument—three pieces of music which have been selected from the programme that you performed this evening at the *Châtelet* Theatre."

The words of the man before me conveyed a command rather than a request; so, putting aside my natural curiosity, not unmixed with resentment at the peremptory manner in which my professional services were demanded, I bowed to the circle of silent men facing me, and seated myself at the piano.

I was dead tired, and even the pleasure of touching such an exquisite instrument as the piano proved itself to be could not arouse within me the energy to do justice to the music I set myself down to interpret. I was haunted, too, by the sight of the man's face who sat bound hand and foot in the chair, which I could dimly see gleaming with dull metallic lustre in the shadows at the further end of the room.

I fancied that, as I played, the man's face grew more haggard, and blanched to an even more ghastly whiteness. I played my first piece—a valse capricieuse of Liszt's; it was received in solemn silence, the chairman of the assembly—he who had first addressed me—alone giving a sign, by gravely bowing his head, that the music had been heard.

The dead silence of the room began to affect my nerves, already overwrought and unstrung by the strange proceedings of the past hour.

As I began the second piece marked for my performance, I could have sworn that a husky cry for mercy burst from the lips of the captive in the metal chair; his face was working convulsively, and I could see that the fingers of his tightly-strapped hands were twitching. The sight of it, added to the mystery of his being there at all, and the utter indifference of the other men in the room to his position, broke down what little of nervous force I had still left to me. I dropped my hands from the keyboard, and turned to the chairman of my grim audience.

"I cannot play more!"

He rose from his seat and came to my side. His full face, with its large, prominent eyes, looked strangely excited.

"You *must* play; you *must* perform the pieces marked on that programme."

"I must know before I do so the reason of this unnatural concert. Why is that man there bound into his chair; why does he watch my every movement with such horrible anxiety; why do you sit around me in such unbroken silence? I must and will know the reason of these unnatural proceedings."

For the space of a few seconds the man did not speak; he regarded me with a strange, fixed stare, that seemed to draw from me all power of resistance to his will, whatever it might be. I felt in the presence of a mesmerist, one who could compel me by the exercise of his powers to bend before his force of intellect, his concentration of mind.

"You *shall* know, and that without loss of time, the meaning of your surroundings. That man whom you see bound yonder is doomed to die, and he will meet his death at your hands! Sit down, Monsieur Kaiservitch," for I had started from my seat in horror. "You cannot by any possibility escape from being the medium through which the vengeance of an all-powerful society shall be wreaked upon one who has disobeyed its laws.

"Listen! All that you see in this room are members of a mighty organisation for the suppression of social abuses, a vast community that is spread over the face of the entire civilised world. By our laws certain offences committed by members are to be punished by death; equally by our laws that death is to be inflicted by someone not belonging to the society. So shall our hands be free from blood-guiltiness! Do you understand now?"

I began to grasp his meaning! I was to be the slaughterer, by some means yet unknown to me, of that wretched man bound so fast in the metal chair! Was there no escape? Could I not work upon the feelings of this diabolical crew to spare the intended victim? I looked, my hands trembling, my lips dull and parched, upon the face of the man who awaited his deathblow. His eyes met mine, but in their glance I read but the misery of hopelessness; he doubtless knew better than myself the character of the men who had doomed him to death.

The chairman resumed his explanation, still holding me fascinated by his dark, gleaming eyes.

"The manner of this man's death will be as follows: —You will play the Chopin Nocturne in B flat that already you have performed to the delight of thousands this night; again you shall play it, but this time every note that you strike will bring mortal terror to the man who has broken the laws of his fraternity. This piano is connected with a powerful electric battery; *upon a certain chord in that Nocturne being played the communication will be made*, and a charge of electric current more than sufficient to kill ten men will enter that man's body, and he will then have paid the penalty of his disobedience!"

I sprang to my feet once more and faced my informant, who with set smile on his pale face regarded me fixedly.

"But this—this will be sheer murder, nothing less than murder," I cried. "Nothing on earth shall make me touch this piano again!"

He forced me with strong hand down upon the chair once more.

"You *will* play, Monsieur Raoul Kaiservitch. You *will* play!"

So saying, he took my two hands into his own and steadily looked at me. A sense of utter helplessness overcame me—my will seemed to disembody itself, to detach itself from my personality, to leave me powerless and weak, a puppet in the hands of the man who stood over me, never removing his eyes from my face.

"Play!"

Obediently I turned to the piano; my fingers involuntarily began the opening phrase of the Nocturne. I played as one in his sleep; no power of resistance came to my aid. I was a mechanical automaton worked by the mesmeric power of a stronger will than my own.

The notes dropped one by one from under my fingers; the first movement of the Nocturne, with its searching, plaintive melody, was finished, and I passed without pause on to the minor scheme of exquisite beauty. I watched as in a dream the face of the doomed man, knowing that as chord by chord formed themselves under my hands, the knell of death was sounding in his ears. Nearer and nearer drew the fatal harmony that would release the dread force which brought eternity to him; there was no hope, no possible accident that could spin out the threads of life for him.

Mechanically, and with no will of my own, I struck the long-sustained minor chord that forms the modulation wherein the melody returns to its first and earliest cry.

As I did so, I noticed that the faces of my audience turned with one accord towards the chair that stood in the shadow!

I, too, looked!

The eyes of the doomed man were closed, a slight froth appeared on the parted lips, the muscles of the neck and hands stood out tense, but, as I dropped with horror my hands from the ivory keys, resumed their ordinary appearance; the jaw fell; I understood! The long-sustained chord had been that selected to deal the death blow; the man was dead, and I, Raoul Kaiservitch, was his executioner!

I dropped unconscious on to the floor, knowing and hearing nothing further.

ഇൗൽ

When I recovered myself I was lying in the shade of a doorway in the Rue des Sept Chiens; daylight was breaking, and I was alone, faint, weary, and hungry. Staggering to my feet, I regained in a few moments the house for which I had been bound when these dread things fell upon me.

Success has come to me, and as the years pass, fame has been coupled with my name: but never since that night have I played the B flat minor Nocturne of Chopin. I am haunted ever by the sight of a face, pale and livid, wherein the eyes watch my every movement with horrible intensity; I can hear the long-drawn minor harmony that opened the gate of the land of shadows to a helpless fellow creature who had done me no wrong.

Who were the men who thus entrapped me for their fell purpose?

What devilish Brotherhood was it that used me as the handle wherewith to deal death to one of their number?

I do not know; from that night to the present time I have seen or heard nothing of my companions of that dread hour in which my hands struck the Harmony of Death.

The Peculiar Gaze of the Hypnotized.

The Mystery of Turkentyne

By Julian Hawthorne

Mason, Jordan, and I had been lunching together at the club, and were smoking peaceably in a corner of the smoking-room when Dr. Dwight came in with a copy of the *Evening Instigator* in his hand. His face was serious and bore traces of excitement, and his bearing was pregnant of news. He walked up to us, nodded, and sat down, holding the paper across his knee.

"Smoke?" said Jordan, languidly drawing a cigar from his waistcoat pocket.

"A nip of brandy, if you'll touch the bell," replied Dwight. "Have you heard about Turkentyne? It's in the paper, I see, though it was only 11 when it happened. I was with him."

"Has he been getting drunk again on lemonade and seltzer?" interjected Mason. "It's a funny thing, by the way; have you noticed it? It's been going on for the last three or four weeks. Little Turkie always had the best will in the world to get off on sprees with the boys, but fate in the shape of an impracticable stomach made liquor of any sort an impossibility for him. He actually can't touch so much as a glass of claret without undergoing disastrous reverses in his epigastric region. I've seen him following a knot of the fellows about, watching them toss off their cocktails and straights with eyes green with envy, but never daring to chip in himself. The jollier they got the more down in the mouth would he grow; and he once confided to me that he would give half his fortune for the digestion and constitution of a man like Greenwood, for example—who, for his part, can drink all day if he can only get somebody to pay the shot."

"I guess Greenwood must have found his paymaster, then," I remarked; "for I have noticed the past month or so that he has been hilarious every evening; and I've seen him ordering fizz—and paying for it, too—as if it was water."

"What I was going to say," resumed Mason, "Turkentyne has been strangely festive of late for no substantial reason that I could ever discover. I've never seen him put anything stronger than lemon juice into his glass, and yet he's been whooping it up as if he were loaded with the best stuff in the cellar."

"He gets inebriated through sympathy," said Jordan; "I've heard of such a thing. He's probably of a peculiarly sensitive and sympathetic nature."

"Sympathetic as a fish!" retorted Mason scornfully. "A fellow who's made his money working wheat corners as Turkie has isn't going to suffer from the pangs of an impressionable imagination. No, sir; there's a mystery there and I'd like, to hear an explanation of it. The man gets roaring drunk on nothing at all; that's the long and short of it; and yet I'll wager he hasn't swallowed a pint of liquor in three years. I know what I'm talking about."

"Maybe he's a haschisch or chloral fiend," I suggested.

"I am able to answer for him as to that," put in Dwight, who has been silently sipping his brandy all this while. "I'm his physician and I'm in a position to affirm that he has never touched drugs of any kind. He had a peculiar organisation and could stand no sort of stimulant, not even tobacco."

"There," exclaimed Mason triumphantly; "and is it not nevertheless true, doctor, that he has been exhibiting all the symptoms of the practised rounder?"

"All but one, I admit," replied Dwight.

"And what's that?"

"Why, that every night, at about 2 o'clock a.m., he has suddenly become as sober as a judge and gone to bed with a head as clear as crystal. And when he got up in the morning there wasn't the faintest symptom of feverishness or discomfiture of any description. That of course is proof positive of his actual abstinence."

"By Jove!" drawled Jordan, "if the fellow has discovered a means of enjoying all the delights of the rounder without suffering any of the penalties I should like to sit at his feet and imbibe his wisdom. What do you make of it doc?"

"I must inform you gentlemen," said Dwight gravely, "since you evidently haven't heard it, that our poor friend is dead. Yes, he died this morning in my presence at five minutes before 11 o'clock."

We all uttered exclamations. After all, we had liked poor little Turkie. He had been a vain, shallow, voluble, absurd creature; but he had possessed some warm human qualities. He had been fond of us; he had fulfilled his conception of friendship toward us; he had been generous with the only quality of attraction he had—his money; he had longed to make us like him and admit him to the charmed circle of our good fellowship. The charmed circle in question was verily a paltry enough object of ambition; but, such as it was, Turkie had craved it, and his mortification over the constitutional weakness which had disabled him from partaking of what our civilisation chooses to regard as the emblem of good fellowship had been so comically sincere and acute as to have attracted our amused attention. The spectacle of the strutting, crowing little man mourning because he could not share our excesses was enough to upset the gravity of an Egyptian idol. And then the phantasmal fashion in which, daring the last few weeks, he had contrived to accomplish the appearance of carousal, without employing the concrete means to that end—had rioted in wassail, without absorbing so much as a drop of the grape—was just such a grotesque kind of miracle as seemed to suit his character. But that Turkie should, thus suddenly and without warning, wrap himself about with the majesty of death was a fact quite out of keeping with the humble measure of his personality. There is dignity in death; but who could associate dignity with the thought of Turkentyne? The atmosphere of social dram-drinking had suited him well enough; but the chill majesty of the last great change—could that really have fallen upon Turkentyne?

"What did he die of? How did it happen?" I asked after a pause.

"What the cause of death actually was I am unable even to conjecture," Dwight replied. "But every symptom pointed to heart-failure superinduced by acute alcoholism. In fact, it was preceded by as startling a fit of the horrors as ever I witnessed."

"Why, then, he has been drinking after all," said Jordan. "He must have done his loading-up in secret. Though I don't see what his object could have been in that either. But if imagination or sympathy can make a man drunk it's too much to believe that it can give him the D.T. and kill him."

"I am certain, at all events, that he has touched nothing stronger than soda-water during the last four-and-twenty hours," remarked Dwight. "He has not been out of my sight during the whole of that time. We lunched together yesterday; he went down to Long Branch with me in the afternoon, where I was called on professional business; we came back to town on the 6 o'clock train and he dined and spent the night at my house. And it was there he died."

"How did it come on him?" asked Mason.

"When he came to lunch he was as quiet and cool as I am now—or more so. I may mention, by the way, that his heart has always been as sound as a dollar. He drank a weak cup of black tea with his lunch and at half-past 1 we took the train. We hadn't been aboard ten minutes when he began to show signs of liquor. His face flushed a little and he talked volubly and foolishly. I should have said (if I hadn't known to the contrary) that he had just swallowed a stiff horn of brandy. To make a long story short, he grew more and more noisy and boisterous all the afternoon. By the time we got back to New York he was drunk—there's no other word for it. His eyes were wavering, his speech was thick, and he was unsteady in his gait. He proposed all sorts of things, as drunken men do; I had some trouble getting him to my house. There he became so bad as to make me uneasy, though I knew all the time that there was absolutely no cause for his condition. At midnight he suddenly jumped out of his chair, his skin cold and clammy, his eyes staring, his body trembling—well, if you've ever seen a man with the mania-*a-potu* you know how he appeared. I applied the same treatment as if he really had the disease. But he grew rapidly worse; it was a terrible night. I had to call assistance at last and put him in a straitjacket, to prevent his doing himself or some one else an injury. At 10 o'clock this morning he grew very weak; we removed the jacket and got him into bed. He lay there muttering to himself and occasionally shivering for half an hour or more. Then he suddenly sat up, reached out with his arm, gave a gasp or two, and fell back dead. That's all there is to tell, gentlemen; but what it means I can't pretend to guess."

During the silence which followed the doctor's narrative Jerry Wallace, the dramatic critic, a clever man, but rather prone to dissipation, entered the room. He looked pale and dishevelled, and he shuddered nervously as he dropped into a chair and ordered a glass of absinthe.

"Poor Tom Greenwood is gone, boys," he said in a husky voice. "Pegged out this morning a few minutes before 11. I was with him all night. It's been a siege, I can tell you. I'm as limp as a rag. Poor old Tom!"

"Tom Greenwood dead, too? What ailed him?" demanded Mason.

"Shakes!" replied Jerry briefly and shuddered again.

"How long was he ill?" enquired Dwight.

"He'd been drinking ever since before 2 o'clock yesterday; started in with champagne and by 6 o'clock was working the brandy bottle. I kept with him, though I couldn't keep up with him—he was drinking two to my one. We made the rounds, but a little before midnight I managed to get him home to his rooms. He went right to the cupboard, pulled out a quart bottle of brandy, and took a drain at it. The next thing I knew he'd got 'em and he had 'em bad, I can tell you. I tackled him the best I could and tried to quiet him down, but he wore me out after a while and I had to call up the folks and send out for a doctor. We tried everything, but it was no use. At 10 this morning it was plain he hadn't much further to go. He lay on the bed quivering and mumbling; and along towards 11 he raised up and cried out, "Look out for Ned Turkentyne! By —, I forgot him." Those were the last words he said. In five minutes he was dead. The doctor called it heart-failure."

"What an extraordinary coincidence," murmured I to Dwight, who was sitting near me. "From start to finish it's Turkentyne's case over again. But what could he have meant by that last remark of his?"

Dwight seemed much agitated. "It recalls to my mind something I had forgotten," he said, in a low voice. "Several times during his last hours Turkentyne cried out—"Tom has forgotten—Greenwood has forgotten!"

I had no idea what he meant and took it for part of his ravings. But now it seems to look as if there were something behind it. Do you know anything in the nature of a compact or understanding between the two men?"

I shook my head. "They were on friendly terms and that sort of thing. I remember Turkentyne enjoying Tom's power of disposing of liquor and once he said jokingly that he would be willing to pay him a good salary to acquire his faculty. That was the night we three went together to Professor Blade's seance."

"Blade, the spiritualist, you mean?"

"Spiritualist, or magnetiser, or conjuror—whatever you choose. It was the usual show; but Turkie had never seen anything of the kind before and was a good deal interested, especially with the hypnotic experiments. The professor took a swallow of port wine and the subject smacked his lips; you know the kind of humbug."

"And afterwards he said that to Greenwood, did he?"

"Yes, as we were walking home together. Greenwood, I believe, was something of a hypnotiser himself. I recollect his answering that maybe he could earn that salary after all, or words to that effect. But it's of no consequence."

"Was that all that either of them said about it?"

"That's more than I can tell you. I left them on the next corner and they went off together."

"How long ago was that?" enquired Dwight, after a pause.

"A month ago, or more, I should think."

"Ah! and it's about a month ago that Turkentyne began to go on his barmecide sprees and since Tom obtained the means to pay for champagne and brandy."

"Why, what have you got in your head now?"

"And there's another point that I didn't mention before," continued Dwight, not noticing my interjection. "The other day, when I was at Turkentyne's rooms and we were talking together, I picked up a cheque-book of his that was lying on the table and unconsciously, as it were, began to read off the stubs. There were four or five of them with Greenwood's name and for a hundred dollars each. The date of the first was about a month back. When I realised what I was doing I put the book down."

"I must confess, doctor, I don't quite see what you're driving at."

"I don't quite see myself; but here is a series of facts. First, Turkentyne expresses a willingness to pay Greenwood a salary if he can acquire his power of holding liquor; secondly, from that time on Greenwood comes into some money, which he spends on liquor, and Turkentyne begins his barmecide dissipations; next, from that time on Turkentyne pays money to Greenwood at the rate of about a hundred dollars a week. Once more, Turkentyne and Greenwood die at the same moment of time and exhibiting similar symptoms, and both speak of something having been 'forgotten'. Add to those the fact that you instruct a transference of sensation at the professor's seance and all the evidence at present at our disposal is in."

"Well, it's queer, certainly; but what does it prove?"

"You are as well able as I to form an opinion," replied the doctor evasively. "More things are possible in this world than some are apt to imagine. You say Greenwood was a hypnotiser. I should say that Turkentyne would be a good hypnotic subject. But we shall probably never know anything more about the matter than we know now. Meanwhile I have an appointment to keep. By the way, an autopsy will be held on Turkentyne to-morrow at which I shall attend. Would you like to come? I am anxious to hear what the verdict will be."

I consented to be present, and with that understanding we parted.

The scene of the autopsy was dreary and depressing. A small, bare room; half a dozen indifferent men; a policeman at the door; and in front of the window a table, on which was extended a figure swathed in a white cloth. This cloth was presently unwrapped, exposing to our view the body of poor little Turkie. The face looked natural and I should have supposed, under other circumstances, that the man was merely asleep. The body was well nourished and the skin remarkably white and clear.

After some general conversation among the professional gentlemen present, in the course of which the peculiar circumstance attending the death were discussed, it was decided to examine the heart of the deceased and Dr. Dwight was requested to perform the operation. He approached the table, took a case of instruments out of his pocket, and opened it. I saw him select something bright and sharp and bend over the body; and then I became suddenly convinced that I did not care to assist at an autopsy and started to leave the room. I was feeling acutely uncomfortable and I daresay I looked so, for I noticed that one of the attendants glanced at me with a significant grin.

I had my hand on the door-knob and was just turning it when a quick exclamation from behind arrested me. It was followed by a confused chorus of voices and a general gathering together of every one present round the table. I turned, but could see nothing but the backs of the company as they bent eagerly over the body. What had happened? Had poor Turkie's interior revealed some unexpected monstrosity? As I stood hesitating whether to go or stay the babel of voices suddenly became hushed and out of the silence emerged a thin, falsetto groan like the last remonstrance of an exhausted bagpipe, followed by these words, pronounced in a tone of feeble but indignant complaint—"Take that razor away, doctor! What the deuce have you done with my clothes?"

Such were the words and the voice was the unmistakable voice of Turkentyne. He was not dead after all. I have no distinct recollection of the course of events after that, until an hour or two later Dwight, Turkentyue, and I were together in Turkentyne's rooms with a lunch before us. For a man who had so lately returned from the other world Turkentyne was looking pretty well, but he had a bad scare and his own voice vibrated and broke occasionally as he propounded to us in interrupted sentences the surprising story of his experiences during the memorable month just passed. The doctor listened complacently, for as the tale unfolded itself it substantially confirmed the diagnosis at which he had darkly hinted in his talk with me at the club.

"It was that fellow Blake that suggested it," said Turkentyne. "That is, he gave me the idea, and Tom and I afterwards worked it out between us. The principle of the thing is that when a fellow is hypnotised he can be made to feel all that the fellow who hypnotized him feels and act just like him, though there's nothing real in it, you understand—only he believes there is. Well, as soon as we settled on the principle we set to work to experiment. In the first place Tom hypnotised me; it was a little difficult at first, but after a while we got the hang of it, and he could send me off with a wave of his hand. Then we got down to business. I got a couple of quarts of champagne, and he and I shut ourselves up in my room, and he hypnotised me—only very lightly, you know, so that nobody would have known that I wasn't in my normal state; and then he drank the wine. Before he had finished the first bottle I was just feeling as jolly as a grig, and by the time they were both gone I was just about right. Well, that experiment settled the question whether the thing could be done, and then we made our bargain. I was to pay Tom so much a week, and he was to use the money in drinking all the wine and liquor he wanted. He was to begin at a certain hour each day and not get too full until after dinner; and it was stipulated that he was not to get dead drunk at all unless by special arrangement with me. We started in on that basis; but the morning after his first spree I woke up feeling like the deuce, for the hypnotic current hadn't been switched off, so to speak, and of course I was undergoing the same after effects that he was. I went over and had a conference with him, and we fixed it up easily. When he hypnotized me after that he gave me an order to wake up from the trance at a certain hour, say about at 1 or 2 o'clock in the morning, so that I should come out the next day without a coated tongue or a headache. As I was putting up the money for the job you see it was no more than fair that he should have all the bad hours to himself. From that time on we got along famously. The only awkward part of it was that sometimes the fellows wondered how I managed to get tipsy without drinking any thing; but that didn't amount to much and I was generally able to bluff them by pretending that cider was champagne and water gin and ginger ale whisky or brandy, and as a general rule they didn't notice what I was drinking at all. Of course I had to depend on Tom to keep his end up and not to overdo it, and he did first-rate until the last—poor old fellow."

"By the way, how do you account for the catastrophe?" I asked.

"Well, there's only one explanation of that. You see, we had got the hypnotising business down so fine that Tom could send me off just by an act of will without the necessity of our being actually together at all. All he had to do was to say, at a certain hour, 'Go to sleep, Turkie, and don't wake up till such and such an hour.' Then, wherever I was, off I'd go. But, as luck would have it, he must have forgotten day before yesterday to mention the waking-up hour, and afterwards, when he got the horrors, of course he was too busy with that to remember anything. So I had to go in for the whole thing. I suspected what was the matter, but I couldn't wake myself up. And when he died I suppose I died too, though if I did I don't see how I managed to come alive again. By George, it's lucky I did come alive before it was too late, or I might have been buried..." He broke off and became very pale.

"It was the autopsy that brought you to," said Dwight. "The first incision that I made started up your circulation and woke you out of your trance. But the case raises some interesting questions as to the possible extent of hypnotic power. Possibly, if you had had a weak heart you might have died in good earnest. I only wish poor Tom could be as easily resuscitated as you were."

"He shall have a bang-up funeral, any way," said Turkentyne, with a sigh, "and I'll foot the bill. And this thing has taught me a lesson, fellows, that I shall never forget. The moral of my story is—avoid the appearance of evil, I used to write in my copy books when I was a kid and I remember it now. Drinking is a bad thing and getting drunk on hypnotism is every bit as bad as on whisky. I'm done with it. I've been a fool and worse than a fool, for if I had been content to keep within the bounds of my own stomach, as it were, maybe poor Tom Greenwood would have been alive to-day!"

This was an edifying conclusion, and I have reason to believe that Turkie has, ever since that episode, remained as blameless in appearance as he already was in fact.

The Lion-Tamer

By Dora Sigerson Shorter

I.

"Up! Hector, Brutus, Nero." The lion-tamer cracked his whip; he strode smiling cruelly among the snarling animals; he knew no fear; his pleasure was in the danger of his position. The strong, brutal natures always on the look-out for a sign of weakness in him to attack—he lashed them as he would disobedient curs if they did not obey him, and they crouched to him. Sometimes one would face him for a moment, and the two would look into each other's eyes, till the brave beast would turn tail, subdued by the superior courage in the man's gaze. Often it was but the weight of a straw in the balance who would have the victory. But the man always came from the conquest with a smile upon his lips, while the women in the audience would give little cries of fear, and lean fainting upon their male companions, envying the woman the while who might call such a man her master. Had they but known it, she stood over there by the door in the gold and scarlet costume of a lady gymnast—a nobody to be the wife of such a man! Now she did not even look as the lion-tamer strode amongst his animals—a figure that a sculptor might copy for a god. All the women's eyes in the theatre followed him except hers; hers were downcast and turned away.

"Nora," a voice said low in her ear, "he has beaten you again?"

Her eyes flashed as she turned them upon the speaker, then fell; a deep flush spread over her neck and face.

"He has never beaten me," she said coldly; "how dare you say so!"

"He has beaten you," the voice said, "as he will beat you again, and yet again."

"He has not beaten me." She spoke angrily, stamping her foot, her fierce gaze even yet not meeting the eyes of her questioner.

"Why are you wearing that silk scarf around your neck? It is not customary—not becoming."

"Because I have a cold. Is it not enough?" She looked him up and down, challenging a denial, but he did not answer, gazing sadly before him at the crowded benches of the applauding house. The lion-tamer, astride a lion, was riding round the ring.

"I hate the life"—the woman spoke after a pause—"I hate the men's eyes. I am not one to smile when my soul is full of bitterness, or to dance lightly when my heart is heavy; neither can I uplift my face for the admiration of men, nor do I care to twist and distort my body for their amusement. Every night, as I swing above their heads and prepare to launch myself into the air, I smile upon them, and hate them, hate them—the cruel faces with their look of mock terror upon them, all waiting for me to fall, to miss my mark, to become a crushed mass of death."

"Nora,"—the man's voice was strained,—"don't."

"I tell you, they are waiting for me to fall. What else do they come for? What else are they watching for there"—she waved her hands towards the cage of lions—"but the death that walks with the man behind those bars? Sometimes I say to myself up there above their heads: 'Look how they sit with their breaths indrawn with suspense! Give them their sensation—miss this time,' And I—whom no one loves, who has no hope, no happiness—I do not miss."

"Whom no one loves?" The man's voice rang eager and broken.

"Whom no one has a right to love." She spoke hastily and coldly, seeming to answer the question in his voice. The man turned away his face from her.

"What a handsome couple of gymnasts!" some one said from the audience. "I wonder if they are married?"

The man's hand clenched. The woman drew her scarf more tightly round her.

"It is cold here," she said, as if she had not heard. "I wish I could go home." And again she repeated softly, full of yearning, "O God! I wish I could go home."

"Home!" the man echoed. "The trees are well in leaf there now, and the little birds are quarrelling over the placing of their nests; there is peace in the valley, and the great hills are yellow with golden furze."

The woman laid her hand upon his arm pleadingly. "Be silent!" she whispered "Oh, be silent!"

"Far away from London, from its darkness, its weariness, its soul-killing noise and crowding," the man continued, as though speaking aloud to himself. "There is silence from the crash of human tongues; only God speaks in the moving of the leaves and the falling of the waters."

"And the countless eyes," Nora whispered, as though afraid of being heard, "the eyes always watching for me to fall—they are not there, nor the ears always astrain to hear my dying cry."

The man shuddered. He drew nearer and, laying his hand upon her arm, gazed intently into her eyes.

"Wherever you go, eyes are watching you," he said, "ears are listening to you, tongues are ready to be busy with your misfortunes in this great city. But at home there are no eyes to watch you save of those who love you. There are no ears to listen save of those to whom your voice is music. There are no tongues to speak of you except with kindliness."

The woman, crying silently, drew back into the shadow of the passage. The man followed, and, taking his place before her, gazed into her eyes. From the theatre came the sound of clapping and "bravos." The attendants of the circus were busy; the two stood alone.

"Beneath the moon the fair valley smiles"—he spoke low and distinct. "The peat smoke curls upward, half seen in the faint light; its perfume is in the air. Here and there, among the purple gloom of fern and little trees, the star of a cottage light is seen. The contented lowing of lazy cattle, the bark of a watchful dog, or the chirp of some awaking bird is all that breaks the silence." He made a downward motion over her face with his hands. She lay back against the wall half in a trance, his eyes seemed to command her soul, she was passing into his power under the mesmeric influence of his voice. He continued softly, "The shadowy mountains encircle all. The light of the passing moon moves like a benediction over the land. The scented breeze is warm, and the cottage doors stand open. There is no enemy here to bar them against, and the night is not yet begun. In one cottage alone there is mourning, an old woman sitting in solitude by a hearth where the turf lies grey, the fire in its heart."

Nora passed her hand across her eyes, as if to see clearer. She sank upon a bench and spoke as in a dream.

"I see her," she said. "Her hand is to her side. No tears come from her eyes—she is too old to weep—but her heart is crying always. She is ill and miserable."

The man put his hand upon her forehead. "What does she say?" he said.

"She is calling 'Nora, Nora, Nora," nothing but 'Nora.'"

"Is there no reply?"

"There is a woman far away who is trying to reach her; but she cannot—she is tied, she is held back by some one very strong and very cruel. She is crying in her heart too, but she cannot go. She dare not go. God and man have bound her, so she must not break loose and go."

"And the old woman?"

"She is growing older and more weary. She is drifting away; she is dying. She cries, "Nora, come to me. Oh, my little Nora!'" She moved uneasily, as though in pain. The man passed his hand downward over her face.

"Tell her," he said slowly, "tell her you will come. Tell her you will be strong and cast the chains from about you that are killing you. Tell her you were young, and had no knowledge of what life was when you left her. Tell her that as an inexperienced girl you thought all nobleness dwelt in a body that God had made strong and beautiful above other men, how you left everything you held dear for his sake. But now, disillusioned, loveless, a woman who has suffered, you are going back to her again." He paused a moment, and continued with an effort: "Tell her that there is one who loves you as his own soul, one who you could not care for long ago. Tell her you love him now, and that he will shield you from all misfortunes, and take you away from suffering. Tell her, tell her."

Nora pressed her hands together, as though in great pain. "I cannot tell her that," she said, "I cannot tell her that."

The man drew his breath in with a sob.

"No, of course not; I was mad. Be calm. Tell her you will go home alone."

The woman opened her lips to speak, but the man passed his hand upward over her face a moment and disappeared. A strong hand fell upon her shoulder.

"Mother!" she cried, with a breath of joy or relief, "I have come home."

"Asleep?" a hard voice said in her ear. "Why are you not outside in your place, you lazy sloven?"

She started to her feet, passing her hand across her eyes, staggering into consciousness.

Her husband seized her by the shoulder, shaking her. "By God!" he growled, "if I thought you were drunk I would lash the hide off your bones."

"Don't dare to speak to me like that!"—she faced him now like one of his lions—"and take your hand off me at once!"

"I'll speak to you as I like and use you as I like." He shook her to and fro, then pushed her roughly from him. "Don't give me any of your infernal jaw, either."

She seized the loaded whip he had laid beside him when he came upon her, and raised it above her head. Her hot Irish blood coursed madly through her veins. In her passion she stood high as himself. Her trained sinews stood out on her arms. She came upon him like a thunderbolt, but he seized her by her wrists, as in a vice.

"I am not afraid of you," he said, and laughed. "I will tame you as I tame my lions, in spite of your claws."

He twisted the whip from her hands, and for a moment held it over her, as though to strike. She crouched for the blow, but met his eyes with a gaze so like one of his beasts when he ill-treated it, that he flung the whip aside. His fearless, cruel soul was momentarily ashamed beneath eyes that reproached and condemned him. Sometimes in the arena he had felt the same look bent upon him, and shame had turned him that fear never stayed, and his lash would fall unsatisfied to the ground.

"I have never struck a woman in my life," he said roughly, "but you are enough to make a man begin."

She laughed, and did not answer. The light shawl fell from about her shoulders, and on the white of her skin he saw the black track of a cruel grasp.

"I have never struck a woman," he repeated, sauntering away.

She sank down on a bench, drawing the scarf about her again. She could hear the rattle of ropes and pulleys. They were fixing the wires for her performance. She stood up, waiting her turn, and looked from her shadow into the theatre.

"Oh, the eyes! the eyes! the eyes!" she muttered, "all waiting to see me fall. Let the end come soon, God, if it be your will. I am weary, weary, weary of being alive!"

II.

There had been serious trouble at the Imperial Circus a few nights after this. The "shooting star," the beautiful Madame Blumenthal, would not go through her performance. The manager had spent his patience and his time in remonstrating with her; her husband had argued with more force than effect. "For the first time in his life," as he said himself, "he had struck a woman"; and the manager had looked on and not interfered. He was only sorry that he had no legal right himself to chastise her. He raved at her for a pig-headed coward.

A coward! And that was the reason the wonderful Madame Blumenthal was afraid to go through her performance, afraid to do the amazing flight through the air that all London was crowding to see. She sat and cried and trembled till her eyes were swollen and the red mark of her husband's blow became even more vivid on her pale face.

"Oh, forgive me!" she sobbed; "let me off this one evening. I have never felt like this before, never been afraid."

And the man who could not understand fear dragged her on to her feet,—

"If you are not ready in five minutes, God help you!" he growled.

"They are all watching for me to fall," she whispered. "There's a man there that has followed us for the last six months, ever since I began my dangerous leap. He has followed us to Paris, to Vienna, to London—everywhere. He is a ghoul waiting for my blood; he gloats over my danger. I see his eyes as I go out and bow. They follow me as I climb the rope and mount into my seat. All the life in me trembles. I am afraid of him—afraid of all the eyes."

"If you are afraid to go on you will be more afraid to stay away," her husband said cruelly, his eyes on her. "Do you think I will stand being ruined by you? Here, enough of this fuss!" he shouted; "get yourself ready! The trapeze is up, and everybody will soon be waiting."

She drew herself together and clenched her teeth. "I will go," she said hoarsely. "After all, what does it matter?"

When she came into the ring she was smiling as usual. No one noticed that the beautiful Nora had rouged to simulate the natural roses that had left her cheeks, or that a dark scar was hidden beneath the powder on her face.

No one noticed she was troubled but Malachy O'Dermod, who loved her; and he said nothing, but clenched his teeth so that the blood came upon his lip.

"Hold my hand tight, Nora," he said, as they went through one of their performances together. "You are not as fit as usual."

The sound of his gentle, strong voice soothed her. She smiled, feeling braver. "Imagine I, was afraid! But I am not, now that you are here to avert the evil eyes!"

"Trust me," he said, looking into her face, and seeing that she was afraid. "Nonsense!" he laughed. "After all this time!" He spoke to her, cheering her, to turn her thoughts from herself. He became nervous, thinking of her great jump through the air.

"I don't know what it is to-night," she said, smiling, "I feel as if something were going to happen."

The rope was lowered, and she clung to it till it left her almost out of sight of the audience, up under the sparkling roof-lights.

Malachy O'Dermod swung in his place, his soul in his eyes. "O little figure, so lonely," he said through his teeth, "God protect you!" and he kept clenching and unclenching his hands, while she prepared for her spring into the air, saying all the time, as if he did not know he was speaking aloud, "God help me! God help me! God help me!" He turned over in his swing, holding on by his feet. He was to catch her. The terror of his position overcame him as it never had before. In a minute he would know if the precious weight hung upon him. If not, he resolved to loose his feet and drop head foremost to the ground, avoiding the net. His soul cried to her, "Come to me straight, be strong, do not miss," till he felt she must hear and obey. But she, far away, alone under the roof, did not hear him, but, pale and trembling, prepared to gather herself together to spring. For the first time she knew what intense fear was and the facing of death.

"It is my husband," she thought. "His continual ill-treatment of me is wearing me into a coward. Even the lions, who hate him, are afraid to strike. I am not as brave, and my spirit, too, is broken." She saw Malachy turn over on his swing and reach his hands out ready to catch her. Far away she saw the crowd of white faces of the audience uplifted and staring at her. "The place is all eyes," she whispered, "all eyes." She groaned as she thought what she had to do to amuse them, and felt more lonely than ever she had done in her life, standing up there with the crowd of upturned faces and eager eyes demanding her, by their gaze, and saying—"Come; we are waiting: do not keep us." She crouched to spring, and, flinging herself into the air, opened her lips in a low, terrified cry. She felt she had sprung short. No one heard it but Malachy, and he hung upon his swing like one dead and blind. The next second hands grasped hands, and he heard the loud applause of the audience. Never had he enjoyed the agony of her weight as now, when it fell upon him almost unprepared.

"Why did you cry out?" he moaned. "You have almost killed me."

They swung hand from hand, recovering themselves. "I thought I had missed," she gasped. Then they dropped one after the other into the net. Hand in hand they bowed before the audience, delighting in the light and gaiety of the circus. In the memory of their terror they felt as though they had gone through the horrors of death, and out of the darkness had passed to the glory of day and living. Smiling, they went together out of the arena. When they reached a quiet passage outside they could hear the great cage rising round the ring in which her husband was to perform with his lions.

She sank down upon a box with a laugh. "I feel quite tired, like as if I had walked for miles," she said, lifting her damp hair from her forehead as she spoke.

Malachy leant forward, "I feel as if you had been lost and I had just found you," he whispered; then saw upon her brow—almost across her eyes—the vivid wound of a knotted whip lash. "My God!" he cried, his face changing. "Has he done that? Where is he?"

Nora started to her feet. She had never seen him so angry. She put her hand upon his arm to keep him. "Let him be," she said; "it is no use worrying. I am all right—it does not hurt. He was very angry because I would not go at once for my performance."

"Nora!" He grasped her hands in his. "Nora, leave it all, leave it all! It is no marriage of God's that keeps you tied to that brute. You do not love or honour him; he does not love or cherish you. My little Irish sweetheart, I have loved you beyond all telling since you were a tiny child."

Nora drew her hands away. "Do not dare to talk to me like that, or I shall hate you," she said; and then some one spoke behind her sneeringly,—

"A pretty scene, indeed, to come upon."

They turned, and faced her husband.

Malachy threw himself before the lion-tamer and caught him by his coat. He was not a small man, yet did not come much over the other's shoulder.

"You have struck her," he said hoarsely, between his teeth. "You cowardly hound! you shall take the blow back from me."

The other forced him from him, and raised his whip. "I shall cut you in two if you lay a hand upon me."

Nora, without thinking of anything, only to separate them, flung herself between them, and the blow fell across her shoulders, making her cry out. Her husband laughed when he saw where the blow fell.

"That comes of being in the wrong place," he said, striding out into the circus.

Nora heard the applause that greeted him, and missed Malachy from her side. She sprang up, frightened. Where had he gone? She suddenly came upon him in the shadow, an iron bar in his hands. He was creeping towards the bowing figure in the ring. He made a spring as she came up, but the lion-tamer saw him, and with a smile slipped into the cage amongst his lions.

Nora caught the man by the arm, and pulled him roughly towards her. "What were you going to do?" she cried. "What were you going to do?"

The bar dropped from Malachy's hands. "Nothing," he said. "I was mad for the moment; I hate him. Would to God he were dead; but I shall not be his slayer."

Nora let go his arm. Her heart echoed his words, then ran cold at its own guilt.

"What is he making of us both?" she whispered; and thought of herself as she was when a girl—so innocent, so glad of the joy of living in herself and everything else; how she had welcomed the young birds whose nests she knew and would not harm; and the children, how they loved her! Now she looked upon young things with pity, feeling that they would come to misery with years, as she had done. Misery, aye, and even crime; for in her heart now was the unspoken thought, "As there is no other way, O God, separate us by death." That glorious gift of life she once so revelled in she was now ready to throw away; or was it possible she thought of gaining her freedom by another's death? She hid her face in her hands. "How can I bear it?" she thought. "My life is embittered and ruined, I am beaten and insulted at every turn, my love is cast back upon me, my tenderness repulsed. How can I help but hate him, O God?"

She looked up, and saw her husband smiling among his lions. The beasts crouched and growled when even he approached. She saw the vast audience staring at him with admiring eyes—the women, perhaps, envying her for the possession of his beauty, the little children applauding with shrill voices every performance of the beasts, that had been taught them with cruel tortures. "If you only knew," she whispered to the women and children, as her eyes set again upon her husband. The great feat of the night was being prepared, lion after lion taking his position in the ring. Two of them refused for a moment to go, and she saw the smile come upon her husband's face that she knew so well. It was his smile of power, of his superior strength and will over anything that set itself against him. Now the lash fell upon the disobedient beasts with a biting shriek through the air. One of the lions crouched as if to spring upon him, and he smiled again and struck it across the eyes. Half-blinded, it slunk away.

One after the other they mounted into their places upon the platform prepared for them. Over the backs of these he was to climb, and mounting the central lion, hold aloft the united flags of England and America, the whole forming a tableau that he had done for many seasons, under many flags. Nora watched him making his last bow to the audience before he mounted into his place. The lions were ready in position, some growling softly to themselves, others licking their comrades, as they leaned towards each other.

"These men always get killed in the end," she heard some one in the audience say; and her companion tittered, "I hope it won't be to-night."

Nora looked at her husband again. She saw him stand a moment and brush the hair back from his forehead. What was the matter? Why did he not move? He seemed to draw himself together, then make a step towards the impatient beasts. Then he stopped again and looked around. Was he afraid at last? No, there was no fear upon his face—only bewilderment. He brushed his hand again across his eyes and walked towards the lions. One of them made a stroke with its paw towards him, snarling. He did not seem to notice. Some of the attendants seemed to think something wrong, and crowded to the bars, whispering together. One of them called out, but the lion-tamer did not answer. He attempted to get upon the back of the first lion, and slipped; the brute snarled and half turned, but the cruel foot was again upon his back, and he fell into his accustomed place. The man mounted and stepped on to the next beast, then slipped again, and went down on his feet between them.

She heard a voice in the audience mutter, "This may be good for show, but, by Heaven! I don't like it." And some one from the theatre pushed by her, saying, "My God! is the fellow drunk? If he had fallen he was a dead man." Again she saw her husband mount the back of the next lion in a bewildered way, as though he were half asleep. She saw the impatient animals growing conscious of something amiss. The angry lashing of their tails and the low, fierce growling was growing worse.

Even the audience became aware that all was not right, and relapsed into horrified silence. Some one called to the lion-tamer to come back, for God's sake, but he looked round with a cruel smile upon his face and made a step forward; he prepared to mount the centre beast, and drew the two flags from his breast. The lions were snarling and moving impatiently from their positions. He shouted at them to go back; they obeyed him reluctantly, and eyed him with hatred. He put his foot half across the beast nearest him. Nora saw it was not the central lion, but a vicious brute which he could never trust. Her face was like death as she gazed round the audience. What in God's name was the matter with her husband? She opened her mouth to scream, and her gaze fell upon Malachy O'Dermod. He was standing in the passage, his eyes fastened upon her husband like two burning torches, his face white and his thin lips muttering. She stretched her hands towards him, and then suddenly put them before her face. As she did so a great stricken cry arose from the theatre—women and children screaming and men shouting, the whole place in a tumult. She was hustled and jostled amongst the panic-stricken crowds and useless would-be helpers. She heard some one saying, "This is his wife; poor thing!" and knew she had shrieked out in horrible laughter before she fell under their feet unconscious.

III.

A year after this, in a green valley in Ireland, a woman went alone amongst the long fern and purple foxglove. Her face was raised from the lovely things at her feet and fixed upon the blue distance before her. Yet in her eyes, as she went thus, grew a great loneliness and longing. She clenched her hands and held them across her brow, as if in pain. As she passed, a man stepped out from a group of yellow furze straight in her path. He held out his hands to her, calling upon her name,—

"Nora! my Nora!" he cried.

With a great sob she turned, and held him as if he might slip away into a dream.

"Malachy! oh, Malachy!"

"I have waited a year," he said, "since I brought you home. You did not know me then, Nora, when I took you from among their feet. Ah, my love, it was hard to watch others nurse you and see you slowly coming back from your fever and madness; but I knew it was right and best not to let you know till now."

The woman drew herself back from him with an awful cry.

"O God! I had forgotten, and only remembered the agony of having lost you. Malachy, Malachy, we are outcasts from the happiness of God. Our ways are separate; we must not meet again."

He took her by the two hands and looked into her eyes. He thought the fever that had burnt in her poor brain was returning.

"What do you mean?" he said tenderly. "We shall never part again."

She drew her hands from his and stood before him like one turned into stone.

"The mark of Cain is upon you and upon me," she said.

"What do you mean?" he stammered, a horror growing in his eyes.

"I mean you drew the strength from my husband's limbs and the reason from his brain. You made him fall amongst the lions; you mesmerized him: and I knew, and could have stopped you, but I let him die."

The man grew white as death, and staggered from her.

"Yes, it is true!" he gasped. "I did not know my own power, but I hated him and wished him dead. I watched him that night, and my spirit went out and encircled him in numbness and death. I knew it, I knew it; but dared not breathe it to myself."

"We are murderers," the woman said, in a hard voice. "There is a dead man's body between us and happiness for ever. Bid me good-bye and leave me."

The man fell upon his knees before her, kissing her hands again and again.

"Is there no escape?" he groaned. "Is there no pardon? Is there no punishment less terrible than separation?"

"There is no punishment so just," she said; then fell upon his shoulder weeping. "But I have seen you once more. Oh, my love, I have seen you once more!"

Then they fell to tears and embraces and long good-byes; and she, feeling him depart, slid upon the ground, her face amid the fern, crying, "Malachy! Malachy! Malachy!" as one cries upon the dead.

The Higher Hypnotism

By Charles Fleming Embree

When they found Cristoforo, a third of the blade was buried in his breast, and the rest of the machete stood straight up. Though Maria lay on the pavement of the court before the church not far away, all her muscles were paralysed, remained so for months; and even after she recovered, it was proved that she could not have had the strength to drive that machete so deep.

Yet it was now clear from Cristoforo's papers that at the time he returned from abroad, his calm exterior hid a terrible thirst for revenge because she would not wed him; and that, even while he mingled in society, life was but bones to him; and he had sworn the destruction of them both.

In San Angelo, an hour from the City of Mexico by electric cars, is a Cosmopolitan circle. Editors, travellers, Basque musicians, poets, astronomers, a world of eccentric genius; no American thimble-parties to dawdle over; no English teas. Bohemianism lifted into philosophy, science and its occult shadow rushing from brain to brain—such is their unusual life. It it an upper, rarefied stratum of the Mexican society.

Don Cristoforo, back from a year in Paris and Vienna, sat next to Flora at one of her 11 o'clock suppers. Opposite was Maria (whom all the world knew he had tried so hard to marry) as placid, as glorious Andalusian beauty, as ever, and just as able to look him straight in the eye. Because it used to be hinted that Cristoforo had even tried hypnotism in his desperation to win Maria, Flora, the malicious (who would have given her head to marry the Machiavellian fellow herself), would keep the conversation on that science; which nettled Cristoforo.

"The old stupid sort of hypnotism—controlling one mind by another—is a back number," said Cristoforo, stroking his lean, sallow face after a custom of his, and looking solemnly cunning. "It is as bungling as telegraphy with wires."

There was a general outburst; ladies forgot their dessert; musicians ceased sipping black coffee. Flora cried out: "What! He has brought home to us some new European mystery. Explain. Is the new hypnotism to be more—ah—more effective than the old?"

Some of the company politely chortled in their throats. That was a direct stab at his failure to win Maria. Cristoforo turned his cold eye from Flora to Maria (who answered it with wide glowing orb of self-possession) and back again. Then piqued, daring, he replied: "It is."

"Oh, tell us!" cried a dozen men and women, leaning eagerly over the board.

Cristoforo cleared his throat and toyed with his coffee cup. "The higher hypnotism has arrived," said he, slowly. "As in telegraphy, we are now on the point of doing away with cumbersome wires, and send the spark of intelligence leaping the sea by Marconi's system, so in hypnotism. The old way is stupid, my mind is acting on yours, leaving yours to move your muscles. But as psychology, electricity, and chemistry are now approaching one another, and the greatest minds begin to see that life is electricity, so hypnotists begin to comprehend that the mind of one person may act directly on the muscles of another—that is, upon the nerves that move those muscles—with no clumsy substituting of the second mind. The spark of my brain's power might leap the gulf between me and your hand, and move that hand. Your mind would play no part in that. In a few years the hypnotist will no more act upon the subject's brain, clumsily suggesting that it move the muscle. No. The hypnotist's own brain will move it!"

The company gazed on Don Cristoforo's sharp, leathery countenance. Flora sneered. Maria's full red lips smiled idly, but her eyes were winking in curious fashion.

"What!" cried Flora, sarcastic, "will you be able to move the other person's tongue, too?"

"I?" asked Cristoforo, cold and surprised. "Not I. The hypnotists."

He had a queer, strained look, as though all his muscles were power-fully contracted. His brow was moist as with great effort. His eyes wide, motionless, stared at the coffee cup. Across the table the lids of Maria's black Andalusian orbs were batting with unwonted rapidity. She put up her hand and rubbed them, surprised at their nervous tricks. A long sigh as of immense effort suspended, escaped Cristoforo; his own lids shut and opened; he let down from his tenseness, and turned with polished, clever ease to Flora.

"As for tongues," he said, "some day when you are inclined to be cutting, I may, at a distance, hold yours."

The company applauded that breezily. Flora was one of those women who think they may finally win an old bachelor after all, if they keep jabbing at him long enough. An editor, an astronomer, and a dilettante in art took up the subject. The conversation became rare, imaginative, racy.

Maria was always wearied by Don Cristoforo. She was inclined to yawn. She thanked her stars that she had not been fool enough to marry so repulsive a man; and sat looking at a diamond that flashed on her right middle finger. As she did so, the finger twitched. It seemed that she was extraordinarily nervous. Then unawares this finger lifted itself, made a tiny circuit, and fell back. She shivered, sweeping the company with furtive glance. All were absorbed in the higher hypnotism—save Cristoforo, on whose forehead she saw the gleaming beads of sweat. Again she heard that long sigh of effort suddenly suspended.

"Do we intend to linger with Flora all night?" said he, with easy camaraderie; and the company arose. Maria was dumb, as she retired with her uncle, the astronomer, to that old walled domain of theirs, just beyond the great trees of the Plaza de San Jacinto.

Cristoforo kept bachelor rooms in the house of a French acquaintance, who was rapidly ruining himself at Monte Carlo. The building was opposite a quaint church, with a paved court, surrounded by a wall. In his bedroom, Cristoforo looked at his eyes in a mirror.

"They smart; they are inflamed," he said.

Then he wrote in a journal:

"February 3rd. — Succeeded in controlling eyelids. Find that it reacts on my own. My eyes smart as though they had been held open too long. Succeeded in controlling finger. Find that my own is a little stiff so that I write with difficulty."

There are no others of God's creatures so calm as certain Mexican-Andalusian women like Maria. But as the days went on, she grew nervous, suffered from insomnia, lost colour and flesh; and among her friends it was whispered that she had grown eccentric.

On a Sunday, Maria and Flora, went to mass together. As they entered the little paved court of the church they passed Cristoforo going in, too, dressed as for a promenade on the Parisian boulevards. Maria, haughty and splendid being, did not even look at him, but Flora made one of her polite jabs at his expense. The women knelt bareheaded on the stone floor of the church, he seating himself on a bench behind them. The devil was in him.

All of a sudden the shapely right arm of Maria raised, made a circle through the air, and landed a blow on the head of Flora. An instant's profound amazement, then Maria toppled over in a faint. A hubbub arose; Flora, at first angry, then excusing the act as a nervous accident, got her now reviving companion home.

Immediately upon the fainting of Maria, Cristoforo had been seen walking briskly out of the church. In haste he had retired to his rooms, where he arrived in an exhausted condition, heart failing him, cold sweat dripping from his brow, yet with a demoniac exultation expressed by every line of that cunning, leathery face. His right arm hung stiff at his side. Having lain down for an hour till his exhaustion was relieved, he wrote in his book:

"February 24th. — Progress is on the whole rapid. Succeeded in controlling whole arm. But the reaction on self becomes more and more plain. Using the power on her seems to impair the use of it on me. My right arm was helpless for an hour, and is now so numb I write with difficulty."

When he had written that, he sat for a long time with his head in his hands. His arm was paralysed. So terrible were the possibilities into which his thoughts ran; so dreadful the results that might ensue, did he succeed to the utmost in his diabolical plan of revenge, that at length when he arose he looked like a physical wreck.

"I will not give it up if it kills me," he said. "She has ruined me as it is; I shall conquer her and die for it if I must."

Two weeks went by; it was whispered about that Maria was certainly crazy, so queerly she acted; also that Don Cristoforo, her old lover, was losing his health alarmingly; he suffered from an intermittent paralysis. Ah—how powerful his love for her had been, that these mental eccentricities of hers so affected him. No wonder that Cristoforo looked like a wreck, when he loved Maria so that all Europe could not keep him away from her; when she still drove him to despair with scorn; and when to cap the climax, before his very eyes was the magnificent beloved losing her mind.

Even yet, however, both occasionally appeared at little social functions of the distinguished circle in which they had been wont to move.

Again into Flora's dining-room (hung with tapestries of the Empire, by the way) the same guests appeared on a night in March. Through the doors they trooped, gayly chaffing Cristoforo about some occultism or other. Maria was before him; he, like a skull, a smile dried on his lips, walked after. It was then that there occurred a thing so unaccountable and distressing that the company halted where they were, as though attacked with some sickness. Maria had just uttered a particularly scornful sentiment derogatory of his position in some psychological matter. Then it was that her long antagonism so maddened him that the whole of his queer power leaped up to humble her. He stopped. His muscles seemed drawn into knots. His eyes were on the floor; his face became ghastly; and the force began to act.

She suddenly ran before the guests, and, wheeling so that she faced them, deliberately sat herself down upon the table and swung her feet like a school-girl sitting on a fence. But the puerility and misplaced frolic of that act were offset, rendered sickening, by the agony of struggle depicted upon her countenance. Her free mind protested, fought for her body's liberty, and as she sat she shrieked, and fell senseless across clattering dishes.

They carried her out; but here was Cristoforo fallen to the floor.

"Help me up," he said, hoarsely. "I've lost the use of my limbs, somehow."

He, too, was borne home. There was no supper at Flora's that night, but the guests remained there another hour to hear news of the two stricken ones.

"Plainly insane," whispered they. "Terrible! Terrible! And poor old Don Cristoforo, how incredibly her misfortune affects him!"

Grim, Cristoforo lay gritting his teeth in his bed. He had a nurse sent to care for him. His legs were completely paralysed, and many of the muscles of his trunk were temporarily useless.

In a few days he had himself wheeled out in an invalid chair. Sometimes he could hobble a few steps himself. He met all his old associates in the Plaza de San Jacinto, and sat there on a bench chatting with them, scoffing at their sympathy. Always his eyes looked hither and thither, searching for Maria.

One day she, ghost of herself, came walking near, unconscious of him. Cristoforo lay in his invalid chair under the big trees chatting with a Basque musician. The musician saw his muscles stiffen, saw the sweat upon his brow, saw the glare in his eyes. Then he perceived that Maria, walking yonder, acted strangely. She raised her arms, and went crying out in a loud and solemn tone: "I have loved Don Cristoforo all my life!"

This she cried three times, her face drawn into an expression of horror; the while she walked before the public of San Angelo. Staggering like a drunken woman, she disappeared into her uncle's house. And Cristoforo lay dumb.

They wheeled him home, and his friends, coming there, shook their heads over him, and whispered of the latest, freak of the mad Maria. Could it be? Had she really loved him all this time? What was the awful thing, then, that had held them apart—that was slaying them?

Cristoforo slowly grew a little better. He could speak thickly; he could move his legs and arms a little. But his will would not give up yet; the last ignominy was still to be heaped upon her. See how surely he recovered— though slowly— after every fresh blow.

One week later they wheeled him into the plaza. It was noised about as a sort of gala occasion for Don Cristoforo, that being his saint's day, whereon he was going to celebrate the fact that the paralysis was leaving him. A dozen of his friends came through the plaza to cheer the bachelor up, and the astronomer, too, walked yonder with his niece, Maria, approaching. Here was Flora, still bantering Don Cristoforo, and here came the editor, the musicians, the dilettantes in art. The supreme moment was at hand.

It seemed that Don Cristoforo was all at once thrown into a cataleptic fit. Staring at him, the company was alarmed by the terrible look on his face, the sweat there, the knotted muscles, the diabolical smile. He lay stretched out in his invalid chair, still, cold, staring up at the trees of the beautiful Plaza de San Jacinto.

Maria yonder disengaged her arm from that of her, uncle, and approached. Her face wore its look of horror. Solemnly she came forward among the sympathetic company of her friends, and, pausing before Cristoforo, bent down and kissed him on the lips.

"I love you," she said. "I want to marry you."

The mad act stupefied them. Don Cristoforo, with a last effort that seemed to crack his bones, and was the fierce fight with the paralysis that then accomplished his doom, cried out in exultation, guttural and thick, "Woman, what do I want with you?"

As usual, she became helpless; and they carried her home. Cristoforo was also taken to his house, being now dumb and motionless. Hardly any of his muscles could he move; but after a day he was able to whisper a little again and make his wants known.

Now, her humiliation fully accomplished, he, with no real desire for life, nevertheless bent his mind toward health. He watched his muscles for a week; they improved no more. A month. They improved not. His mind staggered; his doom was surely at hand, He had gone too far. Calmly, he decided to slay himself.

But how accomplish that self-destruction now at last so passionately desired? He had some little use of his own limbs to be sure; but no power to strike a blow, no means of obtaining poison. Throughout the unspeakable hours of a dozen lonely nights he lay planning. And the new science, the accursed secret, should die with him—but how? Ah—illuminating thought at last. True that he had no control over his own muscles; he had transferred that control to hers. Hers would still, perhaps, obey him.

"Juan," muttered he to the servant, "come; put me in the chair; wheel me out to the churchyard. I want to bask in the sun of that still spot."

The summer day was beautiful and warm. The paved court of the church was very lonely when they came through the big wooden doors and rested therein.

"Leave me, Juan, and go buy me some oranges," muttered Cristoforo, stretching out stiff in his chair and turning his eyes to the sky. "I want to swallow a little of the juice. You can squeeze it into my mouth for me, Juan."

Juan's white clothes, Juan's sandals, Juan's black hair, disappeared.

The church doors yonder were closed; the shadows of trees lay on these paving stones; and here in a secluded and lonely corner lay Don Cristoforo stretched out stiff, like a mummy.

For the last time the muscles on his face seemed knotted, and the cold sweat stood out in beads. For ten long minutes thus he lay.

In the astronomer's house, beyond the beautiful Plaza de San Jacinto, Maria, who had seemed better of late, arose from her chair. Her face wore its look of horror again! its evidences of fight between the free mind and the enslaved, controlling muscles. On the wall hung swords, daggers, machetes—a style of ornament affected by her uncle and familiar to her friends. One of the machetes she took, huge, heavy, blunt thing, and withal murderous.

Out of the house, under the trees, Maria walked steadily; the whole width of the plaza, and on into a narrow street. Here was the high wooden door, giving entrance through the wall into the court of the church. Maria walked through. All was still, warm, the air dreamy with summer; yonder lay Don Cristoforo, the sweat glistening on his forehead, his body stretched out. Maria came to him, and both hands, holding the machete, were raised. She tried to shriek; a convulsion shook her body; her whole soul strove against the crime. But he, too, strove. His eyes wore shut; his face was drawn and quivering; his nerves were like wires that break. For one instant their minds fought; conflict terrific. But the spark of command leaped the gulf; he operated the muscles of her arms. She raised them high. She struck.

Suggestion

(Translated from *Le Petit Journal*, of Paris, by Edyth Kirkwood)

"What do you think of it, doctor?" asked the prisoner's counsel.

The physician, a celebrated specialist and authority on mental diseases, shook his head gravely in a non-committal sort of way.

"You followed up the clue I gave you?" persisted the lawyer.

"Yes."

"And you think——?"

"I shall examine him again to-day, replied the doctor. "I have seen several experts in the new science and they all agree that poor Julian is an impressionable subject, a ready-made victim to any one who might have wished this deed done by proxy; but the motive? Probably some lover's quarrel, some revenge; they say the girl was pretty and coquettish. There is something baffling about the affair," added the doctor with a slight relaxation of his professional caution. "While I have never had too much confidence in this idea of 'suggestion,' I am not prepared to say there is nothing in it."

"Let me go with you to-day, doctor. I will slip in without speaking, listen to the story he relates, and one of us may chance on some word or idea to give us the indication we seek."

So it was agreed.

"How do you feel to-day?" asked the doctor kindly, as they entered the prisoner's cell.

The man was lying on his hard bed, staring in front of him, with hollow, vacant eyes.

"My thoughts," he replied, "flutter about aimlessly; sad, oh! sad as long snow-covered plains under the light of the moon. I have worn myself out with walking to and fro. My limbs ache as if I had been beaten. I feel very cold, but the palms of my hands are burning with fever, and I have a dull pain at the base of my brain."

The physician nodded gravely and said a few soothing words, then requested the patient to relate all he could remember about the crime.

"But, doctor," objected Julian, "I have already told you twenty times and more. It will be monotonous to go over all that again, though, to be sure, there is nothing better to do here... Well then, place yourself there, opposite to me, so that you will hide that white wall; it looks to me like a canvas on which is painted that unfading image; the coffer with the head upon it! ... When you go away my terror will return. If they would only soil that wall a little; it seems to me the slightest stain would obviate this fancy.... I tried to soil it, and the jailer scolded me as if I had been a schoolboy."

"Go on with your story," said the doctor quietly.

"I was walking along aimlessly when from a long, dark, narrow street I emerged on the thoroughfare. Lights were shining here and there under the trees like great flowers of flame. The yelling of showmen, the music and bells of the merry-go-rounds, the trumpets and drums, hurdy-gurdys and squeaking playthings of the children made a most horrible din, for the annual festival was in full tide.

"Cornered by a group of curious people, I was crowded and crushed, raised off my feet and carried along before a booth. Above the door I read the word: *Metempsychosis.*

"A fat man was selling tickets; he was pitted by small-pox and had one eye smaller than the other.

"Inside it was very, almost quite, dark.

"Before us a square of light opened in the canvas which was stretched at the further end of the booth. Within this frame appeared a table with a gauze screen separating it from the spectators.

"The fat man passed around a pasteboard head such as milliners use for bonnets. When it had gone from hand to hand and was acknowledged to be truly what it appeared to be, he placed it on the table and fastened the gauze screen. The light brightened; by transitions impossible to catch, without anything seeming to move, as the man announced a transformation the pasteboard head turned into a vase full of flowers, then into a cage full of birds, after that into a death's head which became the mask of celebrated statues representing successively Venus, Juno, Cleopatra, Anne of Austria, Marie Antoinette, and so on and on, until the showman said: 'Instead of pasteboard and stucco you shall now see living flesh.'

"Slowly the face dislocated, the features became hazy, confused, to form again little by little and appear distinct, animated, *humanized.*

"'An ingenious trick,' I thought; 'I don't even care to know if it is accomplished by the aid of mirrors.'

"The head of a young girl, sweet and fair, had formed behind the gauze. She opened her great black eyes, which, without definite expression, followed me with the strange fixity of a portrait, while across her face flitted the rather silly smile of the antique statues.

"This steady stare seemed to turn me to stone. My limbs grew rigid. I felt very strangely, though it was neither fatigue nor pain, and there was something oddly familiar about the head. Where I could have seen it before under different circumstances and in different attire I can no more remember now than I could then.

"When the crowd of spectators left, I remained. The showman seemed surprised, but sold me another ticket. "I remained through another representation. When the young girl appeared in the last act I experienced the same singular sensation of torpor, and could not move hand or foot until she vanished from the square.

"The showman walked toward the door and I followed him.

"'Why, I asked, 'did you write *Metempsychosis* on your sign instead of *Metamorphosis*?'

"'Then I must have been mistaken!' he said. 'Bah! never mind; very few will know the difference.'

Profiting by a push of the crowd, I slipped behind him and hid against the canvas. He went out saying:

"'Don't be impatient, Milie; I am going out to get something for supper.'

"I raised the canvas. On a large coffer, covered with some Algerian stuff and ornamented with copper nails, I saw the pasteboard head. A young girl, tall and thin, dressed in a gray wrapper, was combing the long hair that fell over her face. She threw back her hair as she heard my step and recoiled so that the floor of the booth rattled. It seemed to me as if she was trying to break through the boards to escape from me. She looked pale, supernaturally pale. It might have been an effect of light, for the gas was directly above her head.

"I gazed alternately at her bloodless face and at the white face of the manikin; they seemed to grow confused in my mind.

"The girl's eyes shone, haggard and dilated like those of a somnambulist. Her pallid lips moved:

"'You have come to kill me?'

"'Kill you? Nonsense! What weapon could I use?' I remember, laughing as I said these words, ... and that is all...."

"Collect your mind. Force your memory to obey you," said the doctor anxiously.

"That is all I can remember. The next thing I recall is that a man's hands closed around my throat and the man was shrieking with sorrow. His grasp must have been furious, yet I felt nothing.

"Over his shoulder I peered about to see the coffer without trying at all to free myself. The coffer was still in the corner, and the head was still on top of it. There was blood on the floor. The head looked like the pale young girl. Beside it lay a shining sword of curious shape, like an African weapon."

"'The sword was in the booth," explained the physician; "you took it to cut off the girl's head. Then you substituted her head for that of the manikin. All that was accomplished with a strength and rapidity only explicable by vertigo—temporary insanity—aberration, call it what you please."

"Decidedly, you insist upon it as firmly as the examining magistrate," said Julian. "Yet I can never admit myself guilty of an act I am unconscious of having done."

"You were out of your mind," said the doctor. "What happened next?"

"I remember gendarmes with drawn swords... A walk past the booths of the showmen. And I think they hooted and jeered. All the clamor mingled and confounded and became one great sound of rushing waves, then that noise resolved itself into a harmonious concert with dominating chords of deep, sweet sound. After that I found myself here, and you know the rest. You, doctor, felt my, pulse, my forehead, and questioned me searchingly; but without succeeding in establishing my irresponsibility. I have never been subject to epilepsy, nor to somnambulism, and my brain is not diseased. My own opinion? I have given it and been laughed at. Yet if I really did this hideous thing I am accused of, the very thought of which freezes the blood in my veins, then I have been the instrument of another's crime, a victim of *suggestion*. I am excessively nervous and susceptible to hypnotic influence, and have submitted to experiments until I have become a 'good subject.' I have no hope of this theory being accepted. I offer it merely as my own conviction."

"Have you arrived at any conclusion?" asked the lawyer three days after, as he entered the doctor's office with a curious expression on his keen face, and a certain pallor and subdued excitement that at once attracted the physician's attention.

"Why no; I am just where I was," replied the latter. "I can make nothing of it. And you? You have found some solution?

"The solution—the motive—all," said the prisoner's counsel, unfolding a package of manuscript. "The girl had been insane, melancholy, suicidal mania, and all that; but had been cured, as it was supposed, and was not considered dangerous. The *idée fixe*, however, still enthralled her brain, and, like all demented women, the more fantastic the *mise en scène* of the crime, the better it would please her warped imagination. She conceived the idea of employing hypnotism, attended lectures and *séances*, and became an expert pupil. At one of these pseudo scientific gatherings, which were frequented by some medical students of the Latin quarter, she met Julian and—incredible as it seems—hypnotized him and suggested her own murder. This MS., found a few hours ago among her effects, contains a calm statement of the facts, and completely exonerates the prisoner."

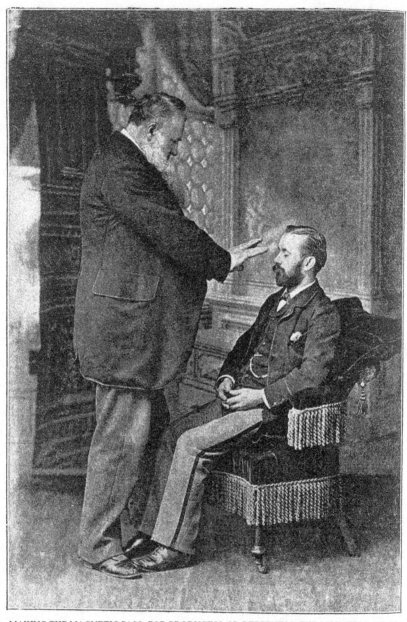

MAKING THE MAGNETIC PASS, FOR PRODUCING OR DEEPENING, THE MESMERIC SLEEP.

The Hypnotist

By Ambrose Bierce

By those of my friends who happen to know that I sometimes amuse myself with hypnotism, mind reading and kindred phenomena, I am frequently asked if I have a clear conception of the nature of whatever principle underlies them. To this question I always reply that I neither have nor desire to have. I am no investigator with an ear at the key-hole of Nature's workshop, trying with vulgar curiosity to steal the secrets of her trade. The interests of science are as little to me as mine seem to have been to science.

Doubtless the phenomena in question are simple enough, and in no way transcend our powers of comprehension if only we could find the clew; but for my part I prefer not to find it, for I am of a singularly romantic disposition, deriving more gratification from mystery than from knowledge. It was commonly remarked of me when I was a child that my big blue eyes appeared to have been made rather to look into than look out of—such was their dreamful beauty, and in my frequent periods of abstraction, their indifference to what was going on. In those peculiarities they resembled, I venture to think, the soul which lies behind them, always more intent upon some lovely conception which it has created in its own image than concerned about the laws of nature and the material frame of things. All this, irrelevant and egotistic as it may seem, is related by way of accounting for the meagerness of the light that I am able to throw upon a subject that has engaged so much of my attention, and concerning which there is so keen and general a curiosity. With my powers and opportunities, another person might doubtless have an explanation for much of what I present simply as narrative.

My first knowledge that I possessed unusual powers came to me in my fourteenth year, when at school. Happening one day to have forgotten to bring my noon-day luncheon, I gazed longingly at that of a small girl who was preparing to eat hers. Looking up, her eyes met mine and she seemed unable to withdraw them. After a moment of hesitancy she came forward in an absent kind of way and without a word surrendered her little basket with its tempting contents and walked away. Inexpressibly pleased, I relieved my hunger and destroyed the basket. After that I had not the trouble to bring a luncheon for myself: that little girl was my daily purveyor; and not infrequently in satisfying my simple need from her frugal store

I combined pleasure and profit by constraining her attendance at the feast and making misleading proffer of the viands, which eventually I consumed to the last fragment. The girl was always persuaded that she had eaten all herself; and later in the day her tearful complaints of hunger surprised the teacher, entertained the pupils, earned for her the sobriquet of Greedy-Gut and filled me with a peace past understanding.

A disagreeable feature of this otherwise satisfactory condition of things was the necessary secrecy: the transfer of the luncheon, for example, had to be made at some distance from the madding crowd, in a wood; and I blush to think of the many other unworthy subterfuges entailed by the situation. As I was (and am) naturally of a frank and open disposition, these became more and more irksome, and but for the reluctance of my parents to renounce the obvious advantages of the new regime I would gladly have reverted to the old. The plan that I finally adopted to free myself from the consequences of my own powers excited a wide and keen interest at the time, and that part of it which consisted in the death of the girl was severely condemned, but it is hardly pertinent to the scope of this narrative.

For some years afterward I had little opportunity to practice hypnotism; such small essays as I made at it were commonly barren of other recognition than solitary confinement on a bread-and-water diet; sometimes, indeed, they elicited nothing better than the cat-o'-nine tails. It was when I was about to leave the scene of these small disappointments that my one really important feat was performed.

I had been called into the warden's office and given a suit of civilian's clothing, a trifling sum of money and a great deal of advice, which I am bound to confess was of a much better quality than the clothing. As I was passing out of the gate into the light of freedom I suddenly turned and looking the warden gravely in the eye, soon had him in control.

"You are an ostrich," I said.

At the post-mortem examination the stomach was found to contain a great quantity of indigestible articles mostly of wood or metal. Stuck fast in the oesophagus and constituting, according to the Coroner's jury, the immediate cause of death, one door-knob.

I was by nature a good and affectionate son, but as I took my way into the great world from which I had been so long secluded I could not help remembering that all my misfortunes had flowed like a stream from the niggard economy of my parents in the matter of school luncheons; and I knew of no reason to think they had reformed.

On the road between Succotash Hill and South Asphyxia is a little open field which once contained a shanty known as Pete Gilstrap's Place, where that gentleman used to murder travelers for a living. The death of Mr. Gilstrap and the diversion of nearly all the travel to another road occurred so nearly at the same time that no one has ever been able to say which was cause and which effect. Anyhow, the field was now a desolation and the Place had long been burned. It was while going afoot to South Asphyxia, the home of my childhood, that I found both my parents on their way to the Hill. They had hitched their team and were eating luncheon under an oak tree in the center of the field. The sight of the luncheon called up painful memories of my school days and roused the sleeping lion in my breast. Approaching the guilty couple, who at once recognized me, I ventured to suggest that I share their hospitality.

"Of this cheer, my son," said the author of my being, with characteristic pomposity, which age had not withered, "there is sufficient for but two. I am not, I hope, insensible to the hunger-light in your eyes, but—"

My father has never completed that sentence; what he mistook for hunger-light was simply the earnest gaze of the hypnotist. In a few seconds he was at my service. A few more sufficed for the lady, and the dictates of a just resentment could be carried into effect. "My former father," I said, "I presume that it is known to you that you and this lady are no longer what you were?"

"I have observed a certain subtle change," was the rather dubious reply of the old gentleman; "it is perhaps attributable to age."

"It is more than that," I explained; "it goes to character—to species. You and the lady here are, in truth, two broncos—wild stallions both, and unfriendly."

"Why, John," exclaimed my dear mother, "you don't mean to say that I am—"

"Madam," I replied, solemnly, fixing my eyes again upon hers, "you are."

Scarcely had the words fallen from my lips when she dropped upon her hands and knees, and backing up to the old man squealed like a demon and delivered a vicious kick upon his shin! An instant later he was himself down on all-fours, headed away from her and flinging his feet at her simultaneously and successively. With equal earnestness but inferior agility, because of her hampering body-gear, she plied her own. Their flying legs crossed and mingled in the most bewildering way; their feet sometimes meeting squarely in mid-air, their bodies thrust forward, falling flat upon the ground and for a moment helpless. On recovering themselves they would resume the combat, uttering their frenzy in the nameless sounds of the furious brutes which they believed themselves to be—the whole region rang with their clamor! Round and round they wheeled, the blows of their feet falling "like lightnings from the mountain cloud." They plunged and reared backward upon their knees, struck savagely at each other with awkward descending blows of both fists at once, and dropped again upon their hands as if unable to maintain the upright position of the body.

Grass and pebbles were torn from the soil by hands and feet; clothing, hair, faces inexpressibly defiled with dust and blood. Wild, inarticulate screams of rage attested the delivery of the blows; groans, grunts and gasps their receipt. Nothing more truly military was ever seen at Gettysburg or Waterloo: the valor of my dear parents in the hour of danger can never cease to be to me a source of pride and gratification. At the end of it all two battered, tattered, bloody and fragmentary vestiges of mortality attested the solemn fact that the author of the strife was an orphan.

Arrested for provoking a breach of the peace, I was, and have ever since been, tried in the Court of Technicalities and Continuances whence, after fifteen years of proceedings, my attorney is moving heaven and earth to get the case taken to the Court of Remandment for New Trials.

Such are a few of my principal experiments in the mysterious force or agency known as hypnotic suggestion. Whether or not it could be employed by a bad man for an unworthy purpose I am unable to say.

The Crime of The Rue Auber

By J.E. Muddock

Enthusiasts have spoken of Paris as one of the most beautiful cities of the world. The Parisians themselves go farther than this, and say it is *the* most beautiful city. The Parisians may be forgiven for their pride, for if we confine ourselves to the Paris of the Boulevards it is beautiful. But there is another Paris which the ordinary traveller does not see. It is a Paris of hideousness, of squalor, of all that is hateful and revolting in human nature. This gay capital, in fact, is a city of the most extraordinary and striking contrasts. And there is another aspect, too, which the observant writer cannot over look; it is the city of original crimes. It has been reserved for Paris to exhibit human nature in such hideous and cruel forms, that one shudders and bows his head in shame and sorrow as he thinks of it. Of course, other cities have their plague spots and human fiends, but it is to Paris the world looks for novelty in the way of crime. But perhaps one of the most mysterious and novel crimes that even Paris has placed upon the records is that which has come to be known as "The Crime of the Rue Auber."

The Rue Auber, let it be understood, is not one of the slums of the city. It is not situated in the plague spots of Clichy and St. Ouen. It has no connection with the notorious St. Denis or Belleville, and it is far removed from *Ménilmontant*. Nor is it part of the Bohemian Quartier Latin. No, it is a thoroughfare of almost frigid respectability, lying just to the west of the Grand Opera, and forming part of a line of connection between the Boulevard des Italiens and the magnificent Boulevard Haussmann which runs north. The houses in the Rue Auber are marked by a monotonous regularity of architecture. They are all large apartment houses and rise to a height of five storeys, each storey or flat representing two households. At No. 13 in this street—according to superstitious people thirteen is always an unlucky number—and on the third *étage* or flat lived Monsieur Henri Didet and his wife, together with one servant, Eugenia Suchard, a woman about fifty years of age. Didet was a young man, a little over thirty, and he was remarkable for his handsome appearance. He was the average height for a Frenchman, with a grace of carriage and perfection of figure. He had a mass of dark hair that fell over his white forehead in a wealth of tiny ringlets. His face was clean shaven, except for his dainty moustache, which was always scrupulously trimmed. His peculiarly mobile face seemed capable of almost any change, and his eyes, which were dark and piercing, appeared to possess the faculty of looking right through you. In disposition he was insincere, incapable of anything like serious thought, and he abandoned himself to the whirl and gaiety of Parisian life. It might be said that he passed his time in planning pleasure for the morrow and in thoroughly enjoying himself the day before. He was a Parisian of Parisians, and life for him had no higher meaning than to live; and his interpretation of "to live" was gaiety of every possible kind, and hourly and daily ministration to the carnal pleasures. He had for some time been in business as a chemist, though his want of seriousness prevented him from succeeding. That, however, did not matter. His handsome person won him a lady who brought him a large *dot*; and just after his marriage an aunt died and left him a small fortune, so he sold the chemist's business, and retired to lead the only kind of existence that charmed him.

Madame Didet was a *petite* woman; not bad-looking, but somewhat insipid. She was fair, with blue eyes, and rather wanting in expression. She was delicate, with a fragile form and a dreamy eye and a general languid appearance. Although she did not suffer from any actual illness, she was subject to attacks of hysteria. She was devoted to her husband, but exceedingly jealous of him; not, however, without good cause. He seemed to possess remarkable influence over her, an influence due to a certain magnetic power he exercised, and by which he was enabled to bend her to his will in almost every conceivable way.

It is necessary to say that Eugenia Suchard, their servant, was rather a stupid kind of woman; but she had been with Didet long before he was married, and she was much attached to her master and mistress.

When the Didets first went to live at 13 Rue Auber, the other half of the flat upon which they had their residence was not occupied. It had been without a tenant for some months, as people complained that the rent was too high. But soon after the Didets went there, the other half of the flat was taken by a Monsieur Charcot, who had been an officer in the army, but had been compelled to retire, owing to a wound he received, which unfitted him for military service. He was married, and between him and his wife was considerable disparity of age. He was about fifty, while she was not more than thirty, and was remarkably handsome. He was a reserved man, somewhat retiring in disposition, while she was volatile and fond of gaiety.

Between these two families, being close neighbours as they were, an intimacy soon sprang up. But it was not long before it became evident to Madame Didet that her husband was paying more attention to the pretty Madame Charcot than was consistent with mere neighbourly feeling. This led to some unpleasantness between Didet and his wife; but he assured her, vowed solemnly in fact, that is as solemnly as such a man could vow, that she was mistaken. She was satisfied, and things went on harmoniously again for some time. But during this time Didet was falling desperately in love with his pretty neighbour, and she did not seem to object.

One day a picnic had been arranged between the two families, and Charcot and Didet, accompanied by their wives and another lady and gentleman, went out for the day. It was summer time and they took train to St. Germain. This is a favourite resort of the Parisians in the summer. It is a charming spot, a little paradise. There is a magnificent forest, many miles in extent, with romantic glades and entrancing walks, and there is a celebrated hotel, the Hotel de Louis Quatorze. It stands in extensive grounds on a terrace that commands a magnificent panorama of the valley of the Seine, with the tortuous river threading its way with many folds and twists, like a silver serpent. Here in the grounds of this hotel are numerous bowers under the trees, and it is delightful to sit there on a summer day, the air languid with the scent of flowers and musical with bird-song, and partake of the exquisite dinner for which the hotel is famed.

The little party enjoyed themselves with all the abandon peculiar to the Parisian when out for the day. A *recherché* dinner was partaken of, and several bottles of choice wine were discussed, and over the cigars and coffee there was much laughter and joking. The French people are a light-hearted people. They live in the to-day. The to-morrow is but a dream, a vague shadow, to them. Madame Didet was particularly vivacious. The wine had heightened her colour and brightened her eyes, and as she toyed with a dainty cigarette, her laughter was silvery and light, as though she had not a care in the whole world.

The day was deepening to its close. Already the purple shadows were creeping along the valley, and the river was growing tawny in the fading light. Beneath a group of trees at the end of the terrace in the hotel garden, a man and a woman stood, all but hidden by the darkness caused by the trees. The man was Didet; the woman Madame Charcot. They had stolen away from the others, she first, he following some time after. He held her hand, though she was trying to disengage it; and into her ear he was whispering in impassioned language these words: "Agathe," he called her by her Christian name, "Agathe, why did Fate not bring us together years ago?"

"Ah!" she sighed.

"Agathe," he cried, growing more excited as her sigh told him that his words found an echo in her own breast, "Agathe, je t'aime!" She started at this declaration, and in accents that told of her distress she said:

"No, no, Monsieur Didet; you must not talk to me like that. Remember my husband!"

"Mon Dieu!" hissed Didet fiercely, under his breath, "I always remember him. Which devil was it that gave you a husband and me a wife before you and I met?"

"Hush, hush!" she said appealingly, "we must be satisfied with our lot. *We*, we must not talk of love."

"Agathe," he murmured in stricken tones, "have you no love for me?"

She averted her face from him, and whispered: "I might have had."

"You might have had!"

"Yes."

"But why have you not now?"

"Because I am already a wife," she sighed.

He threw his arms round her and drew her to his breast; but at that moment a man sprang forward, and, seizing her arm, he twisted her round, almost flinging her to the ground, and then with blazing eyes and white face he confronted Didet. The new-comer was Charcot, and, in a voice hoarse with passion, he exclaimed:

"I suspected this. You are a snake, and your very breath is poison! But beware how you tamper with my wife, lest I am tempted to kill her and you."

Didet had nothing to say. He did attempt to stammer forth something in the nature of an excuse, but he knew his guilt, and the words stuck in his throat.

It was hardly possible that this scene could be kept from Madame Didet. She saw by her husband's face that something had happened, and guessed what that something was. And when Charcot took his wife away, and went back to Paris without the rest of the party, she knew that her guess was right. Then ensued a pitiable scene. She went into violent hysterics, and rent the air with her screams, and so unmanageable did she become, and so excited, that her husband decided not to return to Paris that night, but to remain with her at the hotel. All night long she raved, but towards the morning sank to sleep, waking up three hours later prostrated and ill.

Her husband went on his knees before her, and vowed that he was deeply repentant, and would never sin in the same way again. She sealed her forgiveness with kisses, and in the afternoon they returned to Paris perfectly reconciled. And when he arrived home he sought out Monsieur Charcot, and craved his pardon too, and so earnest did he seem, so humble was he—he shed so many tears, and made so many protestations—that Charcot, who was not a vindictive man, was moved, and said he would think no more of the matter. Thus the neighbourly relations were resumed, although the little episode had undoubtedly left some frigidity behind it.

If the serpent had not been in the garden of Eden, Eve would not have fallen; and had Charcot taken his wife away Didet might not have been tempted. But for weeks and months after that affair at St. Germain he saw her, and seeing sighed. And possibly, nay probably, something in her face, some look in her eyes, answered him.

It was a winter night. Snow was falling over Paris, but nevertheless Monsieur Charcot and his wife had gone to the theatre and taken Madame Didet with them. Didet himself would not go. He pleaded a splitting headache and general vialaise. His wife wished to remain and nurse him, but he would not hear of it. He said that he desired to be alone, to be perfectly quiet for a few hours, and insisted on her going. An hour later he gave his servant a couple of francs, telling her that she could invite Charcot's servant to a *petit souper* at a neighbouring cafe, and when they had gone he sprang from the couch on which he had been reclining with a towel round his head. He dashed the towel to the ground. His *malaise* seemed to have flown. He went on to the landing and listened. No one was coming up the stairs, or down from the other flats. All was silent as death, save for a gas jet on the next landing that hissed like an angry snake, in the cold blasts of air that rushed up the stairway. Didet took a latch-key from his pocket, and noiselessly opened Charcot's door. Then, with a pair of pincers and a screw-driver, he so altered the position of the check that held the latch when it was let down as to make it useless. The consequence of this was that any one letting the latch down would not be aware that the check was damaged, and, of course, would imagine the door was fastened, whereas it could still be opened with a latch-key from the outside. Didet's object in doing this we shall presently see.

His work completed he went back to his own house, and smoked heavily, and drank some cognac. But at one o'clock, when his wife returned, he was asleep on the couch. She was tender and loving to him, and told him all about the play, and how she and the Charcots had supped at a cafe, partaking of oysters and *bouillon*, and *côtelettes à la tomates*, and pudding *au riz avec sauce* à *la rhum*, followed by *gruyère*, and some *petits fruits*, and for wine there had been a bottle of Graves and a bottle and a half of *Château* Margaux, for Monsieur Charcot, when he went to the theatre, liked to sup well, and he was a connoisseur in wines. And then as a *finale* there had been *café noir* and a *petit verre*.

"Ah, mon mari!" she exclaimed, as she threw her arms round his neck, "the supper was splendid, but mon cher, mon prince, I was so lonely without thee."

He laughed, and kissed her. But it was a Judas kiss.

So Judas kissed his Master.

Then they went to bed, and through the snowy air the bells of Paris were booming two.

Silence!

Through the snowy air the bells of Paris were booming three.

Monsieur Didet rose from his bed, and arrayed himself in a thick woollen dressing-gown. A shaded lamp was burning low, but gave sufficient light to render objects in the room visible. He bent over his wife. She was sleeping soundly. The *petit souper* had not disagreed with her. He passed his hand over her head, first from back to front, and then from side to side. She moved, she half turned, she sighed deeply; but he made other passes, and she became passive. Presently he stood erect, and waved his hand up and down slowly. Then she rose. Her eyes were open, but fixed. Her face was pale. Her lips moved as if in speech, but no sounds issued.

"Get up!" said her husband softly.

She slipped from the bed with no apparent effort, and stood before him motionless, her white *robe de nuit* falling about her like the drapery of a statue. He opened a drawer in the dressing-table, and took out something. It was a weapon. He drew off a leather case, and revealed a long, sharp, and glittering stiletto. He grasped her hand, and then bent her white fingers round the handle of the deadly weapon. He next placed a small phial with a glass stopper in her other hand. That done he whispered something in her ear, and she began to move towards the door.

Through the snowy air the bells of Paris were booming half-past three.

He preceded her, opened the door and she passed out; a little shudder seemed to shake her as her bare feet came in contact with the cold stones. He crept across the landing, and with the latch-key opened Charcot's door. Then waving his hand he motioned her to enter. A dim light burned in the passage, and Madame Didet looked like a ghost. All was silent in Charcot's house. The woman moved without a sound, going first now. Didet crept after her on tiptoe. She reached Monsieur Charcot's bedroom. A lamp burned low there also. Charcot slept soundly in one bed, his wife in another. Madame Didet bent over Charcot for a moment or two, then raised her arm high and plunged the long stiletto into his breast. The blood spurted from the wound and encrimsoned Madame Didet's night-dress.

The *petit souper* had caused Madame Charcot to sleep soundly, and she was all unconscious of what was going on.

Again Didet waved his hand, and his wife drew the stopper from the bottle she held. Then she placed the mouth of the phial to her lips. It was filled with a white, colourless fluid, and she poured this fluid down her throat. That act completed, Didet slipped away, leaving Charcot's door open, and his own open; but in his excitement he saw not a figure that cowered against the wall in the passage. He gained his room, and threw himself on his bed.

Through the snowy air the bells of Paris boomed four.

Didet rolled himself in the blankets, and fell asleep. It is astonishing how some men can sleep under every and any circumstances.

Through the air—it had ceased to snow—the bells of Paris boomed seven.

A little later the *laitier* (milkman) came up the stairs with the morning milk. On reaching the Didet-Charcot landing he was surprised to find the doors of both houses open; it was so unusual for them to be open at that time of the morning. He stood at Charcot's door, and called the servant, who had only just got out of bed. She could not account for the doors being opened. Moreover, in her master's door was a latch-key. What did this mean? In alarm she went to her master's room, and soon she uttered a cry of terror, for she saw a woman lying on the floor, and thought it was her mistress. The *laitier* went in and turned up the lamp. Then it was seen that Madame Charcot was in bed and awake—the cry had awakened her— while the night-dress of the woman on the floor was stained with blood. The man drew the curtains of Charcot's bed, then staggered back appalled, for the clothes were all red with blood, a long dagger was sticking in Charcot's breast, and he was dead.

With a scream of awful fear Madame Charcot now sprang up. She recognised the woman on the floor as Madame Didet. She was dead, and in her cold, marble-like hand she tightly grasped a phial.

The milkman rushed over to the Didets' house. Eugenia Suchard was already at the door. She looked like a corpse, so ghastly white was she.

"Mon Dieu! it's awful, awful!" groaned the man.

"Where's monsieur?"

"Sleeping soundly in his bed,' answered Eugenia with considerable firmness.

"There has been murder," said the *laitier*. "Mon Dieu! it's awful, awful!" Then he clattered down the stairs to spread the alarm. In wild terror, Madame Charcot rushed into Didet's house, and threw herself on to the floor. He came to her and tried to soothe her.

Presently the gendarmes arrived, and over the neighbour hood flew the news, and crowds collected, and the most wild and wonderful rumours were circulated. The tragedy was surrounded with mystery. But so far as the investigation of the police went, they were enabled to report that Madame Didet seemed to have stolen from her husband's bedroom; to have entered Charcot's house by means of a duplicate key, had then stabbed him to the heart, and had poisoned herself at his bedside.

The motive?

Well, it could only be guessed at; but, no doubt, there had been some guilty *liaison* between the pair. Possibly—so it was suggested—he wanted to throw her off, and she had resolved to kill him and herself. It was by no means an unfamiliar story in Paris. So in a few days the gay Parisians shrugged their shoulders and said: "These things will happen. How sorry we are for poor Madame Charcot and poor Monsieur Didet! Mon Dieu! it is terrible!"

And so with this sympathy they dismissed the subject, and went on with their gaiety again.

In a few weeks Monsieur Didet gave up his house in the Rue Auber, for he said he could not live in it. The associations were too terrible. The veuve Charcot also changed her residence, and went to live in the same neighbourhood, in fact in the next block of buildings. Four months later Monsieur Didet announced that he was going to marry the pretty veuve Charcot. Then his servant Eugenia Suchard, whom he had retained, said:

"No, monsieur, you shall not marry that woman."

Didet thought that his poor old servant had got a little cracked, and laughed heartily. But with terrible emphasis Eugenia repeated:

"No, monsieur, you *shall not* marry that woman."

"Why?" asked her master, growing serious.

"Because I forbid it."

"You?"

"Yes."

Didet was ashen now. Something in Eugenia's manner caused his blood to chill.

"What do you mean?" he gasped.

"I mean what I say. I have held my peace all too long. I loved my mistress, and I have loved you, but I will not see this last outrage committed."

"You are mad!" he said, as his courage came back, for he mistook her words. "Madame veuve Charcot and I will assuredly become man and wife."

"No," said the woman sternly, "for I'll denounce you first." Once more Didet's face assumed an ashen hue. "On that fearful night I saw all," she added. "I had supped with the Charcots' servant. I had drunk some bad wine, and it gave me cramps, so that I could not sleep. I heard you open the door, and was alarmed. Coming to see what was the matter, I saw you and madame go out. She was in her nightdress and asleep. You had mesmerised her. I followed you like a shadow, and saw madame plunge the knife into Monsieur Charcot's body. Then I fled in horror."

Didet was almost paralysed with surprise and fear. He thought that no human eye had witnessed the deed, and that no human soul had even deemed it possible that he had done this dreadful thing. Here was a revelation. He had committed a fearful crime in order to gain the woman to whom he had given his guilty love. When he had somewhat recovered himself, his first impulse was to kill this sole witness of his guilt, and he endeavoured to seize her. But she escaped, and ran screaming into the street. He knew then that he was a doomed man, and in the madness of despair and fear he shot himself. And thus Nemesis revenged the dark crime of the Rue Auber, and the gay Parisians, when they heard of the sequel to the Rue Auber crime, shrugged their shoulders, and talked of it for an hour or two; then they said: "Ah, these things will happen!" and so they went on with their gaiety again.

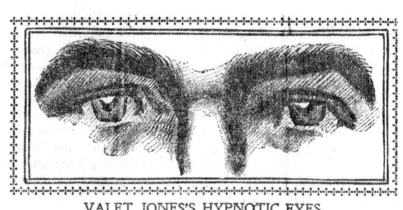

VALET JONES'S HYPNOTIC EYES.

A Queer Coincidence

By Charles B. Cory

"You say," said Doctor Watson, as he rested one arm on the mantel and looked thoughtfully at the open fire,—"you say there is no proof of the actuality of what is called telepathy or thought-transferrence, and perhaps you are right, but I have several times in my life had experiences which were very difficult to explain except by some such theory, and if you care to listen I will tell you one of them which I have in mind."

Our chorus of approval evidently left no doubt as to our desire to hear the story, for Watson smiled, and lighting a fresh cigar he began as follows:

"On the seventeenth of January last year there was a slight wash-out on the Northern road not far from Chicago, and the forward trucks of one of the cars on train 61, on which I was a passenger, left the rails, but luckily the train was going slowly at the time and there was little damage done except a general shaking up of the passengers in the car as the forward wheels bumped roughly over the sleepers for a few yards before the train stopped. The other cars did not leave the track, and only one man was seriously injured.

"This man had been standing on the platform at the time and was thrown between the cars and badly crushed. I was close to the end window and saw him fall, and when the conductor called for a doctor I responded at once.

"I found the man lying on a blanket surrounded by a number of the passengers. He seemed to suffer but little pain, and I feared, from a casual examination, he was badly injured internally, although he was perfectly conscious; he was bleeding at the mouth, and his legs seemed to be paralyzed. He asked faintly if I thought he was going to die, and I cheered him up, as is customary in such cases, but shortly afterwards he developed such serious symptoms that I felt forced to tell him I feared he was seriously hurt, and it was quite possible he would live but a few hours.

"Upon hearing this he became very much agitated, and whispered to me that he wished to speak to me alone, saying he had something of the utmost importance to communicate.

"I thought it was probably some message to send to some members of his family, or some instructions regarding his affairs, but after a few words I became very much interested. He talked for fifteen minutes, part of the time being sustained by the use of stimulants. His story, which was a very strange one, I will repeat as nearly as possible in his own words. After repeatedly asking me to assure him there was no possible chance of his recovery he said:

"'It is not necessary for you to know my name, but it is sufficient for me to tell you that I received a good education in my youth and graduated with high honors at one of the large universities in this country. I always had more or less interest in the study of physiology, and during my college course conducted a series of experiments in hypnotism, and made some interesting discoveries regarding the exaltation of the senses, and especially in relation to illusion and hallucination by the aid of post-hypnotic suggestion.

"'It had been my earnest desire to occupy the position of professor of physiology in one of the universities, but failing to obtain a position of this kind, and having no means of support, I gradually became poorer and poorer, earning a livelihood as best I could, until I became discouraged and attempted to make money in a way not quite so honest.

"'The idea suggested itself to me during a series of experiments which I had conducted with a friend of mine. It so happened that this friend was paying teller in one of our well-known banks of Chicago, where he is to-day. He is a thoroughly honorable man in every way, but I found that he was a good hypnotic subject, or sensitive, as we call it. At first he could not be considered first class, but he was much interested in the subject, and allowed me to hypnotize him repeatedly. After a few evenings he became very easily influenced and one of the best subjects I had ever had. I could put him to sleep in a moment, simply snapping my fingers and telling him I wished him to sleep; of course this can only be done with sensitives who have been repeatedly hypnotized.

"'Under these conditions I succeeded in making him do very many wonderful things, especially in the way of post-hypnotic suggestions; a post-hypnotic suggestion is a command given to hypnotized subjects that at some future time they perform a certain act. In most cases, in waking from the hypnotic sleep they have forgotten that the suggestion has been given them, but at the time set they perform the act unconsciously, as though by their own volition. Not only will they do this, but after the act is performed they usually sink into a quiet sleep, from which they awake after passing into the normal sleep, and, as a rule, have forgotten that they did anything unusual, or that they have been hypnotized, and take up the thread of thought again at the point where they first entered the hypnotic condition. They do not remember what they have done or seen. Their mind is a blank as to all that occurred during the time they were hypnotized.

"'For the last two years I have been rather fortunate, in a small way, speculating in stocks. My capital being small, the amount of money I could make was, of course, comparatively little; yet I succeeded in doing very well until about three weeks ago, when, by two or three unfortunate speculations, I found myself absolutely destitute, and without a penny in the world. It was then the idea suggested itself to me to hypnotize Mr. Herrick and make him bring me money from the bank. This of course was perfectly possible, if no accident occurred, or no unforeseen difficulty presented itself, which I had not previously thought of, as the cashier would act simply as an instrument, being governed entirely by my directions. I asked him in a casual way several times about the affairs of the bank, and learned one day that the bank would have an unusually large balance in settling with the clearing-house. It was the custom for Mr. Herrick to lock up his own funds, and simply state to the cashier that he had done so.

"'According to a carefully arranged plan, I hypnotized him last evening and commanded him to take all the money and securities he had in his possession, after settling with the clearing-house, and instead of locking them in his vault to put them in a bag, of course taking precautions to do this when no one was observing him, and then leave the bank in the usual manner.

"'He was to take a carriage and drive directly to a small, unoccupied house which is situated on the corner of Blank and 117th streets.

"'It was my intention, as I had gone so far, to go still further. I knew that Mr. Herrick would bring me the money and securities, and that I should find him asleep in the house, but what I did not know positively, and what I feared was, *that he might not forget what he had done when he awoke.* As a rule, sensitives obey the command to forget, but in the course of my various experiments I have found sensitives who had a vague idea of what occurred, perhaps nothing tangible, but still sufficient, in a case like this, when there would be a great row about the lost securities, to suggest a possible clue.

"'It is a very cold day, six degrees below, I think, and I had deliberately intended to leave Mr. Herrick asleep after I had taken the money from him and let him take his chances, sleeping without any fire or covering, in an hypnotic condition, with the temperature below zero, and you can judge what his chances would have been. This scheme I thought out deliberately, and what seems strange, I had not the least repugnance against arranging for the death of my friend. After I had once made up my mind to make him steal the securities his disappearance seemed to be the only way to insure my safety. Of course no one could know I was connected with this matter.

I would not go near the bank, and unless he was followed, which was most unlikely, as he had been with the bank some years and was a thoroughly trusted official, there would be absolutely no chance of my detection.'"

Watson relighted his cigar, which had gone out, and continued —

"While he had been speaking another train had arrived with a lot of workmen who were busily engaged jacking the car back on the rails. The train was about to return to Chicago, so I inquired the name of the bank and its president, and the address of the house, writing them down so there could be no possible mistake. I then hastened on board the train, leaving my patient under the care of Dr. Morse, a local physician, who agreed to notify me as to the condition of the man later in the day.

"Upon arriving in Chicago I immediately drove to the bank, but found it closed. I was told, however, that Mr. Bartlet, the president, was attending a corporation meeting in an office in the same building. I immediately hunted him up, and, upon hearing my story he hastily ordered a carriage and we drove to the house as described.

"On our way out we stopped and picked up Dr. Marsh, who as you know is very much interested in such matters. It was quite a long drive, but we found the place without difficulty. It was unoccupied, and many of the windows were broken, and altogether it presented a very dilapidated appearance, such as the cheap houses on the outskirts of a great city often do after having been unoccupied for a year or two. We tried the door and found it unlocked. On the first floor the rooms were entirely empty, loose papers scattered about, and no signs of any one having entered the house. Upon going upstairs we found the door on the first landing at the head of the stairs closed, but not locked. At the back of the room was a cracked wooden stool and a dilapidated hair sofa, which had evidently been considered too used up to be of any value. Part of the cover was torn away, one of the legs was broken, and some of the hair stuffing was lying scattered about the floor. On this lounge lay Mr. Herrick apparently sound asleep; his lips blue with cold, his face pale, and the general appearance of a man half frozen to death. He was breathing very quietly, however, and his heart action was still fairly good, although somewhat slow. By his side lay a small bag, which, it is needless to say, was pounced upon by Mr. Bartlet. It contained some valuable securities, and a great bundle of bank bills of large denomination. Both Marsh and I considered Herrick's condition as decidedly interesting and unusual, and we were both of the opinion that, as part of the story had proved true, it was very likely the whole would turn out just as described.

"If this proved to be the case, all that now remained to be done was to restore Herrick to his normal condition, which might or might not be easy to accomplish. The first thing to be done was to get him out of such a low temperature. We tried various methods of restoring consciousness, but without success. What we did not like was that his heart action was gradually becoming weaker. We gave a hypodermic injection of strychnia, and the heart was soon acting in a much more satisfactory manner. There was no return to consciousness, however, so taking him in the carriage we drove back to Dr. Marsh's house, and arriving there we all turned to and did what we could to restore Herrick to consciousness. Now that he was in a warm room the drawn expression and the blue look left his face, but otherwise he appeared to sleep as soundly as ever. The heart was now acting very well, and aside from the coma the condition of the patient gave us no cause for anxiety. As time went on, however, and we absolutely failed to waken him, and the heart again showed signs of weakness, we began to feel somewhat uneasy.

"You see," said Watson, "we did not know what suggestion was given the patient; these post-hypnotic suggestions are peculiar in their action upon some sensitives. If, as it is fair to suppose, this man was ordered to sleep, he should in the natural course of events sleep for a number of hours and then awake, after passing from the hypnotic sleep to the normal sleep; but we know very little of the effect on some nervous systems of post-hypnotic suggestions. Another thing, in many cases the patient will not waken or cannot be wakened except by the person who put him to sleep. The reason for this is plain enough. Part of the effect on the mind of hypnotic suggestion is due entirely to sleep. The skilled hypnotist commands one of his sensitives to sleep under certain conditions. The sensitive expects to be awakened by the same voice and in the same way, and habit and association have fixed in his mind certain conditions which he associates with the order to awake. There is no doubt whatever that Mr. Herrick heard what we were saying when we spoke to him in a loud voice, but he heard it without understanding, much as a person in a sleepy condition hears noises about him without trying to comprehend them. It is undoubtedly true that the man who put Herrick to sleep could have wakened him in a moment, while we, with all our knowledge and experience, were unable to make his brain regain its normal condition. We decided to let him sleep; and if, at the end of a few hours, he did not regain consciousness, we would try again what we could do to assist him, of course watching the heart in the meanwhile and using nitro-glycerin or strychnia if indicated.

"At that moment Herrick suddenly spoke, at first huskily and then in a loud, clear voice, shouting, 'Yes, yes, I hear you; I am awake.' Then he sat up, asking in a dazed way, 'Where am I? What does this mean?'"

"As he did so the old-fashioned clock in the hall struck the hour of seven."

The queerest part of this story is suggested by a letter received from Dr. Morse the next day, which read as follows:

Dear Watson: You asked me to write you about the injured man, and I do so now to tell you he is dead. He died a minute or two before seven o'clock last evening; I know the hour exactly, because I was watching him at the time, and for some moments he had been whispering and muttering to himself, but all I could catch was something about, "I withdraw my command;" when, suddenly raising himself, he shouted, "Wake up, wake up!" and fell back dead just as the clock in the church-yard struck seven. I should be much interested to hear whether his story was true or not. Drop me a line about it when you have time.

Very sincerely yours,

F. Morse

Philip Darrell's Wife

By B.L. Farjeon

The unexpected news that my friend, Philip Darrell, was married gave me no pleasure. I regarded it, indeed, as a kind of treachery. We had agreed never to marry, and had planned our annual summer holiday in the Tyrol, which, of course, must now be abandoned. The secrecy of the proceedings annoyed me, and this secrecy was kept up even in the affectionate letter in which he announced the event. He married in Rouen, where he had not a friend. "I have the handsomest woman in Europe for a wife," he wrote. "I enclose her portrait. In a couple of months we shall be in London."

Mrs. Philip Darrell was a magnificent creature, if her portrait told a true tale. Dark, lustrous eyes, with noble eyebrows and eyelashes, large mouth and nose, rather sensuous and inviting lips, low forehead, and a wealth of black hair. Her age I judged to be about thirty-five, which would make her seven years older than Philip. A discomforting discrepancy.

The features in Mrs. Darrell's face which principally attracted me were her eyes. After the first examination of the portrait my eyes wandered involuntarily to hers, and a dreamy sensation stole over me to which I insensibly yielded. When I became conscious of this fascination, I wrested my attention from the picture, and presently I found myself wandering again to those compelling orbs, which seemed, as it were, to hold me charmed. I put the portrait hastily away in a drawer; it was not pleasant to feel that it exercised over me a mysterious power, for which I could find no intelligent reason. In the middle of the night I awoke and saw Mrs. Darrell's eyes shining upon me in the dark. Why should I light a candle, rise from my bed, take out the picture, and gaze upon it with a perturbed spirit, seeing only the lustrous eyes which followed every remonstrant movement of my head? My folly mad me angry, and I thrust the portrait back in the drawer beneath a mass of papers. There it remained for a week, by which time I had recovered my composure, and felt once more master of myself.

At the end of this week there came to dine with me two gentlemen who were also on terms of friendly intimacy with Philip—Dr. Lessing, a celebrated specialist in mental diseases, and Mr. Storey, manager of an important life assurance company. The conversation turned upon Philip, and learning that they had not heard of his marriage I mentioned that I had a portrait of the bride, and produced it. Dr. Lessing was the first to examine it, and I observed that he devoted a considerable time to a study of the picture. He then passed it over to Mr. Storey, who gave utterance to a startled exclamation.

"If I am not mistaken," he said, "I know the lady."

"Ah," I exclaimed, with a feeling of satisfaction, "that is capital. You can tell us something about her. What is your opinion doctor?"

"Most men would consider her handsome," was the reply. "Such a face on the stage would be very attractive. I should like to see her play Lucretia Borgia. Observe the eyes of the portrait. It is not that they follow you whichever way you look—that is the case in many portraits—but that they exercise a fascination over you. There exists in them a haunting power."

"I have felt it," I said, greatly startled.

"And your mind has been disturbed—you have become gloomy, pessimistic. They haunt you, I repeat, and haunt you for evil."

"Wonderfully true."

"Nothing wonderful in it. I should advise you to avoid this woman."

"That I shall not do. When Darrell comes to London I shall court her society."

"Be on your guard. Unless my experiences and studies are at fault she possesses a strong mesmeric power, and as determined a will to give it effect. My judgement of Darrell leads me to the conclusion that he is not a strong-minded man; in which case his union with this woman can hardly be a happy one."

"You are condemning upon theoretical grounds," I said, and turned to Mr. Storey. "You, however, can give us facts."

"I side with Lessing," he said.

"Your facts, your facts!" I cried impatiently.

"They form a little story. Did Darrell tell you the name of the lady he has married?"

"No."

"Strange, is it not? The inference is that she pledged him to silence. I will supply the omission. Her name was Madame Van Loop."

"Madame! A widow?"

"Twice widowed. She is a Dutchwoman. Her first husband was a gentleman of the name of Kempden, and with him she lived four years. He died, and she afterwards married Mr. Van Loop."

"What did her first husband die of?" inquired Dr. Lessing.

"Of a rope. He hanged himself."

Dr. Lessing smiled gravely, and asked if Mr. Kempden was insured.

"There was an insurance on his life for *£10,000, and* there was a difficulty about it. Eventually the widow accepted a third of the sum. Mr. Kempden's fortune—not so large as she expected, I believe—was left unreservedly to her."

"A proof," I interposed, "that he loved her and had confidence in her."

"Shortly after her second marriage a proposal was made in our office for an insurance on the life of Henry Van Loop, for no less a sum than £20,000. It was a sound life; Mr. Van Loop had not an ailment. Nevertheless I declined it. Fortunately."

"How fortunately?"

"Her second husband died within two years of his marriage."

"What did Mr. Van Loop die of?" asked Dr. Lessing.

"Well, it was a curious coincidence. He, also, died of a rope. He hanged himself. He was rich, and she inherited everything; not a shilling was left to any of his blood relatives."

"You seem to be intimately acquainted with her history," I observed.

"When an important proposal is made to us and refused, our interest does not end there. We ascertain all possible particulars relating to the applicant."

"Were there any children?"

"None, by either marriage."

"Let us hope," said Dr. Lessing, "that Darrell's life is not insured."

"Is not this going too far," I remonstrated. "It is admitted that her two husbands committed suicide, and you are virtually proclaiming her a murderess."

"I made no accusations," said Dr. Lessing, "but you will admit that there is something peculiar in Mrs. Darrell's matrimonial career. In the course of my professional investigations I have met with many strange experiences, and I know for a certainty that crimes may be committed by suggestion, and that what looks like suicide may be actual murder."

"A startling theory."

"It is not theory; it is fact. Relatively, according to the strength of their will-power, human beings can influence one another for good or evil. Call it what you will, magnetism, mesmerism, hypnotism, we know that it exists, and it has to be reckoned with. An actor, by sheer force of earnestness and self-concentration, can move a multitude to tears or laughter. How much more potent is it when the full strength of the magnetic current is brought to bear upon a mind which has been prepared for the evil suggestion that leads him to commit murder or suicide? The guilt lies not at his door, but at the door of the person who exercised this influence over him. The law, however, as it stands, cannot touch the actual criminal" —I think it was my earnest gaze that caused him to break off suddenly and to say, "And now let us talk of something more agreeable."

We did so, but whatever we talked about my mind continued to dwell upon the subject we had dropped. I was glad when my guests took their leave, and I could give full play to my morbid imaginings. The portrait was on a side table, and a stronger power than my own compelled me to set it before me to gaze upon it, until my mind became enfeebled, and I was no longer master of myself. There are influences which, when a man yields to them, afford him pleasure, plunge him for a time ecstatic delirium. The drunkard, the opium smoker, have periods of exultation; they are carried to the heights, they revel in delightful dreams, they are deliciously maddened by fancies and visions. But the effect produced upon me now was one of profound, hopeless depression. The salt was gone out of my days—there was nothing to live for. Light, beauty, the joy of living, were clothed in funeral garb. There was a grey, leaden sky, the wind sobbed, the trees swayed with mournful moans. Was there no escape from this universal misery? One, and only one—the grave!

At three o'clock in the morning I awoke, shivering. I had fallen asleep in my chair. Wine, spirits and fruit were on the table. The decanter nearest my hand contained brandy. Blindly, unthinkingly, I half filled a tumbler with liquor and drank it off. In a moment my depression took flight; courage, resolution, returned. I seized Mrs. Darrell's portrait, and tearing it to pieces flung it into the grate, in which the fires was still smouldering. Bending forward, I watched the strips of cardboard curl and twist like the writhings of serpents, until the picture was utterly destroyed. Even then my feverish fancy traced the fatal eyes in the white ashes. I drank more brandy, and went to bed.

Four months elapsed before Philip returned to London with his wife. In the meantime I had received three or four letters from him, written in high spirits; he was the happiest man in the world, his wife was an angel, and so on, and so on. His last letter, however, was written in a more despondent mood. He said his liver was out of order, in which respect I had a fellow feeling for him.

His arrival in London was announced by an invitation to dinner at the Langham, and to the Langham I went, tingling with curiosity. They gave me a cordial welcome. Mrs. Darrell was as beautiful as her portrait, and my conscience pricked me as I thought of the fate of the luckless picture. Her manners were gracious and pleasant, and when dinner was over, and we were at our claret, she referred quite openly to her being older than Philip.

"Confess now," she said, "that you were alarmed when you heard that Philip had married a woman older than himself."

"He did not tell me," I replied. "I was inclined to be angry with him for being so uncommunicative. Between such old friends as ourselves—"

She interrupted me. "There should be no secrets."

"I was about to say as much."

"O," she said vivaciously, "but everyone has secrets. Yourself, for instance. Have *you* not a skeleton in your cupboard? Dear me—those skeletons? Eh, Philip?" He nodded, gloomily it appeared to me. "Ah, Well, don't let us talk of them. Shall I sing to you?"

She sang beautifully in French and Italian, and showed herself to be an accomplished woman.

"You remain in London, I hope," I said.

"Oh, yes; it is Philip's wish, and therefore mine. We shall take a furnished house for six months; that will give us time to look about us. We have packets of letters from house agents, and to-morrow we commence the hunt."

So we chatted on till it was time for me to leave. Philip walked part of the way home with me, and it was only when we were alone together that it struck me how small a part he had taken in the conversation. I asked him if he was not well.

"Not very bright," he said. "That fiend dyspepsia had tight hold of me. What do you think of my wife?"

"She is a beautiful and accomplished lady," I answered.

"Yes," he said, and seemed to be considering. "Let us meet often; you do me good."

He spoke of mutual friends, and inquired after Dr. Lessing and Mr. Storey.

"I intend to ask Storey to insure my life," he said.

I started. "Your own wish, Philip?"

"I suppose so. My wife and I were talking of such matters, and it came into my head."

"Now," thought I, "did she put it there?" But I said nothing of the conversation between our mutual friends and myself relating to the insurances on the lives of Mrs. Darrell's two former husbands. I wondered if he knew anything about them.

As I anticipated, the policy was not granted, and Philip expressed his surprise to me. I suggested that the doctor's report was unfavourable; I had to say something.

"That may be," Philip replied, "but this particular doctor is an ass. I have had myself examined by two physicians who are connected with life assurance companies, and they say there is nothing whatever the matter with me. True, I am suffering from an unaccountable depression, but it will wear off in time. The singular part of the affair is that I have been rejected by other offices on grounds not stated."

I could have enlightened him, but did not. There is a freemasonry among insurance companies, and Mr. Storey had struck the warning note.

Meanwhile, the furnished house had been taken, and I was invited to inspect it. It did not meet with my approval. The neighbourhood was gloomy, and the windows at the back faced a churchyard. Philip's low spirits would have been better served by a brighter outlook. The more I saw him the greater grew my anxiety concerning him. All my endeavors to dispel his melancholy were in vain. I remonstrated, I scolded, I preached— and I might as well have talked to a stone. I spoke also to Mrs. Darrell.

"Yes," she said, "it is a pity that Philip is inclined to mope."

"He never was," I remarked.

"Ah, but then, you see," she rejoined, in her brightest manner, "we all of us live two lives, an outer life and an inner life. And O! the care we take to keep the curtain down. Quite right, too. What should we see if it were raised? Dry bones, grinning skulls, withered hopes, miserable tragedies. We cannot escape from them; it is best they should be hidden."

She covered her eyes with her hand, as though suddenly overcome by sad thought, and only removed it to wipe away her tears. But I asked myself if she were acting.

One evening I dropped in upon Philip, unaware, and found him alone. His wife had gone to a theatre, and he was sitting with his elbow on the table, and his chin resting in his hand. Before him was a striking photograph of Mrs. Darrell, with her haunting eyes. I inquired why he had not accompanied her to the theatre, and he replied that she had said he would not like the piece that was being played. Now, it was a comedy, which I had seen, and laughed at rarely, and I told him so.

"Just the kind of thing you ought to see; it would wake you up."

"She knows best," he said. "You have no idea how considerate she is. I persuaded her to go."

"Then it was your idea in the first instance?"

"No, it was hers. She can't get much enjoyment out of my society."

He was utterly spiritless, and do what I might I could not rouse him out of the fatal lethargy which had fallen upon him.

"Look here, Philip," I said at last. "You should see a doctor."

"A doctor! What for? There is nothing the matter with me—nothing. I am as well as you are. It is only this horrible depression—"

"Which has been upon you too long. It ought to be attended to."

He gave the usual answer—

"O, it will wear off."

When we conversed he hardly looked at me. When his eyes were not fixed upon the portrait of his wife they were turned to the floor; we were sitting on opposite sides of the table, and thinking a glass of wine would do him good I asked him to join me. He pointed to the sideboard saying there were glasses and wine and spirits there, and rising to get them I saw at his feet a coil of rope.

"What is that rope there for?" I asked.

"Nothing. It is the rope my poor wife's last husband hanged himself with."

"For God's sake, Philip," I cried, and grasped his arm. He shook me off, and exclaimed—

"Are you crazy? There's no harm to it."

"Who gave it to you?"

"No one. My wife showed it to me."

"But why keep such a horrible memento?"

"Why not?" he retorted. "It is a link in her life—and mine. What do you keep gazing at it in that way for? Do you think it is alive, that it can speak, that it can move?" He pushed it under the table with his foot. "There, it is out of sight; don't let us talk about it any longer. By the bye, you haven't seen the upper part of the house. Everything is in apple pie order now, and I am sure my wife would not object."

Glad to get away from the symbol of a ghastly tragedy I followed him upstairs, and he took me through the rooms. We came to one on the top floor, used as a box room, and as he held up the candle I noticed a stout beam stretching from wall to wall, about three feet over our heads. Philip's eyes were fixed upon it with strange intentness. This beam, and the rope downstairs, sent a shiver through me, and I hurried him below as quickly as possible.

Now I must leave others to decide whether I was justified in carrying out an idea that occurred to me. I felt as if some desperate effort should be made to pluck Philip from his morbid state, to drive him as it were, out of himself, to make him forget. I had tried fair means and failed: I would try violent means. I determined to make him drunk.

I succeeded. Drinking moderately myself I plied him with liquor, and at eleven o'clock he sat before me in a helpless state of intoxication. My plan had served one good purpose; as he drank, his despondency abated, and for the first hour he was even cheerful. I then endeavoured to persuade him to get to bed, intending afterwards to take my departure; but I did not succeed, and I could obtain no assistance from the domestics. The only alternative was to wait for Mrs. Darrell's return from the theatre, and hand Philip over to her care.

It was past midnight before she came. She let herself in with her latch key, and her movements were singularly quiet. She stepped softly to the room in which we sat, and seemed to listen at the door before she opened it.

"You here!" she cried, and then, in a voice of alarm, "Has anything happened to Philip?"

"Only—you see," I answered, feeling rather awkward as I pointed to her husband, whose arms were stretched upon the table, and his face hidden on them.

She raised his head, and he looked at her with a foolish smile. Her eyes travelled to the glasses and bottles.

"Yes, I see," she said, and if looks could kill I should have fallen dead at her feet.

"Can I help you to get him to bed?" I asked.

She answered by throwing open the door. "Leave my house," she said, sternly.

"But Mrs. Darrell," I remonstrated, "I assure you—"

"I will call the servants to turn you out if you do not go instantly. I have suspected you all through. Now I know you."

I saw that there was no arguing with her, so with a bow, and a few stammering words that I would explain all to-morrow, I stepped towards the street door, she followed me with a candle. I was glad when I found myself outside, but it was with a disturbed mind that I walked home to my bed. On the following day I called at the house. Mrs. Darrell came to the street and forbade me to call again.

Thus was a long and tried friendship broken by a woman of whom I had a profound distrust, and from Philip I did not receive a line; nor did I hear anything of him for five or six weeks, and then the news was startling. It was conveyed to me by Dr. Lessing and Mr. Storey, who, late in the night, paid me an unexpected visit.

"Have you heard?" they asked simultaneously, as they entered the room.

"Heard what?"

They handed me the latest special edition of an evening paper, and pointed to an article, headed, "Melancholy suicide."

My friend, Philip Darrell, had hanged himself.

I was inexpressibly grieved, and yet, when I thought it over, it all seemed so natural. The rope, the beam, his wretched despondency, her haunting eyes—indeed, there had been moments when I had not dared to acknowledge to myself the fear of such a tragedy.

"Philip is the third," said Dr. Lessing. "She has committed three murders by suggestion, has inherited three fortunes (for you will see that the poor fellow has left her his sole heiress), and there is no law to touch her."

"Public opinion," I suggested.

"She will be pitied. Say that we had the courage, or rather the hardihood, to air our impressions—the effect her portrait and then her personality had upon you, and my theory, as you called it—we should be scouted as calumniators and defamers of an unfortunate lady. The law could reach us, but not her."

"There will be an inquest."

"Yes—nothing will come of it. He has been suffering some time from depression. She called in a doctor, I believe, and I will undertake to say that he was never allowed to see Philip unless she was present. She should have called in me."

"You were a true prophet," I remarked.

Dr. Lessing shrugged his shoulders. "It was not very wonderful. I have my eye on other cases quite as simple, which in the judgment of the public, will end in mystery. There is no mystery in them whatever. Cause and effect—nothing more. A certain influence, a certain result. Studies in psychology. We are speaking here in confidence, and I do not hesitate to pronounce this woman a murderess of a most dangerous type; but I would not dare to express myself in such a fashion outside this room. She is a murderess, and she knows she if safe."

"Is she human. Has she any feeling?" I cried in indignation.

"Yes, why not?" There is a wide range of human feeling. I could give you the names of a score of wholesale poisoners and murderers of both sexes, some of whom were exceedingly pious. History supplies examples."

"Philip hanged himself in a room at the top of the house."

"The room with the beam which he took you to see on the last evening you spent with him. I have little doubt that Mrs. Darrell selected the house with an eye to that beam. How often did poor Philip wake up in the night, and see in the darkness the beam and the rope, the spiritual ghost of himself gliding up the stairs to put them to their destined use?"

The image sent shudders through me. Dr. Lessing has a most distressing method of conviction in every word he utters.

It all turned out as he predicted. There was an inquest with the usual verdict. Unsound mind, and an expression of commiseration with the widow, whose grief was publicly poignant. And she inherited the whole of Philip's fortune.

80(08

Twelve months afterwards, in Paris, I saw two persons issue from a jeweller's shop in the Rue de la Paix and step into a carriage that was waiting for them. One was a youngish man, fair, blue-eyed, with a weak face, the other a beautiful woman, who gave him a beaming smile as he took his seat by her side. The man I did not know. The woman was Madame Van Loop, as I prefer to call her.

Was the young man the fourth, and were there a beam and a rope waiting for him?

A Moral Murder: Hanged on Circumstantial Evidence

Frank Airlie was a favorite with most people. Brilliant rather than reflective, clever rather than talented, he was charming, good-natured, generous, and open-hearted. As he also possessed considerable personal advantages, his friends were by no means surprised when one day he announced that he was engaged to be married. He had been accepted by Miss Charlotte M'Farlane, a young lady with whom he had fallen violently in love at first sight, and who now monopolised his thoughts and time, though he had only known her for a few weeks. He was eager to be united with this peerless woman (as he thought her); and, though his friends enjoined patience, and assured him that there was "no hurry," Frank would listen to no one. When he was not in his lady-love's society, his only pleasure was to talk of her; and his friend, honest Jack Fanshawe, was doomed to many an evening of boredom, in which Miss M'Farlane and her perfections formed the one topic of conversation.

Indeed, she was very lovely, with a kind of ethereal beauty, which seemed scarcely human. But many people thought her stupid, or shy; and no doubt she had a habit of "wool-gathering," which was the preverse of flattering to those who were trying to interest her. Perhaps with Frank she behaved better. Anyhow, he regarded her as an angel. The truth was, that the girl's temperament was lympathic to a very unusual degree. She was, apparently, an ideal subject for the mesmerist, and seemed not unlikely to develop the symptoms familiar to the student of hypnotism. But this was nobody's business as long as Frank was satisfied; and that young gentleman was simply enthusiastic. To do her justice, Charlotte had latterly become less absentminded; she came down from the clouds, so to speak. She grew increasingly lively as her wedding day approached, and showed a real pleasure in making arrangements for it, and for the furnishing of her new home.

It was a little more than a week before the day which would make them one that Frank and his affianced bride were walking together along Bond-street, in London. They had been drinking chocolate together at Charbonel's, when, as they left the shop, Charlotte glanced across the road with a terror-stricken expression of face, and uttered a sharp cry. Following the direction of her gaze, Frank saw only a well-dressed man, who smiled quietly as he raised his hat. Charlotte seized her lover's hand, and hurried him away, replying to his anxious questions that the stranger was a man whom she knew slightly, and whose name was Bazalgette. "I hate him!" she said, fervently. She accounted for her strange behavior by saying that she had been "startled;" and, though Frank could not discover how a quiet and gentlemanly person on the other side of the road could have "startled" her, he thought it best to make as light of the occurrence as she by this time did herself. When he bade her good-bye that evening she looked eagerly in his face for a second, and seemed about to make some important communication. But she evidently thought better of it; and in response to Frank's "Well?" she said, "Nothing."

In a few days the matter had altogether faded from his memory. In the best of spirits, he looked forward to unclouded happiness; and now the last day of the probation, which, although unusually short, had seemed so long to the ardent Frank, arrived. For the last time before marriage the happy pair strolled together along Piccadilly. Everything was ready for the morrow's event. When he saw her next she would be standing before the altar. They were about to enter a cab together, and drive to Charlotte's home when Charlotte, who looked pale and strange, begged to be allowed to go home by herself. Frank, although slightly disappointed, immediately gave in to her wish, and endeavored to account, to himself for the somewhat strange proceeding. Having seen her into a cab he turned to stroll toward his club, when he remembered that he had forgotten to give her a small present with which he had come provided. Hailing another hansom, he told the driver to follow the first cab, which was now disappearing round a corner. In this way Frank thought to catch her on her father's doorstep before, she entered the house.

But what was his surprise to find that Charlotte's cab passed by the house where he knew she lived, and proceeded in the direction of Victoria Station! Frank Airlie would not have been human if he had not felt hurt by such a want of candor as this seemed to imply. True to his orders, his cabman kept the first hansom well in sight, and drew up immediately behind it before a large hotel.

Charlotte M'Farlane alighted, and looking neither to the right nor the left, walked straight forward into the hall. Frank sprang out in his turn, paid his driver, and followed. Many people were coming and going. Inside the hotel no one seemed to notice the fresh arrivals. She walked on. Up a flight of stairs, down a corridor. Frank was always behind. He need have had no apprehension of her seeing him. She never looked round once. Without the slightest hesitation she at last stopped before room No. 57. She turned the handle of the door and entered, saying, readily, "Here I am."

The door stood open. Frank looked fiercely into the room.

Good heavens! Standing before the fireplace was Bazalgette, the stranger they had seen in Bond-street—the man whom Charlotte had professed to hate! Burning with indignation, he was about to rush in, when something in Charlotte's appearance caused him to pause and watch. The girl was under the influence of a magnetic spell. There could be doubt of it. Whatever had brought her to that hotel, Charlotte was innocent of any thought of evil. She was here against her will; and Frank, feeling instinctively that he was about to be a witness of strange proceedings, allowed his curiosity to outweigh all other considerations.

Bazalgette made a pass with his hands across Charlotte's eyes. She started, and came completely to herself, looking with terror at the unfamiliar surroundings and the face of the operator.

"Now," said the latter, "I want you of your own free will, to give up this Frank Airlie, and to accept me in his place. You know I could force you to do so; but I do not wish to win my wife in that way. Your answer, please. You know how I have loved you," he proceeded, with some feeling; "all these years I have waited and longed for you. Forgive me for using my power over you to secure this interview, but once my wife, I swear I will never have recourse to it again. Charlotte, my darling, we are made for each other."

Charlotte was strongly agitated. "How can I break faith with Frank?" she said, piteously. "Besides, I love him so! Have mercy on him and me."

On hearing her speak of her love for Frank, Bazalgette abandoned his conciliatory tone, and, drawing a pistol from his pocket, laid it quietly on the table.

Frank now sprang into the room. To his immense astonishment, Bazalgette betrayed not the least symptom of surprise beyond the slight raising of his eyebrows. Charlotte, on the other hand, made a convulsive movement toward her lover. But her outstretched hands fell powerless at her side on an exclamation from Bazalgette.

"Well met!" observed the latter; "I was about to ring the bell for a waiter. You have saved me the trouble. I only need a witness; and you will do as well as anyone else. Who are you, by the way?"

Frank felt mystified. What was a witness required for? The man spoke with such assurance that he began to wonder whether he was awake, or only in the grasp of a nightmare.

Bazalgette was now looking intently upon Charlotte, as if endeavoring to impress his thoughts upon her unspoken. The girl's features lost every sort of expression. Her face became a mask of vacuity. Suddenly, without the slightest warning, she seized the pistol; and before Frank could interfere she had blown out her brains.

"Murder!" shrieked Frank, as he sprang upon the human devil; "you have killed her."

"She has committed suicide while of unsound mind," returned Bazalgette coldly. "You saw her shoot herself."

Then Frank understood why the "witness" had been required; and, dreading lest the gallows should be cheated, he darted into an empty room, where he remained concealed until a small crowd of servants and residents in the hotel, alarmed by the report of the pistol, had swarmed into Bazalgette's apartment. The mesmerist was at once secured; and but a short interval elapsed before the police appeared upon the scene. The prisoner smiled, and said—

"Gentlemen, there is a grave misunderstanding here. This is a case of suicide, not murder. A gentleman is here who witnessed the deed."

"Where?" cried a dozen voices.

"He was here a moment ago. He must be somewhere about," said Bazalgette, turning rather pale.

But several witnesses testified that when they arrived there was no one in the room besides the prisoner and the corpse.

The policeman nodded significantly; and the mesmerist was removed in custody. Appearances were against him. In his room a lady was found shot with his pistol, while he stood by.

Late that night, as Jack Fanshawe was getting into bed, a violent knock at his front door made him jump. Hastily going downstairs, he opened the door. But no one was to be seen. Shutting the door again, he was about to re-ascend the stairs, when his candle shone upon a letter which had been evidently pushed under the door. He opened it, and read—

Dear Jack, —I am going away. I shall not return to England until after a man called Bazalgette, now in custody on a charge of murdering Charlotte, has been hanged. —Yours ever, FRANK AIRLIE.

Bazalgette never again saw his "witness," in whose existence neither judge nor jury seemed inclined to believe when the case came on for trial. Here was a girl, engaged to be married the next morning, found shot in a mere acquaintance's room. Some comment was made upon the absence of her intended husband. But the judge interposed by saying that he could quite appreciate the poor fellow's feelings which would make his presence particularly painful, and there really was nothing which he could bear witness to. "The theory of suicide" added this legal luminary in his summing-up, "has been advanced. But it is for you, gentlemen, to consider whether you think it probable that a girl would have been likely to destroy herself on the eve of a marriage to which she looked forward with pleasure, and also whether she would have been likely to do the deed at a hotel rather than at her own home. In any case, the prisoner supplied the pistol; and should you come to the conclusion that he is guilty of murder, a motive for the crime might perhaps be found in the jealousy and chagrin which he may have felt at her impending union with another."

Frank Airlie is back in England now. But he looks twice his age. He lost his bride in awful circumstances; and he shudders to think that his silence caused the death of a fellow-creature, however guilty he may have been. For Bazalgette was hanged on circumstantial evidence.

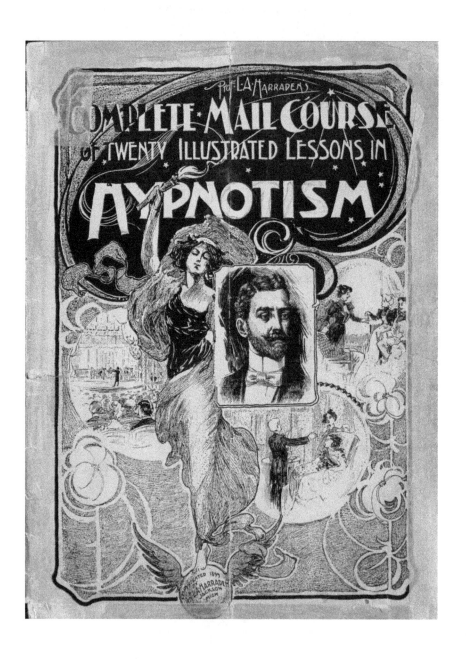

A Hypnotic Crime

By Willard Douglas Coxey

The first occasional meeting of the Society for Psychical Research drew together an even dozen kindred spirits. It was a motley party, to be sure, but of their enthusiasm for the subject that mutually attracted them there was no room for doubt.

There were two or three lawyers, a clergyman of a liberal type, several physicians with more learning than practice; an amateur hypnotist, whose experiments were conducted after long hours of wrestling with abstract columns of materialistic figures; an Irish Spiritualist, with pronounced views on reincarnation and a distressingly unremunerative collection business; a deputy coroner, whose presence was, perhaps, peculiarly apropos in view of the uncanny nature of the society's investigations; and, finally, a newspaper reporter of wide travel and peculiar experiences, with leanings toward Blavatskyism in its most acute phases.

ℰℭ

"Then you believe that the hypnotic influence may be reproduced in a subject without the knowledge or suggestion of the hypnotist?" said the clergyman to one of the legal gentlemen.

A leading remark, after the formal organization had been effected, prompted the question.

"Experience has convinced me that there is something in it," was the quiet reply.

"In other words," persisted the questioner, "you would imply that hypnotic conditions may be continued without outside influences—that, in fact, a subject may have the suggestion of the hypnotist perpetuated without the volition of either?"

"Precisely."

The circle had become noticeably interested. When the clergyman shrugged his shoulders, and murmured something that sounded like a doubt of the lawyer's position, there were some evidences of disapproval. It was, however, the amateur hypnotist, who had been given the place of honor in the chairman's seat, who spoke.

"Our legal friend undoubtedly has something interesting to relate in connection with his avowed belief," he said. "We are here to exchange experiences in things occult. Let us hear the facts before throwing doubt upon his contention."

"Exactly," responded the attorney, "let my story speak for itself. The incident I am about to relate," he added, "occurred under my own personal observation, in a certain city in Illinois, where I had just been admitted to the bar. When I have finished, the society will at least acknowledge that the case had all the elements necessary for a modern mystery."

THE LAWYER'S STORY.

I.

It was a strange case. It baffled the skill of all who had any connection with it. If ever there was a case of murder, this was one; and yet, in spite of the most compromising circumstances, it was almost impossible to believe that the man who was charged with the crime, and who had been hurried off to jail by the detectives, could be the culprit. His character had hitherto been unimpeachable. His whole life was known to his neighbors. The most skeptical could not find a blemish on it.

So far as the outside world knew, he and his wife had lived the happiest of lives. If there was any lack of harmony between them, none of their many friends knew it.

And yet, one morning, John Ransome, according to his own statement, awoke to find his wife lying beside him, dead, her sightless eyes staring into space, and her round, white throat bruised and blackened where cruel fingers had clasped it with a grip of steel until the last vestige of life had gone.

In the midst of his real or marvellously simulated horror the detectives accused him of murdering his wife. In a dazed way he protested his innocence. He was apparently too greatly shocked to care what became of him, but the ring of his voice when he said, "Do you think I could have done that, and slept beside her all night long?" was that of an honest man. "She spoke to me when I came in," he said, "and then I fell asleep. When I awoke this morning she was dead."

The circumstantial evidence against him was, however, strangely complete. He had been out late the night before. The servant girl, frightened half out of her wits by the detectives, said she had heard him come in after midnight. She recognized him by his step and a peculiar, hacking cough. This Ransome did not deny.

In response to further questioning, the girl said that, about six o'clock in the morning, she went upstairs to the room occupied by Mr. and Mrs. Ransome, with a pitcher of hot water, as was her custom. She rapped on the door, and a moment later the key was turned in the lock, and then Mr. Ransome reached out his hand and took the vessel. Almost immediately afterwards she heard Mr. Ransome's cry for assistance, and hastily returning to the room, saw the accused bending over the dead body of his wife.

Nothing could shake the girl's statement that the door of the bedroom was locked on the inside when she went upstairs. Later, it was noted as a peculiar fact that both windows in the room, facing the lawn, and entirely inaccessible from the outside except by means of a ladder, were also securely fastened. One of the officers asked Ransome if he had fastened them, and he unhesitatingly answered that he had done so, the previous evening, before leaving the house. The most minute search failed to show any displacement of the grass or shrubbery, such as would have been inevitable had anyone attempted to climb up from the outside.

The detectives had therefore established, by only a few minutes' work, what seemed to be an unbroken chain of circumstantial evidence, clearly pointing to Ransome's connection with the crime. Ransome was locked in the room with his wife. Both windows, as well as the door, were securely fastened on the inside. There was no other means of entrance or escape. It would have been impossible for any one to have left the room and then secured the fastenings. The woman was not dead when Ransome entered the room to retire, for he acknowledged that she had spoken to him. No coroner could resist such evidence. Ransome was committed to jail without bond to await the action of the grand jury.

Perhaps the man did not suffer much during his incarceration. He appeared stunned, and unable to realize the gravity of his position. The inquisitorial powers of the police were used in every conceivable way to wring a "confession" from him, but he persisted in his asseveration of innocence. He made no attempt, apparently, to conceal anything that had occurred either before or after his alleged discovery of his wife's death; he unflinchingly admitted that to the best of his knowledge and belief he was locked in the room with her, and he guilelessly told the chief that before leaving the house on the night of the tragedy, he and his wife had some sharp words, and he had left her in anger, but that his ill-feeling had all disappeared before returning home. No one had known of this, and the admission was prejudicial to his case, but he seemed to have no desire to conceal anything—except how the crime was committed and his own agency in it.

This was what puzzled the police. The man was daily strengthening the web of evidence that had been woven about him—doing it with a guileless air of truth and honesty that was astonishing—and still he vehemently protested that he knew absolutely nothing of the murder.

Ransome's counsel was in despair. The evidence against his client, of which he could not fail to be cognizant, was unanswerable. The only possible hope for the prisoner was the plea of "guilty," and an appeal to the court for mercy, and this the lawyer urged upon him.

"The case against you is terribly black," he said. "The evidence of the prosecution is practically without a flaw."

"I know it," Ransome replied—"I know it as well as you do."

"The only chance I see for you is to plead guilty," continued the lawyer.

"But I can't do that," was the quick reply.

"Why not?"

"Because I am not guilty, and I would not say I killed her, even to save my life."

The lawyer gazed at his client with a puzzled look in his eyes. Was the man really innocent? It was difficult to believe it—the evidence against him was seemingly so conclusive. And yet the eyes of the prisoner looked into his without flinching, and his face had no incriminating blush of guilt.

"It's a strange case—a very strange case," he muttered, as he left the prisoner's cell.

II.

Ransome stood in the witness box. He was on trial for his life. The servant girl had been sworn and examined, and battled over on technicalities by the opposing counsel, and cross-examined until her head was in a whirl and her speech incoherent; the detectives had told their stories; the defense had produced a score of witnesses to testify to the good character of the accused, and now, after a long and acrimonious argument between the prisoner's lawyer and the state's attorney, Ransome had been placed upon the stand in his own defense.

Unheeding his lawyer's instructions to say nothing except in answer to the questions of counsel, Ransome had just burst forth with a strenuous asseveration of his innocence, when the hundreds of eager eyes that watched him, saw his head fall forward on his breast, and his fingers clutch convulsively at the rail.

"Do you mean to tell this honorable court and these worthy jurymen that you knew nothing of the death of the deceased until after the servant girl had left your door?"

It was the state's attorney who spoke, but there was no reply. The prosecutor looked inquiringly at the prisoner, and then at the judge.

"You must answer the question," said the court.

"My client will answer, Your Honor," said Ransome's attorney, and he leaned over and whispered to the prisoner. What he said was indistinguishable, but the court and the spectators were surprised to see him draw back and look at the accused with an air of puzzled wonder. The next moment the lawyer was forgotten, and the eyes of judge and prosecutor, jury and crowd, were rivetted upon poor Ransome.

Slowly he raised his head, and those who saw his face were startled by its expression. His eyes were wide open and staring, but it was evident that he saw nothing of the scene about him. They seemed to be fixed with terrible fascination upon something pictured in space. Suddenly a look of anger flashed in his eyes, and then the breathless crowd saw him reach out and grasp some invisible presence, and clutch, and tear, and strangle it, and, finally, with a muffled cry of horror, throw the unseen object off, and sink back against the rail, panting and exhausted.

For a moment the crowd and the group of lawyers within the rail were awed into silence. Then the state's attorney sprang to his feet.

The judge raised his hand.

"Wait," he said, "let us see the climax to this strange scene."

The state's attorney resumed his seat. As he did so, the prisoner seemed to revive. His eyes began to assume their natural expression. He gazed at the eager faces around him, and a look of wonderment came into his eyes.

"What has happened?" he whispered to his attorney, who had been immeasurably shocked by the scene that had just transpired.

"You were—ill," he answered, hesitatingly.

"Yes, I was ill," said the prisoner.

The next moment a look of terror came into his face. It was not a trance now. His eyes were clear, but those who saw the horror pictured in them knew there was something more to come.

Suddenly, with a wild cry that rang through the courtroom, he shrieked:

"I—I—I *did* kill her—I know it now—it all comes back to me—I am her murderer!"

There was a restless movement in the crowd; an instinctive pressing forward; a low murmur of horror. The court officers rapped for order, and poor Ransome went on.

"I remember it all now—while I have been standing here it has all come back to me!"

His attorney tried to stop him.

"You are hanging yourself," he whispered.

"Never mind," was the loud response—"I will hang then. When I said I was innocent I believed I was telling the truth—now that I know I am guilty I will not deny it.

"The night my wife was killed," he continued, "I attended a hypnotic seance. I had always been greatly interested in hypnotism, and that night, although a stranger to the company, I offered myself to the hypnotist as a subject. Subsequently, I was told that, under suggestion, I had entertained the company by committing an imaginary murder. That night, in my sleep, I re-enacted the whole horrible scene, but instead of an imaginary murder, I—I killed my wife!"

The voice of the state's attorney broke in upon him.

"Mr. Ransome, did you not say at the inquest that you had no recollection of where you spent the evening previous to the murder?"

"It is true—I swear it! Until this moment the occurrences of that night have been a total blank. Now it all passes before me like a panorama—the seance—the hypnotic trance—the —murder! Do with me as you will—for I killed her—I killed her—I killed my wife!"

For the second time the prisoner collapsed. As he fell backward an officer caught him and placed him in a chair.

There was another excited movement in the crowd. The voice of the judge interrupted the tumult.

"Court is adjourned," he said—"the prisoner is remanded to jail."

Ransome was taken back to his cell. The next morning he was found dead. Unable to endure the memory of his hypnotic crime, he had committed suicide.

෫෩෪

"A good story," admitted the clergyman, when the lawyer had finished.

"And a valuable beginning in our gathering of testimony in the psychic field," added the chair.

"But what would have been the result of the trial if the prisoner had lived?" asked the deputy Coroner.

"Ah," responded the lawyer, "that is exactly what puzzled the court and the state's attorney."

The Playwright's Story

Syd Percival and I were chums from boyhood. We studied at school together; we made our choice of professions together; and through the first weary years of struggle on the provincial stage we managed to stick pretty closely to each other. Then Sydney's talent began to assert itself. He was a born actor, whilst I was an indifferent one at the best, and he soon left me far behind. He got to London, and began to be talked about as the coming man.

Meanwhile I jogged along, and eventually, mainly through Sydney's influence, obtained a footing in the West End theatres. Soon after this I married a sweet little woman who had often played leading lady to my leading gent, in the provinces. With our joint salaries—for she was then playing in London—we managed to rub along pretty comfortably; and for a time I believe, I was the happiest man on earth.

Sydney Percival, who was a bachelor, was always sure of a welcome to our humble little home, and he was a constant visitor there. Now, for years I had entertained a desire to become a playwright. As an actor, I felt myself a failure, but I had dreams of victory in the other direction.

As a culmination of many previous efforts I had at last written a play which, I felt sure, if I could but get it accepted, would bring success. Ethel was as excited about it as myself, and urged me to get it read as quickly as possible. We were discussing its chances when Sydney came in, and I gave it to him to look over. His face lit up with genuine pleasure when he had read it, and he said it was certain to go.

Well, I had it sent to manager after manager, but invariably the same result. It was always returned with the same little note of polite refusal; and at last I sent it out no more.

In trying to hide my disappointment I grew strangely morose, and so unlike my usual self that I caught Ethel's eyes fixed on me, wonderingly, more than once.

At this particular time my wife was playing in the same company as Percival. One day I fancied I detected a glance which passed between them indicative of a secret understanding.

As the days went on, my suspicions became stronger and stronger. I detected a secret meaning in every look, and thought I could fathom a subtle understanding in each sentence that passed between them.

The climax came one day. I had come in softly from the street. As I neared the door of the sitting-room, which was slightly ajar, I heard voices—my wife's and Percival's. I stopped dead. They had not heard me; my wife was speaking:

"We must persuade him to go to some quiet little spot, away from the world, for a change of air and scenery. Some place where he will hear no news. Then we can mature our plans. Oh, I feel certain of success; what a surprise it will be for him! He must not know of our plot; that would spoil everything."

Then Percival's voice broke in:—

"He shall not know. He cannot suspect. I wouldn't have him find us out for the world. If you could persuade him to go to your relations at that quiet little village on the Cornish coast, it would be splendid. Get him to see a doctor. Tell him you fear his health is breaking. The doctor is almost sure to order him a change of air and scenery. Then will come our opportunity."

I waited to hear no more. I went out noiselessly and staggered along the street like a drunken man.

Blindly, madly, muttering incoherently, I stumbled along until I found myself in Hyde Park. I sank on a seat and tried to think. I could not. My head seemed whirling round, my brain on fire. I retraced my steps and reached home again. Home! The bitter mockery of it. I entered and found Percival awaiting me. The sight of him calmed me instantly.

"Tempest, old man," he began, "I do wish you would exert your skill on me again. Those confounded neuralgic pains have come on badly, and I don't want to give up. Just hypnotise them away for me, and once more earn my everlasting gratitude."

Now, I must mention that as a hobby I had taken up the study of hypnotism some years before, and had acquired considerable power in that direction.

I placed him in an easy, comfortable position now, and very soon he was under my influence. When at last he sank back, my heart gave a great throb. He was my enemy, my undoer, in my power—entirely at my mercy. Yes, my turn had come! They should both suffer. I pulled myself together, and in calm, decisive tones, addressed him thus:—

"To-night when you are playing 'Bernard' to my wife's 'Millicent,' in the last scene of the second act, you will forget that you are only acting a part and will strangle her in real earnest. You understand; I command you to strangle her in very truth. Answer me!"

"I understand," he said, in dreamy tones.

"You will remember nothing of this when you awake." I went on. Then I brought him out of the sleep.

"Thanks, awfully, old man. I feel as fit as a trivet now," said he, as he shook himself, "and now I must be going."

He was gone, and I—I paced the room with great strides and panting breast, like a wild beast yearning for its prey.

My wife came in before going to the theatre, and putting her arms round my neck, kissed me adieu.

Yes, I would go! A horrible fascination drew me towards the house where so terrible a tragedy was to be enacted. I went, and placed myself where I could see, without being myself observed.

The curtain was rung up for the second act; one scene—two—and now the last. She came on, and the house rose at her and cheered itself hoarse. She surpassed herself. Then through the secret panel at the back came Percival as "Bernard," the discarded lover. With passion in his voice he pleaded to her—in vain.

"By heaven!" he cried, "if you cannot be mine in life, at least nothing shall part us in death."

He seized her in his arms and planted one wild, frantic kiss on her lips; and then—then—his fingers coiled round her slender throat, and they swayed downwards together.

How I trembled! I almost fell. The house was quiet—so quiet. They did not know what I knew. They saw only the make-believe, I—ah, my eyes were rooted to the spot where the grim struggle was going on. My head seemed bursting and my vision was getting blurred. I remember stumbling forward and being caught by someone, and as I fell, my eyes still riveted on the struggling figures, I saw something big and swift fall from the flies and strike the head of Sydney Percival. Then came a blank, I knew no more.

✂✀✃

The first thing I became aware of was the sound of subdued voices, and they seemed a long way off. Turning my head ever so little, I saw two figures seated at one side of the bed. They heard me move, and one of them bent over me and met my glance.

"Thank Heaven!" she said. "The crisis is passed. He is saved."

It was my wife. She kissed me, and I felt the hot tears drop to my face.

"You must keep very quiet, dear," she said. "You will soon get stronger, now."

"How long," I asked, in a whisper, "have I been here?"

"Six long weeks," she replied, "but you will soon be yourself again now."

She went from the room, and left the other woman, whom I found to be a nurse, by my side.

The nurse, seeing my restless condition, gave me a sleeping draught, and once again I sank into unconsciousness. The days went on and grew to weeks, and I began to leave the bed and get about the room. I had said nothing to Ethel of what so occupied my mind. I could not broach the subject; but trusted to time to make all things clear.

During all that time Sydney Percival did not come nigh, and his name never passed between us.

I was rapidly approaching convalescence, and was nearly fit to leave the sick-room, when a thought suddenly struck me one morning. During the few weeks I had been conscious I had not seen a newspaper.

As I stood there I heard a newsboy calling out the main items of news in the evening papers. A sudden resolution took possession of me. I went downstairs to the street door, and, waiting for him to come along, bought a paper.

I had barely glanced at it when I started up with a sudden cry. What was this?

To-night Mr. Sydney Percival, the deservedly popular actor, will commence his career as actor-manager, when he will produce at the Colosseum Theatre a new five-act play by Mr. John Tempest, a new playwright, entitled "The Awakening of Harold." Mr. Sydney Percival himself takes the part of "Harold," and Mrs. Ethel Tempest will play "Beatrice."

The paper dropped from my fingers. Good Heavens! What did it mean? My play—my great effort that I had staked so much on—to be produced to-night, and by Sydney Percival. I was as one suddenly bereft of reason. I glanced at the clock. The hand was just pointing to eight. Hastily gathering up a coat, hat, and muffler, I rushed downstairs—all my weakness gone in the whirlwind of excitement which possessed me.

My feet carried me swiftly along, and I reached and entered the Colosseum. I went in and took up a position where I was not likely to be seen and recognised from the stage. The curtain had just gone up, and the play was proceeding.

How they acted—those two! I had never seen anything like it, and the audience rose at them after each act.

At last the fifth act was on, in which occurred the great scene of the piece. The house was silent as death; I sat as one entranced. Ah, it was over!

Then burst out the applause that knew no stinting. Again and again the principal actors came before the curtain. I could see that Percival was making a speech, but I could not hear his words. All I had ears for was the cry of "Author! Author!"

I turned to leave, and was passing out when I felt my arm grasped, and a voice, which I dimly recognised, said:—

"By Jove, Tempest, old man, they said you were not here! Come along; we shall never get the people out else."

He led me along, half-dazed, to the back of the stage. I saw my wife and Percival as in a mist; could just discern their start of surprise, and then I was before the house listening to the applause of the people I could not see. For a mist shut everything from my vision, and a merciful unconsciousness fell on my poor, dazed brain, and even as they clamoured wildly for a speech I fell prone upon the stage. When I came to myself Ethel and I were alone; she had a cab waiting, and together we entered it and drove home.

We entered the little sitting-room, and my wife, Heaven bless her! putting her arms around my neck, sank on my breast, and shed tears of joy.

I tried to disentangle her arms from my neck.

Don't touch me, Ethel; I am not worthy. You do not know what a wretch I am—what, but for an accident, I might have become.

"John," she said, "I know all, and it makes no difference. Percival knows, too, and you may still count him amongst your dearest friends. Think no more about it. Let the past go; the future looms up brightly before us from to-night."

In my ravings during the weary weeks of brain fever I had disclosed the hideous secret, and had explained the occurrence which almost ended in a tragedy, and would have done but for a piece of wood falling from the flies and striking the head of Percival, rendering him unconscious.

This then, was the secret understanding between them—the plot which I had so vilely misinterpreted! They had resolved to produce my play, Percival being confident of its success. He resolved to take a theatre under his own management, and produce it with Ethel in the cast. They did not wish me to know anything of it until success had been assured, and so desired to get me away where I should be little likely to see any theatrical news. It was to be produced on my birthday, and was to be a glad surprise.

Next morning when Percival came in and, greeting me with a hearty hand-shake, said, in that earnest way of his, "I'm so glad, old man." I felt too full for words, and could only stammer, brokenly: "Heaven bless you both, and forgive me."

"There is nothing to forgive," said Percival. "Think of it no more."

My Hypnotic Patient

By L.T. Meade

"Very well," I said, "I will call to-morrow at the asylum, and you will show me round."

I was talking to a doctor, an old chum of mine. He had the charge of a branch hospital in connection with the County Asylum, and had asked me to take his post for a few days. His name was Poynter—he was a shrewd, clever fellow, with a keen love for his profession, and a heart by no means callous to the sufferings of his fellow-beings. In short, he was a good fellow all round, and it often puzzled me why he should take up this somewhat dismal and discouraging branch of the profession.

Poynter had been working hard, and looked, notwithstanding his apparent *sangfroid*, as if his nerves had been somewhat shaken.

When he begged of me to take his post, and so to secure him a few days' holiday, I could not refuse.

"But I have no practical knowledge of the insane," I said. "Of course, I have studied mental diseases generally; but practical acquaintance with mad people I have none."

"Oh, that is nothing," answered Poynter, in his brisk voice; "there are no very violent cases in the asylum at present. If anything unforeseen occurs, you have but to consult my assistant, Symonds. What with him and the keepers and the nurses, all we really want you for is to satisfy the requirements of the authorities."

"I am abundantly willing to come," I replied. "All the ills that flesh is heir to, whether mental or physical, are of interest to me. What hour shall I arrive to-morrow?"

"Be here at ten to-morrow morning, and I will take you round with me. You will find some of my patients not only interesting from a medical point of view, but agreeable and even brilliant men and women of the world. We keep a mixed company, I assure you, Halifax, and when you have been present at some of our 'evenings,' you will be able to testify to the fact that, whatever we fail in, we are anything but dull."

This statement was somewhat difficult to believe, but as I should soon be in a position to test its truth, I refrained from comment.

The next morning I arrived at Norfolk House at the hour specified, and accompanied Poynter on his rounds.

We visited the different rooms, and exchanged a word or two with almost every inmate of the great establishment. The padded room was not occupied at present, but patients exhibiting all phases of mental disease were not wanting to form a graphic and very terrible picture in my mind's eye.

I was new to this class of disease, and almost regretted the impulse which had prompted me to give Poynter a holiday.

I felt sure that I could never attain to his coolness. His nerve, the fearless expression in his eyes, gave him instant control over even the most refractory subjects. He said a brief word or two to one and all, introduced me to the nurse or keeper, as the case might be, and finally, taking my arm, drew me into the open air.

"You have seen the worst we can offer at present," he said; "now let us turn to the brighter picture. The people whom you will meet in the grounds are harmless, and except on the one mad point, are many of them full of intelligence. Do you see that pretty girl walking in the shrubbery?"

"Yes," I said, "she looks as sane as you or I."

"Ah, I wish she was. Poor girl, she imagines that she has committed every crime under the sun. Her's is just one of the cases which are most hopeless. But come and let us talk to Mr. Jephson; he is my pet patient, and the life of our social evenings. I have considerable hopes of his recovery, although it is not safe to talk of giving him his liberty yet. Come, I will introduce you to him. He must sing for you when you come here. To listen to that man's voice is to fancy oneself enjoying the harmonies of Heaven."

We walked down a broad grass path, and found ourselves face to face with a gentlemanly man of middle age. He had grey hair closely cropped, an olive-tinted face, good eyes, and a fine, genial, intelligent expression.

"How do you do?" said Poynter. "Pray let me introduce you to my friend, Halifax. Dr. Halifax, Mr. Jephson. I am glad to be able to tell you," continued Poynter, addressing himself to Jephson, "that I have just made arrangements with Halifax to take my place here for a week or so. You will be interested, for you have kindly wished me a holiday. I start on my pleasure trip to-night."

"I am delighted," responded Jephson, in a genial tone. "If ever a man deserves a holiday, you do, doctor. Your patience, your zeal, your courage, fill me with amazement at times. But such a life must be wearing, and a complete change will do you a world of good."

"You will do what you can for my friend here," said Poynter. "At first, of course, he will be a stranger, but if I place him under your wing, Jephson, I have no fear for the result."

Jephson laughed. The sound of his laugh was heart-whole. His full, dark eyes were fixed on me intently for an instant.

"I'll do what I can for you, Dr. Halifax," he said. "Come to me if you are in any difficulty. Poynter will assure you that I have a certain influence at Norfolk House. There are few of its unhappy inmates who do not come to me for advice—in short, who do not count me among their friends."

At this moment Poynter was called away to speak to someone.

"Yes, I'll do what I can to make your stay amongst us pleasant," continued Jephson. "But, dear, dear, at the best it's a sad life, and those who come under its influence must at times be troubled by melancholy reflections. When all is said and done, Dr. Halifax, what are we but a set of prisoners? Banished from those we love, and who love us! If there is a class of human beings whom I truly pity, it is the insane."

"Mr. Jephson, will you come and talk to Miss Whittaker for a minute?" said the shrill voice of a quaintly-dressed lady, who I was told afterwards imagined herself to be Bathsheba.

He turned at once, bowing courteously to me as he did so.

Poynter returned and took my arm.

"Well, what do you think of him?" he inquired.

My reply came without hesitation.

"He is one of the handsomest and most intelligent men I have ever spoken to. Why is he here, Poynter? He is no more insane than you or I."

"In one sense you are right, but he has his mad, his very mad, point. He imagines that he is the richest man in the world. Acting on this delusion he has done all kinds of eccentric things—written out cheques for sums which never existed, misled no end of people, until at last his friends found it necessary to confine him here. But I have hopes of him—he is better, much better, than he was. Let us take this path to the left, and we will come upon him again. I see he is talking just now to poor Miss Whittaker. Introduce the subject of money to him while I have a chat with Miss Whittaker, and note his reply."

We very quickly came up to the pair. Mr. Jephson was holding an earnest conversation with a very pretty, very sad-looking, young girl. He was evidently trying to cheer her, and his fine face was full of sympathy.

"How do you do, Miss Whittaker?" said Poynter, as we came up to them. "Allow me to introduce my friend, Dr. Halifax. Jephson, I am sorry to interrupt your chat, but as I am going away to-night, I want to have a word with Miss Whittaker. Will you come this way, Miss Whittaker? I shall not detain you for an instant."

The doctor and the girl turned down one of the many shady paths. Jephson sighed as he looked after them.

"Poor, poor girl," he said; "hers is one of the saddest cases in the whole of this unhappy place."

"And yet she looks perfectly sane," I replied.

"She is sane, I am perfectly convinced on that point. Ask our doctor to tell you her story. Would that it were in my power to help her!"

His eyes sparkled as he spoke, and a smile of profound pity lingered round his lips.

I felt almost sure that the man himself was sane, but to make doubly certain I must press my finger on the weak point.

"Allow me to remark," I said, "that to be confined here must be a great deprivation to a man of your wealth."

When I said this a quick change came over Jephson's face. He came close to me, looked fixedly into my eyes, and said, with sudden, grave emphasis :—

"My dear sir, your remark is more than just. A man of my exceptional wealth must feel this confinement acutely. I do feel it for more reasons than one—you will understand this when I tell you that my income is a million a minute. Fact, I assure you. I have often thought seriously of buying up the whole of England."

He spoke with great emphasis, but also with great quietness, and his eyes still looked sane and calm. I knew, however, that Poynter was right, and hastened to change the subject.

We followed Miss Whittaker and Poynter at a respectful distance. They came to a part of the grounds where several paths met. Here they paused to wait for us. Miss Whittaker raised her eyes as we approached, and fixed them, with an eager, questioning gaze, on my face.

The moment I met her eyes, I felt a thrill of quick sympathy going through me. She was certainly a very pretty girl, and her dark grey eyes, well open and set rather wide apart, were full of the pleading expression I had only seen hitherto in a dog's. Her lips were beautifully curved, her abundant soft brown hair shaded as gentle and intelligent a face as I had ever seen. There is a peculiar look in the eyes of most mad people, but if ever eyes were sane, Miss Whittaker's were as they looked pleadingly at me.

"I will say good-bye for the present, Dr. Poynter," she said, holding out her hand to my friend, "for if you have nothing more to say, I must go into the house to give Tommy his reading lesson."

Her voice was as sweet as her face.

"Who is Tommy?" I asked of Poynter after she had left us.

"An idiot boy whom Miss Whittaker is more than kind to," he replied, "and whom she is developing in the most marvellous manner."

"Look here, Poynter," interrupted Jephson, "be sure you give Halifax a right impression of that poor girl."

He turned away as he spoke. I immediately raised eyes of inquiry to my friend.

"Why is Miss Whittaker here?" I asked at once. "I seldom saw a more beautiful face or a more intelligent-looking girl. When I look at her, I feel inclined to say, 'If she is insane, God help the rest of the world.'"

"And yet," said Poynter, speaking in a low voice which thrilled me with the horror of its import, "that gentle-looking girl is so insane that she was guilty of murder. In short, she is under confinement in a lunatic asylum during the Queen's pleasure, which of course may mean for life."

Just then some people came up, and I had not a moment to ask Poynter for any further particulars. I had to catch the next train to town, but I arrived at Norfolk House again that evening prepared to stay there during the week of my friend's absence.

This happened to be one of the social evenings, and immediately after dinner I had to put in an appearance in the immense drawing-room which ran right across the front of the house. There were from seventy to eighty people present. Most of them were nice looking. Some of the girls were really pretty, some of the men handsome. They all wore evening dress, and dancing, music, and song were the order of the hour.

My quick eyes at once singled out Jephson's fine figure. He looked more striking than ever in his evening dress, and when he sang, as he did twice during the evening, the quality of his tenor voice was so rich and sweet that I abundantly indorsed Poynter's verdict with regard to it.

There was a sudden hush in the rooms when Jephson sang. Restless people became quiet and talkative ones silent. A pleasant melancholy stole over some faces—a gentle peace over others. On the last of these occasions Miss Whittaker approached close to the piano and fixed her beautiful, sad eyes on the singer's face.

If ever eyes told a tragic story, hers did.

"Poynter says that this girl has been accused of murder," I muttered to myself. "There must be a mistake—if Jephson knows her story he will probably tell it to me, but I wish I had had time to ask Poynter to give me full particulars."

During that first evening I had no opportunity to say any special word to the young girl, but her image followed me when I retired at last to my own room, and I saw her sad, pale face again in my dreams.

I am not a coward, but I took care to lock and draw the bolts of my door. To say the least of it, a lunatic asylum is an eccentric sort of place, and I felt that I had better prepare against the vagaries of my immediate neighbours.

I fell asleep almost the moment my head touched the pillow. In my sleep I dreamt of Miss Whittaker. At first my dream was of the tranquil order; but gradually, I cannot tell how, my visions of the night became troubled, and I awoke at last to find myself bathed in cold perspiration, and also to the fact that the noises which had mingled with my dreams were real, and very piercing and terrible.

Shrieks of agonized human beings, the quick, hurrying tread of many feet—and then a rushing sound as of a body of water, smote upon my ears.

I sprang to my feet, struck a light, dressed in a moment, and hurried down the corridor in the direction from where the noises came.

Lights were flashing, bells were ringing, and terrified faces were peeping round doors in all directions.

"Keep back, keep back!" I exclaimed to one and all. "There has been an accident of some sort. Stay in your rooms, good people. I will promise to come back presently and tell you what it is about."

A few of my patients had the courage and self-control to obey me, but others seemed completely to lose their heads, and laughed and shrieked as the case might be, as they followed me in the direction from where the noise came.

I found myself at last in a large room which was evidently used as a sort of general store-room, for there was a huge linen press occupying nearly the whole of one side, while the other was taken up with big cupboards filled with different stores.

My eyes took in these details in a flash. I remembered them distinctly by-and-by, but now all my thoughts were occupied with the scene of confusion which arrested my attention in the middle of the floor. Several nurses, keepers, and attendants were bending over the prostrate figure of a woman who lay stretched in an unconscious state on the floor. Another poor creature was jabbering and talking in a distant corner. I looked quickly at him and saw that he was a boy. He was shaking and sobbing, and pointed his finger at the woman.

"This is Tommy, sir," exclaimed one of the attendants; "he's our idiot boy, and is quiet most times, but sometimes he takes a contrary sort of fit, and once or twice before now we thought he meant mischief. He took a wonderful fancy to her," pointing to the unconscious woman, "and she seemed to be doing him a power of good; but to-night he broke loose, and crept about setting places on fire. That's his craze, and he's always locked up at night. How he got loose to-night there's no telling; but, there—he's more sly and cunning nor a fox. He escaped, and might have had the whole building in flames but that she saw him, or smelt something, or found out. We can't say what did happen, for when I and my mate Jones rushed in here, we found her on the floor all unconscious as you see her, and dripping wet as if she was deluged with water; and here's Tommy—Tommy won't utter a word for the next twenty-four hours, so there ain't no use trying to pump him."

"How do you know there has been a fire?" I asked.

"You look here, sir—this wood is all charred, and we found a box of matches in Tommy's pocket. Oh, and here's her dress burnt too, poor thing. I expect she turned on the water tap and then lost her senses. She gets very nervous at times. Dear, dear—it was brave of her to tackle the fire alone, and Tommy in one of his mad fits."

"Stand aside now, please," I said. "I must see what can be done for this lady; I am afraid she is seriously hurt."

The attendants made way for me at once, and I knelt on the floor, to discover that the pale, unconscious face over which I bent belonged to the pretty girl whom I had admired so much in the drawing-room that evening.

With the assistance of a couple of men, and a kind-looking elderly nurse of the name of Hooper, I had Miss Whittaker conveyed back to her bed-room, and in a very short time we had her wet things removed, and she was lying in bed.

As I feared, she was very badly burnt about her left arm and side. Her right hand, too, was swollen and cut, and one of her fingers was dislocated.

"It must have been with this hand she held Tommy," exclaimed Mrs. Hooper. "Well, she is brave, poor thing; everybody likes her, she's that obliging and tractable. Do you think she is much hurt, sir?"

"We must get her round before I can say," I replied. "I don't like the look of this continued unconsciousness."

The nurse helped me with a will, and in about an hour's time a deep breath from the patient showed that her spirit was slowly returning to a world of suffering. The breath was followed by one or two heavily-drawn sighs or groans of pain, and then the dark grey eyes were opened wide.

They had a glassy look about them, and it was evident that she could not at first recall where she was or what had happened to her.

"I think I have fully surrendered my will," she said, in a slow voice. "Yes, fully and absolutely. Yes—the pains are better. There is comfort in resting on you. Yes, I submit my will to you. I obey you—absolutely."

"What are you talking about?" I said in a cheerful tone. "I don't want you to submit your will to mine, except to the extent of allowing me to dress this bad burn. Will you move a little more round on your right side? Ah, that is better."

She submitted at once. A faint blush came into her cheeks, and she said in a tone of apology:—

"I beg your pardon. I thought you were my friend, Dr. Walter Anderson."

I made no reply to this, but having made the poor thing as comfortable as I could, I administered an opiate, and, telling Hooper to sit up with her, went away to see after Tommy and to quiet the rest of the excited household.

There was very little more sleep for me that night, for the event which had just taken place had aroused more than one refractory patient to a state bordering on frenzy. I found I had to use my soothing powers to the best advantage.

Early in the morning I went to Miss Whittaker's room to inquire after her. I found her in an alarming state, highly feverish, and inclined to be delirious.

"Pore thing, it's partly her madness, no doubt," remarked Nurse Hooper; "but she do talk queer. It's all about giving up her will—as if anyone wanted to take it from her, pore lamb, and that she'd like to see Dr. Anderson."

"Do you know who he is?" I inquired.

"No, sir, I never heard his name before."

I looked again at my patient, and then beckoned the nurse to the door of the room. "Look here," I said, "I see by your manner that you are anxious to be kind to that poor young girl."

"Kind? Who wouldn't be kind?" exclaimed Hooper. "She's the nicest young lady, and the least selfish, as I ever come across."

"But you know what she is here for?"

"Yes." Nurse Hooper tossed her head disdainfully. "I'm aware of what they *say*. You don't catch *me* believing of 'em. Why, that young lady, she wouldn't hurt a *fly*, let alone kill a man. No, no, I know the good kind when I see 'em, and she's one."

"I will sit with her for a little," I said. "You can go and have some breakfast."

While the nurse was away Miss Whittaker opened her eyes. She looked full at me, and I saw that she was quite conscious again.

"You are the new doctor?" she said.

"Yes," I replied, "Dr. Halifax."

"I can't quite remember, but I think you were very kind to me last night?" she said again, and her sad eyes scrutinized me anxiously.

"I naturally did all I could for you," I replied. "It was very brave of you to put out the fire; you saved us all. I was bound to help you."

"I remember about Tommy now," she said, with a little shudder. "Tommy was awful last night. I cannot soon forget his face."

"Try not to think of it," I said. "Shut your eyes and let your imagination wander to pleasant things."

She gave a long shiver.

"What pleasant things are there in an asylum?" she answered. "And I am, you know I am, shut up here for life. I am only twenty-three, and I am shut up here for life!"

There was not a scrap of excitement in her manner. She never even raised her voice, but the dull despair of her tone gave me a sort of mental shiver.

"Forgive me for forgetting," I said. "Some time, perhaps, you will be well enough to tell me something of your story. In the mean time, believe in my sympathy. Now I must attend to your physical condition. Are your burns very painful?"

"Not for the last hour, but I feel weak and as if I were drifting away somewhere, and it seems to me that my life must be nearly over."

"Don't say that," I replied. "At your age, life is little more than really begun." Then I added, driven by an impulse which I could not resist, "It is my earnest wish and desire to help you. I have a strong feeling that there is some terrible mistake here. I would do anything to prove your innocence, and your sanity."

"Thank you," she answered. Her eyes grew dim for a moment—she turned her head away. "Thank you," she repeated again, more faintly.

Nurse Hooper came into the room, and I hurried downstairs.

After breakfast I spoke to Jephson.

"Did you ever happen to hear of a man of the name of Walter Anderson, a doctor?" I inquired.

"Only from Miss Whittaker," he replied.

"We all know, of course, that he is her greatest friend."

"I should wish to know more about him," I answered.

Jephson fixed his fine eyes on my face.

"I am glad you are going to be kind to that poor girl," he said.

"I am not only going to be kind to her, but I mean to get her out of this place," I answered, stoutly. Jephson laughed.

"The kind of speech you have just made is often heard at Norfolk House," he replied. "For at Norfolk House nothing is impossible to anyone—no feat is too daring, no exploit too vast. But you will pardon me for laughing, for this is the very first time I have heard the doctor of the establishment go into heroics. You are, of course, aware under what conditions Miss Whittaker is confined here?"

"You know the story, don't you?" I retorted.

"Yes, I know the story."

"Can you tell it to me in a very few words?"

"In as few or as many as you please."

"The fewer words the better. I simply want to be in possession of facts."

"Then I can give them to you very briefly. Miss Whittaker has come here from London. Her story can be told in half-a-dozen sentences. She was a gentle, modest, rather nervous, very highly-strung girl. One day she went to the house of a man with whom she had little in common, who had, as far as we can make out, never in any way injured her, for whom she had no apparent dislike, to whom she bore no apparent grudge, and forcing her way into his private sitting-room, deliberately fired at him."

"She killed him?" I exclaimed.

"She fired at his head; he died at once—and Miss Whittaker is here for life. It is a short story—none shorter—none sadder, in the whole of this terrible place."

"You believe that she did it?" I said.

"Yes, I believe that she did it—the papers gave full accounts of it—there were witnesses to prove it. Miss Whittaker was brought to trial. As there was no motive whatever for the act, it was put down to dangerous homicidal insanity, and she was sent first of all to the criminal asylum, afterwards, through the influence of friends, here."

"I cannot make head or tail of it," I exclaimed. "You believe that pretty, sweet-looking young girl to be guilty of a horrible deed, and yet you don't think her insane?"

"I think she is as sane as you are, sir."

"Believing this, you tolerate her—you can bear to be friends with her!"

"I tolerate her—I like her much. The fact is, Mr. Halifax, the solution of this story has not yet been arrived at. My firm belief is this, that when it comes it will not only clear Miss Whittaker of any responsibility in the crime she has committed, but also re-establish her sanity."

"Nonsense, nonsense," I said. "If she did this deed, she is either insane or wicked. You say you are convinced that she did fire at the man?"

"She undoubtedly fired at a man of the name of Frederick Willoughby with intent to take his life. She fulfilled her purpose, for the man died; still I believe her to be sane, and I believe that there is something to be found out which will establish her innocence."

"You talk in riddles," I answered, almost angrily. I turned on my heel and walked away.

The whole episode worried and distressed me. I found that I could scarcely attend to my other duties. Jephson's words and manner kept recurring to me again and again. He stoutly declared that Miss Whittaker was both innocent and sane, and yet she had killed a man!

"Why should I bother myself over this matter?" I murmured once or twice during that morning's work. "Jephson is mad himself. His ideas are surely not worth regarding. Of course, Miss Whittaker is one of those unfortunate people subject to homicidal mania. She is best here, and yet—poor girl, it is a sad, sad, terrible lot. I told her, too, that I would try to clear her. Well, of course, that was before I knew her story."

As I busied myself, however, with my other patients, the look in the gentle young girl's grey eyes, the expression of her voice when she said "Thank you—thank you," kept recurring to me again and again.

Try as I would, I found I could not force her story out of my mind. Towards evening I went to see her again. Nurse Hooper told me that my patient had passed a restless and feverish day, but she was calmer now.

I found her half sitting up in bed, her soft hair pushed back from her forehead, her face very pale—its expression wonderfully sweet and patient. The moment I looked at her I became again firmly convinced that there was some mistake somewhere—so refined and intelligent a young girl could never have attempted senseless murder.

"I am glad you are easier," I said, sitting down by her side.

When she heard my voice a faint, pink colour came to her cheeks, and her eyes grew a shade brighter.

"I am almost out of pain," she answered, looking at me gratefully. "I feel weak—very weak; but I am almost out of pain."

"Your nervous system got a severe shock last night," I replied; "you cannot expect to be yourself for a day or two. You will be glad to hear, however, that Tommy is better. He asked for you about an hour ago, and told me to give you his love."

"Poor Tommy," replied Miss Whittaker—then she shuddered, and grew very pale—"but oh!" she added, "his face last night was terrible—his stealthy movements were more terrible. I cannot forget what he has done."

"How did you first discover him?" I asked.

"I was going to sleep, when I heard a slight noise in my room. I looked up, and there was Tommy—he had hidden in that cupboard. He was trying to set the bed on fire. When he saw me, he laughed, and ran away. I followed him as far as the store room—I don't think I remember any more."

"You must try to forget what you do remember," I replied, in a soothing tone. "Tommy had a mad fit on. When people are mad they are not accountable for their actions." I looked at her fixedly as I spoke.

"I suppose that is true," she answered, returning my gaze.

"It is perfectly true," I replied. "Even a gentle girl like you may do terrible things in a moment of insanity."

"They tell me that I once did something dreadful," she replied. "It comes over me now and then as if it were a dream, but I cannot distinctly recall it. Perhaps I *am* mad. I must have been if I did anything dreadful, for I hate, oh, I hate dreadful things! I shudder at crime and at cruelty. You said you believed in me, Dr. Halifax."

"I earnestly desire to help you," I said.

"I have learned patience," she continued, falling back upon her pillows and clasping her hands. "I lost all—all, when I came here. I have nothing more to fear, and nothing more to lose, but I do wish to say one thing, and that is this: If I am insane, I don't feel it. Except for that one dark dream which I cannot distinctly recall, I have none of the symptoms which attack other members of this unhappy establishment. It is my own impression that if I was insane for a moment I am sane again. Dr. Halifax, it is terrible, terrible, to be locked up for all your life with mad people when you are not mad."

"It is too awful to contemplate," I answered, carried out of myself by her pathos and her words. "I wonder you kept your reason, I wonder you did not become really mad when you came here."

"For the first week I thought I should do so," she replied; "but now I am more accustomed to the people here, and to the sights which I see, and the terrible sounds which come to me. For the first week I was rebellious, fearfully rebellious; but now, now, I am patient, I submit—I submit to the will of God."

"Pardon me," I interrupted. "Your speaking of submitting your will reminds me of an expression you made use of when you were recovering consciousness last night; you spoke then of submitting your will to—to a certain human being. Is that the case?"

"Don't! don't!" she implored.

Her eyes grew bright as stars, her face became crimson.

"You must not speak of him. To speak of him excites me beyond reason."

"Tell me his name, and I won't say any more," I replied.

She looked fearfully round her. The emotion in her face was most painful to witness. She was evidently frightened, distressed, worried; but gazing at her intently, I could not see, even now, that there was anything in her actions or attitude which might not be consistent with perfect sanity.

"I wish you would not try to get his name from me," she said; "and yet, and yet, you are good. Why should not I tell you? He is my friend. Dr. Walter Anderson is my dearest friend, and I shall never, never see him again."

"You would like to see him again?" I retorted.

"Like it!" she replied. She clasped her hands. "Oh, it would be life from the dead," she answered.

"Then I will find him and bring him to you. You must give me his address."

"But he won't like to come here; I dare not displease him. You understand, don't you, Dr. Halifax, that where we—we revere, we—we love, we never care to displease?"

"Yes, yes," I replied, "but if Dr. Anderson is worth your friendship, he will come to see you when he knows that you are in sore trouble and need him badly."

"You can't understand," she replied. "My feelings for Dr. Anderson are—are not what you imagine. He is a physician, a great physician—a great healer of men. He soothes and strengthens and helps one, when all other people fail. He did much for me, for I was his patient, and he my physician. I love him as a patient loves a physician, not—not in the way you think. I am only one patient to him. It is not to be expected that he would give up his time to come to me here."

"Let me have his address, and I will try if he will come," I answered.

When I said this, Miss Whittaker was much perturbed. It was more than evident that I presented to her a strong temptation, which she struggled to resist. The struggle, however, was brief, for she was weak both in mind and body at that moment.

"You tempt me too much," she said, in a faltering voice. "The address is in that note-book. Turn to the first page and you will see it. But, oh, remember, if he fails to come after you have gone to him, I shall die!"

"He will not fail to come," I replied. "Keep up your heart I promise to bring him to see you."

I spent some time arranging matters that night in order to make myself free to attend to Miss Whittaker's affairs on the morrow. After my interview with her I was quite resolved to take up her case; nay, more, I was resolved to see it out to the bitter end.

There was a mystery somewhere, and I meant to fathom it. Queer, excitable, nervous, this young girl undoubtedly was, but mad she was not. She had killed a man, yet she was neither mad nor cruel.

With Dr. Walter Anderson's address in my pocket-book I started for town on the following morning. I told my assistant doctor to expect me back in the middle of the day at latest.

"Attend to all the patients," I said when I was leaving, "and in particular, visit Miss Whittaker. Tell her she is not to get up till I see her."

Symonds promised faithfully to do what I wished, and I stepped into my train. I arrived at Charing Cross a little before ten o'clock, and drove straight to the address which Miss Whittaker had given me.

Just before I reached my destination, a sudden thought occurred to me. This Dr. Anderson, whose name was quite unknown to me, was doubtless in his own way a celebrity. Miss Whittaker had spoken of him with reverence as well as affection. She had used the expressions which we employ when we speak of those who are far above us. She had alluded to him as a great physician, a wonderful healer of men. Now, I, a brother physician, had never heard the name, and the address to which I was driving was in a poor part of Fulham. It would help me much in my coming interview if I knew something of the man beforehand.

I pushed my umbrella through the window of the hansom, and desired the driver to stop at the nearest chemist's.

I went in, and asked to be directed to the house of Dr. Anderson.

"Do you mean Dr. Walter or Dr. Henry Anderson?" asked the chemist.

"Dr. Walter," I said. "Do you know him?"

"Well, yes—not that we dispense many of his medicines." Then the man looked me keenly in the face, and I looked back at him. He was young and intelligent, and I thought I might trust him, and that perhaps he would be willing to help me.

I took out my card and gave it to him.

"If you can tell me anything with regard to Dr. Walter Anderson, I shall be very much indebted," I said.

"Do you mean with regard to his special line?" asked the chemist.

"Yes, that and anything else you like to tell me. I am about to see him on behalf of a patient, and as I do not know him at all, anything you can say will be of use."

"Certainly, Mr. Halifax," said the chemist, reading my name off my card as he spoke. "Well, the fact is, Dr. Walter Anderson is a gentleman with whom we haven't much to do. He is not, so to speak, recognised by the faculty. Now, Dr. Henry—"

"Yes, yes," I interrupted, "but my business is with Dr. Walter. Is his practice anything out of the common?"

"Well, sir, I'll tell you what I know, but that isn't much. Dr. Walter Anderson went in for family practice when first I settled in these parts. He did fairly well, although he never placed, in my opinion, enough dependence on drugs. One winter he was unfortunate. There was a lot of illness about, and he lost several patients. Then all of a sudden he changed his mode of treatment. He went in for what you in the profession call fads, and Dr. Henry Anderson and other doctors who have large practices round here would have nothing more to do with him. I cannot but say I agree with them, although my wife holds by Dr. Walter, and says he did her neuralgia a world of good."

"What are his fads?" I inquired.

"He has taken up what we used to call mesmerism, but what is now known as hypnotism. Lots of women swear by him, and my wife is one. I shouldn't suppose you'd place much faith in such quackery, sir?"

"Hypnotism can scarcely be termed quackery," I answered. "It is a dangerous remedy with small advantages attached to it, and possibilities of much evil. Thank you for your information," I added.

I took my leave immediately after wards, and five minutes later had rung the bell at Dr. Walter Anderson's modest door.

"So he is a hypnotist!" I muttered under my breath. "That accounts for poor Miss Whittaker's surrender of her will. I must say I don't like the complexion of things at all. The hypnotist is one of the most dangerous productions of modern times."

I sent in my card, and was shortly admitted to Dr. Anderson's sanctum.

I was greeted by a tall man, with silvery white hair, an olive-tinted face and brown eyes, which gave me at once a mingled sensation of attraction and repulsion. They were the kind of eyes which a woman would consider beautiful. They were soft like brown velvet, and, when they looked full at you, you had the uncomfortable, and yet somewhat flattered, sense of being not only read through but understood and appreciated. The eyes had a queer way of conveying a message without the lips speaking.

When I entered the room they gave me a direct glance, but something in my answering expression caused them to become veiled—the hypnotist saw even before I opened my lips that I was not going to become one of his victims.

"I must apologize for taking up some of your time," I said; "but I have come on behalf of a lady who is ill, and who is very anxious to see you."

Dr. Anderson motioned me to seat myself, and took a chair at a little distance himself.

"I have not had the pleasure of your acquaintance until now," he said. "Is the lady known to me?"

"Yes, she is a great friend of yours—she tells me that you know her well. Her name is Miss Whittaker."

Dr. Anderson turned hastily to ring an electric bell at his side. A servant immediately answered his summons.

"If any patients call, Macpherson, say that I am not at home."

Having given these instructions he turned to me.

"Now, sir," he said, "I am ready to give you my best attention. I knew Miss Whittaker; hers is one of the saddest cases I have ever come across. I shall be glad to hear of her, poor soul, again. Are you her physician at the asylum where she is confined?"

"I am her physician *pro tem*. I am interested in her, because I do not believe her to be insane."

Here I paused. Dr. Anderson was looking down at the carpet. His face appeared to be full of a gentle meditation.

"She was always a very nervous girl," he said, after a pause; "she was easily influenced by those whom she respected. I took an interest in Miss Whittaker; she was my patient for some months. My treatment was highly beneficial to her, and the outburst which occurred was the last thing to be anticipated. When you speak of doubting her insanity, you forget—"

"No, I forget nothing," I said, speaking with some impatience, for I did not like the man. "After all, Dr. Anderson, my opinion on this point is quite wide of the object of this visit. Miss Whittaker is ill, and wants to see you. She has a bodily illness, which may or may not terminate fatally. She wants to see you with great earnestness, and I have promised to do all in my power to bring you to her sick bed."

Dr. Anderson raised his eyes and looked full at me. There was a steady reproach in them, but his lips smiled, and his words were gentle.

"I don't know you," he said, "and I am quite sure you don't know me. I am more than anxious on all occasions to obey the call of suffering. I will go to see Miss Whittaker with pleasure."

"When can you come?" I asked.

"When do you want me to come?"

"Now—if it will at all suit your convenience."

"Miss Whittaker's convenience is the one to be considered. You heard me give orders a moment ago to have my patients dismissed. That means that I am at your service. If you will excuse me for five minutes, I will be ready to accompany you."

He went out of the room in a dignified fashion, and I sat and looked round me. No one could have been kinder or more prompt in attending to what must have been an inconvenient summons; yet I could not get over my prejudice against him. I tried to account for this by saying over and over to myself:—

"He practises hypnotism, and my natural instincts as a doctor are therefore in arms against him."

But when he returned to the room prepared to accompany me, I found that my instinctive dislike was more to the man than to his practices.

We had a very uneventful journey together, and arrived at Norfolk House early in the afternoon. I was met by Symonds in the avenue. I introduced him at once to Dr. Anderson.

"I am glad you have come," he said, looking at the doctor and then at me. "Miss Whittaker is worse. She is very weak. She has fainted two or three times."

I was startled at the effect of these words on my companion—he turned white, even to the lips—his expressive eyes showed the sort of suffering which one has sometimes seen in a tortured animal. He turned his head aside, as if he knew that I witnessed his emotion and disliked me to see it.

"This is too much for her, poor child," he muttered. "My God, who could—who *could* have foreseen?"

"I will just go up and tell my patient that you are here," I said to him. "She longed so for you that doubtless you will have a reviving effect upon her immediately."

"You need not prepare her," he said; "she knows I am here already. You are perhaps aware, or perhaps you do not know, that I study a science as yet in its infancy. I am a hypnotist by profession. Over Miss Whittaker I had immense influence. She knows that I am here, so you need net prepare her."

"Well, come with me," I said.

I took him upstairs and down a long, white corridor which led to the young girl's room.

It was a pretty room looking out on the lovely garden. The western sun was shedding slanting rays through the open window.

Miss Whittaker was lying flat in bed, her arms and white hands were lying outside the counterpane; her eyes, bright, restless, and expectant, were fixed on the door.

The moment she saw Dr. Anderson they became full of a sudden intense and most lovely joy. I never saw such a look of beatitude in any eyes. He came forward at once, took her two little hot hands in one of his, and sat down by her side. I followed him into the room, but neither he nor she saw me. The physician and the patient were altogether absorbed with one another.

I went away, closing the door behind me.

I did not like Miss Whittaker's look. I had already found she was suffering from a critical heart condition owing to the repeated strains and shocks which her delicate temperament had undergone.

I could not attend to my other patients, but moved restlessly about, wondering how long Dr. Anderson would remain with her.

He came out of the room much sooner than I expected.

The look of real trouble and distress was still most apparent on his face.

"She is asleep now," he said, coming up to me.

"You have mesmerized her, then?" I answered.

"Only very, very little, just sufficient to give her repose. She is extremely weak, and I am anxious about her. I should like to talk over her case with you, if you will allow me."

"With pleasure," I replied. "Come with me to my consulting-room."

We went there. I motioned the doctor to an easy chair, but he would not seat himself.

"You do not like me," he said, looking full at me. "You distrust me; I am an enigma to you."

"I do not understand you, certainly," I replied, nettled by his tone.

"That is evident," he retorted. "Notwithstanding, I am going to put implicit confidence in you. I am a man in a great strait. Since Miss Whittaker's arrest, and since the severe sentence pronounced against her, I have been one of the most unhappy men on God's earth. There was one right and straight course before me, and day after day I shrank from taking it. All the same, I knew that a day would come when I should have to take it. When you called on me this morning and mentioned Miss Whittaker's name, I knew that the day and hour had arrived. That was why I desired my servant to dismiss my patients—that was why I, a very busy man, leaping into popularity day by day, gave up my time at once to you."

Here he paused. I did not interrupt him by a single word. I looked full at him, as he restlessly paced up and down the room.

"My opinion of Miss Whittaker is this," he said, stopping abruptly and fixing me with his dark, curious eyes. "My opinion is this, that if she stays here much longer, she will die. Do you agree with me?"

"I have not studied her case as carefully as you have," I replied. "Nevertheless, my opinion coincides with yours. Miss Whittaker is not strong—she is more than usually nervous. The sights she cannot help seeing in this place, the sounds she must hear, and the people she must associate with, cannot but be injurious to her health. Even if she lives, which I doubt, she is extremely likely to become mad herself."

"That is true," he retorted. "She is quite sane now, but she cannot with impunity live day and night, for ever, with the insane. She will die or go mad unless she is liberated."

"She cannot be liberated," I replied. "She was tried for murder, and is here during the Queen's pleasure."

He was quite silent when I said this. After a brief pause in his restless pacing up and down, he turned on his heels and walked to the window. He looked fixedly out for a moment, then turned full upon me.

"You must listen to an extraordinary confession," he said. "In very deed, if justice were done, I ought to be now in Miss Whittaker's place."

"You!" I answered, jumping from my seat.

"Yes—I repeat that I ought to be in her place. Mr. Halifax, you don't believe in hypnotism?"

"I believe it to be a little known science full of dangerous capabilities," I answered.

"Yes, yes; you have not studied it, I can see. You talk from an outsider's point of view. I believe in hypnotism, and I have acquired the powers of a hypnotist. I can exercise great power over certain people—in short, I can hypnotize them. As a physician I was somewhat of a failure; as a hypnotist, I have been an enormous success. I have cured mind troubles, I have made drunkards sober, I have comforted folks who were in trouble, and I have removed by my influence the desire of evil from many hearts. Some of my patients speak of me as little short of an angel from Heaven. I have an extraordinary gift of looking right down into the souls of men; I can read motives, and I can absolutely subdue the wills of those over whom I have influence to my own will.

"This is a great power, and except in the case of Miss Whittaker, I can conscientiously say that I have only used it for good. She was the patient over whom I had the most complete influence. She was the most extraordinary medium I ever came in contact with. Circumstances arose which tempted me to use my power over her in an evil way. The man Willoughby, whom she killed, happened to have been an enemy of mine. It is unnecessary to go into particulars—I hated the fellow for years—he did me untold mischief—married the girl I had already wooed and was engaged to, amongst other trifles.

"Miss Whittaker came completely under my influence. Her health improved rapidly, and I found that by my will I could make her do anything that I pleased.

"It so happened that by an accident Miss Whittaker and Willoughby met together in my presence. She had never seen the man before. I observed that when he came into the room she shuddered, trembled, grew very pale, and turned her head away. I guessed at once that my will was influencing her, and that because I hated him she did the same.

"Instantly the desire came to strengthen her dislike. I willed her to hate him more and more, and so great was my power over her, that she made an excuse to leave the room, being unable to remain in his presence. The next time I met her, she said to me impulsively, 'I cannot get over the terrible horror I feel of the man whom I met when I was last in your house.'

"I made no reply whatever, but hastened to turn the subject.

"She had not the faintest idea that I had any cause to detest him.

"Willoughby had come to live near me—we were friends outwardly, but his hateful presence came between me and all peace. The temptation grew greater and greater to exercise my will over Miss Whittaker in this matter—at last, with the result you have heard. It is true that I did not go to the length of willing her to kill him. This was but, however, the natural result of the hate

I had inculcated. On a certain morning, this innocent, gentle, affectionate girl went to the man's rooms, and because I hated him, and because I willed her to hate him too, she took his life.

"That is the story of Miss Whittaker's insanity."

When Dr. Anderson had finished speaking, he sat down and wiped the moisture from his brow.

"I am willing to tell this story again in open court, if necessary," he said. "My agony of mind since Miss Whittaker was arrested baffles any powers of mine to describe. I am abundantly willing now to make her all reparation. Do you think there is a chance of her being saved?—in short, is there any hope of the sentence against her being reversed?"

"It is impossible for me to say," I replied. "Had you given the evidence you have now favoured me with in open court at the time of the trial, the result might have been very different. May I ask you, Dr. Anderson, why your remorse did not lead you to make this reparation to your unhappy victim at the only time when it was likely to help her?"

"I can give you a plain answer to that question. At the time of the trial I had not the moral courage to deliberately ruin myself by making the confession which I now make to you. You can, or perhaps you cannot, understand what it is to struggle with remorse—what it is daily and hourly to bid your conscience be quiet. In my case, it would not obey me; it would keep calling loudly on me to repair the awful mischief I had done. I have spoken to you to-day—I have reposed full confidence in you. The question now is this: Can Miss Whittaker be liberated, and, if so, how soon?"

"You will stand to the confession you have just made me, even though it lands you in the prisoner's dock?" I answered.

A queer smile crept into his face.

"That will not be my punishment," he retorted. "I shall lose my patients and my chance of success in life, but there are no laws at present to punish hypnotists. Even if there were, however, I think—I think now—that I should be willing to abide the issue."

"In that case we must draw up an appeal to the Home Secretary," I began; "your statement must be taken down in writing—" I was interrupted by an imperative knock at the door. Even before I could reply it was pushed open and Nurse Hooper, very pale and frightened-looking, put her head in.

"Will you come at once to Miss Whittaker?" she said. "She's in a very queer state."

"Let me come with you," said Anderson, springing to his feet.

We rushed up the stairs and entered the sick girl's room.

Dr. Anderson had left her sleeping quietly, but she was not asleep now. She was sitting up in bed, gazing straight before her and speaking aloud with great rapidity. From the look in her eyes, it was evident she was gazing intently at a vision we could not see.

"I gave up my will," she said. "I gave it up when first you asked me. It is yours to do whatever you like with. I have heard you telling me day and night to hate him. To hate him! I do hate him. Now you tell me to kill him. Please don't tell me that. Please stop before you ask that. I'll have to do it if you insist, but *don't* insist. Don't lay this awful, awful command on me. Did you say you must? Did you say you would have to lay it on me? Then I'll do it! I'll borrow my father's pistol, it is over his mantelpiece. I can get it easily. No one will suspect me of hating that man, so I can easily, easily kill him. I know, of course, where this will lead—to prison first, and then to death. But if you ask me, I'll go even there for your sake. Yes, I'll go even there."

Her words were low, intensely horrible to listen to, her face was deadly white. The fierceness, the hungry glare of a tiger gleamed in the eyes which were generally so sweet in their glance.

"This is the house," she went on, in a hoarse voice. "I am knocking at the door. It is opened. I see the servant's face. Yes, he is at home. I am going in. That is his room to the left. Oh, how dreadful, how dreadful is the thing I have got to do! Dr. Anderson, I submit my will to yours. I obey the voice which tells me to—"

"Stop—hold!" cried Dr. Anderson, suddenly. "Take back your will. See, I give it back to you."

He took her hands and forcibly laid her back on the bed. She stared up at him fixedly, and he gazed intently into her wide-open eyes.

"Take back your will, Ursula," he repeated in an imperative voice. "Here it is—I return it to you. Be the gentle—the loving Ursula of old once again."

His words acted as magic. The hungry, angry light died out of the beautiful eyes—they grew soft—then they filled with tears.

"I had a bad dream," she said, speaking as if she were a child. "It is over—I am glad to be awake again."

"I'll stay with you until you are better," he answered—"until you fall into a gentle, healing sleep."

But, strange to say, when Anderson gave Miss Whittaker back her will, his power over her had vanished. Try as he would, he could not soothe her to sleep; by the evening she was more feverish than ever, and her condition was highly critical.

She lay in a state of delirium all through the night, but she did not talk of any more horrors. Her troubled spirit had evidently entered into a happier and more peaceful phase of memory. Her conversation was all of her mother who was dead, and of her own life as a light-hearted schoolgirl.

When the sun rose the next day, Miss Whittaker died.

I have not seen Dr. Anderson since. It is my belief that he will never again try hypnotism, either for good or evil.

Note on the Texts

The following is a list of the sources of the texts included in this volume, listed in the order of their appearance in this volume.

Stanley Percival. "The Tragedy of the Wedding." *Ludgate* Vol. 6 (Oct. 1898): 509-524.

Julian Hawthorne. "The Irishman's Story." In: *Six Cent Sam's*. St. Paul: Price-McGill Company, 1893. pp. 288-315.

Erckmann-Chatrian. "Suggested Suicide." *Romance* Vol. 2 (July 1891): 332-346.

Arthur Conan Doyle. "John Barrington Cowles." In: The *Captain of the Polestar, and Other Tales*. London: Longmans, Green & Co., 1890. pp. 230-266.

Ichor. "Hypnotism With a Vengeance." *Queenslander* (Mar. 7, 1891): p. 449.

Marie Madison. "A Scientific Revenge." *New York Clipper* (Oct. 12, 1895): 499-500.

H. Thomlinson. "How I Committed My Murder." *Strand Magazine* Vol. 24 (Aug. 1902): 161-168.

Ambrose Bierce. "An Adventure at Brownville." In: *The Collected Works of Ambrose Bierce, Volume 2*. New York: Neale Publishing Company, 1909. pp. 247-265.

Hugh Conway. "Paul Vargas: A Mystery." *English Illustrated Magazine* Vol. 1 (April 1884): 439-449.

Havelock Ettrick. "The Harmony of Horror: A Pianist's Most Terrible Experience." *Harmsworth Magazine*, Vol. 4 (April, 1900): 217-222.

Julian Hawthorne. "The Mystery of Turkentyne" *South Australian Chronicle* (Aug. 24, 1895): p. 18.

Dora Sigerson Shorter. "The Lion-Tamer." In: The Father Confessor: *Stories of Death and Danger*. London: Ward, Lock & Co., 1900. pp. 313-339.

Charles Fleming Embree. "The Higher Hypnotism." *Evening Post* (Wellington, NZ), Vol. 67 (Jan. 2, 1904): p.10.

"Suggestion." *Romance* Vol. 3 (Sept. 1891): 186-191.

Ambrose Bierce. "The Hypnotist." In: *The Collected Works of Ambrose Bierce, Vol. 8*. New York: Neale Publishing Company, 1911. pp. 177-184.

J.E. Muddock. "The Crime of the Rue Auber." In: *Stories, Weird and Wonderful*. London: Chatto & Windus, 1889. pp. 294-305.

Charles B. Cory. "A Queer Coincidence." In: *Montezuma's Castle and Other Weird Tales*. New York: Ralph S. Mighill, 1899. pp. 135-151.

B.L. Farjeon. "Philip Darrell's Wife." *Weekly Irish Times* (Aug. 8, 1903): 4.

"A Moral Murder: Hanged on Circumstantial Evidence." *Australian Town and Country Journal* (Jan. 25, 1890): 29.

Willard Douglas Coxey. "A Hypnotic Crime." In: *A Hypnotic Crime and Other Like True Tales: Being a Free Adaptation From the Minutes of the Society for Psychical Research*. Maywood, Illinois, 1896. pp. 5-16.

"The Playwright's Story." *Evening Express* (Cardiff, Wales) (Aug. 31, 1908): 4.

L.T. Meade. "My Hypnotic Patient." *Strand Magazine* Vol. 6 (Aug. 1893): 163-177.

Biographical Notes

Ambrose Bierce (June 24, 1842 – 1913?) b. Meigs County, Ohio. Author and journalist, known for his war stories and tales of the supernatural. Bierce disappeared in Mexico in 1913 while covering Pancho Villa's army campaigns.

Hugh Conway (December 26, 1847 – May 15, 1885) b. Bristol, England. Frederick John Fargus was an English novelist, poet, and short story author who wrote under the pseudonym "Hugh Conway." Fargus published his first novel, *Called Back*, in 1883; the book was a tremendous success, but his death two years later cut short what seemed a very promising career.

Charles B. Cory (January 31, 1857 – July 31, 1921) b. Boston. An American ornithologist, author, and golfer. Cory's publications were chiefly in the field of ornithology, but he also authored several works of fiction.

Willard Douglas Coxey (1861 – August 9, 1943) b. Philadelphia. Journalist, poet, and for many years press agent for Barnum and Bailey Circus.

Arthur Conan Doyle (May 22, 1859 – July 7, 1930) b. Edinburgh, Scotland. Practicing physician in the early part of his life but best known for his detective fiction featuring the character Sherlock Holmes.

Charles Fleming Embree (October 1, 1874 – July 3, 1905) b. Princeton, Indiana. American novelist who lived for several years in Mexico, and Mexico serves as the setting for a number of his works.

Erckmann-Chatrian Erckmann-Chatrian was the name used by the French authors *Émile Erckmann* (1822-1899) and *Alexandre Chatrian* (1826-1890), nearly all of whose works were jointly written.

Benjamin Leopold Farjeon (May 12, 1838 – July 23, 1903) b. London, England. Prolific English novelist, journalist, and playwright.

Julian Hawthorne (June 22, 1846 – July 21, 1934) b. Boston. Author, editor, and journalist, only son and middle child of Nathaniel Hawthorne.

Marie Madison (1865 – June 8, 1913) b. Cincinnati, Ohio. May Fleischman was a playwright, actress, and short story writer whose stage name and pseudonym were "Marie Madison." Author of *The Witch* and several other plays, and a regular contributor of short stories to the *New York Clipper* and the *Philadelphia Evening Call*; later wrote under the name *Marie Madison-Brotman*.

L.T. Meade (June 5, 1844 – October 26, 1914) b. County Cork, Ireland. L.T. Meade was the pseudonym for Elizabeth Thomasina Meade Toulmin Smith, children's writer and novelist. She was a prolific author, producing over 250 books, as well as several short stories and essays.

J.E. Muddock (May 28, 1843 – January 23, 1934) b. Southampton, England. J.E. Muddock was the pseudonym for James Edward Preston Muddock, a prolific author of mystery and horror fiction. He also wrote under the pseudonym "Dick Donovan."

Dora Sigerson Shorter (1866 – January 6, 1918) b. Dublin, Ireland. Poet and journalist; also authored several short stories.

CPSIA information can be obtained
at www.ICGtesting.com
Printed in the USA
LVHW010939230821
695886LV00002B/128